CHESAPEAKE WEDDINGS

THREE-IN-ONE COLLECTION

CECELIA DOWDY

BARBOUR
PUBLISHING

Cover Design: Kirk DouPonce, DogEared Design

Published by Barbour Publishing, Inc., P.O. Box 719, Uhrichsville, Ohio 44683, www.barbourbooks.com

Our mission is to publish and distribute inspirational products offering exceptional value and biblical encouragement to the masses.

 Member of the
Evangelical Christian
Publishers Association

Printed in the United States of America.

Dear Readers,

I'm glad that you decided to read the *Chesapeake Weddings* collection. I grew up in Maryland and have fond memories of visiting the locales where these novels take place.

I got the idea to write *John's Quest* from working at my day job. I work at a place where there are a lot of scientists and learned men who hold PhDs. During lunch one day, I looked at the scientists conversing at their table and thought: *I wonder if they believe in God?* I imagined that there were some scientists out there who doubted God's existence, so the idea for *John's Quest* was born.

I was raised in a rural farming community and I recall visiting the farms of friends while I was growing up. My inspiration for *Milk Money* came to me as I was thinking it would be a neat idea to set a book on a dairy farm. Since I've known several people who've suffered from alcoholism, I thought I'd use this book to show how an alcoholic can accept Jesus and gain His help to overcome his or her addiction. Both Frank and Emily learn that having faith in God helps them get through life's troubles.

For *Bittersweet Memories*, I tapped into my interest in identical twins. I also wanted to show how money can ruin familial and personal relationships. My story provides an example of how we can learn to forgive others over monetary matters.

These stories were a joy to write, and I hope you enjoy your time spent with these characters!

Sincerely,
Cecelia Dowdy

JOHN'S QUEST

Dedication

This book is dedicated to my husband, Christopher.
I love you.

Prologue

The loud banging at Monica Crawford's front door awakened her. Forcing herself out of bed, she glanced at the clock and saw it was two in the morning.

"I'm coming!"

She ran to the door. Looking through the peephole, Monica saw her little sister Gina smiling at her.

Her heart pounded as she opened the door, gripping the knob. "What are you doing here?" Playing an internal game of tug-of-war, she wondered if she should hug her sister or slam the door in her face. Humid heat rushed into the air-conditioned living room. She stared at Gina, still awaiting her response.

"It's nice to see you too, sister." Gina pursed her full, red-painted lips and motioned at the child standing beside her. "Go on in, Scotty."

Gina had brought her seven-year-old son with her. Dark shades hid his sightless eyes. "Aunt Monica!" he called.

Monica released a small cry as she dropped to her knees and embraced him. "I'm here, Scotty." Tears slid down her cheeks as she hugged the child. Since Gina had cut herself off from immediate family for the last two years, Monica had wondered when she would see Scotty again. "You remember me?" Her heart continued to pound as she stared at her nephew. His light, coffee-colored skin glowed.

"Yeah, I remember you. When Mom said I was going to live here, I wanted to come so we could go to the beach in Ocean City."

Shocked, Monica stared at Gina, who was rummaging through her purse. Gina pulled out a cigarette and lighter. Seconds later she was puffing away, gazing into the living room. "You got an ashtray?"

Monica silently prayed, hoping she wouldn't lose her temper. "Gina, you know I don't allow smoking in this house."

Gina shrugged. After a bit of coaxing, she dropped the cigarette on the top step and ground it beneath the heel of her shoe. "I need to talk to you about something."

Scotty entered the house and wandered through the room, ignoring the adults as he touched objects with his fingers. After Monica fed Scotty a snack and let him fall asleep in the guest bedroom, she confronted Gina.

"Where have you been for the past two years?"

Gina strutted around the living room in her tight jeans, her high heels making small imprints in the plush carpet. "I've been around. I was mad because Mom and Dad tried to get custody of Scotty, tried to take me to court and say I was an unfit mother."

Groaning, Monica plopped onto the couch, holding her head in her hands. "That's why you haven't been speaking to me or Mom and Dad for two years?" When Gina sat beside her, Monica took her sister's chin in her hand and looked into her eyes. "You know you were wrong. Mom and Dad tried to find you. They were worried about Scotty."

Jerking away, Gina placed a few inches between herself and Monica. "They might have cared about Scotty, but they didn't care about me." Gina swore under her breath and dug through her purse. Removing a mint, she popped it into her mouth.

"They were worried about you and Scotty," Monica explained. "You were living with that terrible man. He didn't work, and he was high on drugs. We didn't want anything to happen to the two of you."

Gina's lips curled into a bitter smirk. "Humph. Me and Scotty are just fine." She glanced up the stairs. "You saw him. Does he look neglected to you?"

She continued to stare at Gina, still not believing she was here to visit in the middle of the night. "What do you want? What did Scotty mean when he said he was coming here to live?"

Gina frowned as she toyed with the strap of her purse. "I want you to keep Scotty for me. Will you?"

Monica jerked back. "What? Why can't you take care of your own son? Did that crackhead you were living with finally go off the deep end?"

Gina shook her head. "No, we're not even together anymore. It's just that. . ." She paused, staring at the crystal vase of red roses adorning the coffee table. "I'm getting married."

Monica's heart skipped a beat. "Married?"

Gina nodded, her long minibraids moving with the motion of her head. "Yeah, his name is Randy, and he's outside now, waiting for me in the car."

Monica raised her eyebrows, suddenly suspicious. "Why didn't you bring him inside? Are you ashamed of him?"

Gina shook her head. "No. But we're in a hurry tonight, and I didn't want to waste time with formalities."

"You still haven't told me why you can't keep Scotty. Does your fiancé have a problem with having a blind child in his house?"

Gina scowled as she clutched her purse, her dark eyes darting around the room. "No, that's not it at all."

"Uh-huh, whatever you say." She could always sense when Gina was lying. Her body language said it all.

"Really, it's not Scotty's blindness that bothers Randy. It's just that—he's a trapeze artist in the National African-American Circus, and they're traveling around constantly." Her dark eyes lit up as she talked about her fiancé. "This year they'll be going international. Can you imagine me traveling around the globe with Randy? We'll be going to Paris, London, Rome—all those fancy European places!" She grabbed Monica's arm. "We'd love to take Scotty, but we can't afford to hire a tutor for him to travel with us."

"You're going to marry some man and travel with a circus?" Monica shook her head, wondering when her sister would grow up. At twenty-seven, she acted as if she were still a teenager. Since Monica was ten years older, she'd always been the responsible sibling, making sure Gina behaved herself.

Gina grabbed Monica's shoulder. "But I'm in love with him!" Her eyes slid over Monica as if assessing her. "You've never been in love? I think it's odd that you're thirty-seven and you never got married."

Monica closed her eyes for a brief second as thoughts of her single life filled her mind. Since her breakup with her serious boyfriend two years ago, she'd accepted that God wanted her to remain single, and she spent her free time at church in various ministries. She filled her time praising God and serving Him, and she had no regrets for the life she led. But whenever one of the church sisters announced an engagement, she couldn't stop the pang of envy that sliced through her.

Forcing the thoughts from her mind, she focused on Gina again. "This discussion is not about me. It's about you. You can't abandon Scotty. He loves you."

Gina turned away, as if ashamed of her actions. "I know he does, and I love him, too. But I really want things to work out with Randy, and it won't work with Scotty on the road with us. He needs special education since he's blind."

Her heart immediately went out to Scotty. She touched Gina's shoulder. "Scotty knows you're getting married?"

Gina nodded. "I didn't tell him how long I would be gone, but I told him I'd call and visit. Please do this for me." Her sister touched her arm, and her dark eyes pleaded with her. She opened her purse and gave Monica some papers. "I've already had the power of attorney papers signed and notarized so that you can take care of him." She pressed the papers into Monica's hand.

"How long will you be gone?" asked Monica.

"The power of attorney lasts for six months. Hopefully by then me and Randy will be more settled. I'm hoping after the world tour he'll leave the circus and find a regular job."

Monica frowned, still clutching the legal documents.

"Please do this for me, Monica," she pleaded again.

She reluctantly nodded. If she didn't take care of Scotty, she didn't know who would.

Chapter 1

M s. Lattimore, the principal of Scotty's school, closed the folder and patted Monica's arm. "Scotty needs tutoring. He's way below grade level."

Monica sipped her coffee, digesting the news. The aromatic blend slid down her parched throat. As bright sunlight, brilliant as buttercups, streamed through the window, she tried to focus on the principal's words.

She leaned back into the leather chair, gazing at Scotty's teacher and the school principal. Since Gina had left Scotty at her door two months ago, Monica's life had been one hectic cyclone.

"What do you suggest?" Monica asked.

Scotty's teacher, a specialist in the area of visual impairment named Mrs. Brown, gave her opinion. "You could hire a tutor. Scotty seems bright enough, but I just don't think his mother sent him to school very often." She pointed to a folder on the desk. "As a matter of fact, we've got the records from Scotty's old school. It says his attendance was poor, but he was bright and asked lots of questions." She removed a paper from the folder and quickly scanned it. "Ms. Crawford, he barely knows the braille alphabet. He needs help in all of his subjects."

Monica was not surprised. Gina had never been very responsible. Scotty's poor school attendance was another problem she had to solve in her nephew's life.

She'd found that Scotty wasn't used to living by rules. He had a smart mouth and he sulked, refusing to go to bed at the same time each night. Sometimes he cussed under his breath. Each time Monica said a silent prayer, asking God to give her the wisdom to deal with Scotty's negative habits.

It saddened her to learn he had no spiritual training. Hopefully he would learn to understand God's way of life from his now-regular church attendance.

"How do I find a tutor?" Monica asked.

Ms. Lattimore stood and walked to a gray file cabinet. Pulling it open, she removed a piece of paper. "I have somebody who can help you."

Monica accepted the paper and wondered how much this was going to cost. Gina had left no money to pay for Scotty's care. Another lesson Monica had learned since she was now raising her nephew: Little boys were expensive and they ate a lot of food. Having a new dependent was causing her to live on a shoe-string budget. Monica read the name printed on the paper. "Dr. John French?"

Mrs. Brown nodded, her blond hair swinging over her shoulders. "Yes, he's your best bet. He's licensed to teach visually impaired children. He's taught many students over the years. He knows braille, and he's familiar with the methods of teaching math to a blind child using an abacus and a talking calculator."

"Is he very expensive?" Monica asked.

Ms. Lattimore beamed. "That's what's so amazing about him. He doesn't charge for his services. He considers it his contribution to the community. If you'll read farther down on his résumé, you'll see he's a science professor at the University of Maryland at Eastern Shore."

Intrigued, Monica perused John French's list of assets. She truly sensed the Lord had given her this opportunity. After all of Scotty's expenses, she didn't think she could afford a tutor. But since it was for her nephew, she would have found a way to make ends meet. She noticed a phone number listed at the bottom of the paper.

"So I'll need to give him a call?"

Ms. Lattimore shook her head. "No, you don't have to call him. He's here at the school now, since our volunteer tutors are having a meeting." She checked her wristwatch. "They should be getting out shortly. I already told him he should stop by the office after the meeting is over. We've heard nothing but good things about him. He likes helping children, and I feel that he'll be more than happy to help Scotty."

Monica nodded, still praising God for this unique opportunity. Glancing around the office, she thought about Scotty's school experience here in Ocean City, Maryland. She was pleased he was able to go to a regular public school with Mrs. Brown as his visually-impaired-education teacher. She wanted to make sure he interacted with sighted people regularly.

Her thoughts were interrupted as the door opened, squeaking on rusty hinges. Her heart hammered as an attractive man strolled into the office. His skin was the color of dark coffee, and his eyes shone with kindness.

He smiled before speaking. "Hi, I'm John French." He strolled over. Monica felt as if she were the only woman in the room as he looked at her. When he shook her hand, currents of warmth traveled up her arm. She glanced at his fingers and noted he wore no wedding band. She opened her mouth to speak, but before words could tumble out, Ms. Lattimore stood, interrupting their introduction. A blush stained the principal's pale cheeks, and she laughed, placing her hand on John's arm. "John, *it is* nice to see you again." Fluttering her long lashes, she squeezed his upper arm.

Monica's mouth nearly dropped open as she watched the display of affection.

She cleared her throat, wanting to get the discussion back to the matter at hand. "I'm Monica Crawford. Ms. Lattimore told me you might be able to help my nephew, Scotty."

As he nodded, she tried to make a conscious effort not to stare. Strands of gray peppered his dark hair. Releasing his hand, she leaned back into the chair, hoping her palpitating heart would slow down.

Taking a vacant chair, he continued to smile. The woodsy scent of his after-shave filled the room, making her even more aware of his presence. "I've already met Scotty."

"You did?" Monica couldn't hide her surprise.

"Yes, he's sitting right down the hallway on the bench. It was easy for me to figure out who he was."

Monica removed her electronic planner from her purse. "So, when did you want to start?" She held the device in her hand, ready to enter the correct data into her schedule.

He chuckled, his eyes twinkling. "You're a lady that gets right down to business."

Before she could respond, Ms. Lattimore commented, "Mrs. Brown and I feel Scotty needs a tutor at least twice a week in order to bring him up to the same level as his peers."

As Ms. Lattimore and Mrs. Brown gave their advice, Monica tried to pay attention. However, she found herself paying more attention to John.

The group stood after Scotty's academic discussion was finished. Ms. Lattimore rushed over to John and shook his hand. "If you have questions about any of Scotty's academic needs, you can call me."

Monica lifted her purse and turned toward the door, eager to get Scotty home so he could start on his homework. The sound of John's footsteps followed her as she exited the office.

"Wow, you sure are in a hurry." The amused tone of his voice floated around her, making her aware of how rushed she'd become since Scotty had arrived in her life.

She stopped several yards away from where her nephew sat. "I just want to get Scotty started on his homework." She glanced at the little boy. "I'm so worried about him. I know life will be hard for him since he's disabled, but the least he can do is get back on his grade level." Blinking rapidly, she turned away from Scotty's new tutor, not wanting him to see the emotional tears suddenly filling her eyes.

"Hey," John said softly, placing his hand on her shoulder. "Everything will be okay—you'll see. Wait here a second." She continued to blink away tears as John reentered the office. He appeared seconds later with a tissue. She turned and blew her nose as embarrassment filled her soul.

John took control of the situation as he led her to Scotty. "I know this may sound a little forward, but how about joining me for a bite to eat?"

She stopped walking. "Why?"

"So we can discuss Scotty's needs." He gestured toward the office door. "From what I've heard in there, he really needs help. But if we can buckle down, get him right to work, I can almost guarantee I'll have him on grade level by the end of the school year."

She chuckled, throwing her soiled tissue away in a nearby trash can. "We're one week into the semester. Are you sure you can have him back on his grade level by the end of the school year?"

He shook his head, still gazing at her with his warm brown eyes. "Well, yes, I think it's possible." She felt flustered under his scrutiny. "Do you mind if I call you Monica? You can call me John."

She nodded as they approached Scotty. "Well, I don't know about getting something to eat."

"I'm sure I can convince you to share a meal with me." He mentioned going to the boardwalk and visiting the beach. "Scotty might enjoy walking on the beach, and we could get takeout from one of the restaurants."

He squeezed her shoulder. "Come on, Monica, I'm sure both you and Scotty will enjoy yourselves." He released her shoulder and continued walking. "Whenever I get a new student to tutor, I usually spend some time talking to the student and the parent so we all agree that we have the same goals in mind. It'll be my treat." He seemed so intent upon them going to eat with him that Monica couldn't resist accepting his invitation.

She nodded before telling Scotty about John. "Scotty, you've met Mr. French. He'll be your new tutor."

"I'd prefer it if Scotty called me Mr. John," he said.

"Okay," Monica responded. "Scotty, Mr. John will be your new tutor."

Scotty shook his head. "I don't need a tutor."

"You know you need help with your schoolwork. I don't want you to have to repeat second grade." Scotty remained silent as she continued telling him the good news. "We're going to go with Mr. John to get something to eat down at the boardwalk."

Scotty stood, reaching toward Monica as she grabbed his hand. "I sure am hungry," Scotty said.

As they walked outside, the bright sunlight gleamed on her skin, and the ocean-scented wind danced around them, beckoning them to the beach for a walk in the warm September air. John pulled his keys from his pocket. "How about I drive us down to the boardwalk? We can always come back afterward to get your car."

She agreed and was surprised to see his silver Lexus. The vehicle screamed money, and she again wondered why a college professor would end up spending his free time tutoring a blind seven-year-old child. During their short journey, smooth jazz music filled the car, and Scotty bounced on the leather seat.

John pulled into a parking lot.

"Aunt Monica, I want chicken nuggets and fries."

After walking for a few minutes, they agreed to stop at Harrison's Harbor Watch Restaurant to get food to go. Monica noticed the unique spicy scent of Old Bay Seasoning and seafood filling the air as they stepped into the restaurant. The restaurant also featured chicken tenders and fries. After they'd gotten their food, they strolled along the boardwalk, searching for an empty place to sit and eat. Tourists strolled around enjoying the warm weather of the last few weeks of summer.

A few people flew kites on the beach, and a multitude of the colorful objects bobbed in the sky. The brisk wind moved the birdlike contraptions so they filled the expanse with a kaleidoscope of color. Monica stopped walking, lifting her head toward the sky. "That's so beautiful!" She admired the beach as the white-capped waves tumbled onto the sand.

"Why are we stopping?" Scotty squeezed Monica's hand. "I'm hungry, Aunt Monica!"

She bent toward Scotty, telling him about the kites they had stopped to admire. Scotty's request spurred them toward an empty bench. John opened his Styrofoam container holding his fried shrimp and oysters. As they started to eat, Scotty said, "Aunt Monica, can we go on the merry-go-round after we eat?"

She glanced at John. "Since we came with John, it depends if he's willing to go."

"We can go, sport."

They enjoyed their food then walked toward the carnival rides on the pier. John tried to talk to Scotty about school. When John mentioned math, Scotty swore under his breath.

Monica's face grew warm. She pulled Scotty away from John. Holding his cheeks between her thumb and index finger, she placed her face close to his. "Scotty, what did I tell you about that language?" she gently chided. Her heart continued to pound with embarrassment as Scotty sulked.

"Aunt Monica, my mom said stuff like that all the time."

Sighing, she released him, still exasperated about his using the street language he'd picked up from Gina. "Well, it's wrong. Your Sunday school teacher told me she spoke to your class about expressing anger. Don't you remember anything she taught you?"

"She said it's not nice to cuss," he mumbled. Folding his small arms in front

14

of his chest, he changed the subject. "Can I go to the merry-go-round now?" A few late summer tourists still congregated around the pier as the fake animals weaved up and down on the carnival ride.

Scotty didn't sound sorry for his actions, and she was going to make him understand it was wrong to take the Lord's name in vain. Since he'd come into her care, she'd admonished him about cursing on numerous occasions. However, he still cussed as much as the day he showed up on her doorstep. "No, I'm afraid you can't, Scotty." Gently pulling his elbow, she sat him on a bench. "You're going to sit here and think about what you've done. When you decide to stop swearing so much, I'll let you play." His bottom lip quivered, but she left him alone on the bench, giving him time to ponder his actions.

Tears threatened to spill from her eyes as she left Scotty and returned to John. They sat on a bench close by so she could keep an eye on Scotty. John's eyes were full of kindness and understanding. Feeling like a fool, she sipped her soda, upset she'd cried twice since she'd met him. "I'm sorry about that." Shaking her head, she ran her fingers over the beaded condensation on her cup. "I'm trying hard to teach him right from wrong, but it's just so hard to undo other people's mistakes."

Before John could respond, her cell phone rang. She answered it, turning away from him as she spoke with her boss, Clark. She explained where she'd left the manila folder he needed for his meeting the following morning. As she folded her phone shut, she apologized and mentioned she'd had to leave work early to come to the meeting at Scotty's school that day.

"What do you do for a living?" asked John.

"I work for a marketing company that provides Internet marketing services for small businesses. Shortly before Scotty came into my care, I was promoted to senior executive assistant to the CEO. I have two admins under me. My staff and I do anything possible to keep Clark's day running smoothly. We screen phone calls, make travel arrangements, prepare financial reports from the data given to us from the accounting department. I even tally Clark's expense reports to make sure they balance before we send the information down to accounting."

She paused for a few seconds before continuing. "Since I got promoted, my workload has increased, but things have been even harder now that I have Scotty." She glanced at her nephew as he sat on the bench, pouting. "Sometimes I have to leave work early because the school will call me when Scotty misbehaves, and I also have special meetings with his teachers since he has special needs." She sighed. "I just want to make sure I do well in my new job position; however, with Scotty's academic and behavioral problems, it makes my work life more stressful since I'm always so worried about him."

They sat in silence for a few minutes.

"John, do you have children?"

He threw his empty cup into a nearby trash can. "No, I don't. Why do you ask?"

"I just think it's odd you're a college professor, yet you volunteer your spare time helping elementary-school-aged children."

He remained silent for several seconds, not commenting on her observation. "How about we set up a tutoring schedule for Scotty?" he suggested.

Monica wondered why John refused to acknowledge his reasons for helping blind children. What secrets could he be hiding?

Chapter 2

John changed the subject, not wanting to reveal too much about his life and childless state. He watched her reach into her handbag and remove her electronic planner.

He discreetly stared as she pressed a few buttons on the gadget. Her tall, chocolate brown body reminded him of a cover girl. With her short hair and cute face, she could easily win a beauty contest.

Still holding her planner, she glanced at him with her despondent dark brown eyes. "Which days of the week work best for you?"

"You know I'm a professor at the University of Maryland. I have classes during the day, but I'm free all evenings."

Her eyes widened. "All evenings?"

"Yes."

A woman with a baby strolled by. The child shrieked as the mother continued to walk down the boardwalk. John mentally blocked the disturbing sound from his mind, focusing again on Monica. Her red-painted lips enticed him, and the alluring scent of her floral perfume beckoned, competing with the clean scent of the ocean and the spicy scents of the food.

She put her electronic calendar aside. Running her fingers over her cup, she glanced at Scotty, who was still sitting on the nearby bench. "You know, I'm still wondering why you didn't respond to the observation I made a few minutes ago."

"You mean about tutoring children?"

She nodded. "You have to admit, it does seem strange that a college professor would tutor children—blind children at that. Ms. Lattimore told me you even know braille. You took the time to learn it just to tutor children?"

Bittersweet memories of his little brother scattered through his mind like the tossing white-capped waves in the nearby Atlantic Ocean. Forcing himself to focus on the moment at hand, he blocked the memories. "Well, it's a long story about how I decided to get into tutoring." He leaned back on the bench. "I don't really feel like getting into that right now."

"Okay. I don't mean to be intrusive, but I can't help but wonder about it." Her eyes twinkled as she looked at him. "But I am glad you're helping us."

"I'm glad I'm helping you, too." After a few moments of silence, he asked her the question that had been burning in his mind for the last hour. "Do you think we could get together and do something this Saturday?"

She jerked back as she folded her arms in front of her chest. "Mr. French—"

"Call me John."

She gave him her full attention. "John. . .I don't think I can go out on Saturday." Her dark eyes wandered toward Scotty. "I have a child to take care of now. I don't know if I can find a babysitter. Besides, if you're asking me out, the answer is no."

"No? Why?"

She shook her head. "I can't go out with anyone right now. My life is just too complicated. I just told you how much everything has changed since Scotty's been in my care."

"I can imagine it would be hard."

"Hard doesn't begin to describe it. Scotty has a lot of problems, and right now I'm focusing on getting his life back on track. I can't have other things crowding my head right now."

"I think I have a solution for that problem. How about I come by on Saturday for one of Scotty's tutoring sessions? Afterward maybe we can go to the beach? I can talk to you about Scotty's curriculum. Maybe we can go to Phillips Seafood House for dinner afterward. I love their buffet."

"I love their buffet, too, but I can't go out afterward."

His heart skipped a beat, and he hoped there was some way to change her mind. "Why not? I guarantee you'll have a good time."

A slight flush tinged her brown cheeks, and he caught a glimpse of her pearly white teeth as she smiled. "I'm not doubting I'd have a good time. But I've been having so much trouble with Scotty lately. His behavior has been awful, and I don't want to grant him the treat of dinner at Phillips when he's been misbehaving so much."

He nodded, understanding. "How about I come over anyway? The three of us could go to the beach. We don't have to go to dinner afterward."

She glanced at Scotty. "I'm not sure. . ."

"I don't want to pressure you. But I just want to point out that I usually want to spend a little time with my students and get to know them better. It's easier for me to tutor them if I can observe them outside of the lessons. I could offer to spend some time with Scotty alone, but I didn't think you'd want me to do that since Scotty doesn't know me and you don't know me very well either."

She finally nodded. "Well, since you put it that way, there's no harm I guess."

He released the breath he didn't realize he'd been holding.

"But I can't stay up too late. Since I've had Scotty, I've been so tired. It's hard having a kid dropped into your life." Her shoulders slumped as she toyed with her straw.

"Why are you raising your nephew so suddenly?"

She paused, staring at her cup. "My sister left Scotty with me because she felt she couldn't take care of him." Her mouth hardened into a frown, and when no other details were forthcoming, he decided to let the subject drop and ask her about it again later.

"Are you all right?" he asked.

She nodded as her silence continued, so he took up the conversation about Scotty's tutoring again. The urge to help her with her recent predicament grew, and he knew he could make things better for both Monica and Scotty. "How about I come to your house on Tuesdays and Thursdays to tutor him? Would that work for you?"

"That would be fine. I do have a proposition for you, though."

"Really? What's that?"

She picked up her planner and entered the dates for Scotty's tutoring sessions. She put the gadget away before responding to his question. "Well, I understand that you do not accept payment for your tutoring services."

He nodded, wondering why this bothered her. Thoughts of his deceased brother again filled his mind, reminding him why he'd made a promise to himself to make the lives of visually impaired people better.

"Since you won't accept payment, I don't want to make it seem as if Scotty and I are taking advantage of you."

"But I want to help him. I enjoy helping others."

She nodded. "I know." Her dark eyes met his. "I can see that you're committed to helping others, and that's commendable of you. But when you come by on Saturday, I'd like to make lunch for us to take on the beach. As a matter of fact, I'd like you to join us for dinner each night you tutor Scotty." Giving a small shrug, she continued, "It's the least I can do since you're helping me and you're helping him."

Thoughts of tutoring the young boy in reading and math escaped his mind like a brisk wind while thoughts of seeing Monica filled his soul with joy.

She chuckled. "But I have to warn you: Sometimes we might be eating food you're not used to."

"What do you mean?"

"Well, Scotty's diet consists of a lot of Tater Tots and chicken nuggets. I have to fight with him to eat his vegetables. I'm coaxing him into trying some other foods. I think my sister let him eat whatever he wanted."

She stood, and he touched her arm before she could go and fetch Scotty. "So, I'll see you on Saturday around noon?" She told him her address, and he suggested a few things Scotty could do to prepare for his tutoring session.

She nodded, and as he drove them back to the school so she could get her car, his heart skipped a beat as he anticipated their next appointment.

When Monica arrived home, she read the note Scotty's teacher had sent home with him, giving her the appropriate information on his assignment for class the following day. She then made Scotty do his homework.

He did as she asked without swearing, and relief washed over her. He seemed to be in a good mood the entire evening, even humming as he enjoyed his nighttime television show. She hoped that having a positive male role model in his life would help her nephew with his negative attitude.

When Scotty showed signs of fatigue, she sent him upstairs to get ready for bed. When he was finally settled in for the night, she pulled out her foot massage bath machine, desperately in need of some pampering. Thoughts of relaxation entered her mind as she filled the machine with water and plugged it in. She watched the water bubble and swish in the enclosure before she retrieved a towel from the linen closet.

She plopped into her favorite living room chair with her Bible and study guide beside her and placed her feet into the water. The gushing bubbles soothed her feet, and she laid her head back on the chair, basking with relief and wiggling her toes in the soothing liquid. She touched her Bible and study guide. Thoughts of preparing for teaching next week's lesson in her women's study group filtered through her mind; however, she found she didn't have the energy to crack her Bible open at the moment.

A contented groan filtered through her lips as she enjoyed her pampering session. She thought about all that had happened to her that day. She couldn't believe her nephew had such a gorgeous male tutor. Thoughts of John French continued to dance in her mind until a knock at the door interrupted her.

Reluctantly, she took her feet out of the tub and quickly wiped them with the towel before going to the door. Glancing through the peephole, she was rewarded with a view of her best friends. She beamed, opening the door.

"You sure do look beat!" Her friend Anna pulled her into a hug as Karen followed behind her, her petite frame dwarfed next to Anna's. Monica placed her arms around Anna's wide body while Karen thoughtfully rubbed Monica's shoulder.

Anna released her, holding up a bakery box. "I made these éclairs in the bakery today. I had a few left over so I thought you'd like them."

Karen led the way into the kitchen and placed her hand on Anna's arm. "Don't you think you should cut back on your sweets? Your doctor said you're in danger of becoming a victim of diabetes or high blood pressure if you don't lose the extra weight." They placed their purses on an empty chair.

Anna plopped the box onto the table, then sat down. "I'll start cutting back tomorrow," she groaned, waving Karen's comment away.

Folding her arms in front of her chest, Karen sat across from her, shaking her head, causing her stylishly cut dark hair to bounce. "Well, I certainly hope so. Monica and I are very concerned about your health."

Anna turned away from Karen, focusing on Monica. "So, how have you been, girl?"

Monica pulled out a seat, joining her best friends at the table. She immediately changed the subject. "You picked the right time to bring over some éclairs. It's been a rough day."

Karen narrowed her eyes. "Did Scotty get in trouble at school again?"

She placed her head in her hand, still grateful for the support of her two best friends. "Not really."

"Well, what happened?" Anna prompted.

Monica's mouth watered as she opened the box and sniffed the enticing scent. "How about I make some coffee and we enjoy these éclairs before I give too many details?"

"I'll do it," Karen volunteered. After setting three plates on the table, Karen breezed through the kitchen, starting a pot of decaffeinated coffee and gathering coffee cups and napkins for them to enjoy their snack. After the coffee was brewed, Anna and Karen served themselves. Karen poured a cup of coffee for Monica, adding a generous portion of cream and sugar.

As they ate, Monica informed them about her unusual day.

"A tutor would be good for him," Anna said. "I hope everything works out."

Monica lifted the pastry from the plate, inhaling the rich scent. Her mouth watered so she took a bite, enjoying her favorite dessert. "This is so good."

Anna's dark face glowed as she enjoyed her treat. A dollop of vanilla cream fell from the éclair onto her plate. Taking her finger, Anna wiped up the cream and placed the filling onto her tongue. "Well, I brought an éclair for Scotty. Maybe you can give it to him in the morning for breakfast."

Monica shrugged. "If he behaves himself, he can have it in the morning. If he misbehaves, I'll be eating that éclair myself."

Suddenly thoughts of John French swirled through her mind like a fine mist.

Anna placed her large hand on Monica's arm. "You're not telling us something. I can tell."

Anna leaned back into her chair, and it creaked. She grinned, displaying twin dimples in her cheeks. "You almost look happy." She ate the last bite of her éclair. "As a matter of fact, this is the happiest I've seen you since Scotty came to live with you. What happened today?"

Wincing, Monica wished she could keep her attraction to John a secret for a while longer. Under Anna's and Karen's intense scrutiny, she explained herself. "I'm attracted to Scotty's tutor."

Anna burst out laughing, the loud noise filling the small kitchen. Karen smiled, seemingly amused by this news also.

"Anna, will you be quiet! You might wake Scotty!" warned Monica. She folded her arms in front of her chest, narrowing her eyes. "I fail to see why this is so funny."

Still chuckling, Anna covered her mouth with her hand, her dark eyes shining with warmth. "You act like it's a death sentence. What's wrong with being attracted to him?"

"I agree with Anna," Karen admitted. "What's wrong with being attracted to somebody?"

"I'm happy for you," Anna said. "I just think it's hilarious that you can't be happy for yourself! Maybe now you can get Kevin off your mind!"

Rolling her eyes and pursing her lips, Monica glared at her friend. "I am so over Kevin. He's been married for over a year now."

Karen groaned. After finishing her coffee, she walked to the pot, her high-heeled pumps clattering on the tiled floor. After refilling her cup, she returned to the table. "You say that, but I saw the way you looked at him and his wife and child in church last Sunday. I think it's awful the way he dumped you two years ago and got engaged to Tamara six months later."

Turning away from her friends, she took a deep breath and wished they hadn't brought up such unpleasant memories. Since she'd gotten Scotty, she barely spent time thinking about Kevin and her nonexistent love life.

Anna squeezed her arm. "Hey, we didn't mean to make you feel bad."

"Look, I don't feel bad. It's just that since Kevin dumped me, you two always seem to mention him once in a while. I'd appreciate it if you didn't mention him again until I say I want to talk about him."

Anna put her arm around Monica. "I'm sorry. I love you like a sister, and I can tell when you see Kevin that it still hurts."

Karen nodded, placing her manicured hand on Monica's shoulder. "Yes, sometimes when you look at Kevin, you look like you're going to cry."

Monica shook her head. "No, I don't, not really. I'm glad that Kevin and his wife are happy together." When their church had held a baby shower for Kevin's pregnant wife, she discovered how hard it was to put her bitterness aside and purchase a gift for Tamara's child. A lot of the church sisters had given her looks of sympathy, and she wished the fact that she'd seriously dated Kevin for two years could be erased from the parishioners' minds forever.

"Sure, you're happy for them," stated Anna sarcastically. "You mentioned to me right before Scotty came to live with you that you couldn't believe Kevin strung you along for two years."

Monica shook her head, still wishing her friends would drop the subject. The first year Kevin had dated her, he treated her like a princess. She'd fallen in love pretty hard. When the topic of marriage didn't come up, Monica was about to broach the subject with him when his mother suddenly died of a heart attack. He'd been so close to his mom, and their fairy-tale romance took a nosedive after the tragedy. When she finally did try to discuss it with him, he'd stated he wasn't in the right frame of mind to talk about marriage and he was still grieving for his mother. He gave her the same line for almost a year before he dumped her for another woman.

She forced the unpleasant thoughts from her brain, focusing again on Anna and Karen, who still had their hands on her arm. "John is coming by this Saturday for Scotty's first tutoring session. He wanted us to go out, but I didn't think it was a good idea," she said, changing the subject.

They released her, and Anna placed her elbow on the table, propping her chin in her hand. "Well, let me ask you this: Is he a Christian?"

Karen crossed her slim legs and nodded. "Anna brings up a good point. Is he a Christian? If he is, I don't see any harm in going out with him. The eligible bachelors at our church are practically nonexistent. If you find a good Christian man and he's interested in you and you're attracted to him, you should at least give him a chance." She sipped her coffee. "You can't blame John because Kevin was a fool."

Monica shook her head. "I can't go out with him. Not now. Scotty has a lot of problems, and he needs me to be there for him. He needs my support, and I can't support him fully while I'm fawning over some man." She paused for a few seconds. "I'm not sure if he is a Christian. When I was speaking to him, we mostly talked about Scotty's educational needs."

"Have you even prayed about this?" Karen asked.

"No," Monica answered.

Karen shrugged. "Why not? I know you just met the man today, but hand it over to the Lord and see what He says to you. You're always telling others to pray about things. Now I think it's time for you to heed your own advice."

Anna nodded. "Karen does make a good point. Besides, maybe God has placed John in your path for a reason. He might be the one God intended for you to spend your whole life with."

Monica was silent as she finished her snack, thinking about the advice her friends had given her. No longer wanting the conversation to focus on herself and John French, she asked Karen how the hair salon was doing.

"You know how it is, girl. It's busy in that shop. I barely had time to eat my lunch this afternoon, I was so occupied."

"How are things in the bakery and your catering business?" Monica asked Anna.

Anna chuckled. "Okay. A lot of people are preordering pies and cakes for special events. My staff and I are going to be pretty busy filling orders next week. This Saturday we're catering an anniversary party."

Monica filled them in on the details of her job at the marketing services company. "Remember not long before Scotty came to live with me, I was promoted to senior executive assistant?" Sighing, she ran her fingers through her hair. "Clark has me doing all the scheduling for the marketing promo conference next year for the whole company."

"So you just make some hotel arrangements and be sure all the participants have their registrations in?" Anna questioned.

"Yes, but it's harder than it sounds. There are forty people in the company attending the conference. A lot of them have specifications about the kind of hotel room they want, and they all have special travel arrangements." She shook her head as she thought about the humongous project. "Also, a lot of people want to take their spouses and significant others, so I have to book arrangements for them, too."

Karen spoke up. "The company pays for the spouses to go?"

She shook her head. "No, they have to reimburse the company for their spouses' expenses. When they turn in their expense reports for the trip, it makes things harder for the accounting department because a lot of them *forget* to report the amounts of their companion's expenses and give the company a reimbursement check."

Anna shook her head. "I'll bet they're just trying to get a free trip for their spouses. They probably don't forget anything."

"I agree. It's always the same people who make that mistake." She told them how having Scotty in her life was affecting her attitude at work. "It's hard when Scotty's teacher calls me about a problem in the middle of the workday. Clark is sweet, and he understands everything I've been going through, but it's still hard to get used to having a child around while I'm working a full-time job."

They continued talking about their jobs for a while before Anna and Karen said they were tired. They gathered their purses and Monica told them goodbye as they exited her house. As she opened the curtain and watched her friends drive away, she reminisced about the deep bond they'd developed ten years ago when she'd joined their church. Anna's cooking skills had been put to good use when the church opened a soup kitchen for the needy. Anna, Monica, and Karen had been three volunteers who came each week. While ministering to others, they'd gotten to know one another. As each of them struggled with relationships and work-related issues, they'd encouraged one another to focus on God. Due to financial problems, the soup kitchen could not function as often as it used to; however, Anna, Karen, and Monica continued to meet regularly after their soup kitchen duties had ceased, and they'd found solace and comfort in their friendship.

The next day John taught his classes as if he were in a daze. As large classrooms filled with college students asking questions about molecular biology and photosynthesis, he tried his best to focus on listening to them before answering.

After giving a few pop quizzes and assigning chapters to read, he kept thinking about Monica. Afterward he walked from the George Washington Carver Science Building to his office in Hazel Hall and passed several students on campus. Some rode bikes and others laughed and joked as they strolled to their next class in small groups, carrying backpacks full of books.

He opened the door to his building and spotted a young couple standing inside on the steps. The female wiped tears from her eyes, and her male companion patted her on the back.

He shook his head as vivid memories flashed through his mind of the time a woman had tearfully ended her relationship with him. Gritting his teeth, he took the steps up to his office, determined not to let such recollections spoil the euphoria he felt about seeing Monica the following day.

The next morning he wanted to sing from the top of his roof. Humming, he took the mail from his box and minutes later dropped the pile of envelopes onto the glass-topped coffee table in his living room.

Plopping into his favorite chair, he checked his watch, noting he had to be at Monica's within the hour. That woman was like a ray of sunshine on a dark day.

He relaxed for a bit, then entered his bathroom and shaved away his stubble. After showering and dressing in a pair of shorts and a T-shirt, he completed his ensemble with a baseball cap.

He still hummed as he left his house and drove to Monica's, his heart pounding as he thought about the time they'd spend together. He was halfway to her house when he stopped his car. "Oh man!"

He returned to his house and gathered the items he'd forgotten. He needed his braille flash cards, his abacus, and other items to assist Scotty with his studies. After he had all the necessary items, he returned to his car and drove to her house.

The warmth of the day enveloped him. As he stopped at a light, he gazed toward the trees and noted a few leaves were starting to fall to the ground, a sign of the cooler fall weather that was bound to come within the next month. He smiled as he pulled into her driveway. He rapped on her door, eagerly awaiting another opportunity to see her again. When she opened the door, the scent of seafood filled his nose. Her dark brown eyes sparkled. "Scotty, Mr. John is here," she announced.

Scotty soon appeared at the front door beside his aunt. "Hi, Mr. John."

"Hey, sport." John squeezed Scotty's shoulder. "Are you ready for your first lesson?"

The boy frowned. "I guess so," he mumbled.

She guided her nephew into the living room and John followed. She turned toward him. "Come on into the kitchen." He followed her into the adjoining room, enticed by the scent of her perfume.

She was wearing an oversized T-shirt with a wraparound cloth beach skirt. The tangerine color complimented her brown skin.

Her dark eyes met his. "Are you okay?"

He cleared his throat. "Yes, why?"

Giggling, she entered the kitchen, and he followed her. "You've been staring at me since you came into the house."

He shook his head, ashamed. "Sorry. You look pretty today."

She seemed to accept the compliment and removed food from a frying pan. "I made some crab cakes for us to eat on the beach. This is my mother's special recipe, so the cakes should taste good cold. I also have lobster salad and cake for dessert."

"You purchased lobster?"

"Yes, my friend Anna owns a bakery and she has a side catering business, so she can sometimes get me pricey food at a bargain. She gave me the cake also."

"The crab cakes smell good," John said.

Scotty came in and sat at the table. "It sure does smell good! Aunt Monica can cook real good. She cooks more than my mom does!"

John remained silent as he watched Monica continue with their picnic preparations.

"I figured you and Scotty could get started with your lesson as soon as possible," she said as she pulled a cooler from the pantry and dampened a towel to wipe the interior of the container. "I have a few things to do upstairs, so I'll just leave you and Scotty to do your tutoring session."

John finally sat at the table beside Scotty and opened his briefcase. As he usually did with his new students, he tested Scotty's ability with the braille alphabet by using braille flash cards, giving Scotty each card and listening to him as he tried to read each word, running his small brown fingers over the bumpy white paper. The boy hesitated before reading each word aloud.

He next tested his math abilities. He pulled out an abacus and asked Scotty if he knew how to use one. The boy nodded as he counted out the white beads on the small contraption. His math skills were lousy, and John was determined to make him a more adept student before the end of the school year. He was so engrossed in helping Scotty, he didn't realize a whole hour had passed until Monica returned to the kitchen and began placing food into containers. John reached a stopping point, so he wrapped up his tutoring session with Scotty.

John glanced at Monica, smiling. "Are you ready to leave for the beach?"

She nodded and his earlier excitement returned as he anticipated Monica's home-cooked meal.

Chapter 3

M onica wiped her hands on a dish towel, glad to see that Scotty had warmed up to John during the tutoring session—which was a good sign. But she had to wonder about her own attraction to the man. Was he a good, honest man who wouldn't break her heart the way Kevin had?

After enjoying the pleasant, scenic view as they drove to the beach, they now sat on the sand watching the tourists strolling around the water. A few people flew kites, but the beach wasn't as crowded as it was during the tourist season.

John set up the beach umbrella, and she set the picnic basket and cooler on the sand.

"Aunt Monica, I'm hungry," complained Scotty.

"Honey, we're getting ready to eat."

John helped her by guiding Scotty to a spot on the blanket. The lobster salad was packed in three bowls, and she had packed plastic forks. The crab cakes were wrapped in aluminum foil, and Monica chuckled when she heard John's grumbling stomach. "I guess you're hungry," she said. John smiled sheepishly. She took Scotty's hand as John stared at them. "We usually join hands before we bless the food."

John nodded but made no effort to hold Monica's and Scotty's hands.

When his hands remained limp beside him, disappointment filled her soul. The wind blew, fluttering the flaps of their umbrella.

She tried to hide her emotions as she said grace over the meal. Her voice rang clear and strong in the hot late-summer wind as she thanked God for their food.

Nobody said a word as they enjoyed Cokes, lobster salad, and crab cakes. When they finished eating, they removed their shoes and walked along the shore of the ocean, letting the frothy waves kiss their feet. The sun was a brilliant globe in the striking blue sky, and seagulls dipped toward the beach, seeking crumbs of food from beachgoers. Monica described the scenery to Scotty and reminded him about the story of creation he'd learned in his Sunday school class. "Remember God created the birds and animals," she said.

They walked in silence for a few more minutes before Scotty asked a question. "Mr. John, do you go to church?" John held Scotty's hand as he guided him around the edge of the water.

She rubbed Scotty's shoulder, hoping he had not offended John. Since John had not participated in their prayer earlier, she now wondered about his spiritual beliefs. "Scotty, remember I told you that not all people believe the same things about God."

John shook his head. "No, it's okay. I don't mind telling others about my beliefs." His warm brown eyes turned toward Scotty as they continued to walk. "Scotty, I don't go to church. I'm what people call an agnostic."

He scrunched his eyebrows, dipping his toe in the water. "What's that?"

She continued rubbing Scotty's shoulder. "It means that he doesn't know if God exists." She looked at John. "Isn't that right?"

He nodded. "Yes, that's what it means."

She changed the subject, not wanting to discuss his agnostic views in front of Scotty. "Did you enjoy your lesson today?" she asked her nephew.

After the three of them discussed the bit of progress Scotty had made on his first lesson and what they needed to focus on later, they returned to their umbrella and enjoyed the chocolate marble cake Anna had given to Monica. They walked along the shore afterward and made a trip to Dairy Queen for ice cream. The sun began to dip on the horizon, spilling rays of warmth onto the water.

"I think it's time for us to head home," Monica said. She hated for the time with John to end; however, it was getting close to Scotty's bedtime.

Once they had arrived back at Monica's house, Scotty took his bath and Monica helped him settle into bed. John had offered to stay after Scotty fell asleep so they could talk.

She returned to the living room after Scotty was in bed, sporting a pair of faded jeans and an oversized shirt.

"I think Scotty had a good day," commented John.

Monica nodded as she invited him into the kitchen. She prepared to brew a pot of coffee. After measuring grounds into the filter, she added water and turned on the pot. Soon the aromatic scent of coffee filled the kitchen. She poured two mugs and asked him how he liked his.

"Milk and sugar, please," he responded.

She tried to stay focused on her task and not pay so much attention to the scent of his cologne. As she placed the cup in front of him, she admired the way his shirt hugged his broad shoulders. He took a sip. "Perfect." His dark eyes gleamed as he looked at her, and her face grew warm.

"Do you mind if we go into the living room?" she asked.

"Not at all."

He followed her into the living room, and they sat on her couch. The urge to turn on her praise and worship music tugged at her. However, she didn't think John would appreciate her musical tastes. She was about to ask him about his agnostic views, but before she could speak, he made an observation. "This is a nice place you have here."

"Thanks." She stirred her coffee. "Normally I wouldn't have been able to afford a place in this town. Since this house is only a few miles from Ocean City, it's expensive, just like most real estate in this area."

She continued to explain how she happened to own such a nice town house. "I didn't buy this house. The previous owner, Carla Spencer, was an elderly woman who used to be a close friend. When she died five years ago, she had no living relatives, and I was shocked that she willed her house to me. It was practically paid for, so I refinanced. I still have a mortgage, but it's not much more than what I was paying on the condo I lived in forty-five minutes away." She sat on the couch, reminiscing. "I still miss Carla and so do a lot of the members of our congregation." She sipped her coffee. "I'm touched that she left me her house."

They sat in silence for a while before John asked a question. "You mentioned your sister left Scotty with you because she couldn't care for him. I was wondering if she was having trouble finding a job."

She shook her head and sipped her coffee. She rested the mug on a coaster. "No, it's nothing like that. I don't think Gina wants to work. My sister left Scotty with me, but I felt she could have cared for him if she wanted to."

His eyes widened as he placed his cup beside hers. "Excuse me?"

She shrugged, folding her hands on her lap, and told him about the night two months ago when Gina had shown up with Scotty and left him in her care so she could travel with Randy in the circus.

"What about Scotty's father? Can't Gina ask him to take care of their son?" asked John.

Monica shook her head again. "No, she can't. Gina has a history of unhealthy relationships with men. Scotty's father, William, was into some illegal activities involving drugs. Scotty was a few days old when his father was killed as he tried to attack an armed police officer."

John's eyes were full of sadness as he looked at her. "Doesn't anybody in William's family care about Scotty? Aren't there other relatives on his father's side who can help take care of him?"

Monica sighed. "The little bit about his family that Gina told me sounded awful. Scotty's father was white. His family never accepted Gina because of her race, and they weren't happy about her being pregnant. William and Gina weren't even married. She said he kept promising to buy her an engagement ring, but it never happened." Monica toyed with her coffee cup. "Gina has always wanted to travel around the world and now that she's met Randy, she has her chance to make her dream come true. I just wish she'd given her decision more thought."

She didn't realize a bitter tone had crept into her voice until he placed his hand over hers.

"Hey, are you all right?"

She shook her head. "No, I'm not okay. Just like when we were younger, I'm trying to fix Gina's mistakes." She turned toward him, enjoying the warmth of his hand as she released her burden. "She disappeared for two years, and we couldn't find her. My parents were worried because they thought she might be strung out on drugs or dead." Tears came to her eyes as she recalled those dark two years when both she and her parents were filled with worry and dread. "We wondered how Scotty was getting along, since Gina is not very responsible. This wasn't the first time she'd disappeared, but it was the longest she'd been gone. The other times she only disappeared for a few months, before Scotty was even born."

"Did you call the police and file a missing person report?"

"We did better than that. My parents took out a loan and hired an investigator. Gina moved around a lot, and she didn't work very much. When we managed to track down where she was living, she moved right before we could confront her." Monica shook her head. "We let the investigator go when we couldn't afford him anymore, but we did have evidence that she was alive for the time being."

She pulled her hand away, ashamed to show her vulnerability. He handed her a tissue, and she wiped her eyes. "I'm sorry. I've been such an emotional wreck since we found out Gina is still alive and that Scotty is all right. . .well, all right physically, that is." She turned toward him, gazing into his brown eyes. "Do you really think you can help him get back on his grade level?"

He nodded. "I think I can. You know there are no guarantees, but if he works hard and studies, I think he'll do fine. I've already spoken to his teacher a few times this week, and she's given me his list of reading assignments for the year. He should be receiving more of his braille books shortly."

She was pleased he showed such faith in her nephew.

"Have you talked to Gina since she left for the circus?" he asked.

"No, she never calls."

"What about your parents? Can they help?"

She recalled how pleased her parents were when they saw Scotty for the first time in two years. "Yes, they've been a big help. They live near Baltimore, so they don't see him as much as they'd like, but they do call and talk to him a lot. Also, I discovered having Scotty in my care was placing a real dent in my wallet. I hesitated going to my parents for money because they're retired."

"Were they able to help you financially?"

She nodded. "I wanted to care for Scotty on my own. I'm kind of stubborn like that. I recently asked my parents if they could give me some funds to help out while I'm raising Scotty, and they were happy to help me. My dad even scolded me for waiting so long to ask for their assistance." She tilted her head. "As a matter of fact, they're coming up early next Saturday morning to get Scotty and keep him for the next few days since school is out for teachers' workdays the following Monday and Tuesday. A lot of members of their church go on field trips to some attractions in Baltimore, so they promised to take Scotty to some fun places in Baltimore City."

He leaned toward her. "Since Scotty will be gone, you'll be free to do something fun next weekend," he said. "I've got a lot of connections in town. There's a new comedy club that opened on the boardwalk recently. Since I know the owner, I can get us good seats. How about it?"

The smooth cadence of his voice beckoned her, making her want to throw caution to the wind and go out on a real date with a good-looking man. She scooted away, suddenly finding it hard to remain calm while sitting so close to him. "No."

His brow furrowed. "No?"

She shook her head. "No. I can't."

"Why not? Scotty will be gone, so you don't have to worry about him next weekend."

"I need this time to myself to get my head back on straight. I've been a nervous wreck since he came to live with me, and I need this time alone to think and regroup and pray."

He tilted his head, seemingly confused.

"Besides, in spite of my vows not to date since I'm trying to focus on Scotty, I still couldn't go out with you after what I found out today."

"You're talking about my religious views?" he guessed.

She took another sip of coffee. "Yes, I can't go out with somebody who doesn't share my faith in God. My spiritual beliefs are what keep me centered. My faith in Jesus is the most important thing in my life. . . . It has been since I accepted Christ when I was a teenager. I rely on Jesus for everything." Her heart rate increased as she spoke about God, and her raised voice resounded in the living room.

"I just don't understand your agnostic views." She continued to look at him, grappling to understand where he was coming from. "As a matter of fact, you're the first man I've ever met who is an agnostic."

He blew air through his lips. "I'm a science professor, so I guess that partially explains my views. Also, my parents raised me this way. Both of them were scientists, and they always said there is an explanation for everything—until you could prove God's existence they would not believe in Him."

She shook her head, still startled by John's opinion. "But how can you disprove it? Look around you—the beauty of the world, all the wonderful things on this earth, God must exist! I don't see how you can doubt that," she finished in a small voice.

"I could argue with you on that one. What about death, disease, and the turmoil on this earth? Why does God let millions of people starve in foreign countries? If God does exist, why does He allow His people to suffer so much?" He gripped his coffee cup. "It's the way I feel."

"I can't give you all the answers, but I know if you believe in God and accept Him, you are guaranteed the gift of eternal life. Isn't that wonderful?"

He shrugged, seemingly unmoved by her statement.

"So, I guess your parents aren't religious at all? They don't go to church or anything?" she asked.

"Actually, my parents were what you would call 'saved' before they were killed in a car accident a couple of years ago."

Her heart skipped a beat. "Really? Didn't they try to make you understand the gospel?"

He was quiet for so long she wondered if she'd made a mistake in asking the question. She placed her hand over his. "I'm sorry. This is none of my business. You're in my home as Scotty's tutor, and it's not right for me to try and force you to change your religious views."

He squeezed her fingers. "No, it's okay." He released her hand. "It's hard for me to talk about. You see, my parents started going to church about six months before they were killed. I'm not sure what prompted them to start going or why they changed their scientific views, but a few days before they died, my dad had been calling me, saying he wanted to talk to me about something important."

"What did he want to tell you?" she asked.

John shrugged. "I never found out. But after they died, several members of their congregation contacted me, expressing their condolences and offering help with funeral arrangements. I found out about their recent church attendance and newfound faith in Christ, and I knew they would want a church service due to their faith. So I had their funeral at their church and had their pastor speak." He took a deep breath and continued. "I figured my father may have been trying to contact me to tell me about their reformed religious views."

She shook her head, saddened by this news. "I'm so sorry for your loss. I'm kind of surprised you were so open with me about this."

He touched her shoulder. "You know, we just met and all, but. . .I'm comfortable with you."

His words of praise warmed her heart. "Thanks."

"You're a strong, caring woman, and it was big of you to care for Scotty."

She shrugged. "I had no choice. And I wasn't doing it for Gina. I was doing it for Scotty." She changed the subject. "Don't you ever wonder why your parents changed their minds about God and religion? Haven't you ever thought to search this out for yourself?"

He rested his elbows on his knees, placing his chin in his hands. "As a matter of fact I have. Since I found out they'd changed their minds about God, I've thought about going to church myself to try and discover what they suddenly found so appealing about organized religion."

Silently praying for the courage to continue, she told him what was on her mind. "Well, why don't you do that? There's a class at my church every Sunday before services. It's for new believers and for those who have not yet embraced Jesus as their Savior. I've heard nothing but good things about this class, and it might help you put things into perspective."

"Do you teach this class?"

She placed her hand on her chest. "Me? Oh no. I lead the women's Bible study class, and it's taught at the same time."

"I'll bet you're a good leader."

Heat rushed to her face. "I try to do the best I can. We start the study off with prayer, and I just let Jesus lead me into saying the right things."

Exhaustion from the long day hit her. She yawned, picking up their empty cups. John followed her into the kitchen, and she sensed him watching her as she rinsed out the mugs and placed them in the dishwasher. "So, will you at least think about coming to the class tomorrow? That's when the new session starts. You don't have to stay for the worship service if you don't want to, but I just feel you need this class. It'll help you with your struggle."

"Who says I'm struggling?"

"You seemed upset about your parents' new belief in God, and I figure you're struggling to understand how they happened to change their minds." She placed soap into the dishwasher before starting it up. Soon the sound of swishing water filled the kitchen. "Or was it presumptuous of me to assume that about you?"

He gazed at her. "No, you're right. I've been struggling with this for the last two years."

"Well, do something about it. You know, come to think of it, God might not have placed you in my path just to teach math and reading to Scotty. Maybe He wanted me to encourage you to end your struggle."

He shook his head. "I don't know about that. But I promise I will at least think about attending the class at your church each Sunday."

She walked him to the door. He touched her cheek before he waved and walked to his car. She closed the door and looked out the window, watching him drive away.

One week later on Saturday morning, Monica got up early, reading her daily devotions and enjoying a cup of coffee before Scotty awakened. As she began preparations for breakfast an hour later, he came into the kitchen, feeling his way toward the table. "Are you making pancakes today?"

She grinned, heating the griddle. "Yes, I'm making pancakes. You'll smell them cooking in a minute." She removed sausage links from their package and slid them into a skillet. "Did you need help packing your stuff for your visit to Grandma and Grandpa's?"

He shook his head. "Nope. I have everything packed already."

She rumpled his hair. "Your grandfather is taking you to get a haircut on the way to their house today."

After they said grace and enjoyed their breakfast, a knock sounded on the door. Grinning, Scotty pushed his empty plate away. "Grandpa and Grandma are here!" He ran toward the door, almost tripping over a chair.

"Be careful, Scotty!"

Her parents soon entered the kitchen, Scotty holding his grandmother's hand. "Is that pancakes and sausage I smell, Miss Monica?" Her father's teasing voice filled the room as he kissed her cheek.

Her mother's dark eyes were shadowed with concern as she pulled Monica's hands into hers. "Baby, you sure do look thin." She pulled Monica closer and whispered in her ear. "Don't let Scotty run you ragged. Gina makes me so angry!"

"Mom—"

"I just don't understand how Gina could turn out so messed up and you turned out so well. We raised you both the same. . . ." She looked away as if still trying to find answers to her questions.

"Grandpa, when are we leaving?" Scotty demanded, pulling on the old man's hand.

He chuckled. "We'll be leaving soon." He placed his hand on Scotty's shoulder. "Why don't you run upstairs and get your suitcase. We want to talk to Monica for a second."

Scotty bounded up the stairs.

Her father hugged her. "Monica, you're so thin! Don't you ever eat a decent meal?"

Her mother grunted. "That's what I was trying to tell her. She needs to take better care of herself. She can't allow Scotty's behavior to put her own health at risk."

Monica gritted her teeth, not wanting to hear their reprimands. "I promise I'll try to take better care of myself. The two of you are helping me out a lot just by taking him for the next few days."

Her father spoke. "That's what we wanted to talk to you about. Is keeping Scotty too much for you? Did you want us to start keeping him all the time? Since we're both retired, we have more time to devote to his needs."

Her mother nodded. "Yes, we were talking about it on the way up here. We're just concerned that once we take him in, we'll find that we can't handle him as well as we thought we could."

Monica shook her head. "No, Scotty has to stay with me. Besides, he's learning to adjust to his new school, he's making new friends, and I've gotten him involved at the Sunday school at church. He even has a new tutor who can help him with his math and reading." She took a deep breath, thinking of another way they could help her out. "But you can continue to take him sometimes when he's out of school. It's been hard for me to adjust to having him around and trying to teach him not to swear and to learn to lean on God. . ." She paused. "Well, I know I'm doing what needs to be done, but it's a struggle, and at the end of the week I feel like I need a break."

Her parents agreed to take Scotty more often during his school breaks. They talked about it before Scotty came down the stairs again, struggling with a heavy suitcase. Monica hurried toward him, prying the suitcase from his hand. "Scotty, you're only going to be gone for a few nights. You don't need this many clothes." She opened the suitcase, extracting a few items.

"Why don't you let him take all the clothes he wants?" her father said. "It would be easier for Scotty to visit us more often if he had a few changes of clothes at the house."

Monica nodded. "Okay, you can take those."

Her mother took her aside into the kitchen as Scotty continued to chat with his grandfather in the living room. "Your father and I also wanted to talk about keeping Scotty for a week during Christmas break. I think he might enjoy that. We can talk about it later in the year, though."

Monica nodded, glad they were agreeing to help care for their grandson. Before they left, she pulled Scotty into her arms, running her fingers through his dusty-colored hair. "You take care of yourself and mind Grandma and Grandpa. And remember, no cussing." She pulled his chin between her fingers and looked into his unseeing eyes. "Understood?"

"Yes," he grumbled, squirming out of her tight embrace. She waved at them from the doorway until they were out of sight.

They had not been gone for five minutes before she started to miss Scotty. "Oh Lord, what in the world is wrong with me," she mumbled to herself.

She entered the kitchen and cleaned up the breakfast dishes. Afterward she got dressed and drove to Karen's hair shop.

A few hours later, she left the salon enjoying her freshly permed hair. She'd had a chance to speak with Karen about John's agnostic views. Monica had also mentioned that her attraction to John bothered her because she knew it was wrong to be unequally yoked with a nonbeliever. Karen promised to keep John in her prayers.

When Monica returned to her house, she was surprised to see the message light blinking on her answering machine. She replayed the message, wondering who could be calling her. She listened to John's deep voice. It looked like he was coming to church the next day.

Chapter 4

That night Monica tossed and turned, praying about John's decision to attend class. She got out of bed and made a cup of tea. As she sipped the brew, she turned on her favorite Christian radio station and sat in her living room, listening to the music.

She was tempted to call Scotty and see how he was doing, but she resisted, knowing he would be asleep since it was 2:00 a.m.

Instead, she cradled the warm mug in her hands, eagerly anticipating seeing John the following day. Sauntering to her answering machine, she played his message again, relishing the sound of his voice.

With his mellow tones still filling her mind, she yawned and trudged back to bed. Monica awakened hours later and prepared for church as butterflies danced in her stomach. She scanned her wardrobe wondering what to wear.

She chose a black skirt and a white silk blouse. The light-colored garment was adorned with tiny black flowers. After she dressed, she took special care in curling her short hair and applying her makeup.

Later, as she led her women's Bible study class, she desperately tried to pay attention as the ladies discussed women's roles within the traditional Christian church, but she found her mind wandering a lot. She kept daydreaming about John, hoping she could catch him before the service started.

After they ended their study with a prayer, she rushed from the room, going down the hallway to where she hoped John was also being dismissed from his class. She eagerly watched people filing from the room. A few people greeted her, some stopping for short conversations. The last person to exit the room was Pastor Martin.

Confused, she approached the minister.

He greeted her with a warm hug. "How's my favorite women's Bible study teacher?"

"Fine." She still wondered what had happened to John. "Pastor, I'm anxious to know if my friend John made it to your class."

They made their way back up the stairs. "I'm sorry, Monica. I didn't see anyone new today."

Disappointment washed over her, just like the waves crashing on the sands of Ocean City. "But he called me yesterday and said he was coming. I wonder if anything happened to him, like maybe he was in an accident or something."

He squeezed her shoulder. "Don't worry about it too much. I've found when people are seeking religion and God they have to do it on their own timetable. They sometimes get cold feet at the last minute, and it may take awhile for them to find the courage to make it to church and search for the truth." The sound of her high-heeled shoes echoed on the wooden steps as she listened to the pastor's words of advice.

As she entered the sanctuary, her disappointment consumed her. The Lord knew she'd been disappointed in men before, so she should be used to their behavior.

Holy music filled the room, and she took a seat in the pew and tried to sway to the rhythm as Anna and Karen joined her. She was determined to worship Jesus, even though it seemed as if John was determined not to.

❦

Two weeks later, John pulled into the parking lot of Monica's church. The sun warmed the day, and as he left his car he noticed a few dry leaves littering the sidewalk. He clutched his recently purchased Bible as he neared the building.

He thought about the phone call he'd made to Monica a couple of weeks ago and wished he hadn't broken his promise to attend the class at the church.

As he'd tutored Scotty over the last few weeks and enjoyed Monica's home cooking, she had said little about his agnostic views, but her disappointment in his cancellation of their church date was evident. Her dark, pretty eyes were full of unasked questions. . .questions he wasn't even sure he had the answers to. He had originally planned on coming to the class that morning, but again, he'd hesitated. He finally worked up the courage to come and listen to the sermon, hoping he'd find the courage to make it to class the following week.

He climbed up the steps of the white building. A cross sat atop the steeple, and as he entered the vestibule, people approached shaking his hand, introducing themselves. The warm welcome washed over him, almost making him glad he'd decided to come to church.

"John!" Monica walked toward him, her eyes sparkling. "You didn't tell me you were coming today." As she reached toward him, he took her hand. The scent of her perfume enveloped him, and he longed to kiss her, right here in the church foyer. She stepped back, and he released her hand.

He didn't realize he was staring until a warm blush covered her brown cheeks. "I didn't decide to come until this morning. I hope it's all right."

She chuckled. "Of course it's all right. I'm glad you're here."

"I know I was supposed to come a couple of weeks ago, but at the last minute, I just didn't have the courage." He gazed into her eyes. "I'm surprised you

39

didn't ask why I never showed up when you saw me during Scotty's tutoring sessions."

She shook her head. "I figured it was a personal matter for you, and I didn't want to bring it up until you did. Anna, Karen, and I have been praying for you to come here."

"You told Anna and Karen about. . .about what I told you?" He'd never met her best friends, but she'd mentioned them often.

Her grin faded as he dropped her hands. "Yes, I hope that was okay." People continued to bustle around them in the foyer while children scampered upstairs to the Sunday school classes. "I just finished teaching my women's Bible study class."

"Really? What did you study today?"

She brightened as she spoke of her class. "We read the book of Ruth aloud and discussed it."

"Did you enjoy the discussion?" he asked.

"Oh, so much. You know, it's a powerful love story." She pointed to his Bible. "You should read it sometime. I have a study guide to use with my class, but sometimes things go off on a tangent and we get into a deep biblical discussion. It's so refreshing!"

Her dark eyes shone with warmth. "There're still a few minutes before service begins. If you want, I'll explain why I told Anna and Karen about you."

"Okay." As they entered the sanctuary, a few people looked at them with curiosity and some waved at Monica. Parishioners spoke in hushed tones as the small band tuned their instruments. Sunlight streamed through the stained glass windows, illuminating the place of worship with warmth.

She sat beside him. "I told Anna and Karen about you because when we became friends we made a pact."

"What kind of a pact?"

"Well, all three of us are sisters in Christ—"

"Sisters in Christ?"

She sighed. "Yes, all three of us are Christians, we share a deep faith in the Lord, and I'm close to them since our faith binds us together. So if something is bothering one of us, we promised to tell each other so we can pray about it together until God works everything out."

"Really?" Although he still doubted the power of prayer, he was impressed by their devotion to one another. "Does it usually work?"

She shrugged. "God always answers prayers. Sometimes it just might not be the answer we're looking for."

Unsure how to comment on her last statement, he looked around the now crowded sanctuary. "Where's Scotty?"

"He's in his Sunday school class. We won't be seeing him until the end of the service."

As if on cue, the band started playing. Sweet notes filled the air as people stood and sang praises to God. John glanced around the sanctuary as people's voices lifted in harmony. Some were stoic, seeming to merely mouth the words to the popular Christian song. However, others like Monica swayed to the music, raising their hands toward the ceiling as they sang with emotion. A few of the parishioners had tears slipping from their eyes as they praised their God. After a half hour of worship music, the preacher approached the pulpit. John barely listened to the sermon about forgiveness—he was still so awed by the emotion showed by the parishioners as they praised the Lord.

During the service, John noticed Monica glance to the pew a few rows away near the exit. Her eyes became sad as she watched a man and woman with a small baby, obviously a married couple. The woman glanced at Monica. When their eyes locked, Monica hurriedly looked away, as if ashamed to be caught staring.

After the service was over, Monica led him back into the foyer as she waited for her nephew. Scotty entered, led by the Sunday school teacher. "Aunt Monica?"

"Hey, Scotty. Guess who's here?"

"Hey, sport." John rubbed Scotty's shoulder.

Scotty giggled. "Mr. John, I'm surprised you're here since you don't know if you believe in God."

The startled expression on Monica's face spoke volumes as she pulled Scotty aside, gently reprimanding him in a corner.

"You must be John."

John stopped staring at Monica and Scotty, still huddled in a corner, and focused on the woman who'd just approached. She easily weighed over two hundred pounds, but her dark eyes sparkled with warmth. "Yes, I'm John and you are. . . ?"

Another woman approached. She was petite, thin, and wore a dark suit. Her hair was swept up into an elegant style. "Hi, John, I'm Karen and this is Anna. Monica told us you were Scotty's new tutor."

Monica approached, holding Scotty's hand. "Hi, you two. I see you've already met John."

John watched the two friends with amusement. "Well, I'm glad to have met both of you."

He wasn't ready for the day to end but didn't want to invite himself to Monica's house.

Karen saved the day. "We sometimes go to the Bayside Skillet for brunch after church. Did you want to go with us?"

He wondered what Monica thought about the invitation. Did she want him to come?

Monica hesitated. "Yes, John, why don't you come with us?"

After some discussion, Anna decided that everybody should ride with her to the restaurant in her minivan. Monica climbed into the large vehicle, following Karen, Scotty, and John. "Anna, what's a single woman like you doing with a minivan?" he asked.

She placed a gospel CD into her player, chuckling as she revved the engine. "I guess Monica told you I'm a baker, but I'm also a cook." She continued to grin as she pulled out of the parking lot. "I purchased this van because sometimes I do some catering events on the side, and I can remove the seats and store all my food and equipment in here."

Anna dominated the conversation on the ride to the restaurant, telling John how she'd started her own business while Monica stared silently out the window.

"Are you okay?" he asked Monica.

She nodded. "I'm just a little tired. I had a little bit of trouble falling asleep last night."

They pulled into a parking space. As he exited the car, the wind from the ocean blew toward them. The sun warmed the air, and they commented on the nice weather as they walked into the restaurant.

A server approached, wearing a black-and-white uniform. His muscles bulged as he removed menus from a receptacle. "Where would you like to sit?"

Karen spoke up. "Can you give us a large table with a view of the ocean?"

He nodded, beckoning them to the table, then left them with their menus. John helped Scotty into the seat before he held out Monica's chair for her.

Anna stared at the waiter, whistling softly. "Isn't he the finest chocolate-brown man I've seen in months? Mm, mm, mmm."

Karen leaned in her seat, whispering to Anna. "You know your voice carries. He might hear you."

"I don't care if he does hear me!" Her boisterous laugh rang throughout the room, and Karen playfully swatted Anna's arm.

Anna chuckled as they opened their menus while admiring the view of the ocean. The picture window gave a relaxing view of the large white waves as they tumbled over the beach. A few people ran along the edge of the shore, but the ocean was devoid of swimmers.

Monica quietly read Scotty the options from the children's menu.

The server returned minutes later. "What would you all like to order?" He spoke to all of them, but his warm brown eyes remained fixed on Anna.

Anna batted her eyelashes, staring at the waiter. "What do you recommend?"

He chuckled, winking at her. "The seafood frittata and the banana royale crepes are good. Our cook is a local, and he makes the best breakfast you've ever tasted."

Anna laughed. "Don't you need a pad and pen to write it down? I wouldn't want you to forget our orders."

"Oh, you don't have to worry about that. . .uh. . .what's your name?"

Anna put her menu aside, her complete attention focused on the waiter. "My name is Anna Gray."

"I'm Dean Love."

"Your last name is not Love."

He chuckled. "It sure is. Maybe later I'll prove it to you."

"What?"

He shrugged his broad shoulders. "I was talking about showing you my driver's license."

"Oh, okay." She glanced at her menu. "I'll have the banana royale crepes and the seafood omelet, an order of bacon, and a coffee and an orange juice." She closed her menu and gave it back to the waiter.

Karen ordered a seafood frittata. Monica ordered a sausage-and-cheddar omelet with bacon for herself, John ordered a southwestern omelet, and Scotty ordered an American cheese omelet.

John asked Karen about her profession. She happily answered his questions about being a hairdresser.

He soon grew tired of her incessant chatter, and eventually Karen and Anna started their own conversation, ignoring Scotty, Monica, and John.

John touched Monica's hand. "Are you sure you're okay? Are you just tired like you said earlier?" he asked.

"Yes, why do you ask?"

He shrugged, unsure of how to answer. "You look a little sad. Did something happen recently?"

She shook her head, leaning toward him. "Just worried about Scotty, that's all," she whispered.

He looked at her, sensing there was more going on with her than Scotty's behavior problems. Before he could question her further, their server arrived, and scents of seafood and eggs filled the table. As he prepared to dig into his food, the others bowed their heads while Monica led the blessing. He watched her as she thanked the Lord for their food. Her long lashes fluttered as she opened her eyes and looked at him. He returned her warm gaze before enjoying his meal.

After the meal was over, Anna left the table, and John noticed her in the corner, flirting with the waiter. They exchanged slips of paper, so he assumed she was getting his phone number. Anna returned, announcing she was ready to head back. She drove everybody back to their respective cars at the church parking lot.

John watched Monica as she led Scotty to her car. "Monica."

"Yes?" She unlocked her door.

"How about another cup of coffee?"

"Huh?"

He chuckled. "Do you mind if I come by and visit for a while?"

Her hand rested on the door handle. "Well, I don't know. . . ."

"If you have plans, I understand."

"Why did you want to come by?"

He decided to be honest with her. "I wanted to talk to you about something."

"Really? What?" Her voice was full of intrigue as she awaited his response.

"I'll let you know as soon as we get to your house."

"Okay."

Grinning with anticipation, he headed to his car.

⁓

After they arrived home, Monica settled Scotty in front of the TV with a bottle of soda and some cookies. The little boy loved listening to the programs and followed the stories of his favorite characters as easily as she did. She joined John in the kitchen. She had changed into her house clothes and her slippers.

She tried to calm her racing heart as she poured two cups of coffee before joining him at the table. Monica sipped the coffee. "Before you tell me why you wanted to talk to me, I just wanted to thank you."

"Thank me for what?"

"For helping Scotty. I know he still has a long way to go, but since you've been tutoring him, his schoolwork has improved a little bit during the last few weeks. His teacher called and told me about it. She said if he keeps his improvement level up, he'll probably be on grade level by the end of the school year."

He shook his head as if he didn't want to accept her praise. "I enjoy doing this. I sense it's my mission to help kids who have trouble in school, especially blind kids." He seemed thoughtful as he sipped from his coffee cup, gazing at her marigolds in the flower garden outside the kitchen window.

The sun had disappeared more than an hour ago, and the day was now as gray as if it were about to rain. "Why do you feel that way?" she asked.

"Excuse me?" He stopped looking out the window, focusing on her again.

"Why do you want to help blind children so much?"

"Is there anything wrong with wanting to do that? You said you've seen a difference in Scotty."

She touched his hand. "I don't mean anything negative. I think it's nice you spend time helping others." She didn't want to offend him. "I just sense that. . . well, that there's some reason why you're so passionate about what you do. You talk about your volunteer work more than your job at the university."

He focused on their joined hands. "You know, I really like you, Monica." She tried to pull her hand away, but his grip remained tight. "I really do. I know you don't want to date, but I'm glad we can spend time together since I tutor Scotty. I might check out that class at your church and try to get an answer to some of those questions I have about God. I've been wanting to come, but I've been hesitating, changing my mind at the last minute. I think I just need to push my apprehensions aside and come next Sunday."

"The class started two weeks ago, so you're already behind."

He shrugged. "So? I'm a professor—I learn quickly. If I do find that I can believe in God, do you think we could spend some time together—dating?"

She pulled her hand away. "I'm not sure. I don't want to make it seem like I'm trying to sway your beliefs just so we can date."

"I'd never think that about you." His voice had turned husky, and he leaned toward her, running his hand over her cheek. His touch felt delicious, and she wondered if he was going to kiss her.

"Aunt Monica!"

She jumped up as if she'd been burned by fire. "Yes, Scotty!" She ran into the living room, and Scotty held his empty soda bottle toward her. "Can I have some more soda?"

"No, you've already had enough soda for today. I'll pour you a glass of water."

He grumbled under his breath, and she was relieved when no cuss words tumbled from his mouth. She gave him a glass of ice water and returned to the kitchen.

"Now, where were we?" asked John.

She cleared her throat, glad Scotty had interrupted. "I was asking you why you were so passionate about your volunteer work."

He paused, as if hesitant about answering her question.

"What's wrong?" she asked.

"Well, I guess you could say my passion for volunteer work ties a little with my agnostic views."

"What do you mean?"

John leaned back into his chair, took a deep breath, and began telling her about his childhood.

Chapter 5

I told you that my parents were agnostic, and they raised me that way." He sipped his coffee. "But what I didn't tell you was that when I was nine, my mother gave birth to my brother."

"I didn't realize you had any siblings." She knew so little about him after spending so much time with him during the last few weeks.

He shook his head. "I don't anymore. My little brother, Paul, died when he was only eight."

"Oh, I'm so sorry. I didn't realize." She touched his hand.

"Like Scotty, he was born blind, and I guess that's why I have a soft spot in my heart for people who suffer from blindness. He had a rare disease and that's why he died so early, but I recall his going to a special school, struggling with his blindness. And after he died, I was determined to help others like my brother. I learned braille, and when I went to college to get my degree, I also studied and got a special teaching degree, just so I could help visually impaired people. After I finished college, I started volunteering at schools, helping blind children. I've been doing it for years now, and I feel like this is something I have to do."

She carefully thought of her next question. "So is that another reason why you refuse to accept Jesus? You think He let you down when your brother died?"

He nodded. "I guess you could say that. I recall how heart-sick my parents were when Paul died. They just reemphasized to me that if God did exist, He would not have allowed Paul to die."

"And you believed them?"

"Yes, I did. I just don't understand Him, and that's why I find it hard to believe in Him. Also, my parents accepted Jesus into their lives, and they were killed in a car accident months later. What kind of God allows His saved children to die?" His voice dripped with bitterness.

"John, please come to the class at my church. I think it's what you really need. None of us understands God. Not even those of us, like me, who do accept Him as our Savior. We just have to believe even when we don't understand," she stated.

"Okay," he grumbled.

"So you will come? Just give it a try for a while and see how it goes."

He nodded, and she hoped the class would help him find his way to Jesus.

⨟

The following Sunday, John pulled his car into the parking lot of Monica's church to attend the class.

After the leader dismissed the group, John headed to the sanctuary, eagerly looking for Monica. He spotted her sitting in a pew with Scotty, and his heart skipped a beat. She looked beautiful in a dove gray suit. He strolled to the pew, ignoring the curious glances from the other church members. He plopped into the seat beside her. She barely noticed him as she whispered something to Scotty, obviously fussing with him about something.

Unable to resist, he touched the small mole above her mouth. "Hi, beautiful," he whispered.

"Mr. John!" Scotty beamed, recognizing John's voice. "Are you going to start coming to church with us now? Do you believe in God?"

She reprimanded Scotty. "Don't talk so loud in church, Scotty."

The worship band started playing, and the choir filtered onto the stage, their long scarlet-and-white robes swaying. He squeezed her hand. "I'm so glad to see you."

She squeezed his hand back. "I'm glad to see you, too."

Even though he'd seen her during the week when he tutored Scotty, he still found a small thrill in seeing her at church dressed in her Sunday best, worshipping her God.

The choir began to sing "Amazing Grace," and for once John listened to the lyrics, really listened, and found himself a little moved by the music. Monica stood with most of the congregation and closed her eyes as she swayed to the music. A tear escaped from her eye, and he stood beside her and wiped it away. She opened her eyes, giving him a gentle smile as she continued to sway, singing the inspiring words.

When the preaching began, John made more of an effort to listen but found that being near Monica was distracting. The scent of her perfume unnerved him, and he longed to spend some time with her after the service. Again he noticed that she covertly stared at the couple who sat near the exit of the church with their infant. When the woman happened to look back, Monica hurriedly focused on the pulpit again.

Recalling that something similar had happened last week, he made a mental note to ask her about it later. When the service finished, he followed her into the foyer. "I noticed Scotty didn't go to Sunday school today."

"The teacher was sick, and they couldn't find a substitute."

"I was good today, wasn't I, Aunt Monica?"

She chuckled, stroking his face. "Yes, you were."

"You said if I was good during the service we could go to Phillips for lunch."

Anna rushed into the foyer before Monica could answer. She greeted Monica, Scotty, and John before exiting so fast the floor vibrated. "Where is she going? I thought the three of you had lunch together every Sunday."

"Humph. Where do you think she's going? She's got a brunch date with Dean Love."

"Dean Love? You're talking about the waiter at the Bayside Skillet?"

Monica nodded. "Yes, when Anna sees a man she likes, she pursues him with a vengeance. She barely gives the man a chance to ask her out properly. She'll do the asking, and then we'll listen to her complain when things don't work out." She continued to talk about Anna's new love interest as they walked toward the door. "Dean told Anna he's a Christian, but I haven't been around him enough to see if it's really true."

John frowned. "What do you mean? Do you think he's lying?"

Monica shrugged. "It's hard to say. One man that Anna used to date claimed to be a Christian just so Anna would go out with him. After she spent some time with the man, it was obvious he didn't take her faith seriously. She stopped seeing him after that, and she told me the next time she dated somebody, she would proceed slowly to make sure he expressed his faith through his actions."

"Mmm." He was unsure of what to comment about Anna's dating habits. "Where's Karen?"

"She's sick with a stomach virus, so she couldn't make it to church today."

Scotty tugged Monica's hand. "Aunt Monica, can we go to Phillips now?"

"Be patient. I'm talking to Mr. John."

John chuckled, running his hand over Scotty's head. "How about I treat you and your aunt to lunch, sport?"

The little boy did a small jump with excitement. "Can he come with us, Aunt Monica?"

John was rewarded with a charming smile from Monica. "If he wants to come with us, he can."

His heart sped up as his eyes locked with hers. He realized he could get used to this, spending time each Sunday afternoon on an outing with Monica and her nephew.

In the parking lot, he opened the passenger door for her. "Do you mind if I drive, and we can pick up your car later?"

"That's fine."

Scotty opened his door and jumped into the car, buckling his seat belt. He bounced on the leather seat. "I can't wait to eat at Phillips!"

After they arrived and had eaten their lunch, Scotty had a suggestion. "Aunt

Monica, you never took me to the saltwater taffy candy store. You promised we could go last week!"

"Scotty, stop whining." She touched the boy's shoulder. "We can go sometime this week."

John came to the rescue. "We can go now. I haven't had saltwater taffy in ages."

A short time later, they entered the spacious shop. Scents of sugar and chocolate surrounded them, and workers stood behind a glass window, wrapping taffy and beating and pouring fudge. John gazed at the display case, enjoying the view of several pastel-colored round and cylindrical taffy pieces. Multihued mints rested in receptacles, and various kinds of fudge were available.

Scotty jumped up and down, pulling Monica's hand. "Aunt Monica, I smell chocolate! Can I have some fudge?"

John purchased the chocolate–peanut butter fudge for Scotty and Monica, and John decided on the milk chocolate candy. He also purchased a box of taffy for her to take home for Scotty.

The small candy shop had a playground out back. They sat at one of the small round tables to savor their snack.

John enjoyed his chocolate candy, and Monica ate her fudge. Scotty ate his candy in a hurry. "Don't eat so fast," she admonished. "Your fudge is not going anyplace."

Scotty chuckled as he drained the last of the water from the plastic bottle. "Can I go and play in the playground now?"

"Okay, but be careful," she warned as she led him to the abandoned outdoor play area. She let him loose before she returned to the table. Instead of sitting across from John, she sat in the seat beside him because it had a better view of the play area.

"Did you enjoy the class today?" she asked.

He sipped his water. "Well, it was interesting. It gave me some things to think about, and I'm looking forward to attending next week."

She beamed. "You are? That's so encouraging. I certainly hope you find your way to Jesus through this class."

He still didn't know if he'd "find" Jesus through the class, but a lot of his questions about God and salvation might be answered through the lessons. "I noticed today and last week that you were staring at that couple with the baby sitting near the exit of the sanctuary."

She picked up her water bottle and took a sip, tapping her foot. She remained silent, so he continued. "You looked upset when you were watching them, and when the woman looked toward you, you looked away. Are they friends of yours?"

"I'd rather not discuss them." The unfamiliar stony edge to her voice was like a shock of frigid water.

"I didn't mean to make you feel bad. I just wondered, that's all. You don't have to talk about it if you don't want to."

She watched the play area. "Well, I guess I have to say they're friends of mine." Her voice remained hard, and she certainly didn't sound like the Monica Crawford he had been spending time with during the last month. Her jaw tensed, and he encouraged her to continue, hoping she would calm down.

"They have to be my friends since they're members of my church, and they're good Christian people." Her voice was no longer hard, but sad and resigned.

He rubbed her shoulder, offering her his comfort. "He was your old boyfriend, wasn't he?"

"What makes you think that? Did Karen or Anna tell you?"

He shook his head, raising his hands into the air. "I wouldn't talk to Karen or Anna behind your back about your love life. I'm not that underhanded." He looked toward the cream-colored wall, hurt.

She touched his shoulder. "I'm sorry," she muttered. "I wasn't thinking. Please forgive me."

He nodded, still wondering if Monica trusted him after that comment. "Tell me about this guy. Who is he?" He touched her hand. "Why does he make you look so sad? Are you in love with him?"

She blinked rapidly, and for a minute, he thought she was going to cry. But her eyes remained dry as she fiddled with her empty water bottle. "Not really."

"Not really? Sounds to me like you still love him."

She shook her head. "No, that's not true. I dated him for a long time."

"How long?"

"Two years."

"What happened? Wasn't it possible for the two of you to work through your problems and make your relationship work?"

She laughed harshly, shaking her head. "You know, I wish it were that simple, where we had issues we needed to work through and then we could have made it work."

"But it wasn't that simple?"

She shook her head. "No, it wasn't."

He squeezed her hand. "Be honest with me. What's up with this man at your church and his wife and baby?"

"I was in love with Kevin. We dated for two years, and I was ready to settle down and get married."

"And he wasn't?"

"No, actually he was."

He shook his head. "I don't understand."

"You will understand when I finish telling you." The hard edge returned to her voice as she told him about her old boyfriend. "After we'd been dating for a year, I wanted to know where things stood between us. Before I could ask Kevin what his intentions were, his mother died."

"So you never talked about marriage after his mother died?"

"I waited for a while, since he grieved pretty hard after his mother's death. They were really close and I could tell it was a difficult time for him. He was sad and kind of moody after she died, which is understandable, but things changed between us after that."

He frowned. "How did things change?"

"Our relationship shifted. Kevin was obviously going through a difficult time, but he didn't want to talk to me about it. We continued to date, but I could tell something heavy was on his mind. He refused to open up to me and that bothered me. When I finally asked him about marriage, he put me off by saying he was still dealing with his mother's death and he wasn't in the right state of mind to make a marriage commitment."

"You believed him?"

She sighed. "At first I did, but when our two-year dating anniversary crept up, I figured I was kidding myself. I was about to give him an ultimatum when he took me to a fancy restaurant. It was my favorite place to eat, and I figured he was taking me there to propose."

He squeezed her hand. "And he didn't?"

She shook her head. "He told me we would always be brother and sister in Christ and that he would always care for me as a member of the church. But he said he couldn't continue to date me because he didn't love me."

He gasped. "Really?"

She again nodded. "To make matters worse, he showed up at church the following Sunday with the woman he ended up marrying."

"So he was dating both of you at the same time?"

"I'm not sure. He obviously knew her while he knew me, but I never knew if they were dating. Perhaps he wanted to break up with me before he pursued her and introduced her to the congregation as his girlfriend."

He whistled softly. "That's rough. So was that the woman he was with at church today?"

"Yes. They got engaged six months after he broke up with me and married two months later."

"Six months?"

"Yes."

"He probably was seeing her while he was dating you. Did you ever ask him about it?"

"No."

"No? Why not? You dated the man for two years, so he at least owed you some sort of explanation."

She shook her head, and he gave her a hug. "He didn't love me. That's reason enough to break up. I had my dignity to consider. I didn't want to call him and demand to know if he was two-timing me like that. It would have made me look like a lovesick fool who couldn't let go of a man who obviously didn't love me."

He released her. "Well, Kevin is the king of all fools. If you'd let me date you, I promise I wouldn't treat you so shabbily, and I certainly wouldn't be dating another woman behind your back. Do you still think about Kevin often?"

"Not really. When I see him with his wife and child, it's like a cold splash of water in my face, a reminder of what I imagined for myself if things had worked out with us."

"I think you still have feelings for him. You need to get him out of your mind and not be sad when you see him with his family. How long ago did you two break up?"

"Two years."

"You should have moved on by now. Don't let his negative treatment of you make you doubt all men."

"I'm not doing that."

"Yes, you are. You should see the sad look in your eyes when you see Kevin with his wife and baby. Have you even thought about changing churches?"

"No, I couldn't change churches. My parents always taught me to face my problems. They say if the good Lord is on your side then things can't go wrong. If I had switched churches when we broke up, it would be like I was running away from my problems. Plus, Kevin would have known how much I loved him."

"So you never told him you loved him?"

She shook her head. "I started asking what his intentions were after we'd been dating for a year, but I never told him I loved him, and my mother always says if a man loves you, he'll let you know." She shrugged. "I guess Kevin finally let me know his feelings. It just wasn't what I wanted to hear."

Scotty yelled for her. "Aunt Monica!"

She hurried over to her nephew, who complained about being thirsty. She purchased him another bottle of water, and after he drank it, he tried to return to the play area. He whined as Monica led him back to their table. "John, thanks for treating us to candy, but I think it's time for us to get home. Scotty has some homework to do this weekend, and he hasn't even started."

He stood, giving her a hug before he squeezed Scotty's small shoulder. "Hey, sport. Your teacher told me you've been assigned some books to read. I'll be by this Tuesday, and you can read to me."

"Okay, Mr. John," he grumbled as she led him to the car.

The three of them were silent as he drove back to the church so Monica could get her car. The parking lot was deserted. Monica opened her door and helped Scotty out of the car. She turned toward John. "Thanks again for lunch. I'll be seeing you this Tuesday."

"I'm looking forward to it." Their eyes locked like two pieces of a puzzle, and he wished their time together that day did not have to end. He watched them drive away.

When he returned to his house, he changed out of his dress clothes into a sweat suit. He drove to nearby Assateague Island. After getting out of the car, he stretched and admired the wild ponies frolicking in the woods nearby. A beautiful chestnut-and-white horse galloped past, heading toward a car with an open window. The car's occupants closed their windows, adhering to the island's rules of not petting or feeding the wild horses.

He broke into a slow jog before going into a full-blown run on the sandy shore. He breathed deeply, enjoying the cool wind that surrounded him, glad that the mosquitoes around Assateague Island were now gone since it was already October. He saw a few more ponies and a wild deer in the bushes. He continued running. When he could run no farther, he stopped and walked along the shore. He breathed deeply as he watched the golden rays of the sun splash upon the cloudy water. Thoughts of Monica's breakup filled his mind, and he wondered if they could ever find a way to be together. He thought about Jesus, and His claim of being the Messiah while He walked on the earth. Monica and Jesus filled his mind. As the sun sank onto the horizon, he said a little prayer.

God, Jesus Christ, if You are really my Savior, could You show me a sign to let me know these things are true?

Chapter 6

During the next month, Monica relaxed as Scotty continued adjusting to his studies and to his school. John still stopped by for his twice-weekly tutoring sessions, and she enjoyed his fellowship. She thanked God daily for the help he provided Scotty.

As she drove to Scotty's school after work, she recalled that the busy time of year for her job was approaching, and she would need to work some overtime hours. Clark was going to a convention in Washington DC to help solicit more accounts for the company. Not only would she have to make travel arrangements for Clark, but she would also need to provide clerical support for him while he was gone. During a convention Clark called her frequently, requesting she look up information for him and e-mail him documents he might have misplaced. She knew the impending trip would keep her busy, and she wondered if Anna or Karen would be able to babysit on the nights she might have to work late.

She pulled into the parking lot of Scotty's school. The wind blew, and the American flag and the banner bearing the school's crescent logo snapped in the strong November breeze. Escaping the frigid air, she entered and found Scotty chatting with his friends who also stayed for the after-school care program. "Scotty?" she beckoned.

"Oh hi, Aunt Monica."

She helped him fetch his coat and backpack.

After their short commute they arrived home. Monica unlocked the door, and they were greeted by the scent of cooked meat and vegetables. He sniffed, pulling his coat off and throwing it on the floor. "You cooked already?"

"Put your jacket in the closet," she demanded, ignoring his question.

He grumbled, and when a cuss word slipped from his mouth, she pulled him to a nearby chair. "You haven't cussed in a long time. I thought we already talked about this."

His eyes filled with tears. "Why doesn't my mother call or visit? Does she hate me?"

She often wondered the same things herself. Why didn't Gina at least call to see how her son was doing? "What happened today? Why are you suddenly asking about your mother?"

His lip quivered. "We're making paper turkeys for Thanksgiving. Mrs.

Brown and Robby are helping me make mine."

She pulled him into her arms. Thanksgiving was eight days away, and she had been so busy she hadn't given the holiday much thought. "Go on," she urged, kissing his forehead.

He moved out of her embrace as he continued his story. "People talked about where they would spend Thanksgiving. Since it's Family Week at school, my teacher told everybody to tell about their parents and their brothers and sisters." He shook his head. "I don't have a daddy, and my mother is gone. Where is she?"

She rubbed his shoulder. "Your mother didn't tell you where she was going?"

He shook his head. "No. She told me about some circus but didn't tell me where they were going. Is the circus coming to Ocean City? Can we go and see her if it comes here?" His voice was so full of hope that she didn't know what to say.

Instead of answering him, she pulled him into her arms again and in a low voice called upon God to help. "Jesus, please help Scotty during this difficult time. Please keep Gina safe and please place it upon her heart to call us to let us know she's okay. Please make Scotty strong during this period of adjustment in his life. In Jesus' name, amen."

"Amen." He sighed. "So does that mean Mom will call me since you asked God about it?"

She pulled his chin between her two fingers. "I want you to always remember this: God hears all prayers. He might not answer them as we want Him to, but God just heard us, and He has the power to make you feel better. Now I can promise you that."

He still didn't seem to believe her as he placed his coat in the closet. She watched him as he pulled out his braille reading material and began his homework. She shook her head, ashamed that her sister could abandon her child for a man.

She didn't think it was wise to let Scotty know she'd been trying to track down Gina for the last two weeks. She'd called the National African-American Circus information line, trying to find a way to contact Randy, the trapeze artist, so she could get a message to Gina. She had managed to get a few messages through, but she wasn't sure if those messages were passed to her sister.

An hour later she served the dinner that had been cooking all day in the slow cooker. The cubed steak, vegetable, and potato stew was tasty, but she was so upset about Scotty's questions about his mother that she could barely eat. She sipped on a glass of soda, her stomach in turmoil. Closing her eyes, she said another silent prayer for Gina's safety and for Scotty's peace of mind. She also prayed for her own health—if she worried incessantly about something, it always brought on a stomachache. After she whispered her amen, the phone rang. The sound pealed throughout the house, so she walked into the living room and answered it. "Hello?"

"Monica?" Gina's slurred voice carried over the line.

"Gina!"

Scotty ran from the kitchen table so quickly that he bumped the table and his bowl of stew toppled onto the floor. The bowl shattered into pieces, and seconds later he was pulling on her leg. "I want to talk to Mom!"

"Is that my baby?" Gina asked.

She turned away from Scotty, whispering into the phone. "You're drunk! How can you call here like that?"

"Aunt Monica, I want to talk to my mom!" He was crying and grabbing at her like a madman, so she handed him the phone, hoping he was so excited about hearing from his mother that he wouldn't notice she was inebriated.

"Mom! Why haven't you called me before now?" Scotty clutched the phone as he spoke to his mother. "Uh-huh. Yeah."

Monica hovered, listening to his side of the phone call, wondering what Gina was telling him. She wanted to get the phone back so she could give her sister a piece of her mind. The dialogue continued for five minutes before Scotty said good-bye. As he attempted to hang up the phone, Monica grabbed the receiver. "No, I have to talk to her, Scotty."

He shrugged. "She's gone."

She held the receiver to her ear and heard silence. She slammed the phone back into the cradle, trying to control her anger. "What did your mother tell you?"

"Nothing much. She says the circus isn't that much fun, and maybe I can come and live with her again. I'm glad she doesn't hate me. If she wants me to live with her again, she must not hate me."

She picked up the receiver as her heart pounded. Since she didn't have caller ID, she dialed a combination of numbers to find out if she could get the phone number from where Gina had called. When she couldn't do it that way, she called the operator who informed her the call was made from an international location and she couldn't track the number for her. Frustrated, she banged the phone down, muttering under her breath.

"What's wrong?"

"I needed to speak with your mother, and she hung up." She gazed at the mess in the kitchen. "Did you want some more stew?"

He shook his head. "Can I go to my room?"

"Yes, you can go to your room." She was glad to have a few minutes alone after the disturbing phone call. As she cleaned up the mess on the kitchen floor, she couldn't stop her tears from falling.

❧

The following day after the last student had taken his exit, John gathered his papers and his briefcase and headed to his car, eager to get to Monica's house.

Later, he pulled into her driveway. Scotty tugged on John's hand as he met him at the door. "Hey, Mr. John!"

He chuckled. "Hey, sport! How did you know it was me at the door?"

"I heard your car drive up, and Aunt Monica told me to come and let you in."

John entered the house, disappointed when he didn't smell one of Monica's tasty meals cooking. "Mr. John, my mother called me last night."

Intrigued, he looked at Scotty. "Did she? What did she say?"

"I might go and live with her again. Wouldn't that be great?"

Confused, he glanced into the empty kitchen. It was spotless and again he wondered where Monica was. "Where's your aunt?"

"She's upstairs." He pulled John into the kitchen. "Come and hear me read. I got these Dr. Seuss books in braille a couple of days ago!"

John sat at the table but could barely listen to Scotty read the rhyming words in the braille book. When he struggled with a certain word, John forced himself to pay attention and help him out. They continued their reading exercises for an hour, and he was tempted to go upstairs and get Monica himself when he heard soft footsteps plodding down the stairs.

She entered the kitchen. Her eyes were sad, and there were circles beneath them. He stood, sensing she needed a hug. He pulled her into his arms. "What's the matter?"

She shook her head, motioning toward Scotty. "I'll tell you later," she whispered in his ear, obviously not wanting her nephew to hear their conversation.

"Aunt Monica, I'm hungry," Scotty announced.

She looked at John. "I'm sorry. I'm not feeling well and didn't make dinner tonight."

He squeezed her shoulder, noticing how the bone protruded beneath her skin. "You need to eat something. You're getting too thin."

"My parents say the same thing."

"How about I take us out to dinner at Phillips?"

"Yeah, let's go to Phillips!" Scotty jumped from his seat, excited.

She shook her head as she sat at the table. "No, I don't have the energy to go out."

"Aw, Aunt Monica," he whined.

John sat beside her, taking her hand. "How about I have the food delivered? Why don't we order some pizza? What would you like, Scotty?"

Scotty told him his favorite was cheese pizza, and when John asked Monica, she just shrugged. "I'm not very hungry. Whatever you get is fine."

"Aunt Monica likes supreme pizza," Scotty announced.

John placed the order over the phone, and he added an order of sodas. "They said it'll be here in thirty minutes."

When the food arrived, he answered the door and paid for their meal. He entered the kitchen and opened the boxes. Steam floated from the hot pizzas, and the scents of tomatoes and olives filled the air. He set the box in front of her and opened it. "Here, you need to eat something."

She shook her head. "John, I can't." She held her stomach.

Concerned, he sat beside her, rubbing her shoulder. "Are you sick? Did you catch that stomach virus that was going around awhile ago?"

She glanced at Scotty, who was already gobbling his food and guzzling soda. "My stomach gets upset when I'm worried."

He coaxed her to eat a slice of pizza. "Don't get that upset. It can't be that bad. Is it life or death?" he asked in a whisper so Scotty wouldn't hear them.

She shook her head. "No, but it is serious."

"Well, it won't help if you don't eat something." He took a paper plate and plopped some of her food on it. "Eat that and drink some soda. I'm sure you'll feel better when you're done."

He sat beside her with his plate of pizza. He remained next to her until she ate. She tasted the food and drank her soda. He was even more pleased when she reached for seconds.

After dinner he placed the leftovers into the refrigerator and threw away the paper plates and napkins. Scotty asked if he could watch TV until bedtime, and she told him it was all right. After Scotty took his exit, John sat beside her, taking her hand. "Now, what's the matter?"

Tears spilled from her eyes. "Gina wants Scotty again. I can't give him back." She glanced into the living room. "His life was a mess when he came here, and I've done so much work on teaching him about the Lord and about how important it is to do well in school." She shrugged. "If Gina takes him back, he'll revert to the way he was. She never instilled good values in him."

He rubbed her shoulder. "I'm sorry. Did you pray about it?"

She raised her eyebrows, giving him an intense stare. "Yes I did. You believe in the power of prayer?" Her voice sounded hopeful.

He wiped away her tears. "No, but I know that you do. I'm still unsure what to believe about God and prayer, but I do know that it can't hurt to pray." She turned away as he continued to hold her hand, offering comfort. "Besides, how do you know Gina hasn't changed in the last few months?"

She laughed. The sound was loud and grating. "My sister will need longer than a few months to change. It'll take an utter miracle to change her."

"Well, don't you believe in miracles? God is capable of anything. I read it myself in my Bible."

For a brief moment, her sadness seemed to disappear. "You've been reading your Bible?"

"Of course I have. That's why I've been taking that class you recommended and going to church. I'm still trying to figure out this whole God thing."

"I think you'll figure out this 'God thing' in due time. Your salvation depends upon it."

Not wanting to talk about his journey in finding out the truth about Jesus Christ, he changed the subject. "So where are you and Scotty going to spend Thanksgiving? Will you be cooking dinner?"

"No, I don't see the need since it's just the two of us. I usually go down to my parents' house for Thanksgiving. What are you going to do?"

He shrugged. "I'm not sure. Since my parents passed, I can't go and see them anymore for the holiday. Sometimes I'll spend it with a college friend of mine who lives down in Baltimore. But this year he and his family are traveling to Florida for Thanksgiving." He was disappointed Monica and Scotty were going away for the holiday. "I'll probably eat at a restaurant."

"Why don't you come with us?"

"Come with you? Why?" He tried not to sound too startled at her invite.

"I just don't like the idea of your spending a holiday alone."

Touched by her concern, he hoped this gesture was an indication that she would soon change her mind and allow him to date her the way he really wanted to. "Are you sure your parents wouldn't mind?"

"Of course not. My parents would welcome you."

"But. . .don't you think we'd be giving them the wrong impression? You said we aren't seeing each other. Wouldn't they think I'm your boyfriend?"

She shook her head. "I've already told them you're Scotty's tutor. They know how grateful I am for all you've done for Scotty."

"Okay." He hesitated, still unsure of accepting her invite but intrigued by her gesture. His feelings for her during the last few months had done nothing but grow deeper, and if he spent the holiday with her, he suspected it would make his affections go over the top and make him imagine them as a couple even more.

"Hello?" She waved her hand in front of his face. "What are you thinking about?"

"About your invite. Yes, I accept."

"Good!"

"So, what time should I get here?"

"My parents live about two and a half hours away—"

"Two and a half hours! You're going to go only for the day?"

"Yes. I don't think you'd want to spend the night at my parents' house, let alone the whole Thanksgiving weekend!"

"I don't want you to change your plans just because of me."

She shook her head. "You're coming, and it's settled. My parents eat dinner around two o'clock. Scotty and I leave in the morning since I do help my mother a bit in the kitchen. Can you be here around eight o'clock?"

"I'll be here. Did you want me to bring anything?"

"No, my parents will have plenty of food. Sometimes people from their church drop by during the day to eat their leftovers." She leaned back into her chair, her dark eyes sparkling with curiosity. "Speaking of church, how is that class coming along?"

So much had been happening the last few weeks, he didn't even know if he could explain it himself. He thought about the prayer he had issued after that first class session he'd taken. He still wasn't sure about God's existence, but he'd daily sent up a plea, asking for a sign to show that He really did exist. He hesitated.

She grabbed his hand. "You're still struggling, aren't you?"

He nodded, wishing he couldn't disappoint her. "I can't talk about it. I'm still coming to terms with a lot of things." He wanted to tell her about his daily prayer. But he hesitated, not wanting to give her the wrong idea about his spiritual beliefs.

She shook her head. "Don't say anything to me about it. God knows what's in your heart, and He'll straighten you out. You just wait and see." Her voice was full of confidence.

He checked his watch. "Well, I see it's getting late, so I'm going to head home." He was pleased she had cheered up. "Try not to worry about Gina. I'm sure she was just bluffing." Her frown returned as they stood. "I didn't mean to make you feel bad by mentioning your sister."

"It's okay. She would have popped into my mind as soon as you left anyway." She walked him to the door and said good-bye.

Chapter 7

The following Sunday, after John was finished with his class, he entered the crowded sanctuary.

Monica sat in the middle pew alone. He didn't see Karen, but he did spot Anna sitting in the back with Dean Love. They were holding hands and she beamed, her hair bouncing as she focused on the pulpit.

Monica looked great, as usual, in her church clothes, and he noticed she again stared at the couple who sat near the back with their infant. He wondered if she was still in love with her ex-boyfriend. Her mouth drooped with sadness, and he wanted to sit beside her but at the last minute decided not to. Her charming presence would distract him during the service. He found a seat in the back, intent upon looking up the scriptures Pastor Martin had given him. While people sang and swayed in the church praising God, he pulled out his Bible, wanting to find answers to the questions he so desperately sought.

After the service was over, Monica spotted him in the foyer. Her dark eyes were curious, and he sensed she wondered why he hadn't sat with her during the service. Before he could speak, Scotty entered the foyer, led by his Sunday school teacher. "Aunt Monica!"

"Hi, Scotty." She assisted her nephew with his jacket.

John approached. "Hey," he greeted.

"Hi, John. Until a few minutes ago, I didn't realize you were here today," she commented.

"I sat in the back."

"Oh, did you arrive late? Did you not go to your class?"

He shook his head. "No, I was here on time. I just needed to be alone for a while."

She frowned, pulling her coat from a hanger. He helped her put it on. "I'm making sandwiches for Scotty's lunch when we get home. Why don't you join us?"

"I have a lot on my mind, so I think I'll be heading home."

"Mr. John, why don't you come with us?" Scotty whined.

He squeezed Scotty's shoulder. "I'll see you later this week, sport. Didn't your aunt tell you we're spending Thanksgiving at your grandparents' house? I'm coming with you."

"You are?" Scotty turned toward Monica. "Will my mom be there? Is the

61

circus coming to Grandpa's town for Thanksgiving?"

Sadness etched her face as she took his hand. "I don't think so. Maybe she'll call you soon."

"She'll call me on Thanksgiving?" he pressed.

She placed a hat on her head. "We'll have to wait and see. I never know when your mother is planning to call."

John rescued Monica and changed the subject. "I noticed Anna was with her friend Dean Love."

"They were here? They didn't say hello."

"I saw them leave right after service. They were sitting in the back," he explained. "Where's Karen? I wanted to say hi to her."

"She's out of town at a beauticians' convention in Baltimore. She's supposed to come back tonight. Both Karen and Anna said they would drop by tomorrow evening for a visit."

As Kevin and his family walked by, John touched her arm. "Well, you have a nice day, and I'll see you later this week."

He heard her mumble a good-bye as he exited the foyer.

❧

The next day at work, Monica showed her boss the Power-Point presentation she had completed for a meeting with his key executives the following day. As she moved through the motions of doing her job, she struggled to understand why John had refused to sit with her in the sanctuary the previous day. His standoffish behavior was very puzzling, and she wondered if he had found interest in another woman.

She was glad when it was time to go home. She picked up Scotty from school, and she prepared his favorite meal when they arrived home. She pulled the pan of chicken fingers and fries from the oven. "Come and eat, Scotty!"

He hurried into the kitchen, using the wall to guide himself. "You made chicken fingers and french fries?" He plopped onto a chair. "Do we have any ketchup?"

"Yes, we do." She removed a serving of broccoli from the boiling water and added butter and salt. She placed the food in front of him.

He sniffed. "Do I have to eat the broccoli?"

"Yes, you do." She fixed a plate of food for herself, even though she didn't care for chicken fingers and fries. She hoped that by fixing Scotty's favorite meal, she might cheer him up and help him forget that his mother still had not called him back.

After they said grace, they enjoyed their meal in silence. When he ate the last of his fries and fingers, he asked for more.

"You'll get more after you eat your broccoli."

"Aw, Aunt Monica!" He sulked but eventually ate his vegetable. She made another serving of food for him and added another puddle of ketchup to his plate. He chewed happily, humming as he munched his chicken and fries.

She finished her food and rinsed her plate, placing it in the dishwasher. When Scotty was finished, he left the table and returned to the living room. He paced the floor as if he were bored. "Can I go outside?"

She opened the blinds. Dusk was falling, and the temperature had dropped. "You can go into the backyard." She pulled a ball from the closet and gave it to him. "You can play with this out there. But be sure to come inside when you get too cold." He ran to the closet and got his coat, hat, and gloves, then went into the backyard, bouncing his ball.

She was about to use the time to go through her devotional since she'd overslept that morning, but before she could start, her doorbell rang. "I forgot about Karen and Anna stopping by," she mumbled as she answered the door. They entered, bringing in a cold gust of air. They hugged her before removing their coats and laying them on the couch. She invited them to sit in the living room.

"So, how was your conference, Karen?" Monica asked.

Anna folded her thick arms. "After Karen tells you about her conference, remind me to tell you how things are progressing between Dean and me."

Karen fingered her hair. "It's only been a few weeks. Things couldn't have progressed that much between you two."

Anna chuckled. "You'd be surprised. When God allows you to find the right man, you are on His timetable, and maybe He's telling me that Dean Love is the right man for me." She looked at Monica. "Last time I saw, it looked like John was really smitten with you. Is he still tutoring Scotty?"

Surprised at the question, she nodded. "John and I are not in a relationship, though."

"But you like him, that counts for something," Anna commented.

"Of course I like him. I think I'm falling in love with him, and that's the problem."

Their mouths dropped open as they stared at their best friend. "You're serious?" Karen whispered.

Monica nodded. "I can't wait to see him again. He still hasn't accepted Christ, which is why I won't date him." She recalled his cool attitude.

"What's wrong?" asked Anna.

Monica explained his frosty attitude toward her at church the previous day.

"Well, I don't blame him. He's probably falling for you, too, but knows it can't lead to anything right now." Anna's opinion didn't make her feel any better.

Monica suddenly wanted to be alone, wishing her best friends had not stopped by after all. "Both of you are Christians. You know it's wrong to be unequally yoked with nonbelievers."

Anna leaned back into the couch. "I'm not knocking what you're doing, because I'd be doing the same thing if I were you. I'm just saying look at it from John's point of view. You're falling in love with him, and he might realize that." She flung her braided hair behind her back. "He might love you, too. And being around you is hard, knowing you two can't be together. Instead of acting loving and affectionate toward you, he decides to act cool and calm, hoping these emotions between the two of you will dwindle a little until he decides what he wants to do about God."

Karen gazed at Anna. "I'm assuming Dean is a Christian?"

Anna nodded. "He sure is! He was born and raised in the church. I wouldn't be going out with him otherwise."

Karen placed her hand on Monica's arm. "Are you sure you're over Kevin? I see the way you stare at him and his wife at church. Sometimes. . ."

"What?" Monica pressed.

Anna cleared her throat. "Sometimes you act like you haven't gotten over him. You don't talk to him unless he speaks to you first, and you're not exactly friendly toward his wife."

"It's hard for me to get over things. When I see him, it's a reminder of what I lost. Kevin is a charming, good-looking man, and he's godly. You don't know how much I used to fantasize about marrying him."

Karen arched her eyebrow. "You don't still fantasize about him, do you?"

Monica shook her head. "Not anymore. But it's still hard seeing him."

Anna spoke. "Will you ever get over him? Two years is long enough to grieve over a lost love."

Karen nodded. "I agree with Anna. You've told John about Kevin?"

"Yes."

"I'm sure he's seen you looking at Kevin in church. Maybe John thinks you're still in love with him. You need to let him know that Kevin is part of your past and you're over him for good. And stop being so obvious about your pain! Stop looking at him during service. I'm sure John finds it unnerving," Karen said.

Anna offered to pray, and the three of them stood in a circle and joined hands as Anna's loud, strong voice filled the living room asking God for guidance during this difficult time.

When their prayer was over, Monica gave her friends the details about recent events in her life. She told them about Gina's phone call and John's acceptance of her Thanksgiving invite.

Anna threw her head back, her long hair hitting the back of the couch. "Which one of these things do you want to talk about first?"

Karen focused on Monica. "Do you really think Gina will take Scotty back?"

Monica shrugged. "Who knows? Gina lies so much, it's hard to tell when she's telling the truth."

"Your sister has always been jealous of you," Anna offered. "Perhaps she's just trying to get you upset, knowing you've probably bonded with Scotty. I wouldn't put it past her to do that." She seemed to think about it. "And you know if it was her intent to upset you, she's succeeded. I can tell her phone call really bothers you."

Karen looked at Anna. "Monica can't help being upset! She loves Scotty, and she only wants what's best for him. I'll be sure to keep the matter on my prayer list," she offered.

Monica regarded them with warmth. "Thanks so much for your support. If she does take Scotty away and disappear again, I don't know how I'll handle it. I'll be a basket case worrying about him."

"Can't you get a lawyer or something? Try to prove she's an unfit mother?" asked Anna.

"I'm not sure. Right now my hands are tied. Gina is still legally his mother, but I'm leery of taking her to court to prove her as an unfit parent. The last time my parents tried this, Gina disappeared for two years. Right now I have power of attorney, but it's only for six months. When that time frame is over, Gina has to decide if she wants to continue giving me power of attorney or if she wants to take Scotty back."

Karen pursed her lips. "Well, if you had to, you can prove Gina as unfit. She dumped Scotty on your doorstep."

She sensed the Lord did not want her to take Gina to court to get custody of Scotty. "Like I said, I can't risk doing that. Scotty loves his mother, and he misses her."

Anna changed the subject. "Why did you invite John to your parents' house for Thanksgiving?"

"John has done a lot for Scotty over the last few months. He's been patient, kind, and caring toward my nephew, and he doesn't charge us a dime."

"But you make dinner for him every time he comes," Karen pointed out.

"I like cooking for him, but I wanted to do something more. When he told me he would be alone on Thanksgiving, I just knew I couldn't allow him to do that after he'd done so much for us. So I invited him to my folks' house. I've already told my mother about his agnostic views, so she doesn't have the wrong idea about us being a couple."

"Speaking of your folks," Karen commented, "are they still harping on the fact that you're thirty-seven and not married?"

"They haven't been on my case about that since Kevin broke up with me. I think they were disappointed when things didn't work out between us, especially since they met him several times and they both seemed to like him."

The back door banged open, and Scotty ran into the house, dropping the ball on the kitchen floor. "Aunt Monica! I'm thirsty!"

She traipsed into the kitchen, picking up the blue ball. "Young man, put this back where it belongs." He grumbled as he dropped the ball into the closet before removing his hat, gloves, and jacket. "We have company. Don't forget to say hello."

"Hey, Scotty!" Anna hugged Scotty, and Karen kissed his cheek, leaving a smear of lipstick.

"Yuck!" Scotty rubbed his cheek before saying hello. Monica gave him a glass of water. When he was finished, she sent him upstairs to run his bath.

"Was he excited about talking to his mother?" asked Karen.

"He sure was. I'm at a loss. Scotty loves his mother and misses her, yet she refuses to call regularly to check on her own son. She doesn't even leave a phone number where she can be reached. I'm so worried. What if an emergency happens? How will I even be able to contact Gina?"

Anna and Karen murmured words of encouragement as they gathered their coats. The three women shared a brief hug before they went their separate ways.

Chapter 8

During the next couple of days, the college campus bustled with activity as the young people looked forward to the upcoming Thanksgiving break. John wondered what it would be like to spend the holiday with Monica's family.

As he continued to go through his week, he thought about the class he was taking at Monica's church. His whole outlook on life was changing. The thought of there being a creator in charge of the universe was refreshing.

On Thanksgiving morning John awoke early, still having mixed emotions about spending the holiday with Monica and her family. As he spent more time with her, his feelings grew deeper, so deep that he didn't know what to do with himself.

He got out of bed, taking time to read through the study notes for the church class. As a result of his time studying the Bible, he was starting to understand why Christians placed their faith in a God that was so powerful, yet loving and kind. He still wondered about a lot of things, but slowly his questions were being answered, and that was one of the things he hoped to accomplish by taking this class.

He appeared on Monica's doorstep an hour later. The wind howled through the trees, and snow flurried and fluttered to the ground. He buried his hands in his pockets, wondering if the temperature would rise before the end of the day.

Monica answered the door, looking as lovely as ever. Recalling the way she pined after her ex, he held back and simply touched her arm. "You look pretty." He noticed the dark circles beneath her eyes.

She invited him in, and the scents that filled the house made his mouth water. He sniffed the air. "What are you cooking?"

Giggling, she led him into the kitchen. Scotty was finishing his breakfast. "Hi, Mr. John! Did you want to taste Aunt Monica's blueberry muffins?"

John sniffed again. The scent of blueberry muffins and apple pie filled the air. He saw an apple pie and a sweet-potato pie on the stove. A carton of eggs and a plate of bacon sat on the counter. Monica removed two of the eggs from the carton. "How did you want your eggs?" She held the white oval globes, patiently awaiting his response. He realized he could get used to seeing her like this, in his own kitchen, each day, making breakfast for him.

"Mr. John! Aunt Monica wants to know how you like your eggs!"

He shook his head, dispelling the pleasant daydream. "I like my eggs scrambled."

She broke the eggs into a bowl and whipped them before pouring them into the hot skillet. After she finished cooking, she served him his eggs along with two warm blueberry muffins and bacon. John savored his meal. He'd been so engrossed in his thoughts earlier that morning that he'd forgotten to eat breakfast. She served him coffee and orange juice. When he was finished, he pushed his empty plate aside. "Monica, that is the best breakfast I've had in a long time."

After John finished his coffee, they traipsed to her car. As she started to open her door, he took her hand. "Do you mind if I drive?"

"Are you sure?"

"I don't mind driving." He touched her cheek. "You look a little tired. All you need to do is point me in the right direction once we get off the highway."

"Thanks. I appreciate it. Come on, Scotty." She pulled her nephew's hand. "Mr. John is driving us to Grandma and Grandpa's house."

The boy climbed into the backseat and buckled his seat belt. He placed his music headphones on his ears and played his portable CD player, evidently tuning out the adults.

Once they were on the highway, John was about to comment on the weather when a soft snore wafted through the car. He glanced at Monica as she dozed.

She slept for an hour before her eyes opened, and she looked confused as they raced down the interstate, pine trees passing by in a blur. She blinked rapidly. "Why didn't you wake me up?"

"Because you needed some sleep. I figured you've been awake the last few nights worrying about your sister."

She glanced into the backseat and saw Scotty was still occupied with his music.

He squeezed her hand. "Although I don't consider myself to be a Christian, I do have one Christian quality. I'm honest. I haven't been totally honest with you about everything, but I want to rectify that now."

"What are you talking about?"

"Well, if you haven't noticed, I've been a little distant toward you over the last week."

She remained silent as she gazed out the window, looking at the passing scenery. He waited, seeing if she would comment on his recent behavior, but when her silence continued, he plunged on. "Well, one reason I've been cool toward you is because I think you still love your ex-boyfriend, and I don't think you've done anything to get over him. Until you do, I can't see you having a relationship with anybody else."

"You have no idea what I'm feeling, so I'd appreciate it if you kept your comments to yourself." She was shaking. He didn't know if she was shaking with rage or if a sudden chill from the air had crept into her side of the car. He turned the heat up, wishing he hadn't upset her.

"Don't get mad—"

"What gives you the right to tell me how I feel about Kevin?"

Fatigue swept over him like a tidal wave, and he wondered if they should pull over to finish this conversation. He eased the car into a truck stop and turned off the engine.

Scotty pulled his earphones off. "Are we at Grandma's?" His voice was full of excitement.

"No, sport. We're not. I had to go to a rest stop for a minute. Just listen to your music." Scotty shrugged and replaced his earphones, turning his music back on.

He squeezed her hand. "Please don't be mad."

She glared at him. "How can I not be mad? It's one thing for Karen and Anna to say something like that—"

"Karen and Anna said the same thing?"

"Yes, they did, but they're my best friends. You haven't known me for very long. It's wrong of you to tell me how I feel about somebody when you can't see into my heart. Besides, you know there's no hope for us because of your religious views."

"But, I care about you a lot. I'm falling in love with you—"

"John!" She looked at him as if he'd lost his mind.

"I'm just being honest with you. I'm really falling in love with you, and I know we can't be together right now. But I care about you so much that if you can't be with me, I at least want to see you with somebody that makes you happy. You've got so much going on in your life with Scotty and your sister." He stared at a family as they entered the truck stop. "I think you deserve a good man to be with you and help share your burden. If that man can't be me, I need to learn to accept that." He massaged her fingers. "But you should be able to find happiness with somebody else, and until you release your bitterness toward Kevin, then I think you'll be stuck being single."

Her eyes flared with sparks of anger as she jerked her hand away. "What makes you think being single means being stuck? You're the same age as I am and you're single. Have you ever been married before?"

The question surprised him, and he wondered if he'd jumped the gun on his advice. He just wanted her to be happy, and he knew that with her present situation, if she had a good, kind husband to lean on, she wouldn't worry so much and would take better care of herself. "No, I've never been married before."

She folded her arms, still looking at him. "Why not?"

He took a deep breath, wondering how he should answer her question. She was easily the first woman he loved in several years, but it wouldn't answer why he'd never married. "I guess you could say that the one time I asked a woman to marry me, she said no."

"Why?"

He closed his eyes, trying to ease the painful memories. "Because she said she couldn't marry somebody who didn't believe in God."

"A Christian woman seriously dated you?" Monica asked, her anger seemingly forgotten.

John sighed. "When I first met Gabriela, she wasn't a Christian. We were in graduate school, and she was working on her PhD in physics. She always said she didn't need God in her life, so my agnostic views didn't bother her. We'd been dating for a year when her twin sister died of cancer. Her twin was a Christian, and she shared her faith with Gabriela before her death. After Gabriela's sister died, she changed."

"How did she change?"

"She started reading her Bible and going to church. I thought it was just a phase she was going through. I'd already planned on asking her to marry me, so when I did, she told me that her views about God had changed. She told me of her recent decision to accept the Lord in her life, and she wasn't sure if a relationship with me would work unless I shared her views." He recalled how Gabriela's brown eyes had filled with tears as she delivered the news, and she also told him how much she loved him.

Her anger seemed to disappear, followed by compassion. "I'm sorry. I didn't realize." She squeezed his arm. "It's too bad your religious views have kept you from sharing your life with somebody special."

He was tempted to tell her his views were shifting lately, but didn't want to give her the false impression that he'd changed his mind about God. He decided to wait and see what he believed when he completed the class at her church.

He changed the subject. "I'm sorry I said you were stuck. I didn't mean that in a bad way. But you have this sad look when you see your ex, and it seems like you two really had something special. I think you can find that with somebody else, and until you put the past behind you, you'll be stuck with fantasies of your life with Kevin. . .fantasies that more than likely will never come true."

She looked out her window at a trucker running to his vehicle while yelling to one of his driving buddies before getting into his rig.

"Are you all right?" he asked.

She turned toward him. "Look, you might have a point about Kevin. Both Anna and Karen have mentioned the same thing to me, and I just need to let those memories go and not focus on him so much during church."

"That's why I suggested one time that you change churches."

"I told you why I can't do that."

He nodded. "I know, but you need to do something. I'm sure you're making both Kevin and his wife uncomfortable, staring at them like that during the service."

She thought about his advice. "Do you really think they notice? It's not like I sit there and blatantly stare at them."

"Well, you look over there enough. I think they know what you're doing. I see you talking to other church members after the service, but I've never seen you speak to them."

She huffed. "Well, maybe I just don't have anything to say to them."

"Uh-huh," he said. "Aren't Christians supposed to forgive? If you're a true Christian as you claim, shouldn't you forgive him for what happened?"

She rolled her eyes, staring out the windshield. She checked her watch. "Can we continue this conversation another time? My parents will be expecting us shortly, and they'll worry when we don't show up on time."

He started the ignition. The rest of the drive was made in silence.

As John drove through Baltimore, she told him about some of the nostalgic places she used to visit while growing up. She pointed to the Inner Harbor and mentioned the fun she had shopping in the many stores built around the waterfront. A few boats bobbed in the frigid water, and the squiggly wave decorating the Baltimore Aquarium shone in the distance. As they passed the Maryland Science Center, he reminisced about the field trips he'd taken while he was in elementary and junior high school. When he turned a corner, he hoped Monica's mood lifted as they made their way to her house.

After Thanksgiving Monica kept thinking about how much fun she had spending the holiday with John. In spite of their argument, they did have a good time with her parents. The only sad part of the holiday was when Gina unexpectedly showed up on her parents' doorstep with a black eye and wearing a tight dress and high heels. She was drunk, and Monica's father had to pay the taxi driver for Gina since she had no money. Scotty had been so ecstatic to see his mother that he refused to accompany Monica back home.

Monica wondered what had happened to Randy, the trapeze artist Gina was supposed to marry. When Monica's mother questioned Gina about her marriage, Gina shouted that she didn't want to talk about it. Her parents said they'd drop Scotty off during the weekend, so she hoped they were able to convince him to come back to live with her in Ocean City.

Her thoughts returned to John. Having John with her at her parents' house made it seem as if they were really a couple.

As she cleaned her house and pulled a box of Christmas decorations from the attic, she came across a box of mementos she'd collected with Kevin. She opened the box, scanning the pictures of her and Kevin at social events. She even found a printed copy of an old e-mail he'd written to her when he was away on an extended business trip. He claimed how much he'd missed her and that his strong affection for her kept him awake at night. She opened a heart-shaped box next. It had been filled with expensive chocolates. She sniffed the interior, still detecting the faint scent of cocoa.

She stuffed the items back into the box, again recalling how much she had loved Kevin. Since her breakup with him had been so sudden and painful, she wanted to be cautious about loving another man. John had said he was falling in love with her, and she knew her emotions were just as strong.

But what would happen between them if he never accepted Christ?

She knew if he never accepted Him as his Savior, she could never have a relationship with him. As she threw her memorabilia into the garbage and removed Christmas decorations from the cardboard box, she wondered if she would be strong enough to survive another breakup as devastating as the one she'd had with Kevin. Should she continue to spend free time with John, falling in love with him, when he was unsure about his salvation?

She stared at the Christmas decoration in her hand. Her heart was telling her to keep seeing John, but her mind was telling her to be cautious. "Oh Lord," she prayed, "I don't think I'm strong enough to continue seeing John until I know for sure that he's accepted You. Please guide me in saying the right words when I see him at church on Sunday." Tears stained her cheeks as she finished her short prayer. She wiped them away, sensing she'd made the right decision.

❧

The following Sunday after class, John searched the sanctuary for Monica. He saw Anna and Dean before spotting Karen and Monica in the middle pew. Monica looked toward him, and their eyes met. As he took a seat beside her, he noticed her dark eyes looked troubled.

He said hello to Karen before taking Monica's hand. "I hope you don't mind my sitting next to you during the service."

She pulled her hand away, gazing toward the podium. "I don't mind at all." He wondered why she was so aloof but decided she must still be worried about Scotty and Gina. During the praise and worship time, she lifted her hands toward the ceiling, praising God. But her shoulders slumped and she checked her watch often while the preacher spoke. He knew he needed to do something to cheer her up.

After service was over, he said good-bye to Karen before he touched Monica's arm. "What's the matter?"

"My mother called this morning. Gina's been acting up all weekend. She's broke, and she's mad at my parents because they won't buy her alcohol."

He shook his head, helping her with her coat. "They're still bringing Scotty back today?"

"They're supposed to, but they said he's been upset all weekend, crying, not understanding why his mother is so irrational." He opened the door for her, and they stepped into the brisk morning air. The fierce, cold wind blew with a vengeance, and the sky was bright blue and dotted with large clouds. Puffs of white air escaped their mouths as they spoke.

"But they said they were going to bring him?" he asked again as they walked among the crowd to her car.

She nodded as she unlocked her door. "Yes, they said they will. But. . .my sister is so vengeful that she might have something up her sleeve."

"What do you mean?"

She stepped into her car.

"Well, if she's determined, she'll think of a way to get her way. Do you know what I mean?"

He nodded. "I think so. But how can she stop your parents from bringing Scotty?"

She closed her eyes as if fighting bad memories. "Gina will stop at nothing to get what she wants."

He touched her shoulder. "Don't get so upset."

He continued to stand next to her open car door, wondering how he could comfort her. "What did your sister do in the past to upset you so much?"

"One time, when she didn't get her way, she threatened to harm herself."

He gasped. "Would she have done something so drastic?"

She shrugged. "I'm not sure. She could have been bluffing but. . .I don't know. I've been trying to get my sister to give God a chance, but she won't listen to me, and she certainly won't listen to my parents about Christianity or religion. They raised us as Christians, but Gina never wanted to embrace their beliefs."

He rubbed her shoulder. "Did you want me to come home with you? Did you need my support for whatever happens later?"

As she shook her head, the sunlight glinted off her dark hair. "No, it's sweet of you to offer, but. . ." She looked at him with her brown eyes. "To be honest with you, I'm wondering if this whole thing is a mistake."

"What thing?" Confusion filled his mind as he tilted his head.

She invited him to join her inside the car. He entered, and she turned the motor on, letting the heat warm up her vehicle. "I'm talking about us. I know we're not dating or anything."

"We're not officially. But"—he watched a young couple walk to their car—"I'm falling in love with you—"

"John—"

He touched her arm. "Let me finish, Monica. Sometimes I do feel like we're a couple, especially when we spent the day at your parents' house for Thanksgiving."

She gripped her steering wheel, gazing out the windshield. She turned and looked at him. "I feel the same way, and that's what bothers me so much. You've been so nice and supportive, and I understand how you feel about me because I feel the same way."

"You do?" She'd never admitted her feelings to him before.

She nodded. "That's why I think we should put the brakes on our relationship for a while. I can't let myself get carried away, falling for somebody, only to have him exit my life the way Kevin did."

He vehemently shook his head. "But I'm not like Kevin. I would never abandon you like that. I like you too much to treat you so poorly."

"It's more than that. I should never have invited you to my parents' house at Thanksgiving. I should never have invited you to spend time with me and my friends for meals after church." She gripped her steering wheel again. "I was looking for you this morning in the sanctuary, and when I saw you, I was so happy."

He touched her hand. "I was happy to see you, too."

"Don't you understand? My cooking for you and your spending time with me outside of tutoring my nephew have allowed things to escalate too soon. We need to just stop this."

His heart skipped a beat. "Stop what?"

She took a deep breath. "Stop spending time together outside of tutoring Scotty. When you come to my house, you can tutor my nephew, but that's all there is to it."

He gritted his teeth. "So you're saying that when I come to your house on Tuesdays and Thursdays that I'm just supposed to tutor Scotty and that's it? No more talks, social time, or dinners?"

Tears shimmered from her eyes and fell down her cheeks. "I don't want to do this—"

"Then don't!" He tried to put his arms around her, but she pushed him away. "Don't push me away. You're going through a lot right now, and I need to support you."

She shook her head. "We can't keep spending time together. It reminds me too much—" She stopped speaking and looked out the window. Her ex-boyfriend approached his car a few feet away. He placed the baby into the car seat and helped his wife into the vehicle before he got behind the wheel and drove away. "It reminds me too much about how I felt with Kevin. You know how much he hurt me, and if I keep spending time with you, it'll just get worse."

"Don't say that." He tried to touch her again, but she pushed him away.

"But it's true!" She wiped her eyes and reached in her purse for a tissue to blow her nose. "I appreciate all you've done for my nephew, and I hope my decision for us to stop spending time together won't make you want to stop tutoring him."

He flattened his mouth, hurt she would make that assumption. "I told you about my brother and why I like to help blind kids. I would never punish Scotty just because I don't agree with your actions. I don't operate like that, Monica."

As her tears continued to fall, his heart crumbled. "Is there anything I can say or do to change your mind?"

She shook her head and continued wiping her tears. "I'll just make sure I make myself scarce when you come and tutor Scotty. I can't keep sharing dinner with you because it's getting too personal. I fell for Kevin so hard, and it took me over two years to finally get over him." She ran her fingers over her hair. "I don't want to take my chances on another man unless I know for sure that he is a Christian."

"Kevin was a Christian, and look at how much he hurt you. Being with a Christian man won't guarantee you happiness."

She gasped and stared out the window, as if gathering her thoughts. Before she could speak, he got out of the car and slammed the door.

❧

That evening Monica was so upset she called Anna and told her what had happened between her and John. She'd called Karen also, but Karen was not at home. Anna stopped by a short time later and offered to keep Scotty overnight and take him to school the following morning. "I think you just need an evening to yourself to think and pray about this whole situation," Anna said with a hug before leaving with Scotty.

As the hour grew late, Monica continued to worry about her situation with John. She wished her feelings for him weren't so strong. She dreaded going to bed, knowing she'd have a hard time falling asleep. Feeling like a caged animal, she decided to go to Wal-Mart since she still had an hour left before they closed. She needed to get some beauty items. A short time later, she breezed into the huge store, anxious to get her shopping done. Not paying attention, she collided into somebody walking in the opposite direction. "I'm sorry," she said as she looked up into Kevin's familiar eyes. She jerked back, shocked.

"No, I'm sorry, Monica. I wasn't paying attention." The familiar scent of his cologne reminded her of the time they used to spend together. She glanced at the square package he clutched. "Tamara sent me out to get diapers for Tyler." He held the package up. "My life's really changed since he's been born."

She nodded. "I can imagine."

He continued to look at her, his dark eyes full of curiosity. "Are you sure you're okay? You've got that worried look about you."

Monica smiled. Kevin could always tell when something heavy was on her mind. "I'll be okay."

He checked his watch. "Are you sure? I've got a few minutes if you need somebody to talk to."

The urge to tell Kevin about her problems with John came upon her; however, the feeling disappeared. "No, it isn't something I want to talk to you about."

"Well, I want to talk to you about something."

Monica widened her eyes. "You do?" She wondered what in the world Kevin had to talk to her about.

He nodded and pointed to the soda machine inside the Wal-Mart. "Will you join me for a quick soda?"

Still curious, Monica nodded. After they were seated on a bench with their Cokes, Kevin started the conversation. "I noticed since we. . .since we stopped seeing each other that you've been staring at me and my family at church sometimes."

Monica's skin heated with embarrassment. She sipped her soda, hoping Kevin couldn't tell that his sudden break up still made her bitter. Before she could respond, he continued. "I was wondering if you were okay with everything. I know I broke things off suddenly." Monica sighed, setting her can of soda on the floor. "Tamara also noticed that you keep staring at us in church. At first she just ignored it, but she said it's starting to bother her, and she wondered why you haven't gotten over me in two years."

Monica jerked back. "Gotten over you?"

"It's obvious you're still upset about our breakup."

"Upset about our breakup? Kevin, you told me you didn't want to see me again after we'd been dating for two years. I know your mom died and everything, and you told me you weren't in the right frame of mind to make a marriage commitment. Yet right after our breakup you show up with Miss Tamara the following Sunday at church! How do you think that made me feel? Were you dating both of us at the same time? Or did you just happen to meet Tamara the day after our breakup and decide to proudly parade her around our church, introducing her to half the congregation?"

She shook her head, her heart still full of shame. "Everybody knew we were a couple, but the way you abruptly brought Tamara around made people wonder, and I could tell they pitied me. You should have seen some of the looks I got when I left church that day. You could have at least respectfully waited a few weeks before bringing her to church with you. You could have let me know what you were going to do. It was like a splash of cold water in my face when you did that."

His dark eyes widened. "You are still angry."

Her heart pounded, and Monica realized Kevin was correct. "Yes, I am still angry. I know it's wrong for me to feel this way, and I've been praying about it, but I still don't understand what happened between us. I felt that we were dating one minute, then the next you tell me you want to break up, and then you show up with Tamara. Were you seeing both of us at the same time? You at least owe me that explanation."

He sighed. "Not really."

"Not really? What does that mean?"

"I met Tamara at the men's retreat—"

"You met her at a men's retreat? How is that possible?"

"She was one of the volunteers at the host church to provide the food. I started talking to her, and I asked her for her phone number."

Monica sighed, wondering why she even wanted to hear this. "When was the men's retreat?"

"Remember, I went to the men's retreat a couple of months before we broke up."

"So you were dating her while you were dating me," Monica mumbled.

"I didn't see her again until the Sunday I brought her to church. I talked to her on the phone a few times, but I wasn't dating her," he said emphatically.

"Okay, I have a few questions. Why did it take you two months to tell me what was going on, and why did you show up at church with her right after you'd broken up with me? Did Tamara know what you were doing?"

"What do you mean?"

"Did she know you broke up with me days before you brought her to church?"

He shook his head. "No, she didn't know. I'm sorry about the way I handled things. I guess I should have been more sensitive."

"More sensitive? You shouldn't have been leading me on for two years!"

"Look, I liked you, but I knew after we'd been dating for about a year and a half that we weren't going to get married."

Monica jerked back. "Then why did you keep going out with me?"

"I enjoyed your company, and I didn't want to hurt your feelings. But it was wrong of me to treat you that way, and I'm sorry. Initially, when you asked about marriage, I really was pretty messed up because my mom had died. But months later, I knew you weren't the right woman for me." He paused, staring at his soda can as if in deep thought. "You know, before my mother died, she always told me I didn't have much common sense when it came to women, but I didn't mean to hurt you," he repeated. "I know we left a lot of things unsaid, and I just want to clear the air before we move."

"Move?"

He nodded. "Yes, Tamara and I are relocating to Hawaii."

"Hawaii!"

"Yes. Tamara's company is transferring her there, and they offered her a position in the new office. I've been searching on the Internet lately, and I was able to find a job there, too. We leave in a couple of weeks. They'll be announcing our departure plans at church on Sunday. We think it'll be a nice place to raise Tyler."

Monica still felt stunned as Kevin checked his watch again. "I've got to get going because Tamara will start worrying if I don't show up at home soon." They stood, and he pulled Monica into a clumsy embrace. "I feel bad about the way things ended between us, and I hope things work out for you and John."

Monica looked into his dark eyes. "You know about John?"

He shrugged. "Of course I do. It's hard not to know. We're in a small church, and people talk. I know he's taking that class, so I hope he makes the decision to accept Christ. If he does, you never know what might happen between the two of you," he said, a teasing glint in his dark eyes.

Monica watched Kevin walk away. It wasn't her usual routine to get beauty supplies at Wal-Mart late at night. She could only imagine that God had orchestrated her running into Kevin this evening, giving her the opportunity to ask him questions she'd been wondering about for two years.

A few days later, Monica spoke with Karen and Anna on the phone and told them about her accidental meeting with Kevin. She also mentioned his family's departure plans. She assured them she was glad that she was finally able to speak with Kevin in person, just to get some answers to her questions and to officially bring closure to the whole situation. Her best friends were shocked to discover that Kevin and his family were moving so far away. Although she'd reconciled herself to the situation, a part of her was still a little glad that Kevin's family would now be a long distance away.

Chapter 9

During the next couple of weeks, John continued to be plagued with questions about salvation and Christianity. He invited Pastor Martin over for a chat so they could discuss his questions. When the pastor arrived, John invited him into the kitchen for coffee and cookies.

"So, why did you want to meet with me?" asked Pastor Martin.

"I have so much going through my mind that I don't want to bother you with too many details. Suffice it to say my search for the truth continues."

"Have you been getting a lot out of the class you've been attending every Sunday?"

"Yes, I have, but I'm still not sure what to believe."

"You know, the Lord tells us if we seek Him, we'll find Him. We're humans, and we make mistakes. We're by no means perfect, and we need somebody to guide us and protect us. Our Savior does that and nobody else. As humans we walk around the earth living our lives, but we can't be gods over our own lives. God has control over all of the universe, and in order to understand Him, you must accept Him and live according to His commands."

"But what about suffering?" John argued.

"What about Christ's suffering? I know there's a lot of suffering on this earth, but you need to focus on the fact that Jesus died on the cross for us." Pastor Martin shook his head, gazing at John with his wise, kind eyes. "God has offered us the gift of eternal life. Accept His gift, be earnest in your quest to know and understand God. Seek Him with your whole mind and heart, and He'll make Himself known to you."

"But scientifically—"

Pastor Martin shook his head. "Forget science. Forget your agnostic views for a minute. You can't deny the evidence that there has been no man like Jesus that walked this earth. You can't deny the evidence that He did indeed exist. I'm talking evidence other than the Bible. Does it make sense that this man, living on earth as God, would suffer so much pain for nothing?" Pastor Martin raised his voice, as if preaching from the pulpit. "He gave His life for us, and we need to accept His gift."

John closed his eyes, letting the pastor's words sink into him. Pastor Martin took John's hand, and after he said a prayer, John whispered, "Amen."

A few days after his meeting with Pastor Martin, John stood on the frigid, deserted beach. He placed his hands in his pockets as he watched the angry waves tumble onto the brown, grainy sand. *God, are You trying to tell me that You're real?* As he continued to stare at nature, he recalled what he'd read in the book of Genesis. God had created all things, the birds of the sky and the creeping things and the creatures of the ocean. John sniffed the ocean-scented air as feelings of warmth and peace settled upon him.

There was no way this earth just happened to appear due to chance. God created it. As scientific theories about earth's creation, like the big bang theory, fluttered through his mind, he pushed the thoughts aside, instead focusing on God. *Lord, thank You for creating this earth. Thank You for creating me, thank You for giving Your Son for our sins. I accept You, dear Lord, I accept You as my Savior. Amen.* John wiped the tears from his cheeks as he continued to stare at the beach.

❧

During the last few weeks since her accidental meeting with Kevin, thoughts of John had swirled through Monica's brain as she worked at the office. She'd focused on how hard it had been lately. All she'd wanted was to spend time with John again.

She prayed as she went through her day, asking God's help in making her strong enough to accept whatever happened with Gina and with John.

As the days passed, she had become aware of the holiday lights and festive decorations in the malls and on the city streets. Monica, Anna, Karen, and Scotty had even taken time out of their busy holiday schedules to attend the annual Ocean City Carolfest at the Music Pier. Before the free concert started, they'd placed their donated canned goods into the collection boxes for the needy.

When the concert started, Monica had swayed to the music, holding Scotty's hand. Just hearing the sweet Christmas carols warmed her heart. They'd also gone to Ocean City's Winterfest of Lights on another evening. After riding the tram and seeing the beautifully lit displays, they'd stopped for hot chocolate and Scotty had gotten to meet Santa. When Scotty begged to see Santa again, she'd taken him to the Music Pier another cold, blustery night so he could get his picture taken with Santa Claus in a lifeguard boat, as a gift for Gina.

She'd found comfort in prayer and her daily devotions, and she still prayed that Gina was okay and that she would continue to stay with their parents until she got her life back on track. So far, she'd not made any more threats to take Scotty away, and for that, Monica was grateful.

The holiday season was now in full bloom. However, since she'd not been dating John, sadness had hovered around her in spite of her moments of joy.

She missed John like crazy! When he came to tutor Scotty, she'd let Scotty answer the door, and then she'd scamper upstairs. She was a coward, but when she saw his dark brown eyes and heard his deep voice, her insides turned to mush, and she knew she would be in his arms at a moment's notice. She found it easier to ignore the attraction when she was around him for only a few minutes at a time. It had gotten so bad that she'd even dreamed about him. She almost wished she'd never met him so she wouldn't be going through this emotional turmoil.

Days later, she gazed around her living room, enjoying the Christmas tree she and Scotty had decorated together. She'd decided to get a real pine tree instead of using her artificial one this year so Scotty could enjoy the scent.

Since Scotty had gone to bed, she decided to wrap his gifts. She scanned the packages, hoping she had not forgotten anything. The little guy had had a difficult year. She hoped she could make up for it, just a little bit, by indulging him with an abundant number of gifts.

Her gift wrapping was interrupted by a knock on her door. Figuring it was Anna or Karen, she rushed to answer, craving some adult company. She gasped when she saw John on her doorstep, carrying two large wrapped packages. His dark eyes seemed to plead with her. "Hello, Monica."

She swallowed, wondering if this visit was a good idea. "John."

"Don't say anything, just let me come in and talk to you. Please. Don't run and hide upstairs like you've been doing for the last few weeks."

She nodded, her heart pounding as he came into her home and placed the presents under the tree. The Christmas lights twinkled in the semidarkness. "That's a pretty tree," he said, removing his coat and sitting on the couch.

She sat beside him. "I got it for Scotty. I know he enjoys the pine scent."

He noticed the presents scattered on the floor and chuckled. "Looks like your nephew hit the jackpot."

"He's had a rough year, so I thought I'd make sure he had a good Christmas."

He took her hand. "Why did you come by tonight? Just to bring presents for Scotty?"

"No, the presents are not just for Scotty. One of them is for you."

She looked at the tree, embarrassed. "But I didn't buy anything for you. . . ."

He chuckled, squeezing her hand. "The best present you could give me is your company again."

She shook her head. "John—"

He pressed his finger to her lips. "Please, let me finish." He glanced around the living room, as if gathering courage to continue. "As you know, there're only a few more weeks for that class I'm taking at your church."

She nodded. "I realize that." She'd been counting the weeks of the class, paying attention to the lesson plans on the bulletin board, wondering which lesson and which words would sway John to finally accept Jesus.

"Well, I just want you to be the first to know that I've finally accepted Jesus."

Her mouth dropped open, and she couldn't find words to express her joy. He smiled. "It happened a few nights ago. I've kept it to myself, but the Christmas Eve service is only about a week away. That's when I was going to go forward at the altar call and tell the pastor about my new vow to accept Jesus into my heart." He paused and before she could speak, he continued. "A woman named Marilyn Tyndall called me the other night."

Monica furrowed her brow, confused. "Who is Marilyn Tyndall?"

"She was a good friend of my mother's," he explained. "She knew my parents when they were first saved, and she was a mentor to my mother." Monica wondered where this was leading. "Anyway, she found my phone number on a piece of paper in my mother's Bible. She also found a letter that my mother had written to me and had never gotten a chance to mail."

"What did the letter say?"

He was silent, and she wondered what he was thinking. "She apologized for raising me as an agnostic, and she was telling me to give Christianity a chance." He went on to explain that she gave him a few scriptures to look up, including Jeremiah 29:13. He told her of his conversation with Pastor Martin, and his constant thoughts and comments to God. "I found myself talking to God and praying regularly. It was so gradual over the last month, my thinking about God. But when I started praying and talking to Him all the time, it occurred to me that God is real and He hears me." He squeezed her hand. "He hears me, Monica, and you just don't know how good it feels to know that I'm no longer in disbelief and I've accepted Him as my Savior!"

"Oh, John, that's so wonderful!" she gushed, barely able to contain her joy. "I'm so glad you told me." She gave him a tight hug.

He cleared his throat as she released him. "I just want you to keep this to yourself for now. I want the other people in the congregation to know when I step forward on Christmas Eve." He took her hands. "Are you planning to go to your parents' on Christmas Eve?"

She shook her head. "I was going to go there on Christmas Day after Scotty opens his gifts. He wants to spend his holiday with his mother, so I was going to let him stay at my parents' house during his Christmas break."

"So will you be here for the church's Christmas Eve service?"

Her stomach tumbled with anticipation. "Of course I'll be there."

"Are you off next week?" he asked.

"No, I took the week between Christmas and New Year's off."

"Well, you know the college is closed for their holiday break. So since Scotty will be gone for the week, I figured we could spend some time together. That is, if it's okay with you."

"I wouldn't mind at all." Thoughts of spending the holidays with John—seeing Christmas lights, drinking hot cider, gazing at her Christmas tree together—gave her a warm bubbly feeling in her stomach. "I think it's a perfect idea."

He pulled her into his arms. "Okay, it's a deal then?" he whispered in her ear before they kissed.

When she pulled away, she felt breathless. "John, you have yourself a deal."

As Christmas Eve drew closer, Monica's health began failing. Scotty ran around the house excited about Christmas, and she could barely stand the noise. The church had their annual Christmas cantata, and Scotty participated with the rest of his Sunday school class. During the performance, she could barely enjoy the music her head hurt so much. When she went to work the following day, she had to leave early because she was sick. She felt hot and then cold before she broke out in a sweat.

She begged Anna to pick up Scotty. She had enrolled him in a child care center for a few days since he was out of school and her vacation from work had not started. She also asked Anna to get some medicine at the drugstore. John called several times, and Monica told him she'd caught the flu and didn't know when she would recuperate.

"I'm sorry to hear that. Did you need me to bring you anything?"

She told him no, but she wanted to be at that church when John made his public proclamation to God. "I'll try and come to the service tomorrow night."

"No, don't do that! We can celebrate over the holidays. If you don't feel up to it, I'll just come and sit by your side until I know you're feeling better."

In spite of her illness, his words warmed her heart. She hung up the phone and snuggled beneath her blankets. She heard Karen's and Anna's voices in the kitchen as they made spaghetti for dinner. She was thankful that her best friends had been over frequently, taking care of Scotty while she was ill. Her parents had already called and said they'd pick him up on Christmas Day so he could spend his winter break with Gina.

On Christmas Day, Scotty's shrieks resonated throughout the house. Anna spent the night to help out, and Monica heard Anna join Scotty under the tree, helping him with his new toys. Monica swallowed. Her throat was still sore, and her body ached. When she came downstairs, she was surprised to see Karen. "What are you doing out of bed?" Both of them admonished her as she stood on the steps, watching her nephew open his gifts.

"I wanted to see Scotty open his presents." His euphoric mood made her shopping spree worth it.

She returned to bed after the gifts were opened. When she awoke hours later, the sun was no longer shining and her room was semidark. She attempted to sit up, and John came into the room. "You're awake!"

As he approached, she took his hand. She glanced at the clock and noted it was midafternoon. "It sure is dark outside."

"The weatherman is calling for snow."

He helped her sit up. The enticing aroma of chicken soup wafted through the house, and for the first time in days, her stomach growled. "That smells good."

John chuckled as he went to her door. "That's some chicken soup. I made it myself."

She swung her legs to the side of the bed. "I'll come down and eat some."

"No! Don't come down to the kitchen. I'll bring up your lunch on a tray. Your parents stopped by hours ago to get Scotty, and they didn't want to wake you. They left some Christmas dinner for us if you want to eat it later or maybe tomorrow."

She shook her head. "I don't want my mom's Christmas dinner now. I want some of your soup."

"Well, you stay put, and I'll bring you a tray." He left the room. Soon he returned carrying a wooden tray with a bowl of chicken soup, a plate of crackers, a glass of orange juice, and a red rose in a vase. "Oh, this is so sweet." She patted her hair, hoping she wasn't scaring him away with her hideous appearance. The hot soup tasted good going down her sore throat, and she ate the whole bowlful. When she finished, he asked her if she wanted more, but she declined. He set the vase on her dresser and took her dishes to the kitchen. He came back with the package he'd left for her days ago under her Christmas tree.

He gave her the gift. "Merry Christmas."

Smiling, she touched the box. "I feel so bad. I didn't get you a gift."

He placed his finger over her lips. "Don't worry. I accept gifts all year round. It doesn't have to be on Christmas."

No longer able to hide her curiosity, she ripped the paper open and found a large white box. When she lifted the lid, she saw an exquisite cherry red sweater. She fingered the garment, and the knitted material was as soft as a cotton ball. She held it to her face, relishing the texture. "This is lovely!"

"When I saw it at the store, I knew it would be perfect for you. That red color looks good against your brown skin."

She continued to finger the garment. "It sure does. I'm glad you bought it for me. I can't wait to wear it."

He sat in the empty chair beside her bed. "Maybe you can wear it over the holidays. If you're feeling better over the next week, we might be able to spend some time together."

She put the sweater aside and took his hand. "I'm looking forward to that. I really am." Thoughts of how she had acted filtered through her mind.

"Uh-oh. What's wrong?"

"I just wanted to apologize for the way I acted in the church parking lot a few weeks ago. That was insensitive of me."

"Don't say anything else about it. You were just trying to avoid getting hurt, and you were following your beliefs. There's nothing wrong with what you did." He looked into her eyes. "You did hurt my feelings. But I know it wasn't intentional."

"To be honest with you, I hated doing it. My feelings for you didn't go away."

"Mine didn't go away either. As a matter of fact, my feelings for you have grown deeper." He caressed her fingers.

Warmth and compassion flowed through her, making her feel loved and wanted. Being around John was making her crazy. When he released her hand she got out of bed, opening the yellow curtain behind her. "It's snowing! Look!"

He stood behind her, gazing at the white flakes as they floated from the sky. "Looks like we're having a white Christmas," he murmured, pulling her into his arms.

"It looks like we're having a wonderful Christmas." As she spoke, her voice faltered with the enjoyment of being held by him, and she watched the falling flakes of snow.

❧

Monica couldn't remember the last time she'd had such a joyous Christmas away from her family. Her sore throat and stuffy nose put a slight damper on the day. However, when John showed her his loving-kindness, her illness melted away like ice during a spring thaw.

They continued to enjoy his tasty soup for the rest of the day. John lit a fire in the fireplace, and she turned on the stereo. Christmas carols boomed from the speakers, and when her favorite tune, "Silent Night," was playing, John took her into his arms and held her as they softly sang the lyrics together. Monica's voice croaked, and she thought she sounded horrible, but John's voice was smooth and mellow, blending nicely with the music. "You know, you've got a great voice," she declared when the song was over.

He chuckled, continuing to cradle her in his arms. "You're not the first person to tell me that."

"Since you're a member of the church now, perhaps you should get involved with one of the ministries," she suggested.

He ran his fingers over her cheek. Her insides quivered like jelly, and she had to force herself to pay attention to the conversation at hand. Then he raised his thick eyebrows. "What do you suggest?"

She giggled, thoroughly enjoying their time together. "I'm suggesting you try out for the choir. They sound good now, but I think they'd sound even better if you were up there with them."

He nodded at her suggestion. "I might do that. There're so many things I want to do now that I'm a Christian. I feel like I've wasted my whole life, and I'm ready to start anew."

She picked up on the eager tone in his voice and encouraged him to continue. "What kinds of things?"

He hesitated and looked away. She sensed he was hiding something, but she didn't want to pry too much since he was a new Christian and was still searching for ways to serve the Lord. "I've been thinking about various things. My mind isn't made up yet, but when it is, you'll be the first to know."

She nodded, still pleased he was so eager to serve the Lord. "You should speak to the pastor about that. We even have an awesome men's ministry that meets on Thursday nights, and we have several Bible studies."

They stared at the orange flames crackling from the warm fire. The curtains were open, and they watched the snowflakes as they continued to drift from the sky, creating an undisturbed blanket of whiteness around them.

Around six o'clock, Monica took a nap. When she awoke a couple hours later, she saw that the snow had stopped. She crept into the living room and found John sitting on the chair near the extinguished fire, reading his Bible. He looked so handsome reading God's Word that she could just stand there and watch him forever. "Hey, handsome," she crooned.

He closed his black book. "Did you have a good nap?"

"I sure did." She pointed to the window. "Looks like you'll have to stay here. We're snowed in."

He shook his head. "I just heard the news on the radio. The back roads are bad, but the main ones aren't too bad. I'm going to shovel your driveway and go home."

Her heart skipped a beat, and she wished he didn't have to leave. "Are you sure? The weather looks pretty terrible."

"Even though you're sick, you still look beautiful to me. I'll be honest and say that I don't trust myself to stay all night in this house with you."

She widened her eyes, surprised at his boldness.

"I'm a new Christian, and I'm still learning a lot, but I am familiar with what the Lord thinks about premarital sex."

She was touched he was taking his Christian vows so seriously. "Are you sure you won't get stuck out there?"

He put his Bible aside and walked to where she still stood on the stairwell. "No, I'll be okay. I've got some good snow tires on my car, and I'll be sure to call you when I get home." He checked his watch. "It's almost ten o'clock, so I'll just borrow your snow shovel and clear out your driveway. Then I'll be on my way."

"Okay." She was still reluctant to let him go but knew it was best under the circumstances. She walked down the steps toward him, and he pulled her into his arms. He kissed her, and she found warmth and comfort from his strong embrace.

He cradled her face between his hands. "There's an indoor ice-skating rink not too far from here. Maybe we can go there for a while this week sometime. I don't want you out on that ice this soon after you've been sick, but if you're feeling better, we can also go to this neat café called Tea by the Sea. They serve great scones. We can go there and relax while we enjoy a hot cup of tea."

She nodded. "Yes, that sounds like a good idea."

He gathered his coat and gloves and found her snow shovel in the basement. He then headed outside. She turned on the outside light and watched him for several minutes as he shoveled the snow. After the driveway was cleared, John came into her house and placed her shovel back in the basement. He kissed her cheek and said good-bye before he took his exit.

During the next few days, Monica grew stronger as her flu vanished. John called often and came by to see her. She even convinced him she was well enough to go out on the boardwalk to see Ocean City's Winterfest of Lights. Although she had already seen the display earlier that season, she longed to see it again with John. The seashore was illuminated with close to a million Christmas lights. Many pedestrians were bedazzled by the beautiful display, and Monica's heart leaped with joy since she was able to see such an exquisite sight with John by her side. They also went to the indoor ice-skating rink another day, and Monica enjoyed the lemon-flavored tea and cinnamon scones at Tea by the Sea.

She found the energy to clean her house, and she missed Scotty. She wondered if he was enjoying his Christmas presents, so she called her parents and was glad to hear her mother answer the phone. "Hey, Monica!"

"I'm surprised you haven't called me, Mom," she complained. "You know I've been sick."

Her mother laughed. "We didn't want to bother you since we knew you were spending some quality time with John. You know, your father and I were just talking about how nice it is that he's found the Lord. That's truly a miracle."

Her heart felt warmed by her mother's sincere words. "I feel the same way.

You know, Mom, my prayers for John's salvation have been answered. I've been praying about this since I first found out about his agnostic views, and I'm just glad that John has accepted Christ as his Savior."

"Speaking of accepting Christ—" Her mother was interrupted by Scotty's eager voice.

"Is that Aunt Monica on the phone?"

She was thrilled to hear her nephew when her mother handed him the phone. "Hi, Aunt Monica!" He sounded like he was out of breath.

"Have you been running?"

"Yeah! My mom and me made a snowman!"

She clutched the receiver, having a hard time picturing Gina in the snow building a snowman with her son. "That's nice. Did you have a good time?"

"Yeah! We had a carrot for the nose, and we used rocks for the eyes! My mom said it looked like a funny snowman." He chuckled, his voice filled with glee.

She was glad to hear the enthusiasm in his voice; however, she had a twinge of doubt niggling in the back of her mind. Was Gina planning on being a good mother from now on? Did she still want to take Scotty away and keep him permanently? Could Monica stand not having Scotty with her anymore if Gina did decide she wanted to be a parent again? All of these questions swirled through her mind like scattered snowflakes on the wind. She barely paid attention to Scotty's incessant chatter as she wondered what would happen to him now that Gina continued to form a bond with her son.

Her mind wandered so much that she barely noticed when her mother was back on the phone. "Monica, I've been speaking for the last two minutes, and you haven't said a word. What's wrong?"

"Mom, what's going to happen to Scotty now that Gina is back? Is she going to take him away again and disappear?"

Her mother's voice was tinged with excitement as she relayed her news. "Well, I wanted to tell you something about Gina. You'll never guess what I saw her doing today." Intrigued, she clutched the receiver, awaiting her mother's next words. "I saw her reading her Bible."

Shock coursed through Monica's veins when she heard the news. "You're kidding. Are you sure you're not mistaken?"

"No, not about this. She doesn't realize I saw her, so I haven't mentioned it to her. I'm going to leave her alone about it now. I think she's working through some things, and I honestly think she's sorry for abandoning Scotty."

Monica sat down in the kitchen chair, still stunned by this news. When she'd accepted Christ as a young teenager, Gina was only a toddler. However, when Gina got older, her interest in church and the Bible never developed. She never participated in the youth fellowship groups as Monica had and instead remained mixed up in the wrong crowd. She had shunned the Bible and God, drowning her pain with drugs and alcohol. The first time she came home intoxicated, she'd been only fifteen years old. Monica remembered her mother had called, frantic about Gina's rebellious behavior. Since Monica was no longer living at home at the time, she didn't have to witness Gina's antics firsthand; however, she did recall her mother always saying she didn't understand how two women could turn out so differently after being raised in the same house.

She barely remembered saying good-bye to her mother as she hung up the phone. She pressed her hands together, bowed her head, and prayed for Gina, hoping she was on her way to having a permanent relationship with Jesus.

Chapter 10

During the next few weeks, Monica kept her sister in mind, saying prayers daily for her salvation. On Sunday she stayed after the church service, along with the rest of the congregation, to celebrate with the new members. It was New Member Day, and John had been one of the new members to be welcomed into the congregation.

Afterward everybody celebrated in the large mess hall in the church basement. Scotty scampered about with other children, playing games. The scent of roasted pork and barbecued beef warmed the air, and platters of fruits, vegetables, and chips adorned the serving tables. After Scotty was fed, Monica made a plate and searched for John so they could sit together. Dejection spread through her when she spotted him sitting at a table with some of the members of the men's choir. The four people he sat with were single, and he'd been spending a lot of time with them lately. He'd told her one night after Scotty's tutoring session that they talked a lot about the Bible, and he said he'd been learning a lot from them.

She continued glancing around the room until she saw Anna and Karen sitting at a table in the corner. She made her way over with her plate of food. "Hi." She sat down, still wishing she could sit with John.

Karen arched her eyebrow, giving her a sly look. "You're not eating with John?"

She shrugged as she bit into her pork sandwich. It was delicious. She enjoyed her food for a while before responding to Karen's comment. "You see him sitting over there with the choir. I didn't just want to go over there and interrupt."

Anna folded her arms in front of her chest. "Why not? He's your man, isn't he?"

She huffed, still trying to enjoy her food. "Just leave the whole subject alone, okay?"

Karen leaned back into her seat, observing her friend. "My, my, aren't you snappy today! I'd think you'd be in a good mood since John has accepted Christ."

Monica put her fork aside, not sure of how to tell her friends things weren't progressing between her and John as smoothly as she liked. She pushed her plate of half-eaten food away, suddenly changing her mind and deciding to reveal her doubts to them. "I've barely spent any time with him since Christmas."

Anna widened her dark brown eyes. "You're kidding. None at all?"

She shrugged. "Not really. We had such a romantic Christmas holiday. He told me awhile back that he was falling in love with me."

Karen leaned closer. "Are you sure he said that?"

"Of course I'm sure," she stated, surprised Karen would think she would make something like that up.

"Did you tell him you loved him?" asked Anna.

She shook her head. "No, I didn't. Well, not really anyway. I told him that I shared the same feelings he had for me just before I told him we shouldn't spend any more spare time together right after Thanksgiving."

"Monica!" said Karen. "You've admitted to him that you're falling in love with him right before your breakup? You need to tell him how you feel now! He's worked through his issues with God, and now it's time to get your relationship with John back on track!"

"I thought it was too soon to tell him my true feelings. I wanted to see if things would work out between us."

"And?" Anna prompted.

She shook her head. "They're not working out at all. At least not for me. You'd think I'd be happy he's now a Christian, but you know, I'm jealous of the time he spends with God."

"Monica!" Karen grabbed her arm.

"He comes to tutor Scotty, but he doesn't eat dinner with us anymore. He spends time with the new friends he's made in the choir, plus he spends so much time reading the Bible, soaking up knowledge. We haven't spent any time together since Christmas, and I'm starting to wonder if I imagined the joy I felt during the holidays."

Anna voiced a question. "Have you talked to him about it?"

She shook her head. "How can I say I'm jealous of the time he's spending with God and the church when I was the one who spouted how important it was for him to become a Christian?"

Karen nodded. "That would sound a little weird. Why don't you ask him out? Maybe he needs to be reminded that you care about him."

She recalled the present he gave her for Christmas. "He gave me the most beautiful sweater for Christmas, but I didn't get anything for him. Maybe if I get him a thoughtful gift, he'll be reminded of my existence."

Anna shook her head. "It's a shame you sound so dismal. If the man says he's falling in love with you, then he's falling in love with you. Stop griping and just cherish the time you do get to spend with him. He's a new Christian, so he's probably zealous and eager. His getting closer to God is more important than getting closer to you."

Monica pulled her plate toward her, deciding to finish her meal after all. Anna's words were full of truth. She was going to go ahead and buy a special gift for John, but she wouldn't mention how disheartened she'd felt about his recent absence from her life. She glanced at the men's choir table. John was laughing heartily, enjoying the fellowship with his new Christian friends. He looked so handsome that it was hard not to stare. His dark suit fit his trim body nicely, and she wished they could have shared their meal together. She hoped things would work out between them.

≫

Later that day John clutched the bouquet of fragrant roses, hesitating before he knocked on Monica's door. Earlier when he'd sat with his new friends from the men's choir, he'd seen her look of disappointment after she'd gotten her plate of food. He'd been tempted to abandon his friends and go and sit with her after all. He'd glanced in her direction several times as she ate with Anna and Karen, and he could sense she was unhappy.

He hesitated, gripping the flowers in his hand. He'd found a new happiness upon accepting Christ. There was something he needed to do, and so far he had not discussed this matter with anybody, except for Jesus. Monica wasn't going to like what he had to tell her tonight, but hopefully she would understand.

He finally found the courage to knock on her door. Her dark brown eyes widened when she opened it. "John!"

He entered her house, kissing her cheek. As he handed her the bouquet of roses, he glanced around the silent house. "Where's Scotty?"

He followed her as she made her way to the kitchen and filled a vase with water. "He's spending the night with Anna. She promised they could make pizza and have popcorn afterward. She's even going to drop him off at school in the morning."

He watched the clear water tumble into the glass vase. "That was nice of her."

"Yeah, wasn't it?" She placed the vase on the kitchen table and removed the tissue paper from the fragrant buds before cutting the ends and placing the stems into the water. "Thanks for the flowers." An awkward silence followed, and he still didn't know how to tell her his news.

"Remember I once told you how pretty it is walking on the boardwalk at the beach in the wintertime?"

"Yes, I remember."

"Since Scotty's not here, how about we go for a walk?"

"But it's cold outside."

He chuckled, pulling her into his arms. "So? Just bundle up. Plus I'll be around to snuggle with to keep you warm."

Her dark eyes twinkled with pleasure. "Okay. Just give me a few minutes to

92

get ready." He waited in the living room while she went upstairs. She returned wearing boots, corduroy pants, and an oversized gray sweatshirt. She opened the closet and removed a puffy black coat and a knitted hat. He helped her put her coat on. She pulled the hat on her head. "I should be warm enough with all of this on."

"You'll be fine." Their breath came out in frosty puffs as they walked to his car. Minutes later, he pulled into a parking space near the deserted Ocean City boardwalk. Lights illuminated the stark area as a few pedestrians walked their pets. The black sky was littered with tiny silver stars, and the moon was a full white orb. He blinked again, amazed how God created the heavens and the earth. Since his salvation, his whole outlook about the earth and the people on it had changed dramatically.

He held her gloved hand as they walked. A few restaurants were open, but most of the businesses were closed. He stopped under a bright streetlight, inviting her to sit with him on a bench. They silently watched the foamy waves crash on the deserted beach. He was still trying to decide which words he should use when he told her his news. He was silent for so long that she finally squeezed his arm. "John, what's wrong?"

The question hung in the frigid air between them, unanswered. "Why do you think something is wrong?"

She shrugged beneath her thick coat. "It's just a feeling I have. Things have been different between us since Christmas."

He still didn't answer her as he removed her glove and held her bare hand in his, kissing her fingers. Her dark eyes were laced with questions and doubts. "I really do love you, Monica."

She remained silent as he continued to hold her hand, massaging her palm. "Are you cold?"

She shook her head, her dark eyes full of fear. She tried to pull her hand away, but he kept it firmly in his grip. "I'm almost sure you're about to tell me some bad news. I can sense it," she said.

Monica turned away, but he took her chin in his fingers and urged her to look into his eyes. He leaned toward her and kissed her on the mouth. When the kiss finally ended, he found his heart was pounding. "That was an amazing kiss," he murmured.

She looked toward the foamy water before focusing on him again. Her dark eyes glistened with unshed tears, but she quickly blinked them away. "You want to end our relationship." Her voice took on a hard edge as she scooted away from him on the bench. He continued to clutch her hand as he massaged her fingers.

"No."

Her eyes widened. "No?"

"No, I don't want to end our relationship. I'd like for us to keep seeing each other."

"But. . .I thought you had something negative to tell me tonight. I can tell when something is bothering you."

He leaned back on the wooden bench. "You're right, something is bothering me."

He again sensed her shiver beneath her thick coat. "Are you sure you're not cold?"

Before she could respond, he helped her up from the bench. "Let's go to the OC Daily Grind and get something to drink. It hasn't been too long since you were sick. And I don't want to be responsible for your getting ill again by being out in this cold air. Let's stop for a cup of hot chocolate, and I'll tell you what's on my mind."

As they walked toward the establishment hand in hand, the night lost its beauty. The twinkling stars no longer seemed romantic, and the sound of the rushing water no longer enticed him. Monica's sadness surrounded them like a hot, thick blanket, suffocating their happiness.

He opened the door, and warmth rushed around them. Music played softly in the background, and a few people sat at tables drinking hot beverages and reading newspapers. He chose a secluded table with a nice view of the ocean before he left her alone to place their order. He returned minutes later with two steamy mugs of hot chocolate covered with mounds of whipped cream and sprinkled with cinnamon. He set the thick white mugs on the table, and Monica lifted hers, warming her hands on the cup. She took a small sip and a spot of whipped cream clung to her upper lip. He playfully wiped it away, licking the sweet cream from his fingertip.

She tried to smile, but her eyes were still sad. "Please tell me what's wrong."

He took a sip of his sweet hot chocolate, barely tasting it before it traveled down his throat. After taking a deep breath and saying a quick prayer, he decided to tell her his news. "I've decided to join a ministry."

"Oh?" She stirred the whipped cream into her chocolate. "That doesn't sound so bad. As a matter of fact, it's a good idea. I'm sure Pastor Martin will be pleased that you're joining a ministry."

He shook his head. "I haven't spoken with the pastor about it."

Seemingly crushed, she took another sip of chocolate before asking him another question. "Why not? He would be the best person to speak with about this."

"To tell you the truth, the only other person I've spoken to about this, except you, is Jesus Himself."

She stared outside as she seemed to gather her thoughts. "Joining a ministry is a blessing, but you're acting like it's something negative. Why?"

"Because I don't want to hurt you."

"What?" Turning away from the window, she looked into his eyes.

"I would like to join a speaking ministry, one that reaches out to people who don't believe in God. Some of the people I'd be speaking to might even be agnostic, just like I used to be. I would like to take a year and just travel around the country, maybe even the world. I would give talks about how I was raised, my doubts about Jesus, my struggles, and about how I finally came to accept Him in my life. There's a group who does this, and they need volunteers."

Her mouth dropped open as she gripped her cup. "You're leaving?"

He shook his head. "Not right now. I still have to talk to some people and get things arranged. I don't have to worry about working for a year because when my parents died, they left me a large inheritance. I plan to use that to take a year off from my job and travel, telling other nonbelievers that they need Jesus in their lives."

Her bottom lip quivered, but she quickly controlled herself and clutched her mug of hot chocolate. "Why do you feel you want to do this?"

"Because I feel like I've lost so much time not being saved that I think I need to do more than the average Christian to make a difference in people's lives. Monica, I'm almost forty years old, and my life has been a waste since I haven't found Jesus until recently."

She shook her head. "No it hasn't. You've done many good things in your life. One of them is helping blind children."

"I know, but I didn't tell anybody about the gospel my whole life, like I should have. If I take a hiatus from my job for a year and join this ministry, I feel like I could make up for lost time."

"Oh, John. . ." She took a sip from her mug before setting it upon the rough wooden table. "Jesus is not concerned about your making up the time before you came to Him. People usually join ministries like yours when they feel called to do it. Do you feel called?"

He wasn't sure how to answer. He squeezed her hand, unsure of how it felt to be called. "I just know this is what I want to do. But I did want to ask you to do something for me."

"What's that?"

"When I am able to get everything into place for this ministry and I'm able to leave for a year and give my talks on my salvation, I wanted to ask you to wait for me."

"Wait for you?" She pulled her hand away, folding her arms in front of her chest.

He nodded. "I'm not sure how long it will take me to get everything arranged, but when I do, I want to know you'll be in my corner and you'll support me. I want to know when I return to Ocean City within a year that you'll be waiting for me so we can continue our relationship." She looked away, and he wondered what she was thinking.

❧

As the cloud of whipped cream floated on her hot chocolate, she wasn't sure if she should laugh or cry. He wanted her to put her life on hold for a year so he could travel the country and do ministry work?

She pushed her beverage away, no longer wanting to taste the chocolate sweetness. Why did he not mention an engagement—or marriage? He'd certainly proclaimed his love for her, so what was holding him back from proposing? If he asked her to wait for a year, wouldn't it make sense to place a ring on her finger?

Also, did John really know what he was doing? He was a new Christian, and although he was zealous in his faith, she had to wonder if his reasoning for entering this ministry was skewed. "I think you need to speak with the pastor about this. Tell him about what you want to do."

"You don't think I should do this, do you?" His deep voice held a note of accusation as he folded his arms across his chest, awaiting her response.

She shook her head. "I'm not going to answer your question. This is between you and God."

"But you don't like my decision. Why?"

She rubbed her forehead, feeling a headache coming on. "I think I'm ready to go home now."

"No, I'm not taking you home."

"Excuse me?"

"I said I'm not taking you home. Not until you tell me what's wrong."

"I won't be seeing you for a year. Isn't that reason enough to be upset?" Her heart already ached for the impending time they would be apart.

"But I'm doing this for Jesus. I'd think you'd be more pleased."

She remained silent as she stared into her hot chocolate.

"Oh, I know what's wrong." His deep voice broke into her thoughts. "You're upset because I didn't ask you to come with me. I didn't want to ask you because it would force you to make a decision between Scotty and me. I know you can't have Scotty moving around the world for a year, and that's why I didn't ask you to come with me."

She shook her head. "No, that's not why I'm upset."

"Oh, Monica." He tried to take her hand again, but she pulled it away. "When I finally get all the paperwork and arrangements done and leave, I'm going to miss you—a lot. We've already been through so much, and just when it seems as if things were falling into place, I get the idea to join this ministry." He watched the other patrons in the room, looking as though his thoughts ranged elsewhere. "But this is something I feel I have to do. Please, be honest with me and tell me what you think."

The pleading tone in his voice touched something deep in her heart. "I don't know a whole lot about joining ministries, so it's hard for me to tell you my opinion."

"But?" he prompted.

"But since you asked for the truth, I'm going to give it to you." She took a deep breath and looked into his eyes. "I think you're making a mistake. I think you're pursuing this ministry for the wrong reasons."

His mouth hardened as he urged her to continue.

"Like I said before, Jesus wouldn't want you to join a ministry to make up for lost time. He would want you to do this if you feel like He's telling you to."

His voice became harsh. "So you don't think I should go? You think I should abandon my vision for joining this ministry?" He looked away from her as if he was hurt.

"Please don't misunderstand me. If you feel called to do this and you feel deep within your heart that this is what Jesus wants you to do, you'll have my blessing." She tried to gather her scattered thoughts. "But if you're merely doing this to make up for the time you weren't saved, then I think you need to reevaluate this whole thing. You're still a new Christian. Do you even know what the scriptures say about good works?"

"I'm not a child. I know what I want to do," he said tersely.

"Please don't be offended. But you say you love me, so you must respect my feelings. Can't you trust that I'm saying these things for your own good?"

He ignored her question. "I said I loved you, but you never told me that you loved me." He stared at her. "I wonder why that is. Are you really over your old boyfriend? I know he and his family have moved to Hawaii, but I still wonder if you're over him."

She jerked her head back, floored by his question. Thoughts of her accidental meeting with Kevin raced through her mind. She shook her head, not wanting to give him the wrong idea. "It was hard for me when Kevin and I broke up, but I'm not in love with him."

His eyes narrowed. "Are you sure about that?"

She stood, her chair scraping across the floor. "I spoke with Kevin shortly before he left."

"You called him?"

She shook her head, not wanting John to get the wrong idea. "Of course

97

not!" She took a deep breath and calmed herself down before telling John about her accidental meeting with Kevin at Wal-Mart. John didn't comment about the conversation she'd had with her ex-boyfriend.

"I'm still not sure you're over him," he said.

She shook her head, angry. "I think it's time to end this conversation. I'm ready to go home now."

As they exited the shop, the cold wind wrapped around her, and she shivered. Salty tears spilled down her cheeks, but she quickly wiped them away, not wanting John to see the evidence of her pain. She stuffed her fists into her pockets, not giving him the opportunity to hold her hand as he usually did when they were together.

Their brisk walk to his car was full of silence. Minutes later, he was pulling up into her driveway. He didn't say good-bye as she exited the car. She didn't close the door right away, wondering if she should say something. Her mind went blank, and she honestly had no idea what she should say. Instead, angry, sad, and flustered, she slammed the car door shut and walked into the house.

She pulled off her coat and dropped it on the couch. As she heard him drive away, she lifted the curtain and watched his taillights disappear around the corner. *Oh Father God, why oh why does John really want to join this ministry? I thought he was the right man for me, but now I'm not so sure. I'm falling in love with him, Lord, but I'm scared. I'm so scared that I don't know what to do with myself. But I'm going to leave this in Your hands, Lord, and I'll try not to worry about it so much.*

Chapter 11

The following week, Monica shook her head as she pulled into her driveway. Scotty was singing a new song he'd learned on the bus trip he'd taken that day with his Sunday school class. She was glad he was preoccupied because she was still thinking about the lunch she'd had with Karen and Anna earlier that day.

Since Scotty had been on his bus trip, she had shared lunch with her two best friends. However, the conversation had focused on Anna and Dean Love. Things weren't going well between Anna and Dean, and Karen pointed out that Anna was too pushy and anxious and that's why Dean was now avoiding her. Monica had wanted to hear what they had to say about her problems with John, but they'd talked about Dean for so long that she didn't even feel like talking about John. Focusing on Anna's relationship gave her a brief reprieve from thinking about her own problems.

A few hours later, after she'd had dinner with Scotty and sent him upstairs to go to bed, her longing for John's company returned. She sat in her living room, flipping through channels on TV, trying to find something to keep her mind occupied. She yawned, wondering if she should go to bed early. However, she knew going to bed early wasn't going to allow her to get more rest. Thoughts of John would plague her until she fell into a fitful sleep.

Frustrated with the lack of good television shows, she turned off the TV and turned on a soft gospel CD. As the music wafted throughout her living room, she pulled down her book of devotionals, desperately trying to find comfort in the words printed on the page.

When somebody knocked at her door, she dropped her book, wondering if John could be coming by at this late hour. As she opened the door, she checked the clock, noting it was almost 10:00 p.m. John stood on her doorstep clutching a sheaf of papers, his dark eyes apprehensive. "Can I come in?"

She nodded. Her heart pounded as he entered her home. He handed her the papers. "Scotty left these at the school during his last tutoring session. I figured he'd need them since some of the material will be used in his class tomorrow." John had held Scotty's tutoring sessions at Scotty's school since his argument with Monica.

"Thanks." She placed the papers on the coffee table. "I'll be sure he takes them to school with him."

An awkward silence followed, and before Monica knew it, John placed his strong arms around her. He muttered an apology into her ear as she returned his hug. "I'm so sorry for getting angry with you."

When he released her, she was initially speechless. It took her a few moments to gather her thoughts. "I shouldn't have spoken so negatively about something you really wanted to do."

He took her hand as they sat on the couch. "Can we talk?"

She nodded, wondering what he was about to tell her now. "I guess you want to talk about this ministry."

He toyed with her hand, listening to her words. "I'd like to."

"But?"

"But so far I haven't taken any steps into going into the ministry."

She tried to decipher his words. "That's odd. You seemed so intent upon doing this. Why don't you get the ball rolling?"

"I'm still considering it, and I'd like to do it, but I'm still giving the matter some thought and prayer."

Butterflies floated in her belly as he continued to hold her hand. She tried to focus on his words. "Just talk to the pastor about it, John."

"I'm one step ahead of you."

"Really? How so?"

"I called the church office and scheduled to meet Pastor Martin later this week." He ran his hand over his head. "Look, we had a disagreement, and couples need to learn to work through disagreements in order to make the relationship work."

"So you do consider us in a relationship?" The thought pleased her, and she hadn't been sure where she stood with John until this moment.

He scooted closer, pulling her into his arms. She found comfort in his embrace as she listened to his deep voice. "I'd like to think we are in a relationship. I know it's been years since I've felt so strongly for someone. Do you realize how much I've missed seeing you over the last week?"

"I've missed you, too. But by the way you've been acting lately, I just assumed we were finished with each other."

He grunted and encouraged her to continue.

She balled her hands into fists as she recalled the last week. "Well, for starters, you've definitely been avoiding me. You're tutoring Scotty at school now. You obviously don't want to see me, since you haven't been coming to my house." She sighed, folding her arms in front of her chest. "You also refused to acknowledge me at church. It's like I don't exist."

He held her chin between his fingers, forcing her to look at him. "I'm sorry.

That was childish and immature on my part. I should have let you know that you hurt my feelings by not agreeing with my ministry idea." He kissed her, and the butterflies in her stomach exploded. "But I know we can work through this. Let's give it some time. Maybe things will work out with your sister and Scotty, and you'll be able to come on the road with me if I should decide to join the ministry."

She turned away, not at all enthused with the idea of traveling around the world. Although she loved being with John, she didn't know if she could give up her job, her home, and her security to travel for a year. However, she kept those thoughts to herself as she thought about the situation logically.

He had still not mentioned marriage, so she knew the question of her traveling with him was out unless he decided they should marry. She also wondered if God was really calling him into this ministry. Hopefully Pastor Martin would be able to shed some light on that subject. "Well, I'm not sure what'll happen with Gina. I've been praying for her a lot lately."

"Speaking of your sister, how is Gina doing?"

In spite of the turmoil with John during the last week, Monica did see a ray of hope in her life. "Well, I'd mentioned that she's started reading her Bible."

He nodded. "Yes, you did tell me about that."

She sat up straighter, enthusiastic about Gina's progress. "And my mom said she's gone to church a couple of times, even spoke with the reverend once."

"That's wonderful. Do you think she's ready to turn her life around?"

She shrugged, not wanting to get her hopes up. "I'm not sure. Gina can be very sneaky at times. There were times when it may have appeared she was getting better, but she would backslide and go back to her old ways. I wouldn't put it past her to be attending church and reading her Bible just because she knows it's something my parents want her to do, not because she wants to."

He scratched his head, obviously puzzled. "I'm missing something here. Why would she do it just to please your parents?"

"I just said she was sneaky. She may want to ask my parents for a large sum of money and figure if it appears she's cleaning up her life, then they'll give her what she wants."

"Well if she's done that before, wouldn't your parents be aware of what she might be up to?"

She shrugged. "Not really. When Gina gets on their good side, I think they're so desperate to have their daughter back in their lives that they make the mistake of giving her the benefit of the doubt. All we can do right now is pray and hope she's making a change for the better."

"Well maybe it will be different this time. Maybe she's ready to make a positive change in her life. Scotty told me he wished his mother could live with you two."

Her heart skipped a beat. "I know he missed his mother in the beginning, but I didn't realize he still wanted her to live with us."

"I don't think he wanted to mention it to you again because he doesn't want to hurt your feelings. He loves you, too, and I'm sure he senses his mother isn't very stable right now."

She shrugged, saying the first thing that came to her mind. "Well, maybe God will work with His Holy Spirit and make my sister stable."

He pulled her into his arms, kissing her cheek. "Yes, maybe He will."

Chapter 12

The next morning Monica awakened early. The bright sun was streaming through her window, and in spite of the winter temperatures, she heard the faint chant of birds carrying on the wind. While enjoying a few pieces of buttered toast and a fragrant cup of coffee, she read her devotional for the day, soaking up the words of wisdom like an eager sponge. She found peace and comfort in the words and hoped she could recall the timely advice as she went about her day.

She closed the book as she finished the last sip of coffee. She still could not believe John had stopped by the previous day and actually apologized for his actions. She gripped the handle of her cup, still basking in the afterglow of his kiss, still wishing she could force things to work out between them.

She bowed her head, praying God would help her and John to work everything out in their relationship. As soon as she whispered her amen, the pounding of Scotty's feet echoed down the stairs. "Aunt Monica! You didn't wake me up!"

She checked her watch, astonished that so much time had passed. "Hurry up and get dressed! The bus will be here in a few minutes, so you'll have to miss it. I'll drive you to school today."

Thirty minutes later, she rushed to get Scotty to school on time. She went through the drive-through lane of a fast-food place to grab Scotty some breakfast before he got to school. She walked him into the school building, making sure he was safely in his class before she drove to work.

During her workday, she found it hard to focus. Her thoughts wavered between John, his ministerial endeavors, and the future of their relationship. Her boss, Clark, had to keep repeating himself when he spoke to her and at one point asked if she was okay. She hurriedly told him she was fine, so she tried to remain focused on leading her staff with the preparations for the executive board meeting the following day. They were to prepare several spiral-bound notebooks of the company's financial data to distribute to the board members. As she made double-sided copies, she tried to force her mind to stay focused on her job for the rest of the day.

When she arrived home that evening, she kicked her shoes off while Scotty ran into the kitchen, wondering what they were having for dinner that evening.

"Oh," she groaned, wiggling her toes in the plush carpet. "I forgot to take something out of the freezer this morning."

Scotty scampered back into the living room, joining her on the couch. He mentioned a popular restaurant that catered to children.

She groaned, not looking forward to a meal at a place that served chicken fingers and seafood to a child clientele. Before she could comment on his suggestion for a meal, her phone rang. Scotty lunged toward the sound of the phone, not giving her a chance to answer. "Hello," he piped into the receiver. "Mom! Hi!"

She listened, wondering what Gina was telling her son. He just gave a lot of yeses and nos and a few uh-huhs. Finally, he raised the phone from his ear. "Aunt Monica, my mom wants to talk to you."

She took the phone away from Scotty, plopping back on the couch. Her brain felt drained and full of fatigue, and she hoped Gina hadn't called this evening to start an argument. "Hi, Gina," she grumbled.

"Man, don't sound so enthusiastic to hear from me," Gina's voice dripped with sarcasm. Monica's shoulders tensed, wondering if she should put off this conversation for another day.

Monica responded to Gina's comment. "What did you want? I'm tired, and it's been a rough week."

"Hmm," Gina replied. Monica could imagine Gina twirling her hair through her fingers as she tried to figure out what was wrong. "Are you and that guy you brought over for Thanksgiving having problems? You always did have a hard time holding on to a man."

Monica gritted her teeth, ignoring Gina's question. "What do you want?"

Gina sighed, lowering her voice. "Look, I know we haven't always gotten along, but I love my son, and I want to live with him."

Monica's heart skipped a beat as she clutched her stomach, wondering if Scotty would be ripped away from her as soon as she'd grown to love him so much. She glanced into the kitchen and saw Scotty sitting at the table eating a banana. "You can't take Scotty away from me," she whispered, not wanting him to overhear. "I'll call you right back."

She hung up the phone, rushed up the stairs, entered her room, and closed the door behind her. Sitting on her bed, she quickly dialed her parents' phone number. When Gina answered, she closed her eyes, hoping she could find the right words to make her sister change her mind. "Look, you can't take Scotty away. He loves it here. Plus he's doing well in school. The counselor at his school said you let him miss a lot of days, and he fell behind. Since John is tutoring him, he's been doing so well and he seems to enjoy his classes."

Gina responded, "Look, he's blind anyway. His life is already going to be hard enough. What good is this education going to do him?"

She groaned, still wondering when her sister would grow up and not be so naive. "Your son really needs a good education to fall back on. He'll need to find a job and support himself when he gets older." She raised her voice, and her heart pounded faster. Tears trickled down her cheeks, so she wiped them away. "If you come here and take this child away, so help me God, I'll take you to court and prove what an unfit mother you are!" Her hands shook as she clutched the phone. A bead of sweat trickled down her brow, and she wondered if she was going to faint.

"Monica—"

"Do you know how much I worry about him, about what'll happen to him when he grows up?" She suddenly stood, leaning against the cool glass window, staring at the frigid beach in the distance. "Gina, don't cross me now because I have God in my corner, and I want what's best for my nephew." She sniffed and walked to her dresser, grabbed a few tissues to blow her nose, and wiped her eyes. She was so upset that she barely noticed Gina was sobbing also.

"Look, Monica. I know I haven't told you this, but I appreciate all you've done for my son. I didn't call you to start an argument."

Monica clutched her soiled tissues in her hand as disbelief settled into her bones. She held the phone tightly, still suspicious of her sneaky sister. "What do you mean?" she asked in a small voice.

"Look, I've had a hard time dealing with Scotty since he came into this world. He was an unplanned pregnancy, plus he was born blind. It's hard for me to deal with his handicap, but I am learning to accept it."

"Your son is just like other kids except he can't see. You just need to treat him the way you would any sighted child."

"I realize that, but it's taken me several months to figure out that you're a better mother than I am. But I should still be a mother to Scotty since he is my child."

Monica still wondered where this conversation was going. "So what did you want to do? You just said you wanted Scotty to come and live with you. That must mean you want to take him away from me." Thoughts of having Scotty ripped away from her made her heart pound even faster. She lay upon the bed, still holding the phone. "I've worked hard to get Scotty to stop cussing and to start paying attention to his schoolwork. My friend John has also been using his own free time to help him. He doesn't even get paid for doing this."

She heard Gina sniffing, and Monica struggled to calm herself down.

Gina spoke. "Look, I wanted to make a proposition to you."

"A proposition?"

"Can I come and live in your house so I can help raise my son? I promise I'm trying to turn my life around, and I've even started going to church."

Monica stared at the ceiling, still hopeful that Gina would improve her life-style. "Are you sincere about this? You want to be here to help Scotty?"

"Yes, I'm finally making some positive changes in my life, and I want to be there for my son. What's wrong with that?"

Monica shook her head, still shocked. Was this an answer to her prayers? "What about working? Are you willing to get a job?" She certainly couldn't afford to support another person on her income. She was already supporting Scotty.

Gina told of her plans to find employment in the Ocean City area. Monica gave her a lengthy list of rules to follow while residing in her home. "You can't smoke in my house. Also, no illegal drugs, and if I find out you're mixing with the wrong kind of people and exposing Scotty to that mess, I'm calling the police," she warned.

Gina took a deep breath. "I know you're right to be leery of me, and I don't blame you. I just want you to give me the opportunity to prove myself while I spend some quality time with my son again."

So many things were twirling through her mind that she didn't know what to do. She rubbed her forehead, sensing an impending headache. "When did you want to move in?"

"How about in two weeks? You have a lot of empty space in the basement. Mom and Dad said I could have the bed and furniture from their guest bed-room. We'll just rent a van and move it in a couple weeks."

She finally said good-bye to her sister, still hesitant about another huge change that was happening in her life. When she finally exited her bedroom, she was stunned to see John standing at the bottom of the stairs. "John?"

He met her halfway up the stairs, taking her hands into his. "I heard you yelling all the way down here."

"Oh!" She covered her mouth. "Did Scotty hear me?" she whispered.

He shook his head. "When I knocked on the door, he let me in then went out back to play with his ball."

"He knows he's not supposed to answer the door unless I tell him it's okay." She looked away from his concerned warm brown eyes. "Did you really hear everything I said while I was upstairs?" She was ashamed of her outburst and wished she'd handled her anger in a more Christian way.

He beckoned her down the stairs and pulled her into his arms. "I didn't hear everything, but I did hear enough to know you were yelling at your sister."

She still felt dazed about her conversation as he led her to the couch. Her tears had left wet trails, and he ran his fingers over them. Her stomach quivered with delight as he kissed each of her tearstained cheeks. "What happened?"

"Actually, it's a good thing."

"Oh?" He gave her a dubious look, obviously not believing her. "You don't look like it's a positive thing."

"There's so much happening right now." She thought about her sister's heartfelt plea. "Gina wants to move in with me to help raise Scotty and to straighten out her life."

"Oh? Well that's better than taking him away from you. Are you sure the two of you will be able to live together?"

She shrugged. "I'm willing to try, for Scotty's sake."

"Are you sure she'll uphold your Christian values while in your home? She won't be smoking, drinking, and acting up as you say she does?"

She shrugged again. "I told her if she does those things, I'll call the police." Dejected, she wondered how long the conversation would bother her.

"What's the matter?"

"I wish I hadn't yelled at her. I was so furious that I thought I was going to pass out. It's been several years since I've been that angry."

He touched her cheek. "I think Jesus understands your frustration. You've been trying to help your sister for years, and now you're trying to help her son. It initially looked like she was stabbing you in the back for taking care of him."

She shook her head, refusing to be comforted by his words. "I still should have acted like a Christian. Don't you see why I'm so upset with myself? I sense Gina may be trying to find her way to God. What kind of example was I, yelling at her when she wasn't out to take Scotty away from me after all?"

"Don't beat yourself up over this. You can apologize to Gina later, and if she forgives you, everything will be all right. When will she be moving in?"

She gave him the details about Gina's arrival.

"I have an idea. How about we rent a van and go down there and help her move?"

"You would do that for me?"

"I'd do anything for you, Monica."

She wondered if that was true. She wanted to tell him to give up his idea of ministering to agnostics and nonbelievers all over the world but held her tongue. She certainly couldn't convince him not to do the Lord's work if that's what he felt he needed to do.

❧

John clutched his Bible as he entered the church, still surprised that he was actually doing as he'd promised Monica a few days ago. A few children frolicked through the otherwise empty hallways, waiting for parents to pick them up from the church day care.

He found Pastor Martin's door closed, so he knocked, and the pastor invited him in. He entered the office, and the pastor shook his hand. "I was kind of shocked that you called to make an appointment."

"Yeah, I've had a lot of stuff on my mind lately, but I've only discussed it with two people."

Pastor Martin invited him to sit before he commented. "Well, whatever has been on your mind, I hope one of the people you discussed it with was God."

John nodded, taking note of the awards and diplomas adorning the walls. He wiped his sweaty hands on his slacks. "Jesus was the first one I spoke with. I've been praying about this for a while."

"I'll bet the other person you spoke with is Monica Crawford."

He opened his mouth, amazed the pastor was so perceptive. "How'd you guess?"

Chuckling, Pastor Martin leaned back in his leather desk chair. "I've seen the two of you interacting over the last few weeks. I know it bothered her that you weren't saved initially, and I'm glad you made the right decision to find Jesus."

He nodded, glad he'd made the right decision also. "I guess I've been feeling kind of guilty."

The pastor's smile faded. "Guilty? Why? Guilt is not a feeling that's associated with salvation. Once you accept Christ, you're starting off with a new clean slate, and you're forgiven for all sins. Just try to live your life according to His commands the best that you can, and that's all He asks of you."

John hesitated. "I guess you could say I feel I should be doing more in the ministry. I feel like I should have researched this and accepted Christ earlier in my life. I want to make up for lost time and try to get as many people as possible to come to Jesus."

The pastor raised his thick eyebrows. "How do you propose doing that?"

He took a deep breath, explaining the ministry he wanted to join. "I figure if I take a year's hiatus from my job and join this ministry, I could make up for at least some of those years when I was an agnostic."

The clergyman sadly shook his head. Steepling his hands below his chin, he gave John a shrewd look. "That's not a good reason to go into the ministry, son. You need to go because you feel called to do it."

"I guess as a new Christian, I'm having a hard time figuring out if I'm called or not."

"Feeling called is when you experience a certain peace and contentment in what you feel the Lord is guiding you to do," Pastor Martin explained.

"How would I know if the Lord is guiding me?"

"You'll just *know* by the feeling of peace that settles in your gut and a gentle calm that settles upon you when you've made a decision guided by the Lord. What is your heart telling you to do?" John looked around the office. Surprisingly, the pastor's words mirrored what Monica had tried to tell him. "If you feel uncomfortable answering the question. . ."

He shook his head. "My heart is telling me to stay here and be with Monica." He gathered his thoughts. "But my mind is telling me to pursue this ministry. I'm a scientist and a professor, and whenever I've failed in something, I feel I should give more effort to find the right solution."

The pastor stood. "Son, Christianity doesn't work that way. Just look at the scriptures and use that scientific mind to research what God is telling you to do." He took a deep breath before continuing. "Have you signed up to go on our men's retreat at the Princess Royale Resort?"

"Yes, I have."

"Well, Brian Smith, a former agnostic, will be one of our speakers."

"You're kidding! He's in charge of the ministry I want to join." John shook his head. "There must be some mistake. He wasn't on the list of speakers that I saw printed last week."

Pastor Martin grinned. "Bless us all! One of the speakers cancelled, and we found Brian at the last minute. But I think this change was God working behind the scenes as usual. I want you to talk to Brian and see what he thinks about your reasoning."

John stood and shook hands with the pastor. "All right, I'll be sure to snatch him for a few minutes at the retreat."

During the next couple of weeks, John continued to struggle with his decision to join the ministry, but he looked forward to talking to Brian Smith at the men's retreat. He wanted to join this ministry to make up for lost time. However, he didn't want to sacrifice a possible future with Monica to fulfill his ministerial needs. He knew if he did take a year off to go away, he would be thinking about her constantly, wondering if another man would make a move on her, romancing her until she fell in love again.

He continued to stroll around campus and pray about the situation, still not sure of what he was going to do. He wanted God to show him a sign, telling him if he should stay in Ocean City with Monica or travel for a year preaching to others.

Finally, on the day they were scheduled to help Gina move, John awakened, the chant of birds beckoning the new day. He looked forward to seeing Monica that day and visiting her parents. He had to wonder what she had told them about their brief breakup and recommitment. He wondered if she'd told them about his desire to go into the ministry.

An hour later, he picked up the moving van from the lot and signed the paperwork. The van was due back the following day. He then drove to Monica's house, eager to get a start on this day.

As he rapped on her door, he recalled the time they'd spent together the last couple of weeks. Amid his choir practice and socializing with his Christian brothers, he'd made sure he found time to spend with her on weekends. They'd spent one Saturday night at the movies, taking Scotty with them. Although the boy could not see the screen, he still enjoyed the songs and the voices in the newest Walt Disney flick.

He'd also continued to tutor Scotty twice a week. He knew Monica still had doubts about Gina's moving in with her, and he wanted her to know he was there to support her in her decision.

He heard footsteps pounding on the floor. Scotty opened the door. "Mr. John, is that you?"

"Yes, Scotty, it's me."

"Aunt Monica is in the kitchen."

He ran his fingers over the boy's head as he followed him into the kitchen. She looked adorable in her baggy jeans and oversized sweatshirt. He kissed her cheek as she flipped pancakes on the griddle. "Breakfast will be ready in a minute. Scotty is anxious to see his mother."

After they'd said grace and enjoyed their pancakes, they were on their way to her parents' house. The ride was quiet and uneventful. They turned the radio on to a Christian talk station while Scotty listened to his earphones during the drive.

When they were almost at her parents' house, John thought about the van's seating capacity. "Hey, do you think all of us can fit into the front seat of this van on the way back?"

Her warm brown eyes glowed. "Oh, that's right, I haven't told you yet."

"Told me what?" He took an exit off the main highway.

"About what my parents did. They purchased a used car for Gina."

"Really?" He wondered if Gina really deserved a car but decided to keep his thoughts to himself.

"She's going to follow us back in her car. Scotty will ride with her." He was pleased to hear this. He wanted some time alone with Monica on the drive back. "I wish they'd waited. . . . At least until she found a job."

He patted her arm. "Don't worry. Everything is in God's hands."

"I know everything is in God's hands, but I can't help but worry about my sister. I wonder how her presence will affect Scotty."

He tried to be optimistic about the situation. "You say she's been going to church and reading her Bible. That's a good start."

She nodded. "Yes, it is." Then she smiled. "I'm glad you decided to come with me."

He returned her smile. "I'm glad I came, too. I had to miss some church activities today to do this, but I don't mind. I know how hard this is for you, letting your sister move in with you so suddenly, but I just want you to know that I'll be there for you if you need me."

Minutes later, they pulled into her parents' town house complex. After John opened their doors, Scotty scooted out of the cab of the truck. "Be careful, Scotty," she warned.

"I want to see my mom." She led him to the front door.

Gina answered, her long locks covered with a multicolored scarf. As soon as she saw Scotty, she pulled him into her arms. "Hi, baby."

She kissed his cheek before she released him, leading him into the house. John and Monica followed close behind. John watched Gina as she placed some items into a box. He wondered if she really had made a positive change in her life.

Monica's mother hugged him, beckoning everybody into the living room. "Gina doesn't have a whole lot of stuff to move, besides the furniture. I figured we could sit around and visit for a few hours."

John joined the older couple in the living room while Scotty talked with his mother in the corner, telling her about his school and about the advances he'd made during his tutoring sessions. After their conversation ended, Gina approached Monica and asked if she could speak with her privately. Monica trudged up the stairs, following Gina.

As Mr. Crawford tried to engage him in a discussion about the latest basketball games on TV, John could barely listen. He wondered what in the world Gina was saying to Monica upstairs in the bedroom.

❧

Monica followed her sister upstairs, wondering if Gina was going to be the bearer of bad news. She tried to calm her racing heart as they entered Gina's bedroom. Boxes were stacked in the corner, and the bed had been stripped. The hardwood floor gleamed under the bright sunlight streaming from the window.

Monica closed her eyes, asking the Lord to guide her and accept whatever her sister had called her into this room to say.

"You're praying, aren't you?" asked Gina.

Monica nodded. "Yes, I am. You know that prayer has always been an important part of my life. I've been praying for you for years."

Gina plopped on the bed, and Monica sat beside her.

Monica gazed at her sister before she spoke. "Look, I wanted to apologize."

Gina's head jerked back so hard, her multicolored scarf fell off. Her dark eyes widened as she picked up the scarf. "You want to apologize to me? That's a switch. Why?"

"For yelling at you when you called me a couple of weeks ago," Monica explained. "I love Scotty so much, and I wanted to protect him from your old lifestyle. Do you realize how much your son means to me?"

"I think I have an idea how much he means to you. I know he loves you, and I'm glad you were able to help me out."

Monica took a deep breath and continued. "When I yelled at you, I didn't act like a Christian. I took my anger out on you before you had a chance to speak. If I'd been patient and listened to you from the beginning, I would have known that you weren't proposing to take Scotty away from me." She squeezed her hands together, still gathering her thoughts. "I know you've been reading your Bible and going to church, and I just didn't want my actions to color your perceptions about the way a Christian should act." She thoughtfully considered her next words. "I also wanted to apologize about the way I've been acting since you've left Scotty in my care."

Gina furrowed her brow. "What do you mean?"

"I kind of feel like I've been wrongly judging you. I've been upset with you for not acting in a Christian manner when maybe you just didn't have it in you to give your son the attention he needed." Monica shrugged. "It's kind of hard for me to explain, but when you dropped Scotty off, I agreed to keep him, and maybe that's what the Lord felt was best for Scotty at the time. It was wrong for me to hold all of this animosity toward you when you went with Randy to the circus." Monica realized it was wrong of her to expect Gina to live as a Christian when she'd never openly professed to accepting Christ as her Savior.

Gina poked out her full lips, gazing at her sister. "Look, I don't blame you for getting mad, but I do want to ask you to do something."

"What?"

"Be patient with me. I know you've pretty much broken Scotty of the habit of cussing over the last few months and he's doing better in school, but I've still got a long way to go."

"What do you mean?"

"I want you to be patient with me if a cuss word slips from my mouth once in a while. I'm not cussing nearly as much as I used to; I've gotten a lot better."

"Well, try to be more careful when you're around Scotty. It's taken some hard work to get him into more positive habits, and I'd hate to see all that work gone to waste."

Gina nodded as she tightened the scarf around her head. "I promise. Also, I am seriously looking to God for answers to a lot of things, and I've been going to church lately. I know I've been sneaky and untruthful sometimes—"

"Sometimes?"

She shook her head. "Okay, most of the time, but I want you to know that these changes I'm making in my life this time are for real. I really want to become a better person for myself and for Scotty."

Monica hoped Gina's words were truthful. If Gina made these changes in her life and believed in the Lord, her burdens would be lighter due to her faith in Him.

Unexpectedly, Gina pulled her sister into her arms. Monica was shocked by the sudden embrace, but returned the hug, trying to recall the last time she'd been hugged by her sibling.

After Monica ended their embrace, she asked Gina what had happened to Randy. Gina blew air through her full lips. "Girl, he never even married me like he promised. I hooked up with a few other people in the circus, and you saw the black eye I had on Thanksgiving." Monica nodded, and Gina continued to explain. "My latest boyfriend was abusive, and he gave me that black eye."

She laid her hand on her sister's shoulder. "You need to trust God to help you in your personal relationships, Gina."

Gina nodded, silently agreeing with her sister.

Minutes later, they returned to the living room. John stood, his dark eyes full of concern. She walked toward him, and he squeezed her hand. "Is everything okay?" he whispered.

She nodded. "Don't worry," she whispered back.

Mrs. Crawford stood, calling everybody into the kitchen. "I made pot roast and potatoes for lunch, and we've got some sodas to drink. Ya'll come in here and eat before you start loading up the van."

They sat at the laden table and joined hands. Mr. Crawford said a prayer of thanksgiving and asked God to watch over his family as they made the trek back down to Ocean City.

Chapter 13

As Monica got into the seat beside John, he revved the truck's engine, clearly anxious to get on the road back to Ocean City.

As they passed the Inner Harbor in Baltimore, he gestured toward the dashboard. "Open the glove compartment."

She opened it and removed a folder. "What's this?"

"Read it and see."

She looked at an outline of the ministry program he wanted to join. "So you've decided to go?"

"I'm still praying about it. I've spoken with Pastor Martin." He then told her about the men's retreat he was going to attend and about their new guest speaker.

"So you're hoping to make a final decision after the men's retreat?"

"Yes, hopefully I will. I'm also hesitant about going into this ministry because of you."

"Me?"

"Yes, I love you so much that I don't know if I could leave you for a year. I wish you'd wait for me."

"John, I don't know."

"Do you love me?"

She held her breath, remaining silent.

"You're not answering me. I guess that means no."

"There's just so much at stake here."

"What's wrong with telling me how you feel about me?" he argued.

"It's hard for me to tell my true feelings to somebody. Especially a man."

"But I would never hurt you. If you loved me, you wouldn't mind waiting for me."

"How can I be assured you wouldn't be dating anybody else while you're gone?"

"I'm hurt. Of course I wouldn't date anybody while I'm gone."

She shrugged, still uncomfortable about waiting for him for a year. She also hoped that John was spiritually strong enough to make the decision to join this ministry. Was it really the right avenue for him to pursue?

≈

The following week John took Monica out to celebrate Valentine's Day. She'd gotten Karen to babysit Scotty so they could go to a fancy restaurant. The dinner was romantic and tasty, and it was nice to spend the evening with her. They didn't speak about his ministerial plans. On the Saturday after Valentine's Day, John found himself looking for Brian Smith at the men's retreat. The posh hotel had reserved their conference rooms and lodging accommodations at half price since it was off-season. When he finally found Brian in the lobby, he stopped and introduced himself, asking if he could spare a minute to talk to him.

Several minutes later, bundled in thick down-filled coats and holding cups of hot coffee, they stood on the frigid beach, watching the waves crash upon the sand. Both men were comfortably silent as they sat on a bench and watched a few winter surfers sporting wet suits ride the cold waves. "It sure is nice out here," said John as he sipped his coffee.

Brian cradled his coffee cup, gesturing toward the ocean. "Yes, it's magnificent." The elderly man focused on John. "But I'm sure you didn't ask me to come out here to stare at the ocean."

"Well, you know that ministry you started awhile back? After I got saved, I found out about it, and I was thinking about joining it. But I've been undecided over the last few weeks." Not wanting to take up too much of Brian's time, John briefly told him more about his problem, and Brian gave his advice.

"Well, John, when I started this ministry, I wasn't looking for new Christians to join it."

"Why not?"

"Because I know new Christians can be eager and zealous, but, also, they might not be spiritually ready to enter a ministry. When we find out a new Christian wants to join, we have to probe and find out if he feels called to do it." Brian sipped his coffee. "John, as a former agnostic, I can tell you one of the hardest things I did was going to God for help. I wanted to do what *I* wanted to do, not what God wanted me to do."

"But I can't help it. Sometimes it just seems like this ministry is the right thing to do."

"But you can't think about what *you* think is the right thing to do. You need to seek God for the answers to your questions. That's what you need to do."

"But I don't want—"

"Don't think about what you want or don't want. You need to seek God for the answer. I'm sure once you opened your heart and sought out God, He revealed Himself to you, right?"

John nodded, still listening. Brian continued, "Well, you need to seek His will about this ministry. We need to seek out God and not lean on our own understanding. Being a scientist, one of the hardest lessons I've learned is that our minds are limited, but God's mind is limitless." He paused before continuing.

"You say you don't want to leave Monica?"

He quickly nodded. "I love her. I've never loved a woman as much as I love her. It'll make me sick to leave her."

"If your heart is telling you not to leave her, maybe you shouldn't. It sounds like she's going through a lot lately, raising her nephew and dealing with her younger sister. She's got a lot on her plate. Perhaps the Lord is guiding you, through your heart, to stay with her and support her."

Brian invited John to stand, and they walked toward the chilly ocean. As they paced along the shore, John continued to speak. "Since I was an agnostic, I know how other agnostics think. I feel that I could bring more to this ministry than an ordinary nonagnostic person could."

Brian raised his hands. "And?"

"And that's why I feel I should do this. Think about all the good I could do."

Brian placed his hand on his shoulder. "Son, I'll be praying for you. But you've got to remember what the Bible says about Christianity and salvation. Pray about what God is trying to tell you through His Word." He rubbed John's shoulder. "Also, perhaps the Lord placed this ministry on your mind for another reason."

"Such as?"

"Perhaps it's something He wants you to do another time? Maybe when things are more settled between you and Monica, you can reconsider doing this ministry, if you feel you should do it in your heart, and bring her along with you." Brian sighed. "I know what you're going through, and I think that's one of the reasons why the Lord called on me to be here today. I'm glad Pastor Martin asked you to come to me because I went through a similar situation when I was first saved."

John was intrigued. "What happened?"

Brian chuckled. "I know this is a serious subject, but I can't help laughing about how foolish I was back then. I was in college when I got saved, and after I graduated, I went on a mission trip to Sydney, Australia." He shook his head. "I didn't pray about it or ask for any guidance. I was young and hotheaded, and I knew I just wanted to go down under and save as many souls as possible. After I had been there about a month, I realized I'd been able to get only one person to accept Christ. I was mad because I envisioned myself helping others, bringing lots of people to the gospel, getting people saved! I told the pastor I was a failure since I'd helped only one person find Jesus."

"Did the pastor set you straight?"

"He sure did! A month later, it was time to come back to the States, but the pastor told me I should prayerfully seek out what I felt God wanted me to do and to not lean on my own understanding. My thoughts of saving tons of people were skewed. The pastor said if I just helped one person find Christ, that's a blessing.

He said I shouldn't be concerned with the number of souls I save, but to just tell people about the gospel. It's up to them if they want to accept Christ."

They strolled along the shore for several minutes as John thought about Brian Smith's words. "Thanks, I'll think about all this."

"Do better than think about it. I want you to pray about it."

Brian touched John's shoulder before draining his coffee cup. "I have to go now, since I'm leading the small group study in the conference room."

John barely waved to Brian as he took his exit. His mind was now consumed with so many conflicting thoughts.

Two days later, John knocked on Monica's door. She answered it, looking professional in her dark business suit. "John! I didn't realize you were coming over tonight. I just got home from work and was just about to make dinner for Scotty, Gina, and me." Her mouth was set in a firm line as she closed the door.

"What's the matter?"

She glanced up the stairs, as if hesitant to discuss what troubled her lest Gina and Scotty would overhear them, and beckoned him into the kitchen. A package of ground beef thawed on the stove, and a raw onion sat beside the meat. She rubbed her forehead, and he wondered if she was getting a headache. He touched her shoulder. "Are you okay?"

She nodded and composed herself. "Gina is trying to make a change in her life, but it's kind of slow getting that change to take place."

"Really? What happened?"

"Well, when I was in the back of the house yesterday, I saw some cigarette butts in the yard, so I know she's been sneaking outside to smoke."

He took her hand. "Give it some time. I've never smoked before, but I do know several people who do, and I know what a struggle it is for them to quit. It's an addiction. Perhaps she can see a doctor. I do know there are things out there for people to use if they want to quit smoking."

She nodded. "Okay."

"Is that all that's bothering you?"

"No, I smelled alcohol on her breath last night. She knows she can't drink while she's in my home."

"Honey, I know she's still struggling with these things. Has it been really bad? Is she at least attempting to make the changes in her life?"

She nodded. "She doesn't cuss, and she does seem to take comfort in the scriptures."

"Has she been looking for a job?"

"Yes, she looks through the newspaper every day. I helped her get a résumé together, too."

"Well, that's good. Maybe she'll be ready to accept Christ soon."

Monica squeezed his hand. "Yeah, maybe." She looked into his eyes. "I sense you didn't come over here tonight to talk about Gina. You look like something is on your mind. Is everything going okay with all of your church duties? How are things going in the men's choir?"

He squeezed her hand, softening his voice. "The men's choir and Bible studies are going well. I wanted to talk about us."

"Have you decided to join that ministry?"

"Baby, I haven't decided that yet." He told her about his conversation with Brian Smith. "He said some things that made me think."

"And?"

"And I'm still not sure about my decision to go, but I need some space for a couple of weeks to think and pray about it. I'll probably see you in church and stuff, but I wanted to know if you would give me two weeks of privacy while I pray and make my decision."

"Okay, I'll give you your two weeks of privacy as long as you tell me the truth about your decision as soon as this hiatus is over."

He squeezed her shoulder. "I promise." He kissed her before he left.

❧

Monica placed her head in her hands, praying, hoping He would place the right decision on John's heart. As she whispered an amen, her phone rang. She was glad to hear Karen on the line. After they spoke for a few moments, Karen said, "Monica, I can tell something is on your mind. What's wrong? Does it have anything to do with John?"

"Yes. He needs to give our relationship a two-week break."

"Why?"

Monica explained the situation to her, and Karen stated her opinion. "I can understand why he would need this time alone with God. He just wants to make sure he makes the right decision, and he still feels as if he should straighten out his life."

"His life is straightened out. He just wants to make sure that if he decides to go into this ministry it's what God wants him to do."

Karen sighed. "Monica, he must still feel like his life is in shambles since he wants to make up for lost time by saving souls for God. That's not the way salvation works."

"I hope he decides to stay. He doesn't seem to feel the calling of this ministry in his heart, and until he does, I think he should stay in Ocean City until he finds his true calling."

"Monica," Karen said gently, "maybe this is his true calling. If he does decide to go, you can't get angry. You'll need to be behind him 100 percent. Don't be so selfish, thinking about the happiness you'll give up when he leaves. If he's doing this for the glory of God, there's nothing you can do about it. This is between him and the Lord."

Karen's spiritual perception stayed on Monica's mind the entire evening. Even after she had cooked their spaghetti dinner and made sure Scotty had done his homework, she still thought about Karen's words. As she prepared herself for bed that night, she asked God to give her the strength to accept John's decision gracefully.

&

During the next two weeks, John was grateful for time alone with God. He attended his Sunday church services but spent most of his spare time in earnest prayer and studying God's Word. He had highlighted the scriptures Pastor Martin and Brian Smith had given him. He read those key verses numerous times and decided his heart was telling him not to join this ministry right now. As he thought about his ministerial endeavors, he recalled the college students he taught at the university every day. He recalled the Christian organizations on campus and how the students would sometimes invite professors to attend these events. He could tell the students about his quest for God and about how he'd finally found Him. The university was the best mission field for him right now. He knew he should stay here to make a difference in the lives of these students.

Once he finally made his decision, he fell on his knees, thanking God for giving him the wisdom he craved. *Lord, I know I don't feel the desire to go into this ministry in my heart. I know You're telling me to stay right here in Ocean City, and within this church, and reach out to the community and the college campus right here. I know I want to stay here, near Monica, so that, if she'll have me, we can be together in a way that is acceptable in Your eyes. In Jesus' name, amen.*

&

Monica tried to hum as she worked, but found her heart just wasn't in it. Gina had taken Scotty to lunch and a Saturday afternoon movie. Instead of taking this time alone to sit and lament about John, she'd decided to use her energy cleaning her messy house. She turned her vacuum cleaner off and admired her freshly cleaned living room. She'd missed John for the last two weeks but knew she needed to give him his space so he could talk to God and make his decision.

She got a glass of ice water and sat on the couch. Her relationship with Gina was improving, and she had to admit her sister did have some common sense. Gina chastised her about not being truthful with John about her feelings. "If you love the guy, let him know," she'd advised.

So Monica promised herself that when she saw John again, she would let him know she loved him. Even if he did decide to leave for a year, she would take Karen's advice and learn to accept it, and she would indeed wait for him.

A hard knock sounded at her door, disturbing her thoughts. She wondered if it was one of the neighborhood kids selling something for school. She opened it and faced John. He looked handsome in his sweatshirt and jeans. Trying desperately to calm her racing heart, she opened the door. "John. . .hi."

She led him into her home. Before she had a chance to speak, he took her into his arms. She relished the scent of his aftershave as he kissed her. He remained silent, but love and adoration sparkled in his eyes. She swallowed, trying to moisten her suddenly dry throat. "John, before you say a word, I just want to be honest with you about something." He opened his mouth to speak, but she placed two fingers over his beautiful lips. "I love you. I've been in love with you for a while, but I was too scared and insecure to let you know. It was wrong of me not to be honest about my feelings for you, and I'm sorry I didn't tell you sooner."

"Monica Crawford, that's the sweetest thing you could ever say to me." He enfolded her in his arms again before releasing her. "And I want to let you know that I'm not ready to go into the ministry now. I was pursuing it for the wrong reasons, and I want to stay here, with you, right here in Ocean City." He kissed her and took her hand. "Do you think you can find a babysitter for Scotty tonight?"

"I'm pretty sure I can recruit somebody."

He smiled. "Good, because I want to take you out to dinner. Be sure you're wearing a nice dress. I'll be by to pick you up at six o'clock."

Monica continued to smile after John left, eagerly looking forward to their dinner that evening.

That night after Monica had changed into her favorite red dress and Scotty was happily eating popcorn and spending time with Gina, John picked her up. Though he appeared nervous, he was handsome in a very appealing dark gray suit with a royal blue necktie. As they drove to their destination, soft jazz music played from his stereo. He seemed very preoccupied. Every time Monica said something to him, she had to repeat herself.

A short time later, they arrived at Fager's Island Restaurant. The lighting in the fancy dining room was dim, and candles winked at the white-cloth-covered tables. A waiter approached and introduced himself. "Hi, my name is Alex, and I'll be your waiter this evening." He glanced at John for a few seconds before continuing. "Your table is right over here."

Monica gasped when she noted the large floral display of bright red roses gracing their table. There was also a crystal bowl filled with cocktail sauce and large shrimp tapered at the sides. Shrimp cocktail was one of her favorite appetizers, and she was ecstatic that John had planned this wonderful night out to celebrate his decision to stay in Ocean City. Perhaps since he'd decided to stay, their relationship could deepen and turn into something permanent. "Do you like the flowers?" John asked softly.

Her heart pounded as she pulled him into a hug. "Yes, I love them. Thank you."

They walked to the table, and he pulled her chair out for her. She was so excited that she didn't think she could even eat the shrimp. John took her hand. "Before we start eating our appetizer—"

Alex approached carrying a bottle of sparkling cider and two wine glasses. "I'm so sorry. We forgot to leave this on the table as you requested."

John waved the man away as if anxious for him to leave. After their waiter had taken his exit, John pulled a velvet box out of his pocket and pressed it into her hand. Monica opened the box and gasped, staring at the most exquisite diamond solitaire ring she'd ever seen.

"Monica, will you marry me?"

Tears slid down her cheeks as she clutched the box and stared into John's warm brown eyes. "Yes, John, I will marry you." He then leaned toward her and his mouth joined with hers.

As they kissed, she silently thanked the Lord for placing John French into her life.

Epilogue

Monica smiled as she walked down the sandy shore of the predawn beach, her cream-colored wedding dress flowing like liquid satin. As the waves tumbled onto the shore, a gentle warm breeze caressed her skin. Her father squeezed her elbow as he marched beside her, murmuring words of encouragement on this important day.

The enchanting event was so unreal, and her happiness piled up in her so high she thought she would burst. As birds swooped from the sky, a woodwind quartet played "The Wedding March," creating a sense of euphoria in the small crowd of wedding guests. Monica's smile brightened further as she approached her wedding party.

Anna, Karen, and Gina made striking bridesmaids in their royal blue dresses. The silky material of their gowns billowed in the wind as they awaited Monica several feet ahead on the stretch of Ocean City beach.

Monica happily thought about the arrangements she'd made for Gina and Scotty. Since Monica was going to be living with her new husband, Gina had agreed to stay in Monica's house and take over the house payments, eventually purchasing the house from her. Gina had been working for five months now, and she was attending church regularly. Monica was glad she was still going to be nearby if Gina needed help with raising Scotty.

Monica saw Anna glance at Dean Love periodically, and she was pleased that Anna appeared to have found the man of her dreams. Dean had recently proclaimed his love for Anna, and Monica hoped their relationship would lead to marriage.

John's new friends from church wore tuxes as they stood opposite the bridesmaids. Scotty clutched his ring-bearer pillow, impatiently waiting for Monica. However, Monica thought John looked the finest of all. When she was finally standing in front of him, he kissed her before the wedding ceremony began.

Pastor Martin beamed at the couple as he performed the wedding service. After the short sermon was over, and their vows and rings had been exchanged, John kissed his bride again.

MILK MONEY

Dedication

I would like to thank a lot of people for helping me with my extensive research for this novel—namely, the Higgins family. Thanks so much for allowing me to visit your small family dairy farm and for answering my numerous questions. I also appreciate your allowing me to assist with the milking of your herd.

I also want to give credit to my ACFW writing buddies: Pam Hillman, Anne Schrock, and Mary Connealy. Your advice about dairy farming proved to be very useful while I penned this novel.

I would also like to acknowledge Farm and Ranch accountant Patti Randle, CPA, for answering my questions about farm bookkeeping practices.

Chapter 1

Dumbfounded, the accountant gazed at a cow giving birth. He dropped his briefcase when he saw the feet of the baby sticking out of the mother's canal. A rope was looped around the legs of the young animal, and a brown-skinned woman pulled so hard that the muscles in her slender arms flexed. Her eyes squeezed shut while she grunted, reminding him of the noises people made when they bench-pressed weights. She opened her eyes. "Casey, hold on," she cooed. When he watched the birth, his sour stomach worsened, and the bagel and cream cheese he'd managed to eat for breakfast felt like a dead weight in his belly.

Her tears mingled with the sweat rolling down her face. She continued to pull and glanced in his direction. "Oh, thank God you came. Come and help me."

A plethora of unfamiliar scents tingled his nose. He swallowed, losing his voice. What was he supposed to do?

She continued to look at him, pulling on the rope periodically. "I already left a message on your answering service that it was coming out backward." Pushing the door open, he entered the room adjoining the barn, still hoping he wouldn't throw up. She nodded toward the rope, still tugging. "With both of us pulling, maybe we'll be able to get the calf out."

"Okay." He swallowed his nausea and pulled, mimicking the way he used to grunt when bench-pressing heavy weights. He followed her example, keeping tension on the rope and pulling each time the cow had a contraction. She grunted also, and their noises continued until the calf exited the birth canal minutes later. She dropped the rope, and he rushed behind her to look at the young animal. He touched the newborn, awed by the birth. She glanced at him as she cleaned gunk off the calf's nose and mouth.

Her sigh filled the space when she noticed the animal was breathing. "Aren't you going to examine the cow and calf?"

Before he could respond, a young man holding a large black plastic tote entered the pen. "This the Cooper farm?"

Confusion marred her face when she glanced at Frank. Then she focused on the new arrival. The newcomer rushed to the baby cow and began examining it. "I'm Dr. Lindsey's son. I'm taking over my daddy's practice this week since he's on vacation. He told you that, didn't he?"

She nodded, still looking confused. "I left a message on your answering service earlier."

The vet grunted. "I was down the street at the horse farm helping out with another birth, so I couldn't leave."

"Are the cow and calf okay?"

"They both look fine." He stopped his examination and looked at them. "I'm glad you had somebody helping you. You might not have gotten him out in time if you'd been pulling him on your own." He pulled a tool out of his bag. "You have antibiotic on hand for the calf, right? If not, I've got some."

The attractive woman nodded, her dark hair clinging to her sweaty neck as she promised the vet she would give the new calf the medicine. Frank watched, mesmerized by the whole process. A short time later, the newborn nursed from the mother. "Thank you, doctor," said the woman, patting the man on the shoulder.

The doctor shook his head, placing his tools back into his bag. "Don't thank me. You two got him out in time." He told Emily he would send her the bill, and then he left the farm. Emily glanced at Frank, as if taking in his khaki slacks and oxford shirt.

Noticing his bloody hands, she beckoned him over to a room containing a sink and a large steel tank. After ripping off the long plastic gloves covering her hands and forearms and dropping them into the trash can, she turned the water on, pumped out several squirts of soap, and washed. "I thought you were the vet," she said, continuing to scrub her hands and forearms. "I've never met Dr. Lindsey's son, so that's why I assumed you were him." After rinsing, she pulled paper towels from a dispenser and gestured for Frank to use the sink.

Frank shrugged and walked to the sink, placing his hands under the running water. "Sorry. I helped you out, but I didn't have any idea if I was doing it right. It's probably good I showed up when I did. It looked like you'd been trying to help that cow for a long time."

She shook her head. "Cows are tough. They can be in labor for hours before giving birth. When you came, I'd just started pulling the calf out with the rope." She continued to stare, frowning. "Well, if you're not Dr. Lindsey's son, then who are you?"

He offered his recently washed hand, glad the nauseous feeling had evaporated from his stomach. "I'm Franklin Reese, Certified Public Accountant."

❧

Emily ignored his hand, narrowing her eyes. "You're kidding!"

"Why would I kid about this?" He beckoned her over to his abandoned briefcase and slid the golden locks open, removing a sheaf of papers. He held the documents toward her. "It's all right here. You called us to come out here because you said you lost your bookkeeper and you needed somebody to show you how to properly do the accounting for your farm."

She shook her head, refusing to take the papers. Gritting her teeth, she recalled the countless arguments she'd had with her stepmother, Laura, during the last several weeks. "So, you're the accountant from Bryers and Ridge Accounting Firm that just opened in Monkton?"

He nodded. "The main office is at the Inner Harbor. They just opened this new branch to service the Monkton farm community."

She folded her arms in front of her. "I didn't call you; my stepmother did." She failed to admit that she was totally against hiring the accountant.

"Look. . .what's your name?" His mouth hardened into a thin line, and she found it hard not to stare at his cocoa brown, long-lashed eyes.

"My name is Emily Cooper."

He still clutched the papers, looking bewildered. "Did you want to call the office and reschedule?" He gestured toward the barn. "I see you've had a rough morning, so you might not be in the mood to talk about your finances right now."

"Just give me a second, okay?" She stepped away, noting how the cool scent of his cologne wafted around her, teasing her nose. She removed her cell phone from her pocket and hit the speed dial to call Laura. Emily left her stepmother a message, clutching the phone and speaking in a low voice so that Franklin would not hear her. "Mom, I thought we'd agreed you wouldn't hire that accountant until we talked about it some more. He's here now, and I'm not sure what to do." She ended her message and placed her phone back into her pocket. She gazed at the silos in the distance, still wondering how to handle this situation. The heated arguments she'd had with Laura about hiring an accountant played in her mind like a broken record.

"Did you want me to leave and come back another time?"

She jumped when his deep voice sounded behind her. "What's the phone number for your firm?"

He held the papers toward her. She took the cream-colored stationery, noting the number on the top. She called and spoke with the secretary, who confirmed Franklin's appointment.

She snapped her phone shut, and he presented her with a laminated ID card. "I usually show this as soon as I get to a new house. But since you were busy in the barn, my routine was messed up. Did you want to call the office back and reschedule?" he asked again.

Shaking her head, she figured it was wrong of her to go against Laura's wishes. "No, come on." She gestured toward the house, wiping sweat from her brow. They walked to her home, and she opened the door and entered the shaded, screened-in porch. Emily removed her barn boots and noticed dung stuck on his footwear.

"Oh no." She cringed, feeling bad about the mess on Franklin's shoes and clothing. After leaving her boots on the porch, she told him to remove his shoes. They entered the kitchen, and she showed him the bathroom in the hallway. "You can wash up in there. I have some spare clothes you can wear so I can wash your shirt and shoes." He nodded, entering the bathroom. She soon reappeared with an old shirt and shoes that belonged to her father. She heard the water running from behind the closed bathroom door, and she left the clothes in front of the room's entrance.

When he returned to the kitchen, a strange, funny feeling rushed through her when she saw him wearing her father's stuff. "I'll get started laundering your clothes, and I'll clean your shoes. When you leave today, I'll have everything done."

He waved her comment away. "Can you just show me where you keep your files?"

"They're in my father's office." She approached the closed door, hesitating before opening it. She took a deep breath, beckoning him to follow her into her dad's space. Her arms ached from pulling the calf earlier, and the effects of her sleepless night made her want to take a long nap. When Franklin stood beside her, she became aware of his height. He glanced around before focusing on the filing cabinet. "Do you know where your father keeps his P&L statements?"

Emily frowned, looking around the cluttered room. "His what?"

"You know, his profit and loss statements."

Emily shrugged, now wishing she wasn't so ignorant about bookkeeping. "I don't know."

"Okay. How about his tax returns? That'll be a good place for me to start." He gestured toward the cabinet. "Are his tax forms in the filing cabinet?"

Emily glanced around the room, feeling out of her element. "I'm not sure."

"You don't even know where your tax returns are?" She cringed as the exasperation in his voice settled around the room like dust.

Gritting her teeth, she glared at him. "No, I don't know." Wringing her hands, she gazed at the piles of paper scattered around the office.

"Why did you call us for our services if you don't know where the paperwork is?" He threw his hands up in the air. "I feel like I'm wasting my time here. You know we charge by the hour."

She snapped, whipping her head toward the newcomer. "I'm sorry! I don't know where anything is. You're welcome to look and charge us for your extra time!" Hot tears pricked her eyes, and she turned away, not wanting Franklin to see her cry. "I have chores to do in the barn." She turned and exited the house, welcoming the intense heat as she ran down the hill toward the barn.

When she rushed out of the office, remorse flowed through Frank. He shook his head, wishing he had not gotten so testy with Emily. Perhaps her father or her stepmother would arrive soon and show him where everything was. His head pounded, so he removed a bottle of water and some acetaminophen from his briefcase and took the pills. He guzzled the water before he turned the computer on. However, he discovered he couldn't access any files without a password. He put on his reading glasses, continuing to glance through the documents in the office. He would need Emily's help with finding the proper paperwork.

He wondered if his sudden move to Baltimore County had been a mistake. Maybe he should call his boss and get him to send somebody else for this assignment. When he was wondering what to do next, Emily returned. Her eyes were red, and she looked tired.

She took a deep breath. "I'm sorry I lost my temper with you earlier." She shrugged, and his heart melted with compassion.

"I want to apologize, too. I have a quick temper, and when people call us for services and don't have the proper paperwork, I get a little upset." The urge to rub her shoulder and let her know everything would be okay rushed through him. However, the urge quickly disappeared. "Our admin is supposed to send a letter or an e-mail beforehand, confirming our appointment and letting you know what files you need to have ready."

She shrugged. "Either Laura got the letter and forgot to tell me, or your admin didn't send it."

"So you're not sure where your father keeps his financial statements?" He glanced around the office. "Is he around to show me where they're filed?"

She shook her head, and her eyes filled with tears. She looked away for a few seconds and then turned toward him, wiping her eyes. "My father passed away a couple of weeks ago."

His heart skipped a beat. "I'm sorry." Shame for his earlier behavior rippled through his tired body. "I didn't know."

"It's okay. I haven't been myself since he died. My stepmother's taken his death pretty hard, so she left a couple of days ago, and she's staying with her daughter in Florida until she feels better."

He frowned. "You don't know how long she'll be gone?"

She shook her head. "She already had this trip planned before Dad died. My dad and Laura usually go to visit her daughter every year at the same time. She should be gone at least a few weeks. I already left her a voice mail asking her to call me."

"Why do you object to getting financial advice for your farm?" When she remained silent, he popped his briefcase open and again looked at the documents.

"In addition to basic bookkeeping advice, your stepmom also wanted to have your farm audited."

"Audited? Why? I thought that was something the IRS randomly did to check up on taxpayers' returns."

He frowned, placing the paperwork on the scarred desk. "That's true, but people can hire accountants to audit their business to make sure they're following GAAP."

"GAAP?"

"Generally accepted accounting principles. For a farm or ranch, people might also want to know the net worth of their business. For some reason, your stepmother might want to know these things since your father is gone and she's not used to doing the bookkeeping." He gestured toward the computer. "Do you mind giving me the password for your computer? It might help me get started. Maybe your dad scanned or saved the documents."

She sat in the leather office chair, and he watched her slender brown fingers tapping on the keyboard, noticing her extremely short nails. After typing the password, she vacated the chair, gesturing for him to sit. "Where do you want to start?" she asked.

She pulled up a seat beside him, and they discussed where her father may have stored his electronic documents. Wisps of her dark hair escaped from her ponytail and rested on her slender neck. Realizing that he was staring, he forced his thoughts back to the job they were doing. They located some of the documents, and she stood. "I have stuff to do in the barn."

"You're running this farm alone?"

She folded her arms in front of her. "Sort of. We do have a couple of teenage brothers who help us out. They live on the horse farm up the road, but they're not very responsible."

"They don't always show up for work?"

"No, they don't, and it's wearing me down." She gestured toward the computer. "Laura and I never knew much about the finances of the farm, so when Dad died, we knew we needed a little bit of help for the chores, but we didn't want to go overboard and hire more help than we could afford. Darren and Jeremy, our teenage hired help, agreed to take turns helping me each day with the milking. Since it's summer, they have free time, and they each have other part-time jobs. One of them works at the Wagon Wheel."

"The Wagon Wheel?"

"It's a restaurant around here."

Frank glanced at Emily, still trying hard not to stare. "Was one of them supposed to be here this morning?"

She narrowed her eyes. "You got it. When one of them doesn't show up and I confront them about it, Darren will always say he thought Jeremy was coming and Jeremy will always say he thought Darren was supposed to come." She shrugged. "One or the other comes often enough for it not to be a huge problem. That is, not until today. It really would have helped me a lot if one of them had shown up and helped me with the difficult birth." Frank silently agreed with her.

"Why didn't you want your stepmother to hire outside accounting help?" he asked again.

"I have my reasons." He assumed that was her way of saying it was none of his business. "But since you're here and my stepmother wants you here, then I guess you need to get started."

As she turned to leave, he stopped her with a comment. "Oh, I forgot to tell you earlier, I prefer to be called Frank."

Emily nodded. Once she left, he began going through her father's Excel spreadsheets.

He accessed Mr. Cooper's most current document and began doing his job. A few hours later, he frowned. The numbers did not look accurate, and he figured it would take him a long time to figure out the late Mr. Cooper's accounting methods.

Chapter 2

A t five o'clock that evening, Emily opened the gate of the stanchion-style barn, which doubled as their milking parlor, and let the cows into their stalls. The thirty large black-and-white animals stomped into the enclosure, each going into her space.

"Hey, Emily."

She grinned with relief when Jeremy Dawson approached.

"I'm glad you finally showed up. I just finished cleaning the equipment for the milking and gave the cows their feed." She'd already attached the mobile milking units to the pipes so they could start milking the cows.

The lanky, mocha-colored teen ran his fingers over his newly cornrowed hair. "Didn't Darren come this morning?"

She folded her arms in front of her chest, frowning. "No. Your brother didn't show up."

"But I thought he was going to come."

"You boys really need to make up your schedule. I really needed you here today."

He followed her into the stalls. "Why, did something happen?"

"Yes, Casey had her calf, and it came out backward."

The young man winced. She put her gloves on and took out the white bucket of cleaning solution. He went into the back room to wash his hands then returned. "Did somebody help you?" he asked.

He put on his gloves, and she handed him an iodine-filled dipper. After pressing the dipper against the udders of the first four cows, they wiped the iodine off the udders with a clean cloth. Then they turned the vacuum on and attached the mobile milking units to the four cows. As the machines milked the bovines, Emily and Jeremy worked together, cleaning the teats and udders of the next group of bovines.

One of the cows in the next group was especially dirty, so Emily cleaned the udders with the iodine and water solution in the bucket before using the dipper. She then explained how she'd had to use a rope to get the calf out, and she mentioned that their new accountant arrived in time to help her.

They worked together, milking four cows at a time, moving the mobile units from cow to cow before reattaching the units to the milk pipes. Emily found that the rhythmic thumping of the machines and the gentle *swish* of the white liquid going through the clear pipes soothed her frazzled nerves.

"So, you hired an accountant?" asked Jeremy after unhooking one of the machines. Cats scurried around the barn as he moved the unit to the next cow. Jeremy turned the suction on and hooked the machine to the udders of the animal. Emily then sprayed the recently milked cows' udders with disinfectant.

She still felt torn about having an outside person doing their finances. Couldn't she and Laura try to figure out the bookkeeping on their own? "Yes." She told him the name of the firm they were using.

He nodded. "Yeah, my mom and dad hired an accountant a couple of months ago."

"Really? Why?"

The teen shook his head. "I don't know. Something about the IRS and an audit or something." He shrugged. She made a mental note to ask Jeremy's mother about her experiences using an outside accountant the next time she saw her in church.

Jeremy continued to speak as he attached a machine to another cow. "You know, I heard my mama talking to somebody on the phone, and she said that you need to get married to get somebody to help you take care of your farm since your mother doesn't like farming and your daddy's gone."

Her mouth dropped open, staring at the young man. "Jeremy, you shouldn't be repeating your mother's conversations."

He shrugged. "She didn't tell me not to repeat what she said."

Blowing air through her lips, she prayerfully tried to suppress her anger at Jeremy's mom for spreading untrue gossip. She'd always assumed Laura didn't like farming as much as she and her dad did, but she'd never heard her say she didn't like farming at all. She wondered if Laura had confided to Jeremy's mother that she didn't like her husband's profession. She knew Laura would sometimes visit Jeremy's mother and they'd have coffee or they'd sometimes volunteer for the same ministries at church.

She further wondered why Jeremy's mother would even be talking about Emily's single status. Since her breakup with her fiancé a year ago, marriage was the last thing on her mind. At twenty-eight, she felt her life was fulfilled just running the farm and trying to glean a profit from her family's business.

Once the milking equipment was cleaned and the cows, beef cattle, and bull were fed, she told Jeremy he could leave and asked him to make sure either he or his brother arrived at five o'clock the following morning to help milk the cows.

Her stomach rumbled, and she returned to the house after two and a half hours of milking and feeding in the barn. She heard Frank still in her father's office, typing on the computer. She needed to take a shower but felt uncomfortable doing so since Frank was still in the house. Her stomach growled again, and she missed Laura's home cooking. After washing her face, she removed Frank's clothing from the dryer. She needed to return his clothes to him before heading out to get something to eat.

When she approached the office, she caught Frank gathering his things to leave. He placed his glasses into the holder before closing the golden clasps on his leather briefcase. "I'll probably be back sometime tomorrow if that's okay with you."

"That's fine." She held his clothes up. "Here are your clothes. I forgot to give them to you earlier."

"Thanks. Do you mind if I use your bathroom to change?"

"Of course not."

He soon returned to the office, sporting the clothes he had been wearing earlier. He gave her the borrowed clothes, and she made a mental note that she and Laura still needed to go through her father's things and decide what they needed to keep. She removed the keys from her purse and followed Frank onto the screened-in porch and locked the door. She got into her old, battered white pickup truck, and Frank unlocked the door to his burgundy Lexus. When Emily turned the key in the ignition, the engine sputtered, refusing to start. She repeated the gesture, pressing on the gas. The grinding turn of the engine filled the hot summer air before it sputtered and died. Laying her head on the steering wheel, she groaned. "Lord, please let this truck start."

Sweat rolled down her neck when she sat up, turning the key again. When the engine failed, Frank appeared in the open window of the truck. Relief flowed through her like warm honey when she realized he had not driven away yet. Funny sensations danced in her stomach when he stood close to the vehicle. "I can't get my truck to start."

He glanced at the pickup. "How old is this thing?"

"My dad purchased it about fifteen years ago." She gestured toward the hood. "Whenever we had a problem with it, I'd always pop the hood, and he could fix it."

"I'm not very good with fixing cars, but I'll take a look," he offered. She pushed the button to pop the hood. She got out of the truck and joined him, looking down at the engine. The wires and inner workings were foreign to her, and the longing for her dad whisked through her, making her wish he were still alive. She blinked the sudden tears away, again focusing on the engine.

Frank tinkered for a bit before closing the hood. "I think you'll need to get a tow truck."

"I was afraid of that." Blowing air through her lips, she returned to the cab of the truck to retrieve her purse.

"Did you want to call a tow truck?"

"The auto shop down in Monkton is closed." She looked at her watch. "I'm going to call them for a tow tomorrow. They usually close around seven o'clock."

"Don't you have AAA? They'll send a tow out immediately."

She shook her head. "I've never needed AAA since I had Dad and the auto repair shop in Monkton."

"Can I give you a lift?"

She clutched the strap of her purse. "I don't want to hold you up. I might be able to get Kelly or Christine to pick me up."

"Who are Kelly and Christine?"

"My best friends. But I think they're working late tonight."

He continued to look at her, pulling his car keys out of his pocket. "I don't mind dropping you off. Where were you going?"

"I was going to Michael's to get a sub."

"Who's Michael? Your boyfriend?"

She shook her head, wondering why he would ask if Michael was her boy-friend. "No, Michael's Pizza. It's on York Road here in Monkton." She checked her watch, and her stomach grumbled. "I'm starved, and since Mom's been gone, I haven't done much cooking. I've been eating out a lot." She shrugged. "I'm a lousy cook."

He gestured toward his car. "I don't mind dropping you off."

"Well, if you're sure." She followed him to his luxury car and got in. He started the motor and turned on the air conditioning. He pulled out of the gravel driveway, and cool air filled the car, bringing relief to her heated body. "Ah, air conditioning."

He chuckled as he turned a corner and increased the temperature of the air conditioner. "You act like air conditioning is a luxury."

"Sometimes I feel like it is. The air conditioning in our truck conked out a few years ago, and we never got it fixed."

"Don't you have your own car?"

"I've never been able to afford a new car. I had a used one for years, but it stopped working a month ago, and with Dad's death and everything, I haven't had time to try and replace it."

They soon pulled into the parking lot of the small strip mall where Michael's Pizza was located. She exited the car, surprised when Frank cut the ignition and got out of the vehicle. "I hope you don't mind my eating with you. I wanted to talk to you about the little bit you may know about the finances on your farm. Besides, you'll need somebody to drop you off after you eat." He retrieved his briefcase from the backseat, and when she glanced at the floor, she noticed some liquor bottles. She frowned, and he dropped the briefcase back onto the seat. "Would you prefer that I not eat with you?"

She shook her head, putting the image of the liquor from her mind, knowing it was none of her business. "No, I'm okay with it."

He retrieved his briefcase before they entered the establishment. Tomatoes, garlic, and cheese scented the air, and Emily's mouth watered as she sat at one of the two tables located in the carryout restaurant. "Do you mind if we split a pizza?" asked Frank.

She told him she didn't mind, and Frank went to the counter and returned with two Cokes. "They said the pizza will be ready in about twenty minutes. I ordered pepperoni and extra cheese with mushrooms. Is that okay?"

"That sounds good."

A group of rowdy teenagers entered and sat at the table across from them. At first it was hard to talk, but the owner came over and told the teenagers to hold the noise down. When the ruckus stopped, she expressed her concerns about her farm. "I've been calling my mom all day. I think she's avoiding me."

"Why would she avoid you?"

She sipped her drink. "Laura has never been the most straightforward person. She beats around the bush about things and expects you to figure stuff out yourself. It drives me nuts."

"You told me earlier that she was your stepmother. You two must be pretty close if you call her Mom."

Emily nodded. "Sometimes I call her Mom. We're kind of close. My dad married Laura ten years ago, right before I graduated from high school." She shook her head, not wanting to discuss the somewhat complicated relationship she shared with her stepmother. "Believe me, I didn't start calling her Mom right away."

He opened his briefcase and removed a stack of paper before placing his reading glasses over his caramel eyes. She watched him flip through the papers, her curiosity about him sprouting like a geyser. He looked up and caught her staring. She looked away, wanting to put this whole situation into perspective. "What did you want to talk to me about?"

"Number one, I just want you to know that it's going to take me a long time, probably a week or more, to complete the audit for your farm. It'll be costly, but we have payment plans, and Laura has already signed the agreement."

"That figures," she mumbled. "She agrees to your services and doesn't tell me a thing."

He continued to flip through his papers. "I've already accessed a great deal of your father's files, and I think I can help advise you and your mom about budgeting, forecasting, and doing the bookkeeping on your farm." He looked at her, and her heart pounded from his intense gaze. "What I need from you is a description about where all of your revenue comes from. I know you get revenue from the milk, but where else do you get revenue? I just want to be sure your father has everything covered in all his files."

Emily started talking about where money flowed into their farm—from cows, beef cattle, heifers, and crops.

He interrupted her. "So, you have cash crops as well as crops you grow for feed?"

"We sure do. We've always done this, because it's hard to make a living from such a small herd of cows. We usually just plant extra so we'll have some left over to sell."

He continued to write, nodding. "I understand. A lot of smaller dairy farms must have some cash crops to survive."

She explained how they hired outside help to assist with harvesting their crops.

He scanned his notes. "Are there any other sources of income?"

"No." She thought about it for a few seconds, figuring she had covered all of their revenue sources. Then she grabbed his arm. "Oh! I forgot about one thing! It's not a source of income directly from the farm, but it does help out."

Frank flipped to a fresh sheet of paper, encouraging her to continue.

"Well, my mom's back went out on her a few years ago. So bending over, milking the cows, and doing manual labor on the farm just wasn't agreeing with her anymore. Since she didn't work on the farm any longer for health reasons, she got a job down at the elementary school. She works in the cafeteria. She loves being around the kids, and she said the work isn't as intense as farming. Since the school is closed during the summer, she's free to do other things." Emily continued to talk nonstop about the farm for twenty minutes, and Frank took notes. She talked about her cows, telling him their names and describing their personalities.

"You name your cows? I've never seen a farmer do that."

"I don't name all of them, but I name my favorite ones." She explained that she had them trained to go into the same stall each night and that most of the larger farms didn't have such a personal relationship with their animals. Their pizza arrived, but she didn't touch it until she'd finished answering Frank's questions. He removed his reading glasses before he took the spatula and served thin slices of gooey, cheesy pizza onto the paper plates. Emily bowed her head, saying grace over her meal. She noticed that Frank respectfully waited until she finished before he bit into his pizza.

She tasted her food, savoring the spices and the tangy pepperoni. "This is so good."

"It's doesn't beat Chicago-style pizza. That's where I'm from."

"You're from Chicago?"

He nodded, sipping his soda. "Yes, born and raised there. That's where my family lives." His cell phone rang. He excused himself as he took the call. "Hey, sport! Did you guys win the game?" A smile brightened his face as he listened to the other person on the line. "Yes, I remember. What happened after you pitched?" The conversation continued for a few minutes before Frank said he was with a client and had to go. He promised to call back the following day.

He flipped his phone shut and placed it in his briefcase.

"Was that your son?"

Frank shook his head. "That was my nephew, Mark." He frowned and stared at the pizza for a few seconds. "My sister has two kids, and she's been having a rough time with them since her husband left her for another woman a year ago."

"That's awful."

"It's been pretty bad, so I made a point to spend a lot of time with the kids after their dad left." He shrugged as he took another slice of pizza. "I feel that every kid needs to have a dad, and I want to be there for them since their father doesn't appear to have time for them anymore."

They ate in silence for a few minutes before Emily asked another question. "How long have you lived in Maryland?"

"I've only been here a few days."

"Really?"

He nodded. "I relocated here from Chicago."

"Why?"

"It was hard for me to leave my niece and nephew, but a lot has happened, and I just felt like I needed a change. Do you ever feel that way?"

"Not really."

"Well, I did." He finished his slice of pizza and removed another piece from the box. "The accounting firm in the Inner Harbor was expanding, and they opened the branch in Monkton to serve the farming community. Since they recently expanded into farm and ranch accounting, they needed somebody to temporarily head up that new division. One of the perks they offer to customers that many of the other farm and ranch accounting places don't offer is door-to-door service. That's why I came directly to your farm. Some accounting places require farmers to bring their files into their office."

"So you're only here temporarily?"

He shrugged. "I'm not sure. I didn't want to commit to stay long-term until I decided if I liked it here or not. So they said we could play it by ear and see what happens. I work at the office in Monkton, but I also have to go to the main office in the Inner Harbor sometimes, too. I rented an apartment not far from the Inner Harbor."

"So, when they needed somebody, you volunteered?"

He shook his head. "Not initially. They came to me and asked me to do it, and I had to think about it for a bit before deciding to come. I had to get licensed to practice in the state of Maryland before I was able to make the move out here."

She frowned, wondering if he was the right person to be showing them their bookkeeping. "What do you know about farm and ranch accounting since your company just recently started offering it to clients?"

"We have a farm and ranch division in Illinois. I advised a lot of farmers located in rural areas on the outskirts of Chicago. I'll admit you're the first client I've served via the door-to-door service. That's not something we offered in Illinois, but they're going to start offering that soon in that state also." He changed the subject. "You've always lived on your family's dairy farm?"

She nodded, helping herself to more pizza. "I have one sister and two stepsisters. My sister, Sarah, hated farming. She left the farm when she was still in her early twenties. She lives in Idaho." She sipped her soda. "My stepsister Lisa lives in Florida, and Laura is visiting her right now. My other stepsister, Becky, is pregnant, and she lives in California. It's a difficult, high-risk pregnancy, and it's a shame she couldn't come to my father's funeral."

"Is this her first child?" Frank took another slice of pizza and sprinkled red pepper flakes on it. His leg jiggled beneath the table, and she wondered if he was nervous.

"No, she has two more, and she's really struggling right now. She's a stay-at-home mom, and her husband works full-time. Since her pregnancy has been so difficult and she is supposed to take it easy, a lot of people from her church have been helping her out."

"It sounds like you're close to your stepsisters."

Emily shook her head. "We're not really that close. I've seen them off and on since my dad married Laura. I'm not as close to them as I am to Sarah."

They ate in silence for a few minutes before Frank asked another question. "Why are you so against your mother hiring an accountant? You never answered me earlier."

She sighed. "This is a family business, and you are not family. When Dad died, I wanted to try and figure out the bookkeeping myself, and I wanted my stepmother to help, but we kept arguing about it. I asked her if she'd at least wait for a couple of months to give me some time to go through Daddy's files."

"And she didn't agree to do that?" he guessed.

"I guess not, because she's gone and you're here."

"Well, your attitude is not very smart."

She frowned. "Why do you say that?"

He folded his arms in front of him, his leg continuing to jiggle. "Emily, you just admitted that you know nothing about the way your father accounted for the profits to your farm. You need an accountant to help you figure things out. You certainly don't want to be flagged for an audit by the IRS. If you are, it'll make things more difficult if you don't know what you're doing."

Pressing her lips together, she looked toward the counter. He touched her hand. "Hey, don't get offended. I just don't think you've thought through this very clearly."

"Whatever," she mumbled, draining her soda cup.

He chuckled, gazing at the empty pizza box. "I guess we had big appetites tonight."

"I tend to eat a lot of food."

"Do you?"

He seemed surprised, so she explained. "I've always eaten a lot of food, because doing those farm chores every day works up an appetite."

"You can't tell that you have a big appetite by looking at you," Frank said before he finished his soda.

Once he'd gathered his papers and placed them back into his briefcase, he closed it and paid the bill before they returned to his car. After he turned on the air conditioning, she rummaged through her purse. "I can pay for half the pizza."

"It's just a pizza. Besides, I can expense the meal since we were talking about business most of the time, anyway." When they pulled into the dairy farm, he reminded her that he would be returning the following day.

After she had showered and gotten ready for bed, she was about to open her Bible when her phone rang. "Hello?"

"Hi, Emily."

"Kelly, hi. What's up?"

Her best friend told her about the date she was looking forward to. "I can't wait to see Martin again."

When Kelly continued to speak, Emily struggled to listen as fatigue washed over her entire body like a tidal wave. "Did you call just to talk about Martin?"

"No. I was wondering if you wanted to go shopping with me next Saturday. I'm going to get my hair and nails done; then I'm going to look for a new outfit for my date Saturday night."

Emily lay back on her pillows, thinking about how busy she was the following weekend. "I want to go to the livestock auction. Is Christine going shopping with you?"

"I'd ask her, but I don't think it's a good idea."

"Why not?"

"Do you have to ask? Christine loves shopping a bit too much. She admitted that if she doesn't curb her compulsive shopping habit, she'll never be able to get rid of all her debt."

"She just needs to find something else to do in her spare time besides shopping." Emily changed the subject. "How are things over at the bank?" She struggled to listen but had a hard time staying awake. She thought about her crazy day, and her fatigue lifted for a few seconds when her brain focused on other things. Emily told Kelly about the difficult birth and about Frank showing up to help her. She then talked about the meeting she'd had with him at the pizza parlor.

"Oh, Em, it sounds like you had a very stressful day."

"Yes, I just don't know what to do."

"What can you do? Your stepmother is still in charge of the farm. Isn't she the official owner since your dad died?"

"Sort of. Dad's will made her the owner of a larger percentage, but part of this farm is mine. That's why I wish she had told me she'd hired an accountant to look at the books."

"Em, you need to let go a bit. You can't do everything by yourself. When your dad died, Laura had to argue with you about hiring Jeremy and Darren to help with the milking."

"My dad and I always did the milking together."

Kelly's sigh carried over the wire. "But your dad's not here anymore, Em, and you need help."

Tears rushed to Emily's eyes, and she wiped them away. Sniffing, she grabbed a tissue. Kelly was silent for a few moments before continuing. "Have you talked to your stepmom today?"

"No, she didn't call me back."

Kelly spoke again. "When you were telling me about Frank, you sounded a little excited. Is he cute?"

Emily threw her soiled tissues into the trash can beside her bed. "Yes!" She recalled Frank's physical attributes. "He's got medium brown skin, and he's really tall, taller than me. He's got these nice brown eyes with long lashes, and he wears the best-smelling cologne. When I'm around him, it's kind of hard for me to stay focused."

"Sounds like you're interested in him."

"No, I failed to mention that I saw some liquor bottles in his backseat." She thought about it for a few minutes. "We mostly talked about the farm, and I told him about the revenue that flowed in, and he wanted to know the cycles for the crops and about last year's selling prices." She mentioned what he'd told her about his sister's husband and her children.

"Did you have a good time talking to him?"

"It wasn't a bad time, but. . .I don't know. I sensed he was nervous or something. His leg kept jiggling under the table."

"Maybe he likes you."

"I doubt it."

"How old is he?"

"I'm not sure. I think he might be a little bit older than me."

They talked about Frank for a few more minutes before Emily yawned. "I think I'm going to sleep right now. Are you getting ready to go to bed?"

Before Kelly could comment, her other line clicked. "Kelly, I've got to go. That might be Mom calling me back." Kelly said good-bye before Emily clicked to the other line. "Hello?"

"Emily, it's me."

"Mom! What took you so long to call me back?"

"I wanted to give you a chance to cool down before I called. I knew you'd be upset about me hiring that accountant."

Emily huffed, and her fatigue evaporated, replaced with anger. "Why did you hire him without asking me first?"

"I did ask you, but all you wanted to do was argue about it. I felt justified to overstep your wishes since you don't always know what's best. You're just as stubborn as your father, and I didn't think you'd ever listen to reason, so that's why I signed the paperwork so the accountant could show you what to do."

Emily gritted her teeth, still struggling to calm down. She closed her eyes, silently praying for strength. She decided to change the subject since there was nothing she could do about Laura's hiring Frank. "How is Lisa doing?"

Laura groaned. "Not too good. She broke up with her boyfriend right before Paul died, and now all she does is go to work and then come home to mope around." Once she'd talked about Lisa, she said that Becky was still doing about as well as could be expected with her pregnancy. Emily had wondered why Laura would visit Lisa so long when Becky seemed to need her more. She was practically on bed rest. When Emily had asked Laura about it, Laura had sadly told her that she didn't think Becky wanted her to come for an extended visit.

"Mom, Frank will be back tomorrow. We'll probably place you on a conference call so you'll know what's going on."

"Thanks, Emily. I appreciate that." Emily said good-bye to Laura before hanging up the phone, curling beneath the blankets, and drifting to sleep.

Chapter 3

Following the forty-minute drive from Monkton, Frank cruised down Pratt Street near the Inner Harbor. He barely paid attention to the throngs of people walking the sidewalks on the warm summer night. The blue electric wave decorating the Baltimore Aquarium blazed in the darkness, and he sighed, anxious to get to his recently rented apartment in the heart of Baltimore.

Once he'd parked, he opened the door to his backseat and removed the glass bottles filled with liquor. He sighed, riding the elevator to his loft apartment. After unlocking the door, he threw his briefcase onto the couch, opened the refrigerator, and pulled out a club soda. He placed several ice cubes into the plastic tumbler. He then poured a little soda over the ice before pouring a healthy amount of his favorite imported scotch into the container. Sitting on the couch, he sipped his drink, his frazzled nerves slowly calming after he'd drunk half the amount in the glass.

The nervous twitch in his leg stopped when he settled into his nighttime routine. He lifted the remote, turning on the network news, thinking about his weird day. When his boss suggested he take the Cooper client, he felt it was just what he needed.

It turned out he was wrong.

When Emily was around him, he couldn't stay focused. The spark of delight that shined in her eyes when she spoke of her farm warmed his heart. He continued to nurse his drink. Her long dark hair and creamy brown complexion made it hard for him to concentrate on his work.

Before they'd gone into Michael's Pizza for dinner, he noticed her frown when she saw the booze in his car. He'd also noticed that she prayed for her meal before she ate. He shook his head. Emily reminded him so much of Julie that it was scary.

His thoughts continued to wander as he entered the kitchen and fixed another drink. When he returned to the couch, he lifted his wedding photo, touching Julie's face, again wondering when he would get over the pain of losing his wife. Taking sip after sip, his mind grew fuzzy as the alcohol chased away the demons that haunted him.

❧

During the next few days working on Emily's farm, Frank tried hard to ignore his attraction to her. She patiently answered his questions about the farm, providing necessary information he needed to do his job. They called her stepmother via speakerphone, and he consulted with Laura about what he planned on doing about the bookkeeping and the audit. He told the older woman he'd be doing the audit for at least a week or more, and she seemed to accept his presence in her home. He still wondered if his attraction to Emily was a good thing. Thoughts of Julie still hovered in his mind, and Emily was the first person he had met who could make him forget about his wife for hours at a time.

When Frank opened his eyes the following Saturday morning, his head felt like it was going to explode. He checked the bedside clock, glad that it was still early, only six thirty. Once he drank a few cups of black coffee, he would feel ready to go into the office before heading out to Emily's farm. His boss was always hounding him about working too many overtime hours on the weekends, but Frank found he enjoyed working more than being alone in his apartment. Working long hours helped make his mind too tired to dwell on the problems he struggled to forget. His cell phone chirped. He lifted the small black instrument from his nightstand and groaned when he saw his sister's phone number displayed in the caller ID window. He closed his eyes and sighed for a few seconds before answering the call. "What is it, Trish?"

"Good morning to you, too, little brother. I should have had Mark call you from his cell phone instead. You seem happier talking to my children than to me."

He lay back on the pillow, trying to relieve his throbbing headache and ignoring her apt observation. "Do you realize it's six thirty in the morning?"

"Yes, but I've been calling you since you moved to Baltimore, and you never answer your phone, yet you always answer when Mark calls. I figured if I called you early enough, you'd at least think it was an emergency."

He rubbed his eyes. "Is there an emergency?"

She hesitated. "Yes."

"Yeah, I'll bet there is." Sarcasm filled his voice. "What's the emergency?"

"Mom's been pretty upset since you left."

"I've been pretty upset since she rejected my wife." His sister sighed, and he struggled to control his temper. "What does Mom want me to do?"

"She wants you to start talking to her and Dad again. Julie's dead now and—"

"Just because Julie's dead means I need to forget what they've done?"

"But it's been over a year. Don't you think it's time to move on?"

"No, I don't," he grunted. "Look, my head hurts, and I don't feel like talking about this right now."

She ignored his comment. "Dad hasn't been feeling well."

He sat up in bed, his stomach churning from the sudden movement. He calmed himself down before asking, "Is he okay?"

"See, I know you still care."

He ignored the comment. "Is Dad okay?" he repeated.

"He's been complaining a lot about having a headache, and Mom says he's hardly eating."

"What does the doctor say?"

She sighed, her voice wavering. "He refuses to go to the doctor." The siblings were silent for a few seconds before Trish spoke again. "I think Dad's guilt about what happened is eating away at him."

He gritted his teeth. "Trish, you know they were wrong! You finally became friends with Julie. You know how much I loved her. . . . You know why I loved her."

"I loved Julie, too."

"I know you did. She always told me if she were to have a sister, she'd want her to be just like you."

"I know. That's why you really need to get over yourself and stop running away from your problems."

"I'm not running away—"

"But you are. Don't you get it?"

"No, I don't know what you're talking about."

"Yes, you do. I'll bet you're still having nightmares about Julie's death, and you probably have a headache because you got drunk last night."

Frank winced at the truth of his sister's words, refusing to confirm her suspicions. "I'm dealing with it the only way I know."

"Well, you need to find another way to deal with your pain. Alcohol and nightmares are doing nothing to help you."

"Well, what do you suggest I do?"

"If I told you, you wouldn't want to hear it."

"Try me."

"Why don't you do what Julie would have wanted you to do? Why don't you give God a chance? Since Julie led me to the Lord, I've found it so much easier to deal with my problems."

"I don't see how you can talk about trusting the Lord. Your husband left you! Look at all the problems you've been having with Mark and Regina since he left."

"It's been hard, but I'm trying to teach my kids that even though their earthly father is not around much anymore, they have a heavenly Father who loves them and will never leave them." He remained silent. "You might want to give God a try and let Him help you with all that you're dealing with. Another thing you might want to do is not be so angry at Mom and Dad."

"Wait a minute."

"No, you wait a minute. Just hear me out about this. I know Mom and Dad didn't like Julie because she didn't come from a good family, and it was wrong of them to think like that. But you have to remember that money's been in our family for decades, and Mom and Dad have been raised to think this way. It's wrong, but in their own twisted way, they felt this was one way to show their love for us: making sure we chose an appropriate mate from a prestigious family."

He was speechless, unsure of how to respond to his sister's comment. Before he could say anything, she changed the subject. "You'll never guess who I saw at the grocery store yesterday."

"Who?"

"Brian. He said a lot of the kids at the rec center still ask about you, and I told him that you'd moved to Baltimore." She sighed. "You've been so sad and bitter since Julie died. You used to be so happy spending your free time at the rec center helping Brian mentor those teenagers. I remember how you used to look forward to having some kids of your own."

He swallowed, tears rushing to his eyes as he recalled the happier times in his life.

"Look, I have to go now. I need to start making breakfast for the kids. I just wanted you to think about what I've told you and to try and talk to Mom and Dad again."

He wiped his eyes and grunted before he ended the call, not wanting to discuss the matter further. He got out of bed and took some acetaminophen. His stomach still roiled when he made his way to the kitchen. He measured dark grinds into the filter, and the fragrant scent of coffee soon filled the air. Taking a mug from the cupboard, he filled it with his morning brew, sat at a chair in the kitchen, and thought about Trish's advice. He just wasn't ready to forgive his parents for what they'd done—he just couldn't.

A few hours later he dressed and called Emily. He was surprised when she answered on the first ring. "Hi, I thought you would be out milking the cows."

"I'm finished with that already. I do it at 5:00 a.m."

He chuckled. "Actually, I was awake at six thirty this morning."

"Really?"

He sensed she was going to say something else, but when she remained silent, he continued. "Look, I know it's Saturday, but I wanted to know if it was okay if I came to your farm for a few hours today. I need to go to the auction—"

"You're going to the auction over in Westminster?"

"Yes, I was going to head over there because my boss said it was a good idea to see what the livestock are selling for. I agreed to go, so after I do that, I thought I could spend a few hours on your father's files."

"Could I ask a huge favor of you?"

"What's up?"

"Could you pick me up for the auction? My truck is still in the shop, and I didn't want to spend money on a rental. I borrowed a truck from another farmer for a few days to run some errands, but the garage said my vehicle is still not fixed."

Her apprehensive tone made him wonder if she rarely asked others for favors. "I don't mind picking you up. Are you planning on adding to your herd?"

"No, I'm going for another reason. I'll explain when you get here."

He said good-bye and hung up the phone.

A few minutes later he exited his apartment building and stopped as a woman walked by. The ivory suit and high heels reminded him of one of Julie's favorite outfits. The female had a surety to her step as she sauntered by, and Frank felt frozen in time when he watched her.

The woman's dark eyes widened as he stared. "I'm sorry, I thought you were somebody else," he explained, ashamed to be caught staring at a woman who resembled his wife. She frowned and walked away. Frank leaned against his apartment building, the bright sun shining in his eyes. That was the third time since Julie's death that he'd made this error. He closed his eyes, wondering when he'd learn to accept that his wife was dead and move on with his life.

He shook his head, strolling to the small parking lot. Once he got into his vehicle, he stared out the window. Maybe spending the day with Emily at an auction was what he needed to get his mind off his nightmares.

❧

Emily tried to relax the kink in her shoulders, hurrying to get dressed before Frank arrived. Fatigue rushed through her like a tidal wave. She really wanted to take a morning nap, but she wanted to go to the auction today. A knock sounded, and her heart rushed with excitement when she ran to the door and opened it. "Oh, hi." She tried not to let her disappointment show when Cameron, the milk truck driver, entered the kitchen.

"Hi, Emily. I've already put your milk in the tank. I just stopped in to say hello."

She tried to smile. "Hi, Cam."

He continued to look at her. "You look real nice this morning." He crumpled his baseball cap between his thick, dark fingers. She knew he was just trying to flatter her. Emily sensed Cameron staring when she poured a glass of water.

She gulped her beverage before placing the glass in the sink.

He grabbed the back of a chair and pulled it away from the table. Gesturing toward the seat, he said, "You look like you could use a rest."

Cameron's hands trembled. He wasn't a bad-looking man, but she wished he wouldn't stay around so much. If he wasn't so nervous, she could imagine a host of eligible women flocking to the milk truck driver.

Emily poured a cup of coffee and sat in the offered chair. "Would you like some coffee?"

He shook his head. "No thanks. I'm going to be leaving soon anyway." He frowned. "You look tired. Is something wrong?" Concern filled his voice.

She clutched the coffee mug, closing her eyes briefly. "No, nothing's wrong." She took another sip of coffee. "I don't mean to keep you from getting to your next milk pickup," she began, anxious for Cameron to take his exit so she could leave with Frank when he arrived. She glanced at the screen door, and her heart skipped a beat when she saw Frank standing on the porch. "Hi." Her throat was suddenly dry, and she sipped from her mug of coffee when Frank entered the kitchen. The cool scent of his aftershave filled the room with musky sweetness, and she sighed, relishing his presence in her home.

During the last week, Frank had appeared torn about his decision to relocate from Chicago to Baltimore. He'd told her that his nephew called him every day, saying he wished Frank had not left. He regretted missing Mark's Little League games, and since he'd left, his sister, Trish, said that Mark had started misbehaving again. Frank had mentioned that he planned to take a weekend and visit Trish and her children soon and that he was still angry that Trish's husband had abandoned their family a year ago.

Emily found it heartwarming that Frank wanted to be a substitute parent to Trish's children. Whenever he spoke of his niece and nephew, his face brightened, and when Mark called him periodically, Frank immediately dropped what he was doing to see what his nephew wanted to talk about.

She'd been working closely with Frank this week as they went over her father's accounting records. Whenever he looked at her, she became flustered, her heart racing like a horse speeding out to pasture. She couldn't seem to keep Frank from dominating her thoughts—or tempting her heart.

"Good morning, Emily." When he came toward her, she immediately noticed his cocoa brown eyes were red and his mouth was set in a firm line, as if he were angry. He sported a simple white T-shirt and jeans, and the material of his shirt hugged his broad shoulders. Frank's dark eyes were full of curiosity as he gazed at Cameron.

Frank offered his hand. "I'm Frank."

Cameron still clutched his baseball cap in his left hand when the two men shook hands. "I'm Cameron Jacobs." His deep voice wavered, and Emily wondered when he was going to leave. She was sure he was due to the next farm for pickup by now.

Cameron placed his hat on his head. "Well, I'd better get going. Take care of yourself, Emily, and I'll see you in a couple of days." The screen door banged shut when he left.

Frank drew his brows together, glaring at Cameron as he walked toward his milk truck. "Is he your boyfriend?" He sat at the table, still looking at her with those intense eyes. Emily sipped from her coffee cup, refusing to let his presence unnerve her.

"He's been asking me out for over a year."

"I can tell he likes you. You've never gone out with him?"

She shrugged, again wondering why she couldn't control her emotions. Her attraction to Frank was strong, stronger than what she'd ever felt for Cameron, yet Cameron was a Christian and they shared the same passionate faith in God. Why couldn't she feel physically attracted to Cameron?

She finished her coffee and went to the cupboard to get a box of cereal. She poured cornflakes into a large bowl then gestured toward the box. "Did you want some cereal?"

He shook his head and touched his stomach. "I don't want any breakfast this morning."

She peered at him again, and he squirmed beneath her intense gaze. "Your eyes are red."

He sighed, scooting his chair back. "I don't feel well this morning."

She let the subject drop, adding milk and banana to her cereal. She dipped her spoon into the bowl, and he waited a few minutes before speaking. "So, why are you going to the auction today if you're not planning on purchasing any cows?"

In between large bites of cereal, she explained. "My father and I used to go to the auction as a social outlet. We'd talk to other farmers, look at the animals being auctioned off—that sort of thing. Sometimes we'd sell our beef cattle there, but I don't have one that's old enough to sell right now." She stopped eating, gathering her thoughts. "We'd already planned to go today. . .before he passed. And I just want to go because I like going."

When she finished her cereal, she drank the last of the milk from the bowl, and Frank chuckled, gazing at her fondly. "That's the biggest bowl of cereal I've ever seen a woman eat."

She smiled back. "I told you milking those cows every morning and doing chores makes me work up an appetite."

"Did your farm help come this morning?" he asked before she rinsed out her cereal bowl and placed it in the dishwasher.

She nodded. "Yes, one of them did show up, and that was great. They've been doing pretty good since Casey had her calf." When she was finished in the kitchen, she went to her bedroom to get her purse. "Are you ready to go?" she asked as she removed her keys from her handbag. Frank nodded, and she locked the door before they headed to his vehicle.

After they were settled in his car, he turned the air conditioning up as he pulled away from the house. "You'll need to tell me where to go since I left the directions at my apartment." She settled into the leather seat, taking pleasure in the cool air. "Do you know when they're going to get your truck repaired?"

"They had to order some parts. It shouldn't be too much longer before it's fixed. Probably next week sometime." When he stopped at a light, he removed a pair of shades from his glove compartment. He placed his sunglasses over his eyes. "Did your mom ever tell you why she hired me without asking you first?"

Emily sighed, folding her arms in front of her. "Yes." She briefly explained what had been said during the conversation she'd had with Laura after Frank's first day on the farm.

He glanced at her before pulling away from the light. "Do you believe her?"

She shrugged. "I don't know. My stepmother is certainly not prone to lying. She does seem to overstep her boundaries sometimes, though. This should have been a decision we made together." She looked out the window, frowning. "Since my daddy died, I don't know what to believe anymore."

"What do you mean?"

"Nothing is the same. You know, when somebody you love is alive, you just take the days for granted, thinking you'll see them the next day. Now that my daddy's dead, my stepmother hasn't been the same—I haven't been the same. I can't sleep, she can't sleep, and the only solace I seem to find is working with the cows and reading my Bible."

"If God is so almighty, then why does He allow people to suffer so much?" The question startled her.

"I don't know, but my belief in Him and knowing my dad is in heaven gives me some comfort."

He changed the subject. "Is that all your mother said?"

"Pretty much. I've spoken to her a few times since you've started the audit. Ever since she's been in Florida with her daughter, she sounds better, happier. I almost feel like she doesn't want to come home."

"Do you still think she's only going to stay for a few weeks?"

"It's hard to say. The elementary school is closed for the summer, so I guess she's not in a hurry to come home."

"I see. Is that all she said?"

She watched him carefully. "Is there something wrong?"

Tension knotted her muscles when she noticed he clutched the steering wheel. "It's still early in the audit process. Your father's budget looks good, but

I can't tell you about the financial solvency of your farm until I've completed the audit." He sighed when he stopped at another light. "I just found out something interesting yesterday that I thought you should know. I figured your mom would've told you when she called, but she obviously didn't."

"What are you talking about?"

The car behind them honked, prompting them to drive since the light had changed. He quickly turned left onto Highway 137 before responding to her question. "I was looking through your father's computer files, and I found a spreadsheet that he called Estimated Selling Cost. I also found some correspondence he had with a Realtor."

"A Realtor? What Realtor?"

Frank shrugged. "There wasn't a name or address, but it looked like he was drafting a letter or e-mail to a property salesman. The spreadsheet listed properties that were recently sold in the Baltimore County area that were similar to your farm."

"Why would my dad be in contact with a Realtor?"

Frank shrugged. "It's hard to say, but from looking at the files, it appears as if he was thinking about selling your property."

Her heart skipped a beat. "Are you sure?"

He kept one hand on the steering wheel and touched her arm with the other. In spite of her shock, her skin tingled. He shook his head. "No, I'm not sure. I'm only speculating. I can show you what I found if you'd like." Silence filled the car. "Are you okay?"

She toyed with her ponytail. "I can't believe my dad would even think about selling our farm."

"He might not have been trying to sell. I'm only speculating."

Emily breathed deeply, trying to digest this new information.

"Where do I turn?" he asked when they entered a roundabout.

She told him to make a right at the first road. He sighed, taking the first exit. The information about her father sat in her brain like a twisted knot, waiting to be untangled. She definitely needed to speak with her stepmother again.

She watched the passing scenery. "I don't understand why Laura didn't tell me all this."

"Maybe she didn't know." He glanced at her with concern. "Are you okay?"

"No, I'm upset about this news." Her life suddenly seemed to be speeding out of control, and she wondered what other secrets her father may have been harboring.

Chapter 4

When the livestock auction was finished, people cleared out of the enclosure, and Frank touched Emily's elbow as they walked to the car. It was almost dinnertime. "I guess you need to be getting home to milk the cows?"

"Both of the brothers are supposed to come tonight for the milking."

"Did you want to get a bite to eat? I know how much you hate cooking." He opened her door for her, and they settled into his vehicle.

She bit her lower lip, staring out the windshield. "Frank, I don't know—"

"I wanted to talk to you about something."

"Can't we talk about it now?"

"Well, you're hungry, aren't you?"

She nodded, a small smile teasing her full lips. The urge to kiss her flowed through him, and he had to make a conscious effort to ignore the romantic feelings that drifted inside his mind.

"Of course I'm hungry," she said.

"Then let's get something to eat."

"Okay. Let me call Jeremy and Darren to make sure they're doing the milking right now." Once she called and confirmed that both brothers had shown up at her farm and were milking the cows, he drove them downtown to the Inner Harbor in Baltimore. After he parked in a garage, they entered the trendy tourist district. "Do you want to eat at The Cheesecake Factory?"

She nodded as they approached the high-class restaurant. Noise filtered from the dining crowd. When they approached the hostess, she gave them a pager and placed their names on a list. "There's an hour wait," she said above the noise. "We'll page you when the table is ready. Just be sure you don't go too far away."

"A whole hour?" asked Emily.

The hostess shrugged. "We're always busy on Saturday evenings."

Frank took the pager, and they strolled around the Inner Harbor. The breeze blew over the water, and he invited Emily to sit on a bench. Boats bobbed on the Chesapeake Bay, and throngs of people walked by, many carrying bags of purchases from the shops in Harborplace. A jazz saxophonist played his horn, and several people dropped money into his instrument case. The music surrounded them, the mellow notes filling the air.

She tilted her head back, closing her eyes. "It sure is nice out here." The hot wind blew her ponytail, and jealousy filled his soul when several men walked by, giving Emily a second glance.

"Yes, it is nice. Do you come here often?"

She shook her head. "Not much. Sometimes my friends and I come out here for dinner. But we haven't done that in months."

They sat in companionable silence, and he was tempted to hold her hand. But he resisted, unsure if she would want him to. The red lights on the pager brightened when the instrument buzzed. "I guess our table is ready," he said.

❧

Emily's stomach rumbled with hunger. Their server approached. "My name is Allen, and I'll be your server tonight. What can I get you all to drink?"

Frank's leg was twitching, and she again wondered if her presence made him nervous. He ordered first. "I'll have a Coke."

She ordered lemonade and a glass of water. Allen soon reappeared, prompting them to place their food orders. "I'll have the Cajun jambalaya pasta," said Emily.

Once Frank had ordered the Jamaican black pepper shrimp, she voiced her concerns about her father. "Do you really think my father would want to sell his farm?"

He looked at her, frowning. "Are you sure you don't want to talk to your stepmother about this some more?" He sipped his soda.

She took a drink of water. "I guess I should. Mom's hiding something. I can feel it." She looked at him, trying hard not to stare into his gorgeous brown eyes.

He sighed, looking sullen. "Like I said earlier, it looks as if your dad *may* have been planning to sell, but I can't tell for sure."

She gripped her water glass. "You're kidding," she mumbled.

"Sweetheart, I wouldn't joke about something like this."

The endearment rolled off his tongue and settled into her heart. She ignored the feeling, again focusing on the news he'd delivered. "Well, you're wrong. My dad would not sell the farm. I've never met a person who loved dairy farming more than Paul Cooper. Plus, my dad inherited our farm from his father. My grandfather was one of the first African American dairy farmers in Baltimore County. Dairy farming is in our blood, and I can't imagine my father giving that up."

He gazed at her with his warm, dark eyes. "You're probably right. You seem to know your dad pretty well. He may have been contacting a Realtor for a different reason."

A horrible thought occurred to her. "Do you think my stepmother wants to sell, and she just hasn't told me?" The thought sickened her. When her plate of jambalaya arrived, Emily pushed it away, her appetite gone.

Frank massaged her fingers. "Are you sure you're okay?" She didn't answer his question, finding comfort in his touch. Reluctantly she pulled her hand away.

"You didn't answer my question, Frank."

He sampled his shrimp before responding. "Emily, I honestly don't know. Maybe you should call your stepmom tonight and try and talk to her about all of this."

"Yeah, I just might do that." She stared at her food, suddenly wanting to go home and place the call in private. Frank continued to eat, and Emily prayed before she sampled her meal. When they finished, Emily requested a take-out box for her leftovers.

Afterward they walked around Harborplace before they returned to Frank's car. He drove her home and cut off the ignition when they arrived at her farm. "Do you mind if we sit on your porch?"

The thought of sitting with Frank on the porch on a star-filled night made her feel warm and cozy. "No, I don't mind at all." They walked to the porch and sat on the swing.

As they gently swayed, Frank spoke. "Are you sure you're okay?"

She nodded. "I'm okay. I just don't know what kinds of things my step-mother is hiding." She looked at him. "I also don't like what you told me about my dad. I feel like I'm being lied to."

He sighed. "Emily. . ."

She shook her head. "I guess you'll be back next week to continue working in my dad's office?"

"Yes, I'll be back next week. I'm not sure what time, though, because I have some meetings to attend." Crickets chirped in the hot summer air. Emily's stomach flipped when Frank held her hand. Sparks of warmth shot up her arm, and she couldn't gather the courage to pull her hand away. "Can I ask you something?"

She looked at him. "What?"

"I really had a good time tonight. I also enjoyed having dinner with you when we went to Michael's Pizza."

She smiled, her belly curling with warmth. "Yeah, I had a good time, too."

"I wondered if you wanted to get together again sometime next week. Maybe we can go to a movie or something." He squeezed her hand. "I like spending time with you, and I want to get to know you better."

She pulled her hand away. "I'll be honest with you. I like spending time with you, too, but there are things about you that bother me."

"What kinds of things?"

"Well, for starters, when we went to Michael's Pizza, I noticed the liquor bottles in your car."

He grunted. "I saw you frown when you saw the alcohol, but I didn't give it much thought."

The swing rocked as she gathered her thoughts. "Do you drink every day?"

"Yes."

"Why? When did you start doing this?"

He threw his hands up in the air, frowning. "Why is it such a big deal? Why are you asking me these questions?"

"You just asked about us going out. These are things I need to know about somebody before I agree to a date."

He sighed. "When something heavy is on my mind, I drink to forget. I've been doing this for about a year now. I've had problems with it before that, but I was able to quit eventually."

"What's on your mind?"

"It's kind of complicated. My parents did some awful things, and I can't let my anger go."

"Frank, you really need to forgive your parents for what they've done. If their actions are causing you to drink, then you need to do something else to deal with your pain."

"I'm almost afraid to ask what you would do if you were me."

"Are you a Christian?"

"I believe in God."

She shook her head, looking at him. "I didn't ask if you believed in God. I asked if you're a Christian."

"I've noticed that a lot of people say they are Christians, but it doesn't necessarily mean the same thing to everybody."

She sensed he was avoiding her question, so she decided to be more direct. "When I use the term 'Christian,' I'm referring to somebody who has accepted Christ as their Savior and who trusts Him completely. Can you honestly tell me you've done this?"

When he remained silent, she continued. "Do you go to church regularly?"

"No, I don't."

"Do you consider yourself to be a Christian?"

He hesitated before responding. "Not really."

She looked away, stunned upon hearing this news. Her attraction to Frank was deep, deeper than she imagined possible given the circumstances. She loved spending time with him and wished something could develop between them. However, she knew even if this was what she wanted, she had to follow the Lord's Word and not get involved with a non-Christian. She clenched her hands together, taking a deep breath before speaking. "I don't think it's a good idea for us to spend time together socially anymore."

"Why?" Exasperation tinged his voice.

"If I'm going to spend time with somebody, I want to make sure he's a Christian. My belief in God is the one thing that's constant and keeps me centered in this crazy world."

"We can still date and get to know each other better. You can't deny that we're attracted to each other."

Their attraction was so strong that it was a bit scary. Emily didn't know what she'd do with herself if she continued to see Frank and then fall for him. "Have you thought about getting help for your problem?"

"What problem?"

"Your heavy drinking problem. There's an alcoholic support group at my church—"

"I'm not an alcoholic."

"You don't get drunk?" He didn't respond. "Your eyes were red this morning, and you said you didn't feel well. Were you sick, or were you hungover?"

His lips settled into a grim line, and he stared out into the cornfield. Another concern struck her. "Do you ever drive after you drink?"

He shook his head. "No. I only drink after I get home for the night." She was surprised when he abruptly changed the subject. "Are you seeing anybody right now?"

"No."

"When was the last time you were in a serious relationship?"

She knitted her brow. "Why are you asking me this?"

He shrugged. "I'm just curious. I like you, and I want to know more about you."

She sighed, not wanting to talk about Jamal, but decided to humor Frank's curiosity. "I was engaged once."

His long-lashed eyes widened, and he encouraged her to continue.

"I met Jamal in grad school."

"You went to grad school?"

She nodded. "I have a master's degree in agriculture. Both Jamal and I graduated a little over a year ago from the University of Maryland."

"Well, what happened? Why aren't the two of you married?"

"I thought we both wanted the same things. I felt he made some wrong assumptions about me, and he just couldn't accept me for the way I was."

He gazed at the cornfield in the distance. "What kind of assumptions did he make?"

The negative memories washed over her. "Well, for starters, he didn't know

I wanted to continue farming."

"Whoa. I've only known you for a few days, and even I can see how much you love farming. What were you all going to do?"

She gave him a puzzled look. "What do you mean?"

"Well, did you expect him to move into the house with you and your parents?"

She shook her head. "No, nothing like that. Since I thought we were planning to stay in the Baltimore County area, I was going to continue working for my dad. I'd planned on commuting to the farm from our new home."

"I still don't understand what the problem was. Besides, you were getting your degree in agriculture. Isn't that a clue that you'd want to stay in the farming business?"

Emily chuckled, recalling her aborted engagement. "Well, sometimes Jamal was pretty clueless."

"What did he want you to do?"

"He found a good job with an engineering firm, but it was located in Texas, so we'd have to move. He said once we were married and settled into our new lives in Texas, he didn't want me to work."

"What?"

Emily nodded. "He wanted me to be a stay-at-home wife and have kids and be a family woman." She shrugged. "Again, I just assumed he knew what I wanted. I would love to have my own family, but I wanted to be a farmer, too. Since he wanted me to give up my profession, he obviously didn't know me very well."

"Is that the only reason you broke up?"

"Isn't that enough?"

He shrugged. "I guess, but I was wondering if anything else happened between you two."

She continued to think about her former fiancé. "Well, he said he was a Christian, and I thought he loved the Lord like I did."

He frowned. "What made you think that he didn't love God?"

She gathered her thoughts. "We were attracted to each other. We were *very* attracted to each other. When our engagement was official, he started pressuring me to make love to him. I told him I wanted to wait until after we were married, but he wouldn't let it go. We argued about it constantly, and we also argued about my continuing to farm after the wedding." She frowned. "It got to the point where I dreaded his phone calls and visits until I finally gave him his ring back. I started to feel like a prop."

"A prop?"

She nodded. "Yeah. I felt like an actress or something."

"I don't know what you mean."

"Well, after I met him, we didn't date for very long before we were engaged. Everything was so rushed that I felt like we didn't get to know each other very much. I sensed he was desperate to get married and have a family, and I was there, dating him. We were attracted, so he asked me to marry him." She sighed. "I don't think we were really in love. I felt like an actress, playing the role of his fiancée, without his knowing me as a person."

A warm breeze blew, tickling her cheek. When Frank took her hand, the warmth enveloped her fingers. "If you felt that way, why did you get engaged?"

"Initially I wasn't honest with myself. I made excuses for our arguments and his behavior. Soon I got tired of making excuses, and I was just honest with myself. I sensed the Lord was telling me that Jamal wasn't the right man to spend my life with."

She mentally sighed when Frank seemed to be content with her answer. They silently rocked in the swing, holding hands, his leg jiggling.

Headlights of a car turning into her driveway shined on them, and Frank dropped her hand. Kelly and Christine soon strolled toward the porch.

Frank frowned, staring at the women. "Who are they?"

Chapter 5

Emily touched Frank's arm. "That's Kelly and Christine, my friends."

Kelly clutched a white grocery bag, and Christine held a box of Cinnabon rolls. "Hi," Kelly greeted. "Christine and I didn't realize you'd have company tonight," she said, looking at Frank.

Emily gestured toward Frank. "He's not company. This is Franklin Reese; he's our new accountant."

Kelly raised one perfectly arched eyebrow, and Emily sensed she was assessing Frank's physical attributes. She stuck out her hand. "Nice to meet you. I'm Kelly, and this is Christine."

Once Kelly shook Frank's hand, Christine did the same. "Hi, ladies."

She looked at Frank before gesturing toward the house. "I guess I'll see you on Monday?"

Frank stood, causing the swing to rock. "Yes, I'll be here on Monday." He exited the porch and waved to the women before he got into his car and drove away.

Kelly placed her hands on her hips, and Christine stood behind her. "He stood me up! This is the last time I accept a date with that loser!" said Kelly.

They stepped into the house, and Emily turned on the kitchen light. She saw how much time Kelly had taken to prepare for her date. Her black hair was swept into an elegant bun, and she wore a new pantsuit. Expensive perfume wafted through the room as Kelly tossed her grocery sack on the scarred kitchen table and Christine placed the Cinnabon box beside it. Kelly pulled out two small ice cream cartons. "I got ice cream for both of us."

Christine pointed to her treat. "And I brought cinnamon rolls for myself." She rolled her eyes at Kelly. "She had the nerve to interrupt my lazy Saturday night." She gazed at Emily. "I was going to spend this evening lounging around in my silk pajamas and reading a book and eating my cinnamon rolls with a cup of coffee." She looked at Kelly. "Then she appeared on my doorstep, distraught that Martin had stood her up, and she insisted we come to visit you so both of us could cheer her up in person. She stopped for ice cream on the way."

Emily sat, placing her head in her hand. "I'm not hungry now. I'm glad you brought me ice cream, but I can't eat another bite." She pointed to her take-out container. "Frank and I ate at The Cheesecake Factory."

Kelly popped the ice cream carton open and fished a spoon from a drawer. "The Cheesecake Factory?" She sat, giving Emily a hard look. "Since when do you go out to The Cheesecake Factory with your business associates?" She grabbed Emily's arm. "I thought you said Frank wouldn't be a good prospect because of his drinking."

Christine sat beside Kelly, taking a bite of her roll before speaking. "His drinking?"

Emily explained that she saw liquor bottles in Frank's car. "We were talking about his drinking earlier tonight."

Christine spoke. "Oh, I'm sorry, Emily. If we'd known, we wouldn't have stopped by."

"I'm glad you guys came by. Frank didn't want to talk about it anyway."

"He wouldn't talk about his drinking problem?"

Emily shook her head. "He got upset when I asked him about it. I feel like he's denying he has a problem."

"What kind of problems could he be having that would cause him to drink so much?" asked Christine.

"I'm not sure. He mentioned that it had to do with his parents, but he didn't give many details."

"Do you mind if I make myself some coffee to go with my rolls?" asked Christine.

Emily stood, wanting to do something busy. "I'll do it." Fresh coffee soon dripped into the pot. When it was finished perking, she asked Kelly if she wanted some coffee, but she declined, so Emily poured two cups and removed the milk from the refrigerator and carried it to the table. She placed the sugar container beside the milk, and Emily and Christine sipped their coffee.

Kelly placed a large chunk of ice cream into her mouth. "Mmm. This is the best remedy for a broken heart."

Emily scoffed. "You only went out with Martin once. You haven't even known him long enough to have a broken heart!"

Kelly rolled her eyes, sampling another bite of ice cream. "Whatever. I thought he had great potential."

"After only one date?" Christine interjected.

"But last week's date was great!" She dropped her spoon on the table and modeled her recently manicured nails. "See, I even got my nails done." The red, oval-shaped nails matched her outfit, and Emily could hear Kelly's disappointment. "I've wasted my whole day getting ready for Martin, only to be disappointed."

"Did you call him?" Emily asked.

Kelly raised her eyebrows, scowling at Emily. "Of course not. If I call him, he'll see how anxious I am."

Christine spoke. "Maybe you should call him anyway. Something might have happened. What if he was in an accident or something?"

Kelly widened her eyes. "Do you think something could have happened to him?"

"It's hard to say," Emily said. "Why don't you call him, and if he doesn't answer, you could leave him a message."

Kelly pulled her cell phone out of her purse and pressed a few buttons. She spoke into the receiver, leaving Martin a message. She snapped her phone shut. "Hopefully he'll call me back tonight or tomorrow."

Christine spoke. "I wanted you all to see my new purse."

Emily fingered the expensive handbag, and Kelly rolled her eyes. "You know you can't afford that, Christine. If you want my advice—"

"Which I don't."

Kelly pursed her lips. "Whatever. But don't come crying to me to borrow money when you can't pay your bills. If you want to do what's good for you, you'd take that purse back to the store tomorrow."

Emily had learned a long time ago that you couldn't reason with Christine. She decided to tell them about the discussion she'd had earlier with Frank. "You'll never believe what Frank told me tonight." She glanced at the clock. "I wanted to call Mom and talk to her about it, but I'm sure she's in bed now." She told them what Frank said about the files he'd found on her father's computer, implying he may have been planning to sell their farm shortly before his death.

"Whoa!" Kelly interjected. "That's deep. Do you think your stepmom knew about this?"

Emily shrugged. "I don't know. I sense she might be trying to protect me from something. . . ." She thought about it for a few minutes. "It makes my head spin when I think about it too much. My father is the last person who would sell this place. He always said he would farm until he died." She covered her lips when tears came to her eyes. "And he did farm until he died." Her mouth quivered, and she went to the sink and got a glass of water. A few tears spilled onto her cheeks, and Kelly and Christine were beside her in seconds, hugging her. "I miss Daddy so much, guys. It hurts so bad."

Christine squeezed her friend's shoulder. "I wish there was something I could do for you. With the Lord's help, it won't hurt so much after a while." Emily breathed deeply and wiped her eyes. Kelly handed her tissues, and Emily dried her eyes and drank her water.

"There's nothing anybody can do to make me feel better." They returned to the table as she continued to speak. "You know, I feel like such a loser."

"Why?" asked Kelly.

"I loved my dad and I miss him, but I seem to be the only one in my family who's taking his death so hard." She gestured toward the phone. "When I talk to Laura, she sounds happier than she was here at the farm. It almost makes me wonder if she's planning on never coming back."

Kelly slapped Emily's arm. "Stop saying such nonsense. She'll come home. I'm sure a change of scenery is helping her deal with her grief. What about your sister?"

"You know I only hear from Sarah when she needs something. Since she doesn't live nearby, it's not like I can just drop by her house and commiserate about Dad."

Christine sighed. "Emily, you can always call your sister. I'm sure she'd find the time to talk to you. Besides, you don't know how Sarah is dealing with your father's death."

Emily shook her head before changing the subject. "You know, I was cleaning up earlier, and I found a stack of programs from my dad's funeral service. Remember my cousin Monica?"

Christine nodded. "Yeah, she's the woman who just got married a year ago and lives on the Eastern shore. I remember she's older than we are. One summer when she was staying at your farm, she drove all three of us to Baltimore to go to the movies."

"Well, remember she was at the funeral with her new husband?"

Kelly nodded.

"She scribbled her new phone number on one of the programs and told me to call her if I needed anything."

Kelly shrugged. "Have you called her?"

"No, I figured she wouldn't want to hear from me."

"Why?" asked Christine.

"You know how people are at funerals. They always say call me if you need anything, and half the time they don't really mean it."

Kelly snorted. "And half the time they do. You should call your cousin."

"I still might give her a call to talk. She used to like visiting here when she was younger. Maybe I can invite her and her new husband to come over sometime."

"That sounds like a good idea. You can give her a call in the meantime," commented Kelly, scraping the last of the ice cream from the container. Once she ate the last bite, she smiled warmly.

"I can't believe you ate that whole carton of ice cream," said Emily.

Kelly nodded. "I did, and now I feel so much better."

A cow bellowed from the barn. "Frank and I went to the auction today; then we went to dinner afterward because we were hungry." Since Christine didn't

162

know, Emily explained how Frank had helped her with a breach birth.

"Maybe you can invite him to church and try to convert him," suggested Christine.

"Convert him?"

"Yeah, invite him to church and share the gospel with him. Maybe he's bitter about something and mad at God."

"Do you really think I should ask him to visit our church?"

"Yeah, of course. What do you think God would want you to do?" asked Christine.

Emily silently thought about Kelly's and Christine's advice.

Kelly patted her full stomach. "Isn't it a shame? Another good-looking man wasted? All three of us are twenty-eight, and it looks like we'll never find husbands." She gazed at Emily. "Do you remember what you used to tell me when we were teenagers? You used to daydream about your ideal husband."

Emily grinned, recalling those times. "Yes, I used to say that my husband would be living on the farm with me, and we'd be working side by side, taking care of the cows, raising kids together."

Kelly continued. "Well, I'm wondering if any of us is ever going to find a husband. You haven't been serious about anybody since you broke up with Jamal a year ago. You haven't even been on a date since."

Before Kelly and Christine took their exit, the three women joined hands and prayed for one another.

❦

Frank pulled into the liquor store parking lot. He sat in the car for a few minutes, digesting all that had happened that day. He'd struggled all day and all evening about asking Emily out on a date. He was attracted to her, and even though he was upset with her decision about not spending time with him, he couldn't really blame her for her choice. He respected that she stuck with her beliefs, and he felt he needed to make more of an effort to put her out of his mind. When they were sitting on her porch, he had suddenly realized this was the first day in a long time that he hadn't thought about Julie. It was that thought that had bolstered him to ask her on a date.

Her refusal of his invitation was probably for the best. They were definitely not suited for one another. He exited his car, and his cell phone vibrated in his pocket as he entered the establishment. He flipped his phone open and walked toward the shelf that displayed his favorite scotch. "What do you want, Trish?" The sound of his sister crying made him stop. He softened his voice. "What's wrong?"

"Frank, it's Mark."

His heart skipped a beat. "Did he get hurt?" he asked hurriedly.

She sniffed. "No, nothing like that." In a tearful voice, she told her brother that Mark had met some friends that day to go to the movies. Afterward they went to a store nearby, and they were caught shoplifting. "The security guard called me, and I had to go get him." She continued to cry. "Frank, I don't know what to do with my son. He's been so angry since his father left."

"Did you want me to talk to him?"

"No, he's in bed now." She paused for a few seconds. "I wanted to ask if you can come down one weekend soon and spend some time with Mark. His father was supposed to come and visit the last two weekends, but he didn't show up. Mark's gotten worse since his father has stood him up." She choked on a sob. "I'll understand if you can't come."

"No, let me check my workload, and I'll see if I can come down sometime soon." He rang off with his sister as he lifted the bottle of scotch from the shelf.

❧

A few days later the screen door banged shut when Emily entered the house. Minutes passed and Frank figured she was changing out of her barn boots before she entered her home. He noted the late hour before she peeked into the room.

He looked up, adjusting his glasses, when she entered. Tendrils of hair spilled from her ponytail, giving her an earthy, mussed appearance. "Frank, it's almost nine o'clock."

He blinked, pulled his glasses off, and rubbed his eyes. "I know. Why are you just now coming in from the barn?"

Sighing, she sat in a chair. "One of the cows was sick. I was just making sure she was okay. I think I'll call the vet tomorrow." She glanced around the office. "Why are you still here?"

"I'm missing some of your father's files."

She frowned. "What are you missing?"

He explained which financial papers he was looking for. "I'm going to have trouble finishing my audit if I don't find those papers."

"Well, I'm sure they're around here someplace." She stood and pulled out a drawer in one of the filing cabinets. "Have you looked in here?"

He nodded. "There's a few filing cabinets in the other corner that are locked. I didn't know where the key was."

Emily lifted a bright yellow mug from the desk and dumped the contents. Frank helped her sift through the mess, and his fingers brushed against hers. Warmth traveled over his hand. She spotted the key. "Here it is."

She rushed to the cabinet, placing the key into the hole. A soft click sounded as she unlocked the drawer. She pulled, but it failed to open. "Frank, I think it's stuck," she gasped, still trying to open the drawer.

He rushed to her side. Together they opened the drawer, and folders tumbled onto the floor. He whistled softly, gazing at the papers. "Your father sure does keep a lot of stuff around."

Nodding, she massaged her neck, and he wondered if she was tired from a long day of work. "I hardly spent any time in this office. I don't really know what's in here." Pulling out one of the folders, she flipped it open, finding notes written in pencil. "This makes no sense to me. It's just a bunch of numbers."

He glanced at the notes and frowned. "Well, whatever this is, it's not what we're looking for." He glanced at the cabinet again. "But we might need to go through this whole cabinet to find the papers we need."

"Maybe we should do this another time. I don't feel like looking through this stuff right now. It's late."

Changing the subject, he pulled a family photograph off her father's desk. "Is this your stepmother and your sister?"

She nodded, glancing at the picture. Emily looked like she was about eighteen in the photo. "Yes, I think I was telling you about my sister when we had dinner at the pizza place."

He sat, still looking at the photo. "Why do you look so upset in this picture?"

"Because my father had just gotten remarried, and I was not eager to have a new female in this house. That picture was taken right before my sister, Sarah, left home. That's why you see her smiling. She was getting ready to leave the farm, and she was relieved because she always hated it."

"Were you angry that your sister left?"

She shrugged, glancing around the cluttered office. "It worked out okay. I love it here, and I don't mind being the only sister left behind to take care of the family business."

"Do you talk to your sister often?"

"Not really."

"Do the two of you get along?"

"It depends. Sometimes we do, and sometimes we don't. She only calls me when she wants to borrow money."

"Really?"

She nodded.

"Does she usually pay you back?"

"Sometimes she does. We were never really close even though we lived in the same house. My daddy used to say we were like oil and water."

"What happened to your real mother?"

"She died of breast cancer when I was fifteen. Things were pretty rough out here on the farm when she passed."

"Things were rough because you were grieving?"

"Sort of. Remember, I told you Sarah hated farming?"

He nodded.

"Well, when Mom died, she refused to do anything. She wouldn't help out with the chores. She'd yell at my dad; she called me names." She shook her head, looking away. "My dad had to ask our church if they knew about any type of counseling services he could use for Sarah."

He stared at her, wanting to take her into his arms and tell her he was sorry that she'd now lost both of her parents. Instead, he asked another question. "How did you deal with your grief when your mother died? It's obvious that your sister turned rebellious."

"I spent most of my time in the barn or in the field with the cows, alone." She folded her arms in front of her. "It was awful. It took me a long time to get over losing my mom."

"Sarah's reaction reminds me of what my sister is going through now."

"What do you mean?"

"Remember I told you about her husband leaving?"

"Yes, I remember."

He told her about Trish's recent phone call and Mark's rebellious behavior. "I have to find some time soon to go and see Mark. I miss him, and I want to do everything I can to make him feel better."

"I'm sorry your nephew is hurting so much."

"I'm sure my sister's life would have been a lot better if she'd never married that guy."

"Frank, you don't know that."

He gritted his teeth. "I never trusted him, and I tried to warn her, but she wouldn't listen to me. Every boy needs a good, stable father at home, and it makes me mad that Mark and Regina's dad doesn't even seem to care."

"You really feel strongly about this, don't you?"

"Yes, it makes me upset when so many young boys are out there and they don't have fathers to turn to." He told her about the rec center in Chicago and the youth he used to mentor.

Her dark eyes widened. "You used to mentor youth?"

He nodded.

"Have you done this since you've been in Maryland?"

He shook his head, almost sorry he'd said as much as he had. He didn't feel like going into the reasons why he'd stopped mentoring one year ago.

Emily frowned as she looked away.

"What's the matter?" he asked.

"Nothing. I was just thinking about something."

He looked at the bulging pile of paper, no longer wanting to talk about his sister and his activities in Chicago. "We have tons of stuff to go through. I hope we can find everything I need."

"How is the audit coming along so far? I'm sure my father's financial records are in good order."

"I can't comment until I'm finished. Do you understand everything we've been going through together? Are you having any problems with the financial software I showed you how to use?"

She frowned. "I think I understand, sort of." She gestured around the office. "I'm still not used to handling all this. It's a lot of information for me to remember."

"Either myself or somebody in the firm can always advise you about financial matters."

"People are always telling me and Laura that we should have gotten more involved in the finances of our farm, and I'm starting to see they were right." She gave Frank a small smile. "But I'm just concerned about figuring out how this farm is doing and making sure we can continue the routine you've taught me during the last few days for our bookkeeping."

"Well, I still have to start a few audits at some other farms, and I'm at a standstill with your audit." He opened his briefcase and removed a business card. He flipped it over, writing his information on the back. "I'm leaving my business card. My work number is on the front, and I'm writing my home number on the back. My e-mail address is listed there, too." He pressed the card into her hand, relishing the warmth of her skin. He hesitated before pulling his hand away, still trying hard to ignore their attraction.

He sat at the computer and opened a document, his leg jiggling. "Even though we've been through the whole budgeting and bookkeeping process together, I've still typed up notes for you and your stepmom about the accounting process for your farm. I tried to make the file easy for you to use." He pressed a few keys on the keyboard. "Laura might need my detailed notes since she wasn't here when I was teaching you everything."

"So you're all finished?" He wished he could keep coming here each day, but being around Emily was torturous, knowing how she felt about his personal life and beliefs.

He told her the truth. "No, not completely. I have some loose ends to tie up, but I can do those at the office. Remember those papers I was telling you about?"

"Yes?"

"Well, when you find those, I can complete the audit." He glanced at the papers piled on the floor. "I don't want to waste time searching for something since we charge by the hour." He pulled a notebook from his briefcase. "I'm going to write down what I'm looking for." He scribbled the information, sensing Emily watching him the entire time. When he was finished, he pointed to the last two items. "I can't find your father's tax returns for the last couple of years."

Her mouth dropped open. "I know he filed his taxes—"

He touched her arm, and she calmed down. "I know he did. When I was going through his bank statements, I could see the direct deposits in his account from the IRS tax refund. But it'll still help me out if I could find those files." He glanced around the office again. "I know they're around here someplace."

"You want me to look for the things you have listed here?"

He nodded. "Please. When you find them, I can come back out here and complete my job, or, if you prefer that I not come, you can scan and e-mail the files to my office."

Silence surrounded them, and Frank was at a loss for words. Since she'd had her conversation with him about his drinking and her religious beliefs, they'd continued working together in her father's office, sometimes making small talk. The attraction he felt for her refused to go away, so maybe it was best that he not return to her home after all. She finally spoke. "I can probably scan them and e-mail them to you if it's quicker. I don't want to waste your time by making you come out here." She tucked his card into her pocket and sat in the chair beside the filing cabinet, stacking the manila folders into a pile.

Frank stood beside the computer, and his heart pitter-pattered. "It's never a waste of time coming out here." The urge to kiss her rushed through him, but Julie's face hovered on the fringes of his mind. Emily dumped some folders into a box, mumbling about looking through them later. She picked up the container and walked into the kitchen, and Frank followed her, holding his briefcase and car keys. He wondered when he'd see her again. She placed the box on the table and walked him to the door. He stood on the porch and stared at Emily. Before he could stop himself, his lips brushed hers. She backed away, her pretty eyes widening.

"I didn't mean for that to happen," he mumbled. Crickets chirped, and the scent of animals and hay wafted around them. Her mesmerizing eyes were beautiful when she looked at him. He stepped back into the kitchen and closed the door, not wanting to leave anything unsaid between them.

"I'm sorry for kissing you," he said. "I hope you're not upset."

"Your lack of faith in God bothers me, Frank. Your drinking bothers me, too." She walked to the window, gazing at the barn.

"I know." She glanced at him, her sullen expression making his heart ache. "My drinking's been bothering me lately, too." Lately he'd been drinking more alcohol at night to get a buzz, and Trish was still calling him all the time, telling him he needed to get help.

She remained by the window, still looking at him. "Have you had a drink today?"

He shook his head. "No, not yet. That's why I'm still here. I didn't have a chance to tell you the other day that if I work late so my mind is tired, I may not drink as much when I go home." He clutched the handle of his briefcase. "But usually the memories and the nightmares bother me no matter what I do." The drinking always calmed him, soothed him, making it possible for him to fall asleep, even though there was sometimes a price to pay the following day. Since he'd started drinking more, he'd woken up sick to his stomach more often.

"You're haunted by something. What is it?" Her sweet voice softened.

"Nothing I want to talk about right now."

"There's an alcoholic support group at my church—"

He held up his hand. "I don't want to go."

"But it might help you," she pleaded. "You know, your lack of faith in God bothers me even more than your drinking." She turned toward the window again. "Maybe it's best that you've finished most of the audit for us."

The rusty hinges on the door squeaked as he opened it. "I'll e-mail you and your mother a report about what I've done so far. Just let me know when you've found those documents."

The screen door banged shut when he left, and he noticed Emily still standing in the window, watching him as he pulled out of her driveway.

Chapter 6

The next day Emily awakened earlier than usual. She spent a leisurely hour reading a few psalms, finding comfort in the lyrical words. Both Jeremy and Darren arrived to help with the milking. After lunch the boys' father arrived plus a few other people she'd hired to help with the three-day chore of making hay.

The day bustled with activity, and Emily was glad for the extra physical exercise. She hoped that if she was tired enough by the end of the day, Frank wouldn't dominate her thoughts. During the day Emily found herself daydreaming about his kiss. She again wished he'd listen to her and take her advice about accepting Christ in addition to getting help for his drinking. She also found herself thinking about the role he was playing in his sister's life with her kids and about the fact that he used to mentor youth while living in Chicago. She wondered if Frank wanted to have children someday, but she pushed those thoughts from her mind, not wanting to dwell on that subject too much.

Fatigue settled in Emily's bones after Jeremy and Darren had helped her with the evening milking. She enjoyed a sub for supper then took a quick shower and changed before trudging to her truck. The repairman at the shop had stressed that she might want to start looking for a new vehicle. "This one is on its last leg and I don't know how much longer we're going to be able to repair it," he'd said.

She sipped from the thermos of coffee, thinking about the repairman's advice. She knew she would probably have to look for a used truck. She'd already called Laura, telling her what the repair shop had said about the truck and about what Frank had told her the previous day.

"Frank already called and told me everything," her stepmother had said.

"He did?" Emily didn't know why she was so surprised. Frank had mentioned that he needed to talk to her mother since Laura was the one who had requested the services of their firm.

"I can tell that something is heavy on your mind," her mother had said. "Did the accountant explain everything to you?"

"Yes, he explained everything in detail. Mom, when are you coming home? I miss you."

"I miss you, too. I promise I'll be home soon."

She continued to drive, putting the whole conversation out of her mind. She pulled into the parking lot of Monkton Christian Church for her volunteer committee meeting. During the meeting, she could barely keep her eyes open. Christine and Kelly were present, and when it was over, the three friends exited the building together. "Girl, you sure do look tired," Kelly said to Emily. "You're going to run yourself ragged working on that farm."

Emily mentioned they'd cut the alfalfa that day with the haybine. "Once it dries out over the next day or so, we're going to have to bale it."

"Sounds like a lot of work."

Emily nodded. "It is. I'm so tired."

Christine touched Emily's arm. "During the committee meeting, you looked like you had something on your mind."

"I do."

"What's the matter? Has Laura said something to upset you?" asked Kelly as they walked into the parking lot.

"No, I miss Laura like crazy, but that's not why I'm upset."

"Well, what's wrong?" Christine demanded. Their cars were parked side by side, and they stood in front of their vehicles. Emily debated about telling them what happened the previous evening.

"Why don't we go and get a snack at the Wagon Wheel?" suggested Kelly.

"I'll go, but I'm not staying a long time," said Emily.

They were soon seated at the restaurant. After purchasing slices of cake and cups of coffee and tea, they sat at a table in the back. Emily sipped her drink before telling her news. "Frank kissed me last night."

Kelly's mouth dropped open. "Whoa. You're kidding!"

"Are you serious?" asked Christine.

Emily nodded. "Yes, I wasn't expecting it."

Kelly stirred her coffee. "Are you going to see him again?"

Emily shook her head. "No, not unless I have to talk to him about the audit. I don't think it's a good idea for me to see him again. Once I find the documents he's looking for, I'll scan them and e-mail them to him. Once he's finished, I won't have to see him again."

"How long do you think it will take you to forget about Frank?" Christine asked.

"I'm not sure. This is awful, but I miss him already. I know there's no hope for us since he's not even a Christian."

"There still might be hope for you and Frank," Kelly said. "Leave everything in the Lord's hands and see what happens."

"Thanks, Kelly." She glanced at her other friend. "Christine, I notice you're wearing a nice pair of diamond earrings. Were they a gift?"

Kelly sipped her drink. "What do you think, Em? Do you really think it was a gift? You know she probably charged her earrings."

Christine touched her earlobes, frowning. "I got these on sale at a new jewelry store that opened at Harborplace. I couldn't resist since they were a good price."

"Has anything else been going on with you, Christine?" asked Emily.

Christine placed her chin in her hand, gazing at her friends. "I do have a confession to make."

"What's that?" asked Kelly.

"I purchased these earrings for a reason."

"And what reason might that be?" asked Kelly.

"They had a meeting at work today. Some of us are going to be laid off within the next few months."

"Christine, I'm sorry," Emily said, touching her hand. "I know how much you like working there."

"So you purchased the earrings because you were upset about the imminent layoff?" asked Kelly, furrowing her brow.

Emily moved to touch Kelly's hand, knowing how upset Kelly became whenever Christine went on a shopping binge. "I think she's trying to tell us that she purchased the earrings because they made her feel better."

"Whatever," said Kelly, rolling her eyes. "You shouldn't be using material things to make yourself feel better, Christine. You said you might be out of a job soon, so buying a pair of diamond earrings won't make things better."

Christine shrugged. "I know they won't make things better, but they make me feel better. Do you understand?"

Kelly shrugged. "I guess."

Emily spoke to Kelly. "You're awfully quiet about what's been happening in your life lately. Have you heard from Martin?"

"Yes," Kelly responded.

Emily and Christine looked at Kelly expectantly. "Well?" asked Emily. "What did he say?"

"He said he forgot about our date the other night."

Christine asked, "Well, did he at least offer to take you out again?"

"No," Kelly responded.

"How come?" asked Emily.

Kelly's mouth was set in a grim line. "You guys, no offense, but this is not something I'm ready to talk about right now."

Emily hugged her friend. "We don't mean to pry. If something's bothering you, then you know you can talk to me and Christine about it." Christine nodded, her dark eyes full of sympathy.

When they were finished with their snacks, Emily hugged her friends before she drove home. Once she'd read her Bible, she crawled into bed and said a brief prayer before she fell asleep.

Chapter 7

The days passed, and Emily still couldn't put Frank out of her mind. She thought about him daily, even though he no longer came to her house. Memories of his kiss lingered, and she prayed, waiting for the feelings to disappear.

During the July Fourth holiday, she rode to Baltimore's Inner Harbor with Christine and Kelly to see the fireworks. Bursts of color exploded in the dark sky, illuminating the pedestrians and couples strolling the sidewalks. Longing pierced her when she observed couple after couple holding hands or nestling in each other's arms to watch the fireworks.

A few days following the July Fourth fireworks, Emily was thinking about the last time she'd seen Frank when she pulled into a parking space on Pratt Street, across from the Inner Harbor. She opened her purse, searching for coins to feed the meter. After the annual evening meeting with the Maryland farmers' association, she felt like taking some time and walking along the Inner Harbor alone. It was a blessing that both Jeremy and Darren came to milk the cows earlier, giving her the freedom to attend the event. She checked her watch, noting it was eight o'clock. She still had some time to stroll around before the shops closed.

She continued searching for change, thinking about Laura. She missed her like crazy, and the loneliness on the farm was eating away at her. When she'd spoken to her a few days ago, she'd told her about the papers missing from her father's office and that she was searching for the paperwork Frank needed to continue his audit. She'd already found and e-mailed him a few of the files, but the rest of the documents were still missing. When she'd asked Laura about her father selling the farm, she'd claimed it was hard to know for sure what her father had planned on doing.

She gasped when Frank exited the upscale liquor store located on the waterfront of the Inner Harbor. He clutched a large paper sack, and Emily was again reminded about how different their beliefs were and how their attraction seemed to escalate, in spite of their unshared faith. His head was down as he hurried toward his car, and Emily couldn't resist calling out his name. She rolled down her window and yelled. "Frank!" He stopped and looked toward her, his dark eyes appearing startled. He clutched his paper bag and strolled toward her truck.

"Emily, what are you doing here?"

She inhaled the familiar scent of his cologne as she looked at him. "I was at a local farmer's association meeting downtown. I just came over here to take a walk."

He remained silent, and she glanced at the bag. Sweat beaded his brow, so he wiped it away. "I had to pick something up before going back to my apartment."

"Oh." She suddenly felt nervous.

Frank relaxed against her truck. "It's hot out here. Did you want to come up to my apartment and cool off for a bit? I only live a few blocks away. We could share a few drinks."

She eyed the paper bag. "I don't think so."

"Emily, I was going to give you some lemonade. I made it myself. You don't have to stay long. I have some things concerning the audit that I was going to talk to you about."

She swallowed, noting her throat was very parched. A cold glass of lemonade did sound good, so she started the ignition. "Just lead the way."

Once he'd gotten in his car, she followed him to his apartment building. A basketball court was outside, and a group of young people played a game in the intense summer heat. A few of the boys spotted Frank, calling out his name. "Hey, Mr. Frank, you want to shoot some hoops with us?"

He waved. "Maybe tomorrow."

As they rode the elevator, Emily spoke. "You play basketball with them often?"

"No, not too often." They soon entered his cool loft apartment. "Sorry it's such a mess." He picked up a few clothes and threw them into the corner. Takeout Chinese and pizza boxes littered the area, and she assumed Frank hated cooking. She could certainly understand, because she'd been living off sandwiches and fast food ever since Laura left for Florida.

She felt the place could be charming and cozy with a woman's touch and a few decorations. The kitchen was spotless, and she supposed he barely used that room. "How is your nephew doing?"

He lifted a pair of shoes and placed them in the hall closet. "He's doing a little bit better. He recently had a birthday, and I was able to go to Chicago for the weekend for his party."

She smiled, enjoying the grin that split Frank's handsome face as he spoke of his nephew. "I'm sure he was glad to see you."

"He was. We talked a lot, and I tried to get him to tell me what's been going on. I let him know I wasn't pleased with his shoplifting, and I hope my talking to him will influence him not to do it again."

"Did his father show up for his birthday?"

Frank frowned, tossing dirty socks into his room. "No, he didn't show up. He didn't even call." He shook his head. "He's such a lousy dad. I don't know what Trish was thinking when she married that loser."

She fingered the empty scotch bottle sitting on the coffee table. "Did you go to the liquor store to buy scotch?" Her voice wavered, and she continued to look around the room. Empty beer bottles and a half-empty bottle of wine sat on the end table.

He took the bottle away from her and dropped it into the trash. "I told you things have been hectic in my life lately." A hard edge crept into his voice, and he continued to gather items and place them in the garbage can.

Clothes were strewn all over the place, and the hamper overflowed with garments. She wondered when he had last done his laundry. After he placed the paper bag in a kitchen cupboard, he pulled two cups from the cabinet and put several cubes of ice into each. The ice popped when he poured the lemonade. Emily sat on the couch, and he handed her the cup. She took a drink, closing her eyes, relishing the sweet, tangy taste of the lemonade and the clean citrus scent of Frank's cologne. "You made this?"

He chuckled. "Yes, I made it."

She raised her eyebrows, enjoying another sip. "It's good."

"Thanks. All it is, is fresh lemons, sugar, and water." He shrugged. "It's no big deal." Silence filled the room, and Emily drained her glass. "Would you like more lemonade?"

"Please."

He returned to the kitchen with her empty glass so he could refill it. As he performed the chore, she was about to ask him about the audit when she noticed the wedding picture sitting on the coffee table.

She lifted the photo and saw Frank wearing a gray tuxedo, and his arm was around a bride. The woman's skin was the color of ripe blackberries, and her dark hair shimmered over her shoulders. Her arm was casually draped around Frank's waist, and her laughter seemed to jump right out of the picture.

She clutched the picture as he returned with the lemonade.

"You're married?" Her voice wavered.

He shook his head. "I guess I should have mentioned it sooner. She's dead." He placed the picture on the coffee table face down.

She stared at the down-turned picture frame. "Dead?"

"My wife is dead. She was killed about a year ago."

"Killed, a year ago? That's so recent."

"I know. I still think about her a lot."

So many questions filled her mind that she didn't know which to ask first. "She's very pretty."

175

"Yes, Julie was very beautiful."

Silence, thick and heavy, filled the room. She wondered what had happened to Frank's wife. "How long were you two married?"

"Two years."

"I'm sorry."

He stood and walked to the window, parting the curtains. Light streamed into the room from the streetlamps. "You know, I'm so sick of hearing that."

She stood beside him. "Hearing what?" Tears glistened in his eyes, and he quickly turned away. "What's wrong?"

When he didn't initially respond, Emily was tempted to let the subject drop.

He wiped his eyes and dropped the curtain, returning to the couch. Emily joined him, still wondering about the death of his wife. "I miss my wife so much. It's one of the reasons I've started drinking again."

"I think your pain will lessen with time."

"I killed her, Emily. I killed my wife."

"I know you couldn't have killed her."

"It's my fault she's dead."

She touched his shoulder. "What happened?"

"Julie was raised in foster care."

She recalled the sad stories she'd heard about children in foster care. "That sounds rough."

"Yeah, but since she had been through so much with her brother during the time they were in foster care, they were closer than they should have been."

"What do you mean?"

"Her brother was into drugs. At one point, he owed somebody over a thousand dollars."

"Did she loan him the money?"

Frank chuckled, the sarcastic sound echoing in the room. "It could hardly be called a loan, because I knew he would never pay us back. I didn't understand why she kept bailing him out."

"So did she give him the money?"

"I told her not to. She promised me she wouldn't meet him in that dangerous neighborhood where he lived to give him the money."

"But she went to meet with her brother anyway."

He nodded, tears falling down his cheeks. "Yeah, she went. Some stuff went down, and there was a bust when she was there. She was accidentally shot and died a few days later."

She hugged him, silently praying she could say the right words. "Did they catch the person who shot her?" she asked, ending their embrace.

"Yeah, they caught him, and he's in prison. But I tell you what, if they hadn't caught him, I'd be going after him myself. I would have searched until I found her killer if the police hadn't gotten to him first."

"Why do you think this is your fault?"

"I should have realized what she was going to do. I should have gone with her. I knew how stubborn she was about helping her brother. Maybe I could have talked her out of it. If I'd reasoned with her, she may not have gone to meet with him and she'd still be alive."

"Or she could have thought about this with a level head."

He gave her a strange look. "What do you mean?"

"I know you miss your wife, and I can see how much you loved her, but it wasn't your job to ensure she always thought rationally. You're beating yourself up over something you had no control over. Julie knew what kind of crowd her brother hung out with, and I'm sure she knew about the danger of meeting him in that seedy area. Why couldn't she have figured out another way to get him the money? Could she have mailed him a check—"

"The type of people he dealt with wouldn't be waiting on a check."

Emily shrugged, still not deterred from making Frank see reason. "You mentioned to me that you were mad at your parents."

He nodded. "My anger at my parents started years ago when I'd started dating Julie. They didn't like the fact that she wasn't from a good family, and they didn't support my marriage."

"Is that the only reason you're angry with them?"

"Emily, when my parents rejected my wife, it was like they were rejecting me, too. I'll be honest with you and let you know that my parents did do something else besides reject Julie."

"What did they do?"

"When I got engaged to Julie, they did a background check on her and her brother. They didn't think she'd be a suitable addition to the family, so they told me the only way they would support my marriage would be if I made her sign a prenup."

Emily gasped. "A prenup? Do you mean a prenuptial agreement?"

He nodded. "Yes. They felt like she was just a gold digger, wanting to get into the family to get some of their fortune."

"You didn't ask her to sign it, did you?"

He shook his head. "No, I loved her, and I couldn't hurt her like that. When we got married, she wondered about the distant relationship we had with my parents. She was smart enough to know that my parents' cold reception of her was tied to her background, but she never knew about the prenup."

"So they didn't talk to Julie much at all?"

He shook his head. "Not really. It was awful. When they distanced themselves from my wife, my relationship with them changed. When Julie died, they offered no sympathy. I feel like they thought she deserved what happened to her."

"Frank! Are you sure about this?"

He shook his head. "They never said it, but they just acted like they didn't care when she died. They didn't call or anything."

"Maybe they thought you didn't want them to call. Maybe they didn't want to make you angrier."

"You sound like you're defending them."

She touched his arm. "I'm just trying to make you see this rationally. What does Trish say about all this?"

"She says my parents want to start speaking to me again."

She said the first thing that came to her mind. "You'll need to forgive your parents for the way they mistreated your wife. I've told you this before, but the only one who can help you is God."

He gave her an icy stare. "What?"

"What about your faith in God? Haven't you prayed about your pain, asked God to help you forgive Julie's killer and to forgive your parents?" She gestured around the cluttered room. "You can't drown your sorrows with booze."

"I don't care about God, and God doesn't care about me."

"How can you say that when you're not giving Him a chance?"

He huffed, running his fingers over his head. "Julie was saved not long after we were married. She tried to get me to accept Christ."

"What happened?"

His voice thickened. "Julie got killed." His dark eyes stared into hers. "I can't forget about that and accept God."

She prayed that God would lead her to say the right words. "Julie was saved? She's with Jesus now. Remember that."

He clasped his hands together. "Don't be preaching to me." He gave her a scathing look. "Besides, you have no idea what I've been through this past year."

She stood and stepped back, startled by his sudden outburst. She swallowed, her anger brewing like a slow stew simmering to boil. "I just lost my father, and I lost my mother years ago!" She clenched her hands together. "I know what it's like to lose someone you love." She calmed down before she squeezed his hand. "Give God a chance. I still have the church program from last week's service in my purse," she said, opening her purse and pulling out the program and a pen. She circled one of the contact numbers on the back. "The information about the alcoholic support group at my church is on the back." She pressed the paper into his palm. "The worship services are also listed. Devon Crandall is the leader for the alcoholic support group. They have weekly meetings, and I've heard good things about his work with the ministry."

He placed the program on the coffee table. "I'll think about it."

"I'll be praying for you, Frank." Emily embraced him before she left.

※

The following Sunday, Frank awakened and sat up in bed, cradling his aching head. "Oh man." The empty liquor bottle stared back at him, mocking his mistake. His sour stomach churned, and before long he ran to the bathroom and threw up. He relaxed against the cool, white-tiled wall, willing his rapidly beating heart to slow down. "God, I can't go on like this. I just can't." The nightmare about Julie haunted him again the previous night, and he squeezed his eyes shut, willing the unpleasant dream to vanish from his mind.

His cell phone chirped, and he stood on wobbly legs and plodded into the bedroom. He pulled the black instrument from the shelf. Not bothering to check the caller ID, he flipped the phone open. "Hello."

"Hi, little brother."

"Trish." The last thing he needed was a lecture from his sister.

"My goodness, don't sound so happy to hear from me." Sarcasm dripped from her voice, and Frank plopped back onto the bed.

"I'm not feeling great right now."

"You're probably hungover."

He winced, ashamed of his nightly routine. "Are Mark and Regina okay?"

"The kids are fine. I didn't call to talk about them or about your drinking problem. I wanted to talk about Dad."

"What about him?" He cradled the phone between his ear and shoulder, grabbing the large bottle of acetaminophen on his bedside table. Popping the jar open, he shook four tablets into his palm and dropped them into his mouth. He drank from a bottle of water, swallowing the pills.

"He's still sick."

"Has he been to the doctor yet?"

She scoffed. "You know he hasn't. But he was telling me the other day that he wished you would talk to them again."

He shook his head, but the movement caused bullets of pain to shoot behind his eyes. Taking a deep breath, he laid back on the pillows. "I don't have time to listen to this."

"Well, you better make time. I think if you'd talk to Dad again, he might feel better. Maybe he'll be so glad to hear from you that he'll do whatever you ask him to, even if that's going to the doctor."

Still holding the phone, he entered the kitchen, willing his aching head to stop pounding. He opened the cupboard. The canister of coffee beckoned him. He removed the can and opened it, spilling coffee grounds into the white filter. "Trish, I have to go now."

"But, Frank—"

"I'll talk to you later." He snapped his phone shut, throwing it on the kitchen table. Soon drops of coffee splattered into the coffeemaker, filling the kitchen with an aromatic scent. He pulled a mug from the cupboard and filled it with the steaming brew, along with a generous portion of cream and sugar.

He entered his living room and sat on the couch. Waves of guilt washed over him, and he blinked away unshed tears. He turned away from the wedding photo, continuing to sip his coffee. As the caffeine soothed his nerves, he set his mug down and returned to his bedroom. He found a box of his belongings, which he had never unpacked, sitting on the bottom of the closet. He dumped the contents, riffling through trinkets, old magazines, and books. Finally, he spotted his large black Bible, a gift from his deceased wife, among the clutter. Once he'd returned to the living room, he retrieved his mug, still holding his Bible. The old church program Emily had given him that week still sat on the coffee table.

He gazed at the paper, making his decision.

❧

An hour later, Frank sat in a pew at Monkton Christian Church. Once the sermon finished, Frank mulled over the pastor's words about forgiveness. Waves of heat washed over him when he stepped outside. People scurried to their cars, anxious to avoid the dreaded high temperatures.

He glanced around the sea of brown faces and stopped when he spotted Emily. Her white dress cascaded over her slim brown body, and her dark tresses were pulled into a severe ponytail, accenting her high cheekbones and full lips.

Kelly and Christine stood beside Emily. Laughter floated from the three women, and he wondered what they were talking about. Emily lifted her head, looking directly at him. Her smile faltered.

"Hi, Emily." He then gazed at Kelly and Christine. "Nice seeing you again, Kelly, Christine."

Kelly and Christine said hello. A mischievous smile played on Kelly's full lips, and after a few more words to Emily, Kelly took her exit. "I hope she didn't leave because of me," Frank commented.

"No, she's meeting somebody."

Christine spoke up. "I need to go, too. There's a sale going on at some of the stores at the Inner Harbor, and I was going to go and look around."

Emily touched Christine's shoulder. "Is everything okay? I don't want you going shopping, buying things you can't afford just to make yourself feel better."

Christine shook her head. "I didn't lose my job, but I just discovered they only went through the first round of layoffs. They're going to do more within the next couple of weeks." She shrugged. "Maybe I'll just look around the stores and not buy anything."

"Did you want to share lunch with me instead?"

Christine declined and bid them farewell.

They stood awkwardly on the hot sidewalk, and Emily spoke. "I was shocked to see you here today."

Frank didn't comment on her observation. People walked around them, and she touched his arm, leaning in a bit closer. "You don't look like you feel very well, and your eyes are red. Are you sick?" Frank sighed, unsure of how to respond "Did you have too much to drink last night?"

He pulled his arm away. "I don't want to talk about that right now."

"Is there something else you wanted to talk to me about?"

He touched her arm. "I never got a chance to talk to you about the audit the other day when you came to my apartment."

"Oh, I'd forgotten all about that with everything you told me." She clutched the strap of her purse. "I'm getting ready to eat lunch. I could call you this afternoon if you want."

"Were you going out to eat?"

"Kelly, Christine, and I were planning to go to the Monkton Village Market for lunch, but they bailed on me. Christine is pressed to go to this sale, and I don't have the energy to go shopping with her. She shops for hours! So we could go and get something to eat if you wanted."

They drove to the vegetarian restaurant and entered. Emily ordered pancakes with fruit, a blueberry muffin, and a cup of tea. Frank's stomach was still sour, so he purchased a bottle of water. He took out his wallet to pay for their food, telling the cashier their order was together. Once they'd sat at their table, Emily said, "You didn't have to pay for my meal."

He waved her comment away. "This is a business meal anyway."

Emily bowed her head and blessed her food. Her long lashes fluttered when she opened her eyes.

"I'm surprised you're eating at a vegetarian place," Frank said.

"It's just a change of pace. I've eaten at just about every place in Monkton since Laura's been gone. They don't have many places to eat here, and you know that I'm tired of making sandwiches every day."

"Speaking of your stepmother, do you know when she's getting back?" He couldn't keep the anxiety out of his voice.

Emily raised her eyebrows, her dark eyes full of suspicion. "Why do you ask?"

"I needed to talk to her about something important. I can call her, but I'd rather talk to her in person."

"What's wrong? Is the audit not going well?"

"It's not going well at all."

"What's happened?"

He thought about the latest development. "The numbers don't add up."

She frowned, staring into his eyes. "What do you mean?"

"There's something wrong. There are large amounts of cash that are unaccounted for."

She put her fork aside. "So there's money missing?"

He ran his fingers over his head, frustrated. "Yes. When you e-mailed me those missing documents, I was able to piece this information together. I'm still trying to figure out what your father's done. I was wondering if your stepmother might know something."

Emily pushed her plate away. "I doubt it. I already told you we didn't know much about the finances of our farm." She appeared pensive as she continued to speak. "Laura and I are lousy with numbers."

He frowned. "Really?"

"Yes. Back in grade school and even in college I struggled with math courses. The only reason I was able to graduate with my bachelor's and master's was because I hired a private tutor to help me with all my math classes. I can barely balance a checkbook."

"You're kidding."

She shook her head. "No, I'm not kidding. I've struggled with math my entire life, and Laura told me she's never been good with math either. My dad had this natural mathematical ability, so we just let him handle all the money. You probably wouldn't understand since you crunch numbers all day."

His mathematical abilities had always come naturally, so it was hard to understand how someone couldn't balance a checkbook. He touched her hand. "Don't worry about it. I'm sure there's some explanation. Did you find your father's missing tax returns?"

"No, not yet. I've been looking during my spare time." She told him they'd been baling hay recently and the intense heat had been affecting the corn crop. "I've been busy on the farm a lot, and I've also been thankful that one or both of the brothers have been showing up for both the evening and morning milkings."

They sat in silence for a few minutes before Emily began eating her pancakes again and Frank drank his water. Her lovely voice broke the silence. "Have you been okay? You have circles under your eyes."

He set his water bottle back on the table. "Remember you told me about Devon Crandall?"

"Yes, I remember."

"I showed up to a meeting." Her startled eyes met his. "But I couldn't go in."

"Why not?"

"I just couldn't. I stood outside the door for a minute, and I don't think anybody saw me." He gazed out the window at a couple who walked by holding hands. "Maybe I can give up the alcohol on my own."

"You told me that you'd had alcohol problems before when you were in college. How were you able to quit back then?"

He recalled that time in his life. "They had AA meetings near campus. But. . ."

She grabbed his hand. "But what?"

"To tell you the truth, I've been doing some heavy drinking for over a year now. Back when I was in college, I'd only been drinking for a few months before it started becoming a problem. I think it might be harder for me to quit this time."

"Maybe you should give it another try. Maybe you could have somebody go to the meeting with you."

"Going to that group of people makes me nervous."

"Why?"

"I don't know."

"Devon is an understanding man. Maybe you can just meet with him to talk about what you've been going through."

As she ate her lunch, Frank gave Emily's advice serious thought.

Chapter 8

During the next month, Emily's days continued to be filled with farm chores. She was glad when they had almost two straight days of rain. The claps of thunder and bursts of lightning thrilled her, making her giddy. The heat and dry weather had worried her, and the moisture was just what her crops needed to thrive.

She'd called Laura about Frank's questions, but her stepmother was shocked to hear about the missing money. As far as Laura knew, all of her father's financial information was in his office. Laura had mentioned it was certainly possible that there were files elsewhere in the house, so Emily said she'd keep looking around to see if she could find any missing documents that would help account for the missing funds.

One morning when the milking was done, Emily and Jeremy stood at the sink, rinsing the equipment and cleaning the barn. The slender teen turned toward Emily. "My mom told me to ask if your mother was coming home soon."

"She said she was coming home shortly. I've been talking to her every day." She glanced at him, wondering if he understood the pain of losing somebody so close. "I don't want to keep bothering her about when she's coming home. But I do miss her a lot." She gave the teen a smile and continued rinsing her equipment. She was a little hurt that Laura had not called to wish her a happy birthday. "Make sure either you or your brother or both of you are here tonight to milk the cows."

"Oh, we'll both be here." He held up a cell phone. "You can even call us to make sure we're here if you want to."

A few hours later, Kelly and Christine arrived at Emily's farm, and the three women rode to the state fair together. When they arrived on the fairgrounds, they assisted the rest of Monkton Christian Church's hospitality committee. In addition to serving pound cake and bottled water, they'd planned on doing face painting to entice the children to their booth. After working all morning, Emily was ready for a break.

"Hi, Emily." Frank's voice greeted her ears like a soothing lullaby. Turning toward him, she enjoyed the sensations that skittered across her skin when he touched her arm. "Frank. I didn't know you'd be here."

"The fair was advertised in the church bulletin, and you told me you were on the committee." His dark eyes sparkled. "Can you take a break?"

She checked her watch. "Is it okay if I take my lunch break now?"

Kelly completed a child's face painting. "Why don't you go ahead with Frank and have a good time." She reached for her purse beneath the booth. "If you don't mind, you can bring me back something to eat." She told her what she wanted for lunch. The rest of the committee members also produced money for lunches since they weren't interested in walking around the fair.

Frank and Emily strolled away from the booth. "Why did you come to the fair?"

"I came to see you. Since I haven't been coming out to your farm lately, I've missed you."

His words warmed her heart, and she decided to be truthful with him. "I've missed you, too."

They strolled around the grounds then bought hot dogs from a vendor and sat at one of the picnic tables. She bit into her hot dog and drank some soda. "How have you been?" she asked.

"I've been okay." He stared at the crowd populating the fairgrounds. "Well, I wish I could be better."

She took a deep breath before asking her next question. "Have you been drinking?"

"I've been working late, and that helps a little bit, but it doesn't keep me away from the alcohol."

"Did you call Devon Crandall?"

"No."

"Why not? He's very easygoing, and I'm sure he wouldn't mind if you called him." He failed to respond. "Are you coming to church again tomorrow?"

He smiled before sipping his soda. "Yes, I plan on going."

"You should try and talk to Devon after church tomorrow. He's one of the ushers. He's well over six feet tall with gray hair. His wife is so short that they look funny together because of his height."

"Okay, I'll keep that in mind."

She bit into her hot dog. "How are Mark and Regina doing? Does Mark still call you a lot?"

He grinned. "Thanks for asking. Both of them are doing fine. Mark has been calling me just about every day. If I don't hear from him, I'll usually call. I'm glad he hasn't gotten into any more trouble, and he seems excited to be back in school."

"I'm glad to hear they're doing well." She observed the colorful tents on the grounds for a few seconds. "Oh, Frank, I almost forgot to tell you." She abandoned her hot dog and clenched her hands together.

"What's wrong?"

"Nothing's wrong. This morning I found the tax returns you were looking for. There were also some other bank statements, too."

He frowned, finishing his food. "Other bank statements? What kind of account is it? Is it checking, savings, money market?"

She shrugged. "I'm not sure."

"Were they to another account, a different one than the one I was looking at?"

"I think so. I didn't realize he had an account there. This bank is all the way on the other side of Baltimore County."

"Did you check the balance? Maybe that's where the missing funds are."

She told him the sum that was in the account.

His eyes widened. "Whoa. Why would he separate that much money into another account? It must be either a money market, savings, or retirement account."

"You know, it's the strangest thing. . ."

He sipped his soda. "What?"

"I didn't find them in his office."

Frank frowned again. "Where did you find them?"

"They were stuck in a manila folder in the hall closet." She shook her head. "I don't understand why he had all his other tax returns on his computer with the exception of those two. Why would he separate them like that?"

He wiped his mouth with a napkin. "I'm not sure. If you don't mind, I'd like for you to scan them and e-mail them to me as soon as possible. That way I can complete the work for your farm."

Questions popped through her brain. If Frank finished his audit for their farm, did that mean she would have no contact with him anymore? He touched her hand. "What's the matter?"

She shook her head, not wanting to voice her concerns. "Nothing. I'm okay."

When they were finished with their lunch, they strolled the fairgrounds again. Frank walked back with her to the booth before he left the event. Christine and Kelly immediately surrounded her, wanting to know what was going on between her and Frank.

❧

"What's wrong, Emily?" asked Christine as they pulled into her driveway.

Emily shook her head. "Nothing's wrong. I'm just tired."

Gravel crunched beneath their feet as they walked to the front door. Emily yawned, looking forward to getting into her soft bed and going to sleep. She stopped walking, looking at her friends. "Do you guys really feel like visiting right now? I was going to go to bed."

Christine patted her shoulder. "We'll try not to wear you out too much. Let's make some coffee and talk for a bit."

Kelly agreed. "Yes, a cup of coffee sounds like a good idea."

Emily walked up the steps, concerned about the full darkness cloaking her house since she usually left the porch light on. She made a mental note to change the lightbulb. The hinges on the screen door creaked as she entered.

"Happy birthday!" The dark kitchen flooded with light, and a sea of familiar faces filled the room.

Emily placed her hand against her mouth. "Oh my goodness."

"Hey, Emily!" Laura Cooper strolled into the kitchen.

"Mom!" Emily shrieked, pulling the older woman into an embrace. The familiar scent of Laura's jasmine perfume filled Emily with euphoria, and tears gathered in her eyes.

Kelly pressed a tissue into Emily's hand. "Happy birthday, Emily!"

She glanced at Kelly and Christine. "You two kept this from me all day!"

Emily released her mother, wiping her eyes. "Mom, you look thinner since you left."

Laura swatted Emily's arm. "I've been fine."

Emily shook her head, still trying to take in the whole atmosphere. "I was wondering why you didn't call me today!" She ignored the numerous guests, eager to speak with Laura.

"Honey, you know I wanted to call you today, but I can't keep secrets. I know I would've accidentally said something to spoil Kelly and Christine's surprise!"

Emily's joy bubbled to the surface, almost gushing forward. Crepe paper streamers fluttered when the wind blew in from the open screen door.

Emily stared at the crowd, touched. "This is one of the biggest surprises I've received in my entire life."

A strong, unique scent filled the air, and Emily rushed over to the stove, opening the lid on one of the pots. "You made me chitterlings!" The pig intestines, cooked to perfection, were one of her favorite foods. Serving herself, she piled some on a plate and placed a generous amount of mustard on the side. She took a bite, savoring the flavor.

Her friends from church were present as well as Cameron. As she continued to eat her food, Christine took her aside. "I'm sorry about Cameron coming."

"Why is he here?" asked Emily.

Christine rolled her eyes. "When we were at the grocery store getting the stuff for the party, Cameron was nearby and we didn't realize it. He overheard us talking about your party, and he asked if he could come. I couldn't tell him no."

Later, when she opened the gifts, she was pleased to see the assortment of perfumes and lotions people gave her. She also received some gift cards to her favorite clothing store. However, she was shocked Cameron gave her pearl ear-rings. "Thanks, Cameron," she said, giving him a small smile.

The party lasted until well into the night. Once the guests were gone and Christine and Kelly had put away the leftovers, it was close to midnight, but Emily was still high on energy. She sat on the porch with her stepmother on the large swing. They swayed in the gentle summer breeze, and Emily was happy to have Laura home again. "How's Lisa doing?"

"She's fine. We had a nice visit."

"Has Becky been calling you much?"

Laura looked away for a few seconds. "You know how strained things are between Becky and me. She calls every few weeks. I just wish we could settle our differences and have a better relationship. I've been praying for a better rela-tionship with both daughters for a long time, so I'm hoping things can change between us."

Emily patted Laura's shoulder, praying things worked out with her girls. She knew Laura had divorced at a young age and her ex-husband had been granted custody of their two small children. Her husband had hired a good law-yer, and he'd used Laura's past convictions with drugs against her. She'd cleaned her life up by the time she was married and had children, but her husband's lawyer was able to convince the judge that the father would be a better parent because he'd never had the substance abuse problems Laura had had in the past. Laura had told her that she always regretted losing custody of her children, even though she had generous visitation rights. Her daughters were now in their early thirties, and she wondered if the strained relationship they had was due to the fact that Laura did not raise them herself.

Even though they'd talked about it on the phone, she told Laura about the audit and about finding her father's tax returns. "Mom, we really should have been more involved in the financial side of things," Emily commented as the swing continued to sway.

Laura touched Emily's hand. "Honey, I know we should have. But there's nothing we can do but move forward."

Emily again mentioned the correspondence Frank had found with a Realtor in her father's files. "He said it appeared as if he was planning to sell the farm. I told him he must be mistaken. Are you sure Dad never mentioned this to you?"

Her stepmother remained silent as the swing continued to rock.

"Mom, what are you hiding?"

"Honey, I wasn't completely honest with you when you mentioned this to me before. I didn't want to tell you this, but Frank is right. Shortly before your father died, he was contemplating selling this farm."

Emily's mouth dropped open. "But. . .why? Daddy always loved farming!"

"I know, but he confided to me that for the last two years profits had been bad for the farm."

Emily shook her head. "I don't believe it. Why didn't he ever say anything to me about this?"

She touched Emily's arm. "He didn't want you to worry about it, that's why."

"But, I still don't understand. Frank would have said something about our farm not being profitable, wouldn't he?"

"Emily, remember he's not finished auditing the books." She frowned. "What's wrong, Mom?"

"I didn't want to tell you this, but. . .before your father passed, I could see how much the financial strain of the farm was bothering him. I tried to get him to hire an accountant to go through his tax returns and stuff to see if he may have been missing some important write-offs."

"And he didn't agree to do it, right?"

"He reacted worse than you did when I made my suggestion. He got angry with me. You were at a church function that night, and we argued about it for hours. Honey, your father was good with numbers, but he was not an accountant and he was no CPA. I know we hear about farms selling out sometimes, but I knew there were farms that did pretty well. I figured if he got advice from an accountant, he may have gotten an even better return when he filed his taxes and when he invested his money. You always hear about tax laws changing and such, and I wanted him to see a professional about his farm."

Emily rubbed her head. "Is this why you wanted Frank to audit our books?"

Laura nodded. "Yes. I've been worried about this for a long time, and since Paul is gone, I'm even more worried about it. We seem to be making it financially day by day, but I just want to make sure your father knew what he was doing when he accounted for this farm and when he filed his taxes in the past."

This newfound information made Emily's head ache. She silently prayed for strength before deciding to tell her mother something else that was on her mind. "Mom, I think I have a big problem."

"What is it? Has something else happened since I've been gone?"

"Well, you know I've been spending some time with Frank."

"You like him, don't you?"

"Yes, how did you know?"

"You say his name like you're familiar with him. I know he has feelings for you, too."

"How do you know that?"

"Just from talking to him on the phone. He seems concerned about the farm, more concerned than a stranger should be. When I speak to him, I feel like I'm talking to a friend." They were silent for a few minutes as they continued to rock on the swing. "Maybe the Lord is trying to tell you it's time to move on since your engagement to Jamal ended."

"I don't think so." They rocked well into the night, and she told her mother all about why Frank was the wrong man for her.

❧

"God will never leave you nor forsake you. I want all of you to remember that when you leave church today," said Pastor Brown to the congregation. Frank closed his Bible, still thinking about the words. He sat in the pew beside Emily and her mother. After all these weeks, he'd finally gotten to meet Laura.

When the service ended, Emily took Frank's hand, causing sparks of delight to dance through his fingers. She gestured toward Laura. "We're going out to lunch at the Wagon Wheel. Did you want to come with us?"

Frank shook his head. He glanced at the ushers still in the back of the church.

"In case you're interested, Devon Crandall is the one on the left," she told him.

He squeezed her hand. "Thanks," he mumbled. Emily and Laura exited the church, and Frank swallowed, still working up the courage to approach the older man. He breathed deeply as he walked up to the usher. "Devon Crandall?" The man gazed at Frank, his dark eyes warm and friendly.

"Yes?"

"My name is Franklin Reese."

The usher smiled, shaking Frank's hand. "I've noticed you coming to our church recently. It's hard not to notice a new member in a church this small."

Frank sighed, not wanting Devon to get the wrong idea. "Well, I'm not a member of this church."

"If you're a member of God's family, then that makes you a member of this church."

"No, I don't think I'm a member of God's family either."

The man's smile faded, and he squeezed Frank's hand. "You look like you need somebody to talk to, son."

"I don't want to hold you up."

"There's no hold up." He placed his hands on his hips, continuing to assess Frank. "People are always telling me how perceptive I am, and right about now I think you need a friend. Would you like to come to my house for lunch?"

"I don't want to bother you."

"Oh, it's no bother. My wife usually cooks too much food anyway." He patted his gut. "I certainly don't need those extra calories."

"Okay."

Devon beamed. "Good. I'll just let my wife know you're coming. You can follow us to our house."

A half hour later, Frank shared lunch with Devon and his wife. The tiny salt-and-pepper-haired woman welcomed Frank into her home, embracing him warmly. When he'd commuted to the Crandalls' house, his queasy stomach had settled from his drinking binge the night before, and he was able to enjoy the tasty pot roast, mashed potatoes, and green salad. "You and Devon can have your dessert in the library," suggested Devon's wife. After placing coffee and cake on a silver tray and carrying it into the library, she left, saying she had some things to do around the house.

The blinds were open, and bright sunlight spilled into the room.

"So, tell me, Franklin—"

"You can call me Frank."

"Okay, Frank. Tell me why you approached me in church."

Frank stirred his coffee, wondering where to start. Did he explain the anger he had for his parents and the death of his wife, which drove him to drink? Did he tell of his budding feelings for Emily? "Since Paul Cooper died, Laura and Emily needed help with their bookkeeping. They contacted my employer, and I was sent to do the job. Emily mentioned you ran an alcoholic support group."

Devon nodded, serving the cake. "Yes, I do. I've been running it for over ten years. The group is not just for members of our church; it's also there for people in surrounding churches. We meet every week in the basement of the church."

"I know." He mentioned showing up at the meeting the previous week but refusing to enter the room.

Devon didn't seem surprised about Frank's actions. "You made it to the meeting, so that's a big step. You should come in next time. We'd be glad to have you. So, tell me what's been making you drink."

"My parents never accepted my wife because of her background. My family's pretty wealthy, and my parents thought they knew who would be the best wife for me. They didn't support my marriage, and when my wife died, they never apologized for not accepting Julie into the family." He briefly told of how Julie was killed, and then he added, "I felt so bad, Devon. Not only did I lose my wife, but. . ." He looked away and didn't realize tears streamed from his eyes until Devon gave him a tissue. "I lost a child." He shook his head. "A few days before Julie died, she told me she was pregnant." He wiped his wet eyes and blew his nose. "I just wish there was some way I could've stopped her from going to meet her brother that day." He balled his hands into fists. "I feel so bad. The alcohol is the only thing that makes me feel better anymore." Devon squeezed Frank's shoulder.

Once Frank was calmer, Devon asked him a question. "When does the urge to drink happen?"

Frank was truthful, telling Devon the urge usually hit in the evening, after working a full day.

"Frank, I'll be praying for you every day, but you really need to meet with the alcoholic support group weekly." He gave Frank a business card. "You can call me anytime you want to, but I'm warning you, I'll be calling you every day, too." He stroked his chin. "By coming to me, I think you've admitted to yourself that you have a problem. Also, I want to point out that you can't handle this sort of problem alone. Not only do you need help from the support group, but you need to find help in Jesus. If you'll just accept Him as your Savior, then the load you carry on your shoulders will become lighter. Remember what the pastor said this morning: Jesus will never leave you nor forsake you."

Frank certainly felt left and forsaken, but he didn't know if he'd find the courage to surrender his life to Jesus.

Chapter 9

A few days later Frank met with his boss and informed him of his final discovery for the Coopers' farm. "You'll need to meet with the wife since she's the one who initiated the audit," his boss had advised.

Now Frank sat in his car in front of the Coopers' farm. It was midafternoon, and he was scheduled to meet with Laura Cooper alone. When he'd called that morning to make the appointment, she'd said to come that afternoon since Emily would be at the grocery store. His thoughts wandered to the previous night. The urge to drink had slammed into him after Trish called, again saying that their father was not doing so well. He'd picked up the phone to call his dad but found the old anger festering in his heart like a canker sore. Instead of turning to drink, he'd called Devon Crandall, who'd again stressed that Frank needed to find relief in Jesus. Devon had encouraged him to come to the next support group meeting, and he'd also told him to discover more about God. "Read the New Testament, Frank. It'll tell you about Jesus' nature." He'd spoken to the man for more than an hour. After tossing and turning in bed for a long time, he'd finally gone to sleep—without taking a drink of alcohol.

He got out of the car and walked to the screen door. The urge to drink almost consumed him, but he forced himself to think of Emily, the Cooper farm, and the news he had to deliver. Taking a deep breath, he rapped on the door. Laura sat at the table, reading her Bible and drinking a cup of coffee. The woman looked up, smiling. "Frank." She placed a marker in her Bible and closed it. "Frank, come on in." When he sat at the table, she touched his hand. "You seem a bit agitated. Are you okay?"

"Not really."

"Is something wrong?"

"I'm fine. I wanted to talk to you about the audit. I don't think Emily looked through all the financial papers in that file she found."

"What are you talking about?"

"Your husband had Excel spreadsheets keeping track of winnings and losses at a gambling casino over in Delaware. I've found evidence that he was spending large sums of the farm's profits at a casino. He kept records of what he had spent and how much he owed the farm from his gambling debts."

Laura cried softly. "I thought he had stopped gambling. He was going to a support group."

Her reaction caught him off guard. "You knew about this?"

"Yes, he did this a long time ago, but he promised me he'd stopped. I can now see it was all a lie." Frank found a box of tissues on the counter, and he gave them to her.

"Emily doesn't know?"

"No, neither of his daughters knew about their father's bad habit. I didn't think it was necessary to tell them since he'd told me he'd stopped."

If Emily and Laura wanted to start keeping track of the accounting records and tracking the profitability of the farm, then he didn't see how he could hide this information from Emily. He relayed his concerns to Laura.

"I understand. I just don't know how to break it to her. She thought her father was perfect." She blew her nose and looked at him as if to seek comfort. "I don't know how I'm going to tell Emily. But I don't have a choice." She sniffed. "Oh Lord, please help me."

"Mrs. Cooper, that's not all I needed to tell you. I believe your husband falsified his tax returns."

With shaky hands, she covered her mouth, continuing to cry. "Do you mean he owes money to the government?"

"Yes. He grossly understated his revenue, and I know he owes the IRS some money. . .a lot of money. He's falsified his tax returns for the last two years." He told her how he couldn't find the tax returns for the last two years and that Emily found them hidden in the closet. "Did you look at the tax returns before you signed them?"

"Paul took care of all the finances. When he told me to sign the tax returns, I just trusted the numbers were accurate." She wiped her tears away. "Will we have to lose the farm to pay the back taxes? This farm means so much to Emily. She would die if she lost this home."

"You could lose your farm. But you'll have to let her know what happened. Usually in situations like this, the IRS will want their money back. They might work with you and Emily to set up a payment plan or something." When she had pulled herself together, he finally spoke again. "When are you going to tell Emily?"

She wiped her nose. "I'll tell her before the end of the day. She deserves to know."

He tried to make her feel better. "Mrs. Cooper, I think your husband may have been keeping track of all this because he was planning on replacing the money he lost back into the farm."

She nodded. "He's done this before, a long time ago. He thought if he kept at it long enough, he would win the money back. But sometimes, when he did win back the money he'd lost, the temptation to gamble it away again was just too great." She shook her head. "I'll never understand why this happened, but I promise I'll talk to Emily about it today."

❧

Later that day Emily returned from the barn, and fatigue washed through her. She told Laura she was going to take a short nap before doing the evening milking. Sleep consumed her until the phone rang. Emily turned her head on the soft pillow, snuggling deeper into her blankets, hoping to get a few more minutes of sleep before milking time.

Laura's footsteps pounded on the floor, and Emily's door flew open when she entered. "Emily, you've got to wake up." She opened the blinds, and sunlight spilled into the room. Emily regretfully broke her midday nap. "Mom, what's wrong?"

Laura paced the room, her mouth set in a grim line. "Becky's had her baby! They just gave her a C-section at the hospital."

Emily's world tilted, and she sent up a silent plea to God for her stepsister's health and for the baby. "But she's only seven months pregnant. What happened?"

"They think the size of her fibroids caused her to go into early labor." Her stepmother shook her head. She sat on the bed and grabbed Emily's hand, closing her eyes. "Lord, please be with us during this trying time." Her voice filled the room as they lifted up the plight of Becky's baby. When their prayer was finished, she squeezed Emily's hand.

"They say the baby's chances of survival are good." Her mother shook her head. "I've got to get out there."

Emily's heart filled with dread at the thought of Laura leaving again, but she knew it was for the best. "I know you do, Mom."

"I hate leaving you so soon."

Emily shook her head, patting Laura's frail shoulder. "Don't feel bad about it. Becky's got two other children, and since it's the busy season at Keith's job, you know he's going to be working some serious overtime now." Both of Becky's children were under five, so her stepmother would have her hands full. "Don't overdo it, Mom. I don't want your back to go out on you again." The last time that had happened, she'd been in bed for a week, barely able to move without being in pain.

"Honey, I won't." She glanced at the clock. "Since Becky's had a C-section, I know it's going to be hard for her to get around for about a week or so. I want to try and get a flight out of here today."

One of Laura's friends from church soon arrived to take her to the airport.

Emily was sorry to see her stepmother go so soon after returning from her trip to Florida, but she knew it was necessary for her to be there to assist her daughter with her children.

That evening Emily was out in the barn with Darren milking the cows when her cell phone chirped. She told Darren to continue milking alone for a few minutes and flipped the phone open. "Hi, Laura."

"Emily, with all the excitement about Becky's baby, I forgot to tell you about Frank's audit."

Emily frowned. "What about it? Is Frank finished?"

"Emily, you need to call him now. I'm not very good at explaining financial things, and he can do a better job of it."

The phone crackled a bit. "Mom, I can't hear you very well."

"Honey, I think I'm losing the connection, but I want you to contact Frank!"

After ending the phone call with her mother, she called Frank. His deep voice carried over the wire. "Hi, Emily."

Her heart skipped a beat as she spoke. She told him about the birth of Becky's baby. "Mom's already left. She told me that I needed to call you about the audit."

"Can I come by tomorrow night?"

"Can you come by before that?"

"I wish I could, but I've got to finish up some stuff for my boss tonight. I promise I'll be there tomorrow."

Emily ended the call, wondering why Laura sounded so stressed.

❦

Frank entered his car, leaning his head back onto the headrest. After meeting with the alcoholic support group and speaking with Devon, he'd hoped he could stop drinking. When he was at his apartment the previous night, he'd thought he could have just a little bit to drink, just enough to take the edge off his raw pain. But once he'd sipped the alcohol, he couldn't stop himself, and he fell asleep sloshed.

He called Devon this morning, telling him what had happened the night before. Devon had again stressed his group was a Christian support group and in order for Frank to give up the alcohol completely, he would need to surrender himself to Jesus. "That's the only way you can find the strength to quit."

He wondered how he could surrender his life to someone. He wanted to deal with things his way and live his life according to his own rules.

He drove to Emily's, pushing the thoughts from his mind. He slowed his car and parked in the driveway once he'd reached the farm. Frank got out of the car and walked toward the barn, smelling the odors of animals and hay. He watched the black-and-white Holstein cows lined up in their stalls. Emily and a lanky teenager, whom he assumed was Jeremy or Darren, walked between the cows, milking four at a time. They worked together easily, and as the milk flowed through the pipes, the machines made a steady rhythm in the early evening heat.

Emily glanced up and smiled. "Frank! You're a little early!"

She didn't seem to be too upset, and he didn't want to interrupt her milking routine. He gestured toward the bovines. "I don't want to interrupt you. I'll talk to you when you're finished."

He watched her, drinking in her presence like an ice-cold glass of lemonade on a hot day. The joy that radiated from her face was like a ray of sunshine.

Since the milking was done, she sent the teen to feed the cows before she rinsed her milking equipment in the adjoining room. He stood beside her at the sink as she performed the chore.

He touched her shoulder. "Are you ready to talk right now?" he asked, touching the tendrils of her hair that escaped from her ponytail.

"Yes, we can talk now. What's happened with the audit for my farm? Mom sounded worried."

He sighed before he repeated the information he'd relayed to Laura the previous day. Emily's mouth dropped open, and her eyes widened. She backed away, shaking her head. "I don't believe you."

"I wish it wasn't true."

She stormed toward the teenager and told him to finish cleaning the milking equipment after he was finished feeding the cows and the bull. Frank followed her as she walked back to the house. "So, you're telling me that my father was a dishonest gambler?" She covered her quivering mouth. "That's not true! There's no way my father would place our farm in jeopardy."

Frank remained silent as she plopped onto the porch swing, unsure of how to comfort her.

She turned toward him, glaring. "So you're telling me that I could lose my farm, too?" Her large eyes filled with tears. "Is that what you're telling me?"

He ran his fingers over his head. "Yes, but—"

She looked away. "Are you sure you know what you're doing?"

The cold, hard edge to her voice frightened him. "What do you mean?"

"Were you sober the whole time you were auditing my farm?"

He clamped his mouth shut, shocked she would make such an implication. Taking a deep breath, he stood and walked away, unsure if she was serious or if she just needed an excuse because she didn't want to believe the truth about her father.

❧

Emily watched Frank return to his car, and her heart pulsed with anger. She almost called him back, shocked at the words that had tumbled from her mouth. Shaking her head, she turned away from the accountant, staring at the corn and silos in the distance.

She wiped her tears away, her head suddenly aching. Rocking the swing in the warm breeze, she tried to digest Frank's bad news. She jumped when Darren stepped onto the porch. "Sorry, didn't mean to scare you." The teen gazed at her, his dark eyes full of curiosity. "Hey, are you okay, Miss Emily?"

She sniffed. "There's so much going on right now." When he made no attempt to leave, she asked, "Did you need something?"

He nodded, his short braids swinging. "Yes, it's payday. Remember?"

"Oh, yes." Once she had given him his pay and he'd left, she sat back on the porch.

Kelly pulled into the driveway and sauntered onto the porch as it started to get dark, still wearing her business suit and high heels. She plopped onto the swing beside Emily. "I was on my way home from work, and I thought I'd stop by." She peered into Emily's face. "What's wrong?"

Emily stared at the porch ceiling. "I can't even talk about it."

"You look zonked." She grabbed Emily's hand. "Come on inside."

Kelly fixed some peppermint tea and placed a plate of lemon cookies on the table. "Have something to drink or eat. You look awful."

Emily's stomach roiled, and she pushed the tea away.

"Em, drink the tea. Maybe it will help calm you down." After taking several deep breaths, she sipped the tea as Kelly sat at the table with her. "Now, tell me what's wrong."

"Frank said some terrible things about my father." Her voice sounded hoarse.

"What did he say?"

Emily could barely speak as she told her friend about Frank's accusations against her dad.

"Have you called Laura?"

"No, not yet. My mom did call me this morning, but I was out milking the cows. She left a message and said Becky and the baby are doing fine." She blew air through her lips. "I just don't know what to do. I don't know what to believe. And do you know what the worst part of it is?"

"What's that?"

She told her how she asked Frank if he was sober the entire time he was doing the audit.

Kelly gasped, and Emily moaned. "Em, I can't believe you said that."

"Frank looked so hurt when I said it."

"Maybe you should apologize to him," Kelly suggested.

"I probably should. I just got so mad when he said those things. I was angry, and I said the first thing that came to my mind."

"Did you know he's been attending Devon Crandall's alcoholic support group?"

Emily stared at her friend. "I told him to talk to Devon, and he told me he'd tried to go to a meeting but he chickened out."

"Well, I heard through the church grapevine that he's been attending. Maybe he's trying to give up the alcohol, Em."

Emily's mouth quivered. "Oh no. What if my insensitive comment makes him go home and drink?" She closed her eyes. "Kelly, I feel so bad. I just. . ."

Kelly rushed over to her friend. "Give him some time to cool off. I'm sure he knew you didn't mean it."

Emily sniffed. "All those things he said about Daddy—I just can't believe them. I just can't."

Kelly left and returned with some pills. "I found that prescription you filled for your sleeping pills right after your father died. Here's two. Why don't you take them and get a good night's sleep?"

Emily accepted the pills and took them. She found she just couldn't talk any longer after Kelly had taken her exit and the medicine settled into her body. Her muscles relaxed, and she soon stumbled up the stairs to her bedroom. For the first time in her whole farming career, she fell asleep wearing the same clothes she wore to milk the cows.

✌

Frank slammed the door to the accounting office building on Pratt Street. He stood on the corner, gazing at the buildings in the distance. Late evening tourists and shoppers walked by, their arms heavy with colorful store bags. He pulled off his tie, hating the managerial meeting that had occurred that day in the main office. His firm required all upper-level managers to wear business attire to these meetings, and he wasn't in the mood to wear his suit today. His boss had also called him into his office, informing him that he'd appeared irritable and cranky lately and he wondered if something was wrong. Frank couldn't admit that he needed a drink—badly. Emily's comment the previous evening had haunted him all night, and he had almost drunk some of his favorite scotch to dull the pain. He'd finally dumped the scotch down the toilet before tossing and turning most of the night.

Once he got into the car, he dropped his head back on the seat, groaning. "Oh God, I feel so bad right now." He started his car and pulled out of the lot. Forty minutes later, he pulled into a parking space at Monkton Christian Church, feeling a desperate need to meet with the alcoholic support group. He gazed at his Bible, still sitting on the passenger side of the car. Questions about God, life, and salvation filled his mind like unwanted weeds in a garden.

After walking into the practically deserted building, he entered the meeting room for the support group. During the meeting, he spoke of Emily's comment the previous evening and about how it had filled him with shame.

"Why were you ashamed?" asked one of the female attendees.

"Even though I was sober the whole time I was doing the audit, I could see myself getting to the point where I could have been drinking during the day." He went on to say that since he'd started drinking after his wife died, he noticed the amount of alcohol he consumed nightly had increased. "I've been waking up with bad headaches; sometimes I vomit."

Once the rest of the attendees had sprinkled in their words of wisdom and told of their weekly trials, Devon invited everybody to stand and join hands as they closed with a prayer. When the meeting was over, Frank pulled Devon aside. "I wanted to talk to you about something," said Frank.

Devon invited him to return to his seat. "You look upset," Devon observed. His wise, kind eyes bored into Frank.

"My addiction is really starting to bother me."

"I know it is. You're feeling guilty right now. I can tell." Devon's voice softened. "You know what you need to do. You need to surrender yourself to God."

"But that's so hard to do! My wife surrendered her life to God, but now she's dead."

"Her body is dead, but her spirit lives on. She's with Jesus right now, and you need to stop focusing on earthly life so much." He looked at Frank for a few seconds. "You know, Frank, I never did tell you my testimony. There's so much about me that I haven't had the chance to tell you yet." He checked his watch. "Are you in a hurry to leave?"

Frank dreaded the return to his empty apartment where thoughts of drinking continued to consume him. "No, I'm in no hurry."

They sat back down, and Devon began his testimony. "I grew up in a home where alcohol flowed like water."

Frank frowned. "Do you mean both of your parents drank?"

Devon nodded. "My brother and I knew how wine and beer tasted before we even started kindergarten."

Frank gasped, shocked. "Your parents gave you booze?"

"No, they didn't give it to us directly. They were just irresponsible about how they left it around the house. My brother and I could get into the alcohol and drink it. We hated the taste but discovered we could water it down and drink it. It made us feel grown up."

"Your parents never knew what you did?"

"Since both of my parents drank so frequently, they didn't realize what was happening. Steve—that's my brother—and I grew up thinking it was okay to drink and get sloshed. Although our father was an alcoholic, he was always quoting scripture, saying Jesus died for our sins and that it was okay that he was getting drunk every night because God had already forgiven him for that. Steve and I grew up with the philosophy that we could do what we wanted as far as drinking was concerned because it was what we'd been hearing all our lives."

"So what changed your mind?" Frank asked.

"Steve and I were in the car with our father, and he was very drunk. He almost fell asleep at the wheel, and the car swerved into a ditch." He looked at the wall for a few seconds. "None of us were hurt, but at that point, I could see my dad's philosophy about being drunk was skewed. However, I was almost sixteen, and I was used to drinking whenever I wanted."

"Did your father continue drinking after the accident?"

"Not right away. He sobered up for a month or so, but before long, he was hitting the bottle as hard as ever. My mother's drinking was just as bad, and as I got ready to graduate from high school, I found that I wasn't happy unless I was drinking. From the type of household I was raised in, I thought the way I felt and handled things was normal. What really made me change my life was when my brother died from a drunk driving accident." He wiped his eyes. "Losing my brother was the hardest thing I'd ever been through, and his death spurred me to look at myself emotionally and spiritually."

"What did you do?" asked Frank.

"Although I'd been raised by a father who quoted scripture all the time, I realized that I'd never really studied the Bible for myself, word for word, to see what God really said we should do to live a life that was pleasing to Him. I was twenty years old at the time, and I searched around until I found a small church where I felt comfortable. I began studying the scriptures with other believers until I finally proclaimed Christ as my Savior. My father died of liver disease because of his heavy drinking when I was twenty-five, but he'd learned to control his drinking after Steve died. My mom, dad, and I all found the Lord after Steve's death, and I make sure when I convince people to accept Christ that they hear about what I went through as I searched for the Lord."

Devon's testimony sank deeply into Frank's heart, and he still thought about Devon Crandall's words as he drove home that night.

Chapter 10

The following Saturday, Frank opened his eyes, blinking and feeling lousy. He swallowed, thinking about his tormented night. Emily's accusation still felt like a punch in the gut. He'd actually made it through the day without a drink, and he'd been on the phone with Devon last night for a whole hour. The urge for a drink consumed him, and he shuffled over to the coffee pot, making a large pot of the steaming brew. He sipped the coffee, recalling Devon's advice. "Son, you need to accept the Lord. Fall down on your knees and accept Him. Surrender your life to Him. That's the only way you can give up the drink."

The ringing telephone interrupted his musings, and he jumped. Groaning, he picked up the receiver. "Hello."

"Frank? It's Emily." Her smooth, sweet voice reminded him of silk. He relished the pleasure of hearing her speak.

"Emily? I'm surprised you called."

"I wanted to apologize for what happened the other day. I shouldn't have said those things to you."

He tried to think of the right words to say. The hurt from her accusation had pierced through him like a lightning bolt; still, he knew she was justified in her assumption, even though it was wrong. Finally, he spoke. "I. . .can I see you sometime today? I wanted to talk to you about something."

"You haven't had anything to drink today, have you? I don't want you to drive over here if you've been drinking. I know you're trying to quit. . ."

"It's hard to stop completely."

She sighed. "That's what I've heard. That's why I want to make sure you're okay. I just don't want you driving over here if you're drinking. I worry about you, Frank."

"You don't have to worry about me. Remember I told you that I only drink at night after I get home," he reminded her.

They agreed to meet for dinner, and Emily offered to meet Frank in Baltimore, but he refused, telling her that he would pick her up.

❧

Darren showed up for work that evening, so after they milked the cows and fed them, she strolled toward the house as the conversation she'd had with Frank that

202

morning still played in her mind. After removing her barn boots, she entered her home and went upstairs to take a long, hot shower, still contemplating the fate of her farm. After showering, she sprayed perfume over her skin before pulling her hair back into a ponytail. Sporting faded jeans and a large red T-shirt, she was more than ready to meet with Frank to discuss her farm.

The crunch of gravel signaled the approach of Frank's car. Emily bounded down the stairs and exited the house into the humid night. The sun was just beginning to set, and the sky was pink and bright orange. Her heart skipped a beat when he touched her arm.

"It's nice to see you again," he said.

She nodded. "It's good to see you, too."

They were soon in his Lexus, taking the forty-minute drive toward downtown Baltimore. While driving, he told her about his recent conversations with Mark and how Trish still worried about the boy's erratic behavior. "I just wish his father would take a more active role in his life," he said. Emily was touched that Frank was so worried about his nephew. He spoke about it so frequently that he almost seemed like a father instead of an uncle.

"Do you mind if we go to the M&S Grill?" he asked when they arrived in Baltimore.

"I don't mind."

They entered the spacious restaurant, and she wondered why Frank had brought his briefcase with him. Their server approached. "We'd like an outside table," Frank informed her.

They ordered sodas when they were seated, and before the server could leave, Frank asked Emily a question. "Do you mind if I order for both of us?"

Food was the last thing on her mind. "I don't mind."

He ordered the flounder stuffed with crab imperial for both of them. "I've been doing a lot of eating out since I've been here. They make the best stuffed flounder."

His leg jiggled, and she touched his hand. "Are you okay?"

He sighed, looking toward the water. Boats bobbed in the hot breeze, and if there weren't so many issues between them, Emily could imagine having a pleasant time with Frank this evening.

His dark, mesmerizing eyes looked tortured. "No, I'm not okay. I need a drink."

She took a deep breath before voicing her next question. "Have you stopped drinking?"

"Sort of."

She frowned, still touching his hand. "What do you mean?" He told her how he'd stopped but then gotten intoxicated a few nights ago.

"Have you had a drink since?"

"No."

"Well, that's good then. You're on the right track." She tried to remain positive. Groups of teenagers strolled down the sidewalk, laughing as they passed on the busy pavement. "Has Devon Crandall been helping you?"

"Yes, I've been speaking to Devon over the last few weeks. He's a nice guy. He's caring."

"Yes, Devon's been through a lot. Did he share his testimony with you?"

"Yes, but he says I need to accept Christ if I want to find the strength to quit drinking completely."

"He's right. You've got to give God a chance." He ran his fingers over his short hair. "I know what your problem is." He remained silent. "You just like having complete control over your life."

Shock etched his face. "Yeah, so what?"

She shook her head. "But you're not controlling your life. The alcohol is." He winced, looking away. She squeezed his hand. "Frank, you can't control your life. You've got to let God help you."

They silently sipped their drinks for a few seconds before she gestured toward his briefcase. "Why did you bring that?"

Sighing, he removed a thick stack of cream-colored paper. "Emily, here's what I wanted to discuss with you."

He went through former tax returns and worksheets, explaining things to Emily. "Bottom line, you owe the IRS this amount of money." He pointed to a large figure on the paper.

Emily gasped. Their flounder arrived, but she had lost her appetite. The server left their food at the side of the table since they were still looking through Frank's papers. "Does this mean that if Laura and I don't pay this back, we'll lose the farm?"

Frank slowly nodded. "You could lose your farm." He quickly squeezed her hand. "But, there are ways to get around this that might work."

Emily blinked, still trying to drink in all the information. "Like what?"

He opened his napkin, avoiding her intense gaze. "I've already contacted the IRS—"

Her mouth dropped open. "You already reported my father?"

Grabbing her hand, he rubbed her palm, and her anger disappeared like a calm sea after a raging storm. "You know I wouldn't report your father to the IRS without clearing it with you or Laura first." He sighed, still holding her hand. "I just contacted them, without giving any personal information, and asked how I could advise a client about their situation. I didn't give the name of you or your family." He looked at her directly. "You could possibly get a bank loan, but

I doubt it since your father already has that farm mortgaged to the brim."

Emily continued to stare at Frank. "Do you have any other suggestions?"

Frank released her hand. Without answering her question, he pulled their plates from the side of the table, placing one in front of Emily and one in front of himself. He took a large bite of his flounder. She wondered how he could eat at a time like this and why he wouldn't answer her question.

She looked at her plate. The delicate white fish made her stomach churn. Taking her fork, she took a small bite.

Frank sipped his Coke. "Emily, I don't know how you feel about this."

"About what?" She put her fork aside, giving him her full attention.

"Well, I could give you the resources so your farm won't be confiscated."

She gasped. "I can't accept that kind of money from you."

He took another sip of Coke. "It could be a loan."

Gritting her teeth, she gazed toward the Chesapeake Bay. "I don't know if we could pay you back."

"Don't worry about that yet. I just want to do what I can so that you won't lose your farm." She stared at his bent head as he ate.

"Why would you do this for me?"

He didn't respond, and she wondered why he refused to look at her.

"Frank?" She placed her hand over his arm, forcing him to stop eating his meal.

"I. . .I just want to do this."

She looked at the patrons at the surrounding tables eating their evening meals, still trying to comprehend. "But I still don't understand. . ."

"I just want to help out a friend. What's wrong with that?"

She gazed at him, still trying to decipher his actions. She was unsure of what to say. Her deep feelings for Frank rushed through her, but she knew that if she was indebted to him, it would make their situation sticky. She pushed the papers toward him. "I can't talk about this anymore."

❧

Once Frank dropped her off, Emily's mind was spinning. She'd called Laura, but she was in the midst of serving dinner to Becky's family, and there was chaos in the background. "Mom, call me back later tonight when you get a chance. It's okay if you wake me up." Since there was a three-hour time difference, Emily didn't want Laura to hesitate about calling her if she thought she was going to wake her.

She sat on the couch in the dark living room and didn't realize she'd fallen asleep until the phone awakened her. She lifted the receiver. "Hello."

"Hey, Emily. It's Kelly."

"And Christine. Kelly has us on three-way."

"Hi, guys." Emily cleared her throat, still trying to clear her sleep-clogged brain.

"You sound like you're asleep," said Christine.

"Why are you all calling me on three-way?"

Christine responded, "Kelly wanted to tell us about her date."

"Emily, Antoine is the greatest!" said Kelly.

"He is?" asked Emily.

"Yeah, and you know I only met him a few weeks ago."

Emily nodded. "I remember you mentioning that. You said he's a new member of the choir."

"Well, he picked me up and gave me flowers!" She giggled. "And he took me to that fancy restaurant downtown!" She continued to gush about her date, not giving them a chance to respond. "He's so cute! He's got those light brown eyes and full lips that were made for kissing! We talked constantly through the meal, and when he dropped me off, he kissed my cheek, and he wanted to know when we could see each other again!"

Emily smiled. "I can tell you want to see him again."

Christine interjected. "You know she does. That's why she's calling us on three-way—so she can tell both of us about this wonderful man!"

"You guys, of course I want to see him again! Emily, it's been such a long time since I've dated anybody! I don't count Martin as dating since I only saw him twice."

"What happened with Martin, anyway? You never did tell us," said Emily.

Kelly groaned. "Well, I don't want to spoil a good evening talking about Martin."

Christine spoke. "Well, you should at least tell us what happened. You used to talk about him all the time, and then when you stopped seeing him, you wouldn't tell us why."

Kelly was silent for a few seconds before she spoke. "Well, when I was talking to Martin, we were talking about Christianity and faith. He blatantly asked me about, well, you know, having sex with him even though I was a Christian. He said that he was a Christian and his belief in God didn't stop him from doing what he wanted. That's when I decided I couldn't see him again. He said that I wasn't open-minded enough to date him, so that was the end of that."

All three women were silent for a few seconds before Emily spoke. "Well, you did the right thing, Kelly."

Christine sighed. "I'm beginning to wonder if any eligible men exist around here."

Kelly stated her opinion. "You never know. I guess we should just trust God and not worry about this so much."

Christine spoke. "Emily, what's been going on with you?"

Emily stood. "Hold on, my throat is dry. Let me get a glass of water." After filling a glass, she guzzled the cold liquid down, relieving her parched throat. When she sat back down, she told Kelly and Christine about her conversation with Frank.

"He offered you that money because he loves you!" said Kelly.

Emily wondered if Kelly was telling the truth. "Loves me? Frank doesn't love me. He's never told me this."

Christine interjected. "I haven't had a serious relationship in years, but from my limited experience, love is very complicated."

Emily clutched the receiver. "How do you guys know Frank loves me?"

Kelly sighed. "You should see the way he stares at you in church! He loves you, girl. I don't know why he hasn't told you yet, but I'm sure he'll tell you eventually."

"I don't think he loves me."

"Yes, he loves you, Emily," Christine said. "Now stop being so hardheaded about it and accept it for what it is."

They talked for a few more minutes before finally saying good night. But her friends' words rang in her ears as she trudged up the stairs to get ready for bed.

❦

Frank struggled through life the next few weeks. The urge to drink washed through him in waves, and he spoke to Devon daily. The older man had advised him to take it one day at a time. "That way your whole situation won't seem so hopeless," he'd said.

Emily filtered through his mind constantly, and he still wanted her to accept his offer of help for her farm. When his boss had called him into his office again, he'd reminded Frank that his temporary venture to start up the farm and ranch accounting division of their company had come to an end. "You've done an awesome job, and you've worked a tremendous amount of overtime. Would you like to stay as part of the farm and ranch division here in Baltimore, or would you rather return to Chicago? The choice is yours."

He walked along the grounds of the Cylburn Arboretum in Baltimore City, his boss's words running through his mind like a speeding train. Since Frank had agreed that it was best he return to Chicago, his boss had hired a replacement for him. The company event at the Arboretum was a threefold celebration: Frank's going-away celebration, the new hire's welcome party, and a celebration of the success of their new division.

His company had rented a room on the first floor of the building, and when his coworkers drank glasses of champagne, Frank thought he would lose his mind. He'd frowned when the alcoholic beverage was popped open by a catering employee. As the beige-colored liquid was poured into glass flutes, his boss must have noted his reaction when he'd approached him. "Don't frown so much, Franklin. We're off the clock now, so we can have a drink to celebrate our success. We do the same thing when we have our Christmas party every year."

Frank had nodded, heat rushing through him. His boss had placed his hand on Frank's arm. "You look like you could use a drink. Let me get you a glass."

Frank had shaken his head. "No. I'm not feeling too good right now. I think I'll go for a walk on the grounds." He'd practically fled the large mansion and onto the landscaped property. The warm sun soothed him as he walked farther away from the building. He finally found a bench outside in the massive garden. Colorful butterflies fluttered above the large expanse of flowers. The rainbow of blooms created a carpet of color, surrounding him with their scent. The leaves on the nearby trees were turning color, hinting at the autumn weather that was coming soon. "Lord, what am I going to do?"

He continued to take pleasure in his surroundings as thoughts filtered through his brain. He recalled Devon's advice. "Give the Lord a chance, son. That's about all you can do to keep the alcohol away." Emily's sweet face came to mind, and he recalled her words of wisdom as they'd shared dinner together. "Frank, you can't control your life. You've got to let God help you."

He recalled Julie's happiness once she'd accepted Jesus into her life. Tears stained his cheeks as a black-and-yellow butterfly hovered around his bench. He wiped his eyes, realizing he couldn't control his life on his own anymore. He needed help—in the worst way. "Lord, help me. I'm a sinner; please help me, Lord." His shoulders shook as he cried and accepted God's grace for his sins.

❦

A few days later when Emily returned home from running errands, she was shocked to see Frank's Lexus parked in her driveway. He'd been to church the last couple of Sundays but had rushed off before she had a chance to speak with him. Her farm's fate weighed upon her mind, and she realized that once Laura returned, they would need to sit down and decide what to do about the back taxes owed on their property.

She exited her truck, holding several bags of purchases. Frank sat on her screened-in porch, waiting for her. His trusty leather briefcase stood upright on the floor, and she wondered why he had brought it with him. They gazed at each other, silent.

"Hi," he finally greeted.

The bags grew heavy in her arms, and she almost dropped them before Frank came to her rescue. "Here, let me help you with those."

"Thanks," she mumbled. They carried the bags into the house and placed them on the table.

He touched her shoulder. "You look tired. Are you okay?"

"It's been a rough day."

"Did something happen?"

She dropped her purse on the table. "Yes, the inspector showed up this morning." Emily explained how the inspector would show up unannounced periodically, making sure their dairy farm fit the government's standards.

"Did he find anything wrong?"

"No, but he sure tried. He was here long enough, poking around. I just wanted him to leave."

"Did anything else happen?"

"Thunderbolt got out."

"Huh?"

"Thunderbolt is one of the cows. She's feisty and fast. She's new to the milking herd, and when Jeremy and I were letting the cows out to graze this morning, Thunderbolt ran right past us." She pouted. "It was awful. We ran into the road to get her back. It took us a whole hour to coax her back to the farm, and she held up traffic."

He glanced around the silent house. "Is Laura here?" he asked.

She placed a carton of milk in the refrigerator. "No, she's still in California."

"When will she be back?"

Emily sat, suddenly too weary to put the rest of the groceries away. "She'll be back next week. She has to start working at the cafeteria again because school's already started. She called the school, and they said she could start a couple of weeks late. The C-section is about healed, and Becky's getting used to the baby's constant demands." She talked about her stepsister's plight for a few minutes before she realized she was babbling. "I know you didn't come here to get an update on Becky's health."

"No, I didn't." Sunlight streamed into the bright, airy kitchen, highlighting Frank's pleasant features. Emily realized she could just sit and stare at this man forever. She pushed the thought from her mind, realizing there was little hope for them to have a relationship. He lifted his briefcase, placing it on the table. Snapping the gold locks open, he removed a sheaf of papers. "You never took the final paperwork for the audit of your farm." He placed the cream-colored papers on the table.

"Thanks."

"As soon as I leave, I want you to promise me you'll look through all this."

She gestured toward the papers. "I'll get to it eventually."

He shook his head. "Please promise me you'll at least glance through them after I've left."

His dark eyes were full of sadness when he gazed at her, and she wondered if everything was okay. "I promise." When silence weighed heavily in the kitchen again, she spoke. "You just came to bring me the papers?"

He sighed when he sat. He ran his fingers over his short dark hair, and the familiar gesture warmed her heart. "No, that's not the only reason I came." He paused. "I'm going back to Chicago."

Her heart stopped. "You're kidding."

"I wouldn't kid about this, sweetheart."

"But. . .but why?"

"I told you that I was initially here for a temporary time."

"You can't stay?" she mumbled.

He shook his head. "I'd like to but. . ." He balled his hands into fists. "I have to make things right with my folks." He took a deep breath. "I don't think I have much time left, so I have to go home."

"Did something happen with your parents?"

"Trish called me a few hours ago. My dad's had a stroke."

"Oh no! Will he be okay?"

"No, the doctors don't expect him to live long. I have to go home."

She patted his shoulder. "Of course you do. I'll be praying for you and your family." So many questions littered her brain like unwanted weeds in a garden. Would Frank be coming back? Would this be the last time she'd see him? Would he ever accept Christ?

"I don't know when I'll be strong enough to come back."

She took his hand. "Frank, please give God a chance. Just come to Him as you are, and He'll accept you. He'll give you the strength to get you through anything. You don't have to fix yourself before you come to Jesus."

"I've given up alcohol for a short time, and it's been terrible." He told her about his experience at the Cylburn Arboretum. "Emily, I'm a sinner in the worst way. Even before my father had a stroke, I was still planning on going to Chicago."

His words surprised her, and she realized they could find a way to make it work between them with the Lord's help. "Frank, we're all sinners. Although you say you've accepted Christ, it sounds like you're still harboring guilt. Jesus doesn't want us to feel guilty. Let Him take all that guilt and sadness off your shoulders. Jesus has already paid the price for all our sins. If you follow the Lord, that'll give you the strength you need."

"I'm a new Christian, and I'm still trying to make my life right. I don't know how long I can stay away from alcohol, even with the Lord on my side." With his father's predicament, he knew he'd find it hard not to drink. "It's unfair of me to want to be with you, knowing I'm so weak."

His words made her speechless. She stared at him, drinking him in, not knowing what to say or do. Soon he was beside her, and his lips touched hers in a brief, tender kiss. She didn't realize she was crying until Frank gave her a napkin from the dispenser on the table. "Are you coming back?" she asked softly.

"I don't know. I'd like to come back when I feel I'm no longer a threat."

"What do you mean?"

"I'm an alcoholic. You've never seen me when I'm drunk. It's not pleasant. It's not right for me to be with you if I turn back to the bottle again."

"We could try. With the Lord's help, we can make it work."

"I have faith, but I don't think my faith is as strong as yours. I'm still praying about it, asking the Lord to lead me into doing the right things. I know He wants me to return to Chicago and spend some time with my dad since I don't know how long he will live." He glanced away for a few seconds. "My mother's always depended on my dad, and I think it'll break her if he dies." He looked at his watch. "I have to get going."

"So you're driving back?"

"Yes, I had a moving company come and take my stuff to Trish's house. She lives in a large home outside of Chicago, and I'll be staying with her until I've made other living arrangements. The movers left this morning, and Trish is expecting them."

"Can we at least keep in touch? I'd like to know how your father is doing." She also wanted to know how Frank was doing.

"Yes, I'd like that."

She wanted to know if he wanted her to wait for him, but she couldn't bring herself to voice those words. He gestured toward the papers before removing his car keys from the pocket of his jeans. "Be sure to keep your promise to me and read those papers after I leave?"

She nodded, still speechless. The screen door banged shut when he left, and gravel crunched beneath his tires as he drove away from the farm.

She watched Frank's burgundy Lexus until it disappeared from view. She then took the stack of papers he'd left and sat on the porch.

The letter was from Franklin Reese, CPA, stating the validity of the financial papers and the results of his audit. Emily didn't understand most of the terms and language, but she recognized a lot of the stuff Frank had shown her at the restaurant the other day. The papers outlined the violations her father had committed and recommended going to the IRS with a payment plan to repay the back taxes. He'd also placed a side note, stating that his replacement, Melvin Sparks, could be entrusted to contact the IRS on their behalf and with filing the amended returns. If they repaid the money, he doubted there would be a lot of trouble from the government agency.

There was also a bill enclosed, noting Frank's hours, but the bill was marked

PAID IN FULL. Emily fingered the cream-colored stationery, shocked that they did not have to pay for Frank's labor.

Frank had also enclosed a check for enough money to cover the balance due to the IRS. She hugged the envelope to her chest. "Oh, Daddy, why did you have to die? Why did you have to be so dishonest?" She sniffed, crying tears of grief. "Lord, what am I supposed to do now? Daddy's dead, Frank is gone, and Laura won't be back for a while. I feel so lost and alone, Lord. Please help me find some peace."

After much prayer, thought, and deliberation, Emily decided to accept Frank's gift. The day she deposited the funds, she fell on her knees, saying a prayer to God.

Chapter 11

As the months passed following Frank's departure, Emily found that her thoughts of Frank continued to haunt her. He e-mailed her a few times, and she knew his father had eventually died. She'd wanted to call him, but she wasn't sure if he wanted to speak with her. She moped about the house, did farm chores, and helped their hired workers harvest the corn. Kelly and Christine came over often, and they called periodically, but her friends couldn't cheer her up. One day after church in November, Emily and her stepmother went downtown for a lazy afternoon. They stopped at the Baltimore Cupcake Company for a snack. Both of them chose chocolate truffle cupcakes with beautiful floral-patterned icing to go with their cups of Café du Monde.

They sat at a table, and the brilliant sunlight spilled into the space as they ate their treat. When Emily finished her cupcake, she was almost tempted to lick the stray icing from her fingers. "I wish I could have another one."

Laura gave her a mischievous grin. "Why don't we get another?"

"Mom!" Emily patted her hips. "I don't need the extra calories."

"Don't worry about it. You're so thin, and you're always out there doing farm chores. I don't think you have anything to worry about." Feeling naughty, Emily complied and returned to the counter, purchasing vanilla truffle cupcakes. Once they had finished their second round of cupcakes, Emily sipped her coffee. "Are you glad to be back in Monkton?" she asked Laura.

Laura shrugged. "I miss your father. But it is nice to be back and into a routine again. I like working at the school cafeteria and seeing the kids every day." A wistful look crossed her face as she stirred her coffee.

"Mom, what's wrong? You've been acting like something's been on your mind since you returned from Becky's."

Laura shrugged. "It's nothing I feel like talking about right now."

Emily figured Laura would tell her what was on her mind when she was ready. She gazed at the street, thinking about Frank and the last words they'd exchanged before he left for Chicago.

"You're thinking of Frank, aren't you?" asked her stepmother, sipping her coffee.

Emily placed her cup on the table. "How did you know?"

"I can always tell when you're thinking about him." They sat in silence for a few moments, watching the cars pass by on the street.

"I was just thinking about how I got to know him while he was here." She told Laura about the close bond he shared with his nephew and about how he used to mentor teens at the rec center in Chicago. Emily thought he'd make a great father but didn't want to voice that opinion. If she dwelled on that too much, it would just make her long for something that might never happen.

"You know, you've been through a lot lately."

Emily shrugged, sipping her hot drink. "I guess so."

"I have a suggestion to make."

"What's that?"

"I wondered if you wanted to go and visit your cousin Monica in Ocean City for a week."

"But what about the farm?"

"I've already spoken to some people, and we have enough extra help so that you can go on a vacation. You need it. When I was in Florida following Paul's death, it did wonders for my mental health."

"I don't know." She found some solace just spending time with the animals each day.

Her stepmother touched her hand. "You've been moody lately, and I know Frank really hurt your feelings when he left. I think a change in scenery may help you out of your mood."

When Emily finished her coffee, she told Laura she would call and check with Monica. If she said it was okay, she'd take her vacation the following week. Maybe the change in scenery was what she needed.

❧

The following week, Emily arrived at her cousin's house. Monica and her husband, John, welcomed her into their home. She also got a chance to visit with Monica's sister, Gina, and Scotty, Gina's blind nine-year-old son. The child read a lot of braille books and magazines, and Monica confided how Scotty's educational needs were what brought her together with John. She'd explained that John was Scotty's tutor, and that was how they'd met.

One day, following a fun-filled Saturday of sightseeing in Ocean City, they returned to Monica's house for dinner. "I'm going to start the oven," said John, kissing Monica's cheek before heading into the kitchen. He was making lasagna for their meal while Monica visited with Emily in the living room.

"John is very affectionate toward you," Emily commented.

Monica chuckled. "Yes, he is. I just never thought I'd fall so deeply in love."

"I'm sorry I missed your wedding last year. Dad had the flu, and I had to stay and take care of the farm."

Monica smiled. "That's okay." She stood and walked to the other side of the room, opening an oak cabinet and removing a large leather book. "Here are our wedding pictures."

Emily admired the photos. "These are beautiful."

"Thanks." Once she had looked at all the pictures, Monica told Emily some news. "I'm pregnant."

Emily's heart filled with joy. "You're kidding."

"Nope! We can hardly wait."

She hugged her cousin. "I'm so happy for both of you; I really am." When they broke their embrace, tears slipped from Emily's eyes, and Monica handed her a tissue.

She touched Emily's shoulder. "Cousin, why are you so sad?"

Emily wondered if Monica would truly understand her problems, but she had to tell Monica all that had happened since her father's death. "I just can't believe my father was a gambler." She told her about Frank, his drinking, his salvation, and his sudden disappearance from her life. "He's e-mailed me a few times, but I miss him like crazy."

"Why do you like him so much?" Monica asked.

"He's kind, he's caring, he's conscientious, and I like being with him. I like being around him. I hated his drinking, and the fact that he was unsaved really bothered me. Now that he's saved, I'd hoped we could work things out. But it looks like I was wrong. I just wish he wasn't afraid of turning into an alcoholic again, but I can't make his desire to drink go away."

"Does he still talk to you? Other than the e-mails?"

"He doesn't call me, but he is in Chicago right now, and I know his father died. We don't have constant contact, just an occasional e-mail."

"Have you thought about calling him?"

"No. I sense he doesn't want to talk to me." Another thought occurred to her. "You know, maybe he doesn't like me very much."

"He offered to save your farm for you. I think he likes you a lot, but he's working through his issues right now."

She shook her head. "No. There's no hope for us."

"Girl, where's your faith? If the Lord allowed John and me to be together, then I know there's hope for you and Frank."

"What do you mean?"

Monica gazed at the photo album. "John was an agnostic."

"Really? I didn't know that."

"Yeah. He didn't even know if he believed God existed. When he first started tutoring my nephew, we shared an instant attraction, but I knew there was no hope for us because of his beliefs."

"But he accepted Jesus," Emily guessed.

"He sure did. So, since God saw fit to bring John and I together, then He might see fit to bring you together with Frank."

"I just wish I could get Frank off my mind."

"Are you involved in any of the ministries at your church?" Emily told her about the outreach ministry. "Is there a singles group at your church?"

"There's one that started just shortly after Frank left. Kelly, Christine, and I joined, but I just haven't felt like going to the meetings. Why do you ask?"

"It might be more fun and fulfilling to hang out with other Christian singles. I remember when I was in the singles group at my church a long time ago, I never met anybody to date, but I had a good time. We'd have fun and fellowship time, and we'd go bowling, out to dinner, out to the movies." Monica shrugged. "It was fun, and it gave me something to do. Also, what do you like to do in your spare time besides work on your dairy farm?"

"Years ago I used to read novels, but it's something I just stopped doing."

"Well, why don't you start doing that again? If I recall, during the winter you don't have as much to do on your farm as you do during the summer months since you're not harvesting any crops or baling hay. If you're worried about spending a lot of money on books, you could always go to the library or a used book store."

"So you're saying that I need to keep myself busy and not worry about Frank so much?"

"Exactly. I certainly can't predict if he'll come back, but if it's the Lord's will, then Frank will come sweeping back to Monkton to be with you again. But if he doesn't come back, at least you'll be so occupied with your new activities that you'll barely notice. When I was pining after a man, another thing I did was get more acquainted with God. Why don't you try reading some more of the Word and focusing on God? I know it'd help."

"You make it sound so easy."

Monica touched Emily's shoulder. "By no means is it easy. I'm not saying doing all these things will make Frank disappear from your mind, but it might help. I can honestly say that I know how you feel, but you just have to take it one day at a time and try and focus on yourself and God until you find out what Frank's going to do."

Emily pondered Monica's words for the rest of the evening.

Chapter 12

Four months later

Would you like another soda?" Cameron Jacobs held Emily's hand, leading her to their seats at the spring gospel concert. People milled about, trying to find their seats in the arena as several waited near the stage, eager for the performance to start.

"I'm fine, Cameron." She put her cold soda aside, no longer thirsty.

Emily continued to think about Frank periodically and wondered why he had only e-mailed her briefly a few times. She still clung to Monica's hope that Frank would find help for his issues and return to Baltimore County; however, as time passed, her prayers remained unanswered, and she wondered if maybe the Lord was nudging her to let go of her fantasy of being with Frank.

During the holiday season a few months ago, she'd mailed him a Christmas card. She'd hoped and prayed for a response, but she had only received Frank's silence.

She gazed around the arena. The gospel concert was one of her favorite yearly events. This year, however, the festive music failed to lift her spirits. Sighing, she ran her fingers through her hair.

"I like your new haircut, Emily. It looks good on you."

Emily smiled her thanks to Cameron, although "new" wouldn't describe her haircut. A short time after her visit to Monica, she felt the weight of her long, dark hair to be too much to handle. She'd visited her hairdresser and asked for a short, snazzy cut.

The band warmed up, and Emily thought about the last four months of her life—about how she ended up coming to this gospel concert with Cameron.

Weeks following her visit with Monica, Cameron had asked her out yet again, so she finally relented and went out with the man. He was a person of strong faith, and she wondered if the Lord was trying to tell her that Cameron was the man she should pursue.

This was their fifth date, and so far Emily felt nothing for Cameron except feelings of friendship. He barely crossed her mind throughout her day, and he didn't haunt her dreams, unlike Frank.

"Emily!" Emily snapped out of her reverie, gazing at Cameron's confused expression. "The concert is over."

"Oh, sorry." She smiled and stood, gathering her coat. Cameron helped her with her garment, and she watched several other members of the audience retrieve their things as they headed to the large parking lot.

They drove home in silence. Emily gazed at the brightly lit windows of the stores downtown. Huddling into her coat, she was eager to return home and finish reading the Christian cozy mystery novel she'd started earlier that week. When Cameron pulled into the lot, she noticed another car in her driveway.

"Are you and your mother expecting company tonight?"

Emily frowned at the unfamiliar car. "I don't think so. But sometimes people from the church will drop by and visit." She remained silent when Cameron rushed out of the car and opened her door for her.

He walked her to the bottom of her porch. Emily sensed from the eager expression on Cameron's face that he was anticipating a good night kiss or an invitation inside for a piece of Laura's apple pie. She quickly bid him good night and turned away, not even giving him a chance to kiss her.

He stopped her with a question. "You don't like me very much, do you?"

She turned toward him again. "I think you're a nice man."

"Nice? You don't like me the way you liked that accountant that used to work out here. I saw the way you used to look at him in church."

Emily didn't want to hurt Cameron's feelings. "I think you're a strong, good man, and I admire your faith in God."

His shoulders drooped. "I won't ask you out anymore, Emily. I feel like I'm wasting my time."

She didn't want him to feel bad. "Cameron. Don't get mad."

"I'm not mad. It's just. . .whenever I'm with you, I feel like you're not with me."

She frowned, squinting at him in the darkness. "What do you mean?"

"Your mind is always on something. Half the time when I speak to you, I have to repeat myself. I almost get the feeling you can't wait for our dates to end."

Emily inwardly winced, hating that Cameron could read her so easily. "I'm sorry, Cameron." She held out her hand, not wanting things to end on a bad note. "We're still friends, right?"

He gave her a small smile, shaking her hand. "Yeah, we're still friends. I'll be seeing you when I come to get your milk tomorrow." He gestured toward the porch. "Since your house is dark and you don't recognize that car in your driveway, I'll just walk you to your door and make sure you get in okay."

"Thanks." His heavy footsteps followed her up the porch steps as she opened the creaky screen door. Cameron was right behind her as she tried to locate the door handle to the house in the darkness.

"Emily." A figure appeared, and Emily almost screamed when Cameron jumped on the person trespassing on their porch. Cameron and the trespasser landed on the floor, making a huge racket. "Get off me! Emily, it's me, Frank!"

"Oh my." Her voice trembled and her hands shook as she jerked the kitchen door open, turning on the light. The men stood simultaneously, Cameron glaring at Frank.

"You could have let Emily know you were on the porch instead of scaring her," Cameron said. "Emily, do you want me to stay, or are you okay alone with him?" Cameron shot a look at Frank.

"I'm fine, Cameron. Thanks for seeing me to my door." Cameron nodded, took his exit, and drove away, his taillights disappearing as he rounded the corner.

Her fright subsided when she entered the kitchen, and she quickly disarmed their recently installed burglar alarm before beckoning Frank inside. Her heart was pounding so hard, she felt it would pop out of her chest.

Suddenly, Frank was bathed in a warm glow, and Emily noticed the changes in him. He removed his leather jacket, and her breathing intensified when she looked up into his cocoa brown eyes. She gazed at his face, which now sprouted a thick beard and mustache.

"Frank, I. . . Why are you here?" Her voice shook, and she slowly sat at the kitchen table.

He shrugged, continuing to stare. "I came to see you. Laura wasn't home, so I decided to wait for you on the porch. Didn't you notice my car outside?"

Emily nodded. Her legs felt weightless as blood rushed to her head. "It's not the same car you had. . .you had when you left."

He chuckled. "That's right. I'd forgotten that you haven't seen my new car."

She shrugged. "When I saw your car, I just figured we had a visitor. I don't know where Laura is," she began before she spotted the note on the refrigerator. Emily read the note, which said that her stepmother was going to be spending the night with a troubled church member. "Laura won't be home tonight. She's been really busy since she joined the church's outreach program." She placed the note on the table.

"I don't recall Laura being in the outreach ministry before. I thought you were a part of that ministry."

She didn't feel like talking about church activities. But she forced herself to comment on Frank's observation. "I decided to stop being in that ministry, and my stepmother offered to take my place." She shrugged. "I had other ministries I wanted to be involved with." She pointed to the pile of books in the corner of the kitchen. "I've been reading some good Christian novels lately, and I've started a book club at my church. I've also been involved with the singles ministry, too.

These things keep me busy. I still have a lot of chores to do on the farm, but not nearly as many as during the summertime."

When he began asking questions about her farm and her herd, Emily answered before she finally stopped herself, not wanting to act like things were okay between them. "Are you here visiting?" she asked abruptly.

"Emily, I'm back in Monkton for good now." Emily stared at Frank, wondering if this was another dream. "A lot has happened to me over the last six months."

She listened to him, still finding it hard to believe he was in her kitchen, talking as if they'd just seen each other yesterday. He ran his hand over his head, and the familiar gesture warmed her heart. "You know I was pretty messed up when I left."

"You mean with your drinking?"

He nodded. "You know I had a big problem with that. It was the only way I had to deal with Julie's death and my parents' decision not to accept her into the family."

"Have you stayed sober since you've been gone?"

"I haven't had a drink since that day I told you I'd stopped. But it's been a real struggle."

"Has it been more of a struggle since your father passed?"

"Yes. My father's death hit the family hard. It was so much to handle all at one time. My sister helped me out a lot with strengthening my faith."

"How are Trish's children? I'm assuming you spent a lot of time with them while you were in Chicago."

"Mark and Regina are fine. Trish and I are thankful that Mark hasn't gotten into any more trouble, but we still think he feels hurt because his father won't come to visit him very often."

"Did you find a nice church home in Chicago?"

"Yes. Although I have a church family in Chicago, I call Devon Crandall a lot since we've become friends. I also kept thinking about what you told me right before I returned to Chicago. You told me that I didn't need to fix myself before coming to Jesus, that He'd accept me as I am. I thought about that a lot over the last few months."

"I'm glad I said something that could help you. But did your father's death make you want to start drinking again?"

He stared at her with his beautiful brown eyes. "I was tempted to drink, yes. But I didn't. I had to pray to the Lord every day to make it through the day without having a drink." He opened his mouth as if he were going to say more, but he remained silent.

"Were you going to say something else?"

"No." Silence filled the kitchen, almost as if each of them had to digest the presence of the other.

Frank massaged her fingers, and she didn't have the strength to pull away. "I've missed you so much. You don't know how many times I've picked up the phone to call you but then decided against it."

She shrugged as feelings of joy and apprehension continued to course through her veins. "Why didn't you call? I wondered how you were doing. I sent you a Christmas card, and you never responded."

He sighed. "Because I had so many things to sort through and to work out in my life, I didn't want to call you before I'd set my life straight," he repeated.

"So everything is fine with you now?"

"Yes, it is. I asked if I could transfer back to the Monkton office, and they let me transfer."

"And now what are you going to do?"

"I'd like for us to date and get to know each other again."

Emily couldn't believe his words. "Date me?"

He sat up. "I'm a new man now. I'd like for you to get to know me better, and I'd like to spend some time with you again."

"I can't believe you did all this—relocated and everything—without calling me first. You could have warned me you were coming."

"I was sitting on the porch when you were talking to Cameron. I heard everything he said. I know you don't have feelings for him."

Emily inwardly winced, upset that Frank had heard such a private conversation. It was also highly upsetting that Cameron had mentioned Frank when they were talking. Before she could speak, Frank made another comment. "Are you dating somebody else besides Cameron?"

"I don't think that's any of your business." He dropped her hand, frowning. "I'm sorry. I shouldn't have said that."

"You're angry with me."

"I'm just. . .I'm just surprised to see you. You didn't even call me to tell me you were coming. You could have at least called and let me know you'd be here instead of sneaking on my porch and waiting for me."

He frowned. "I wasn't sneaking. It's not my fault that you were out on a date when I decided to come."

"You could have at least warned me that you'd be here."

"I felt the Lord leading me to come back here and live. I should have called you, but I guess I just wasn't thinking clearly. I wanted to surprise you."

"Well, you did surprise me. I—"

"I love you." His voice was so low that she had to strain to hear it.

"What?"

"I said I love you, Emily. I know it's hard to believe, but I do. I've loved you for months, but I knew there was no hope between us until I straightened out my life." He scooted closer to her and kissed her palm.

She pulled her hand away. "I don't know if I'm ready for us to date, Frank."

Frank's face fell. "I understand. Will you at least think about going out with me tomorrow?" When she remained silent, he found pen and paper on the kitchen counter. After writing something down, he placed the paper in her palm. "I've missed you, Emily, and I hope you'll let me take you out tomorrow. Here's my phone number. Just call me and let me know when you've decided if you'd like to spend some time together."

She mutely nodded, still trying to come to terms with his sudden presence in her home. "Remember that I do love you, Emily. Just give me some time to show you how I feel and how I've changed. I'll try not to disappoint you," he vowed.

Emily nodded, watching him leave, already deciding she would go out with him the following day.

❧

Frank whistled as he prepared for his date with Emily the next day, hoping and praying she would willingly accept him into her life. He had purchased a large heart-shaped box of imported Swiss chocolates and an exquisite diamond pendant.

He ran his fingers over the sparkling gem, imagining the jewel nestled against Emily's caramel-colored throat. He then grabbed his coat, headed out the door, and drove down the familiar route to the Coopers' farm.

Since he was now renting an apartment near Monkton, he arrived at Emily's house in minutes and knocked at her door. He heard the sound of high heels clicking on the kitchen floor before Emily opened the door.

His eyes widened when he saw her wearing a fancy burgundy dress with matching shoes. Her short hair framed her face, drawing attention to her full copper-colored lips and the tiny freckles sprinkled across her nose.

He kissed her hand. "Emily, it's good to see you again."

She nodded, leading him into the living room. "I'm glad to see you, too."

He glanced around the silent house. "Where's your stepmom?" They sat on the tattered couch, and he placed his bag of gifts on the scarred wooden coffee table.

"She's upstairs taking a nap."

"Is she okay?"

"She's fine. After work yesterday and today she was with a family in need with the church outreach. She just came home a few hours ago, so she said she wanted to take a nap." Emily frowned as she glanced up the stairs.

"What's wrong?"

She shrugged. "Laura's been different since her daughter had the baby."

"How?"

She shrugged again. "It's hard to say. I know something has been bothering her for a long time, but she won't talk to me about it."

"Maybe you should ask her about it again. I'm sure if it was something important she would have told you by now."

"No. Don't assume that. Laura can be close-mouthed about a problem for a long time before she says anything about it."

"I'm sure Laura will tell you when she's ready." He paused for a few seconds, glancing around the room. "So, how have you been?"

"Okay, I guess."

"Do Jeremy and Darren still come to help you milk the cows?"

"No, since basketball season started, they said it was too much for them to handle with classes and homework and all. They're both on the basketball team, so that complicates things with their schedules."

"So you're doing the milking by yourself every day?"

"Pretty much. I'll probably get somebody to help me when the weather turns warm again. I think I told you last summer that we go through five hay cuttings, so that's one thing that adds a lot of work during the summer months."

The floral scent of her perfume filled the room with sweetness. He took a deep breath, removing the chocolates and the pendant from the bag. He presented her with his gifts. "I bought these for you. I hope you like them."

She smiled, opening the small box and admiring the diamond pendant. "My goodness! You shouldn't be buying this for me." Her large eyes were full of apprehension as he removed the pendant and placed it on her neck. The gem twinkled against her caramel skin, and Frank was pleased with his purchase. "I also brought you some candy."

"You really shouldn't be buying this for me. I haven't seen you for months and—"

He squeezed her shoulder. "But it looks good on you. If you don't want to wear it, I'll understand." He sighed with relief when she didn't attempt to remove the piece of jewelry. He checked his watch. "We'd better hurry if we want to get there before the comedy show begins."

She fingered the pendant before she stood. "Frank, I need to be honest with you. I still feel funny about your being here so suddenly," she began.

"Emily, I know this is sudden. I probably should have handled this differently and called you first. How about we have a long talk about everything after the show?" When Emily nodded in agreement, they drove to Baltimore to see a

Christian comedienne. Frank recalled Emily saying last summer how much she'd wanted to see this entertainer when she came to town, so he was glad he had been able to secure tickets. He tried to enjoy the funny skits during the show, but the sad, despondent look in Emily's eyes haunted him throughout the evening.

Afterward they stopped for hot chocolate at Starbucks. She still seemed sad, so he took her hand, wanting to make her feel better.

She finally smiled, pulling her hand away before sipping her hot drink.

She looked outside at the people passing by the window. "What's on your mind?" he asked.

"I was just thinking that because of you, I'm still living on my farm. Due to the increase of robberies in town, my stepmother insisted we get an alarm system, and we could afford it since you had. . .helped us out financially like that." She squeezed his hand. "Frank, I am truly grateful for what you did for me and Laura. I really am. I promise we'll pay the money back," she said softly, her eyes suddenly filling with tears.

His heart skipped a beat when he moved to her side of the table and sat beside her, pulling her into his arms.

"Emily, I'm not worried about the money. Now, what's the matter?"

He relished the feel of her soft hair in the crook of his neck, her tears splattering against his crisp white shirt. "Oh, it's nothing." Her slim brown body fit into his arms perfectly, and he just wanted to hold her forever.

"Well, something must be wrong if you're crying," he persisted, wondering if he would ever understand why women were so strange.

She sniffed. "My life has just been so crazy since my daddy passed. I had to get used to his death; then you showed up, and then I had to get used to the attraction we shared while I came to grips with the fact that you were an unsaved alcoholic. Then you found that incriminating evidence against my father, and I had to get used to the fact that my father wasn't as perfect as I thought him to be." She swallowed, and he continued to hold her. Her hands were shaking, so he took her hands into his, hoping to calm her down. "Then I wondered if there were other facts about my father that I needed to know about." She gave him a watery smile, and he handed her a tissue. She blew her nose and gazed out the window.

"Go on," he urged.

She sniffed loudly. "Then you helped me save my farm, and then you left." She snapped her fingers to emphasize her point. "Even though you said goodbye, I still wondered if you were coming back. And then, months later, you appear on my doorstep to pick up where we left off like nothing was wrong. Yes, things have been a bit crazy since the beginning of last summer, Frank. I feel like my life has been one big emotional roller coaster."

He released her and faced her directly. Her head was down, so he lifted her chin with his fingers, staring directly into her watery eyes. "I hurt you when I left suddenly?" The realization of what he did hit him like a freight train. She nodded. "I'm so sorry, Emily. I was thinking about turning my life around, getting myself back together in Chicago. Leaving seemed to be the best choice." He blew air through his lips, still gazing at her. "Plus, I knew I was in love with you, and I couldn't stand being around you all the time, seeing you, knowing we couldn't be together because I was an alcoholic. I guess I was too selfish to realize how my actions might hurt you."

He pressed his lips to her forehead. "You know, staying wasn't an option for me. When my dad died, you don't know how close I came to drinking again." He took her hand. "I'm still struggling with my alcoholism, and I wanted to be sure that I'd been sober for a long time before I came back here. I wanted to be here with you. I wanted to see you, but I felt like if I were here and started drinking again, things wouldn't have worked out with us, and I would have hurt you more by being here instead of staying away." He squeezed her fingers. "Please say you'll forgive me. I do love you, and I hope that you'll believe me eventually."

"I understand why you left, but I still have a hard time starting over with you again." She grabbed a napkin and wiped her eyes. "You know, I was wondering why you bought me those gifts."

He frowned. "What do you mean?"

She touched the pendant. "You leave for six months, and then you show up at my house with this necklace, thinking that things are fine between us and we can start dating."

He shrugged again. "So?"

"So, it almost seems like you're trying to bribe me to go out with you. I feel like you want to use your money to buy nice things to fix the situation so that you can get your way."

"What else am I supposed to do?" He threw his hands up in the air, exasperated.

"Frank! This necklace means nothing to me. It's pretty and I love it, but if I could exchange this necklace for some of your time during your six-month absence so that I wouldn't have had to worry about you so much, I'd exchange it in a heartbeat."

He gripped his cup. "Do you mean to tell me that you would exchange the necklace just so you could have had some contact with me when I disappeared for six months?"

She nodded. "If you had just kept me in the loop and talked to me and told me that you might possibly return, my mind would have been more at ease, and I would have felt better." She continued to caress the necklace. "This necklace is just a piece of jewelry, but your honesty is priceless. Do you understand?"

"I think so. I'm sorry. It's just that. . ."

Emily touched his wrist, urging him to continue. "Go on."

"It's just that, growing up, my father wasn't always nice to my mother. He had affairs, and my mother would get upset and cry. He always managed to buy her something—expensive jewelry or a trinket that she would like. Things would be better for a few months before he started acting up again." He sipped his chocolate. "I thought women liked getting nice things, and I thought it showed how much I want to spend time with you."

He looked out the window, staring at the people walking down the sidewalk. "You know how I take a special interest in Trish's children and how I used to mentor boys at the rec center in Chicago?"

"Yes."

"Well, while I was home, I thought about why I'm so passionate about kids having a father in their lives, especially boys. As I've been meeting with alcoholic support groups, talking things out, I've discovered that my passion for that stems from the way I wished my dad had treated me. He always provided for Trish and me financially, but we didn't do a whole lot of things together as a family. He was gone a lot, working long hours, and he was always going away on business trips."

"Frank, you've never told me any of this before."

"Honey, I don't think I even realized half this stuff about myself until recently."

"It sounds like your time away has given you a chance to really think about your life."

He agreed before taking another sip of his hot drink. "Anyway, Julie, when I was married to her, used to complain about my buying her things after we'd had an argument. She said my generosity didn't make the problem go away and that we needed to talk about it."

She nodded. "Julie was right. But you're just following your father's example, so it's understandable why you would think that a new item might make a woman feel better." She changed the subject. "Were you able to straighten out your relationship with your parents?"

"I'm glad I went to Chicago, because both Trish and I were able to spend some quality time with my father before he passed. We convinced him to accept Christ before his death."

Emily squeezed his hand. "That's wonderful, Frank."

He nodded. "Things are still a little shaky with my mom. In my heart, I feel I've forgiven them for the way they treated Julie, but I still feel bad for my mom. She's still not saved, but Trish and I are working on her. She's grieving so hard for my dad, and Trish and I are doing all that we can to console her."

"At least Trish is still there in Chicago with her. Did your mother object to your leaving again?"

Frank thought about his mother. "Yes, she objected a lot, but I felt strongly about coming back and seeing you again, and I didn't think it was right for me to stay away. She accused me of abandoning my familial duties since my dad had passed. I reminded her that Trish and her family were in Chicago to keep her company."

"Does she know about me?"

"Yes."

"Does she know that I'm a dairy farmer? I know she didn't approve of Julie's background. I'm not from a privileged background either."

He didn't want to tell her that his mother already objected to his dating her. Since he sensed Emily was already apprehensive about having a relationship with him, he certainly didn't want to scare her away with that fact. "Let's not talk about my mom right now. Let's talk about us."

She stared at the whipped cream and marshmallows floating on her cup of hot chocolate. "Frank, I'm not sure this is such a good idea."

His heart skipped a beat. "What do you mean?"

She pointed to the hot chocolate. "Us spending time together, drinking hot chocolate, dating, whatever you call it."

His mouth dropped open, and he touched the tiny mole on the side of her neck. "Emily, I've told you how much I've changed over the last six months. The least you can do is give me a chance to prove myself. Why would you not want us to date?"

She looked at him, her eyes sparkling with fear and apprehension. "I can't deny there is something between us, but even though you're saved now, I find it hard to trust you." She raised her hands in the air. "You've been gone for six months with hardly any contact. If we start dating and then I get emotionally involved with you, what's to stop you from leaving again for another six months?" She fingered the paper mug. "What if you leave again and never come back?"

"Oh, Emily." He tried to pull her into his arms, but she pushed him away. "Frank, you need to give me some time and space to think and pray about this. I feel so confused right now."

He closed his eyes briefly, silently praying for a way to make her understand how much he truly loved her. "I'll be praying for you, too, Emily."

She raised her eyebrows. "You'll be praying for me?"

He nodded. "Yes. I'll be praying that God will make you understand just how much you mean to me. I'll also pray that God will soften your heart to forgive me for leaving you for six months." He stopped and swallowed, still trying to find the right words to say. "I'll also hope and pray that Jesus will allow you to trust me. I know you don't trust me right now, but maybe, just maybe, that'll change."

"It just sounds so odd, you speaking of prayer."

He shrugged. "I told you I've accepted Christ. I'm a saved man, so of course I'm going to pray."

She seemed to be thinking about his statement, weighing his words. "I do need some time to think about this." Her toffee-colored fingers caressed the sparkling diamond nestled on her neck. "I also think you should take your gift back. It's not right for me to accept such an expensive item from you if I'm not sure what's going to happen between us."

"Keep the necklace."

"But, Frank, I really don't feel comfortable accepting things from you."

He sighed. "Why don't you keep the gifts until you decide what you'd like to do? Think and pray about it for as long as you want. Take all the time you need. I understand why you're hesitant about spending time with me again. When you feel more comfortable about it, just let me know, and we can talk about it." They were silent as the whirring sound of the espresso machine filled the shop. Frank finally spoke. "Come on, I'll take you home now."

She nodded, then stood and gathered her coat. "All right." She remained silent as he helped her put on her coat, and they walked to his car.

Chapter 13

The following Sunday, Emily stood in the pew, accompanying the choir with the rest of the congregation in the closing hymn. Laura grabbed her arm after they exited the sanctuary. Before Laura could speak, Kelly walked toward them from the front of the church, still sporting her red-and-white choir robe. "Emily, I've been meaning to call you for the last few days, but I've been busy." She seemed slightly out of breath, and tendrils of dark hair fell into her face.

Laura squeezed Emily's arm. "Kelly, did you know Frank was back in town? I just saw him in the sanctuary."

Kelly frowned, staring at the older woman. "Of course I do, Mrs. Cooper! Didn't you know?"

"No, I didn't." She gazed at her stepdaughter. "Now I understand why you've been so quiet and moody the last couple of days. Why didn't you tell me that Frank was back? Have you had a chance to speak with him yet?"

Frank entered the foyer. "Yes, Laura, I've seen your daughter. Twice."

Emily glanced at Frank. "Hi, Frank."

He smiled, touching her shoulder. "Hi, Emily."

Mrs. Cooper spoke to the accountant. "You've changed so much over the last six months, Frank, I barely recognized you sitting in front of the sanctuary. How are you?" She embraced him, and he smiled.

"I've been okay. A lot has been going on in my life since I've been gone."

Laura's brown eyes twinkled. "Well, we're going out to lunch. Why don't you join us and tell us all about it?"

He looked at Emily briefly before focusing on Laura again. "I'm afraid I can't, but you ladies have yourselves a nice lunch." He waved, following the rest of the crowd out of the church.

"Emily Jane Cooper, what in the world is going on here?" Her stepmother folded her arms in front of her chest, impatiently tapping her foot. Kelly stared at Emily also, and Emily felt as if she were being judged by a jury.

"Emily!" Kelly grabbed her arm, and Emily gazed at her best friend.

"What?"

"Let me put my choir robe away. Then we can go to lunch, and you can tell me and your mom what's happening between you and Frank."

"Okay."

"Hi, Emily." Christine approached, wearing a new dress. She held up her purse. "I got a new bag on sale at one of the shops at the Inner Harbor, fifty percent off."

"Why did you buy the purse?" asked Kelly.

Christine pursed her lips. "I had a huge argument with my sister the other day. When I got off the phone, I just wanted something to make myself feel better, so I went shopping. I think I did pretty good since I only purchased two items and one of them was on sale."

Emily's stepmother fingered the purse. "It looks lovely, Christine. We're about to go to lunch if you'd like to join us."

Soon they were seated amid the Sunday afternoon crowd at the Wagon Wheel. Emily told her mother, Kelly, and Christine about the two times she'd seen Frank and about her fears. "I've been praying about it, and I want to date Frank, I really do, but it's just so hard to trust him after all that's happened. Also, I'm wondering what will happen when he has rough times. Will he still turn to alcohol? I know he's saved, but that doesn't mean he's perfect."

"Neither are you," Kelly retorted.

"What's that supposed to mean?" asked Emily.

"Frank explained why he left. He told you himself how messed up his life was before he found Christ. He finally admitted he had a problem with alcohol, he beat his habit, he's accepted Christ, and now he's back. It may have taken him some time to be honest with you, but I can understand why he stayed away."

"But he could have said something before now. He only e-mailed me a couple of times, and that was it."

Laura touched Emily's hand. "Honey, Kelly is right. I'm not saying you need to pick up where you left off, because you're right to be cautious, but maybe you can get to know each other again."

Emily shook her head. "I don't know."

Laura continued to speak. "Emily, I think Frank's silence was just his way of protecting you. He feared he wasn't strong enough to stay away from alcohol. He didn't want you to get emotionally involved with him if he ended up drinking again."

Kelly nodded. "I agree, Mrs. Cooper. I think it's good that you were honest with Frank, Emily. He knows he's made a mistake, and I'm sure he feels bad about hurting you. But I also sense that he felt as if he had no choice, because if he was here and he messed up again, he would have ended up hurting you even more."

Christine spoke. "I agree with Mrs. Cooper and Kelly. You need to date Frank and just take it slow. Get to know each other again. He's already told you that he loves you and wants to give you two a chance." She twirled the pearls around her neck. "You know, if you don't at least give him a chance, I think you'll regret it."

She glanced at her friend. "Do you think so?"

Christine nodded firmly. "Yes, I do think so. I could see you wondering for years and years what would have happened if you'd given Franklin Reese a chance way back when."

Emily ate the rest of her meal in silence, allowing Kelly, Christine, and her stepmother to chat without her input. At one point, Laura pulled out her wallet and showed Kelly and Christine recent pictures of her grandbaby.

Emily's mind was still plagued with thoughts about Frank when she milked the cows later that evening.

⁂

The following Sunday, Emily entered the sanctuary with her stepmother. She anxiously scanned the crowd of parishioners sitting in the wooden pews.

"Looking for somebody in particular?" Laura whispered in her ear.

Emily gritted her teeth, wishing her affection for Frank wasn't so obvious. She wondered where he was. The service was about to start, and he still had not shown up.

The choir entered the choir loft, and the small church was suddenly filled with holy music.

Kelly joyfully sang the opening hymn with the rest of the choir. Emily attempted to sway to the music, but thoughts of Frank and his whereabouts filled her mind.

When the choir completed their selections, Pastor Brown stepped into the pulpit, and his deep, booming voice filled the sanctuary. "Before I start the sermon this morning, I wanted to introduce one of our new members. I assume a lot of you have met Franklin Reese."

Emily's heart skipped a beat as she clutched her Bible. A few of the parishioners nodded in response.

"Well, he's been through a life-changing experience, and he's requested that I allow him to tell you all about it. So, here's Franklin Reese!" He raised his hand toward the pulpit door, and Frank stepped onto the dais. They shared a handshake before Frank stood in front of the microphone.

Emily openly stared at the man who was slowly capturing her heart. He looked handsome sporting a dark suit and a cream-colored shirt and tie.

"Good morning."

Parishioners loudly responded to Frank's greeting.

"I've come to tell you this morning about how I came to accept Christ into my life."

During the next fifteen minutes, Emily listened to Frank tell details of his troubled college years and about the first time he realized he was an alcoholic. He then spoke of his sobriety, his first marriage, his strong love for his wife, her salvation, and her sudden violent death. "Friends, when my wife died, I felt a part of me had died also. I was mad, angry, and bitter. I was upset with my parents since they didn't accept my wife because of her background." He told of his return to alcoholism, the joy and warmth he received when attending Monkton Christian Church, and his support from Devon Crandall and the alcoholic support group. He mentioned there was a certain parishioner who urged him to accept Christ, and without mentioning a name, Frank's eyes met Emily's. He told of his salvation at Cylburn Arboretum and his sudden flee back to his hometown, hoping to put his life back in order.

He ended his testimony by telling how Christ had made a difference in his life. "My life is far from perfect, and I still have problems, but they don't seem like such a burden now that I'm relying on Jesus." A tear glistened on Frank's cheek as he spoke of the deep love he had for his Savior. The congregation stood, applauding Frank's courage in openly proclaiming his salvation journey.

Emily barely heard Pastor Brown's message afterward because she was still thinking about Frank's speech.

⁂

A few weeks following Frank's testimony, Emily walked toward her house after milking the cows. She removed her barn boots before opening the door and entering her home. The scent of chicken filled the air, and Laura removed a pan of biscuits from the oven. "Hi, Emily."

Emily sniffed. "Hi, Mom. You made chicken and dumplings and biscuits?" Her stomach grumbled with hunger, and she looked forward to the meal.

Laura smiled, but her eyes seemed sad as she looked at Emily. "Yes, I haven't made it in a long time, and I know how much you like my chicken and dumplings." Once Emily had washed up and changed, she joined her stepmother at the table. After Laura said grace, Emily piled her plate with food. "I made chocolate cake for dessert." Emily smiled before she stuffed a bite in her mouth.

Laura tapped her foot, sipping a cup of coffee, and Emily savored the tasty meal. "Aren't you going to eat?"

Laura shook her head. "I'm too nervous to eat."

Emily stopped eating, dropping her fork on her plate. "Why would you be nervous?"

Her stepmother's hand shook as she set her cup back on the saucer. "You've probably guessed that something heavy has been on my mind since Becky had her baby."

"Yes. When Frank came back to town, that was one of the first things I told him. I knew something was bothering you, but I didn't know what it was."

Laura sipped her coffee. "Well, you know how I've always wanted to improve my relationship with my daughters."

Emily nodded.

Laura shrugged. "I missed a lot of their childhoods because my ex-husband was granted custody. Although I saw them for a few weeks each summer, I still felt as if they resented me, especially Becky. She was only five when the divorce happened, and I sometimes think she blames me for what happened to her."

"Children are not always rational."

Laura shrugged. "Adults are not always rational either." She stared at her coffee cup as she continued to speak. "I think Becky still blames me a little bit for the divorce, but we've been discussing what's happened over the years, and I think we're getting closer. When Becky had her baby and we spent a lot of time together, she told me that she and her husband had discussed it, and eventually she wants to go back to work. She said she was tired of being a housewife and mother full-time and she wanted to reenter the workforce."

"But Becky has three kids now, and all of them are under five. Won't she and her husband be paying a lot in daycare costs if she decides to work again full-time?"

Laura took Emily's hand, looking directly into her eyes. "They won't have to pay as much in daycare costs if I'm taking care of their kids."

Emily's heart skipped a beat, and she gasped. "You're leaving?"

Laura nodded, squeezing Emily's hand. "Honey, I know when I first married your father, you and I got off to a rocky start, but I've grown to love you as a daughter."

"I love you, too, Mom."

"I've told you how I've always regretted not having a better relationship with my daughters. This is something that I really want to do. I can be there to help raise my grandchildren and solidify my relationship with Becky."

Emily wiped the tears from her eyes. "I'm going to be on this farm all by myself." She did not find the thought to be soothing. She recalled how empty the house felt when Laura was gone the other two times.

"Honey, I know. I've been struggling with this decision since I returned last September. That's what's been bothering me so much. I never said anything, because Becky didn't have a job yet."

Emily sniffed as Laura handed her a tissue. As she dried her eyes, she noticed that Laura was crying also. "So Becky's found a job?"

"Yes. She's going to be starting in one month, so I'm not leaving right away, but I promised her I would be there to help out when it's time for her to start her new job. We've already spoken about the finances, and she'll be paying me an amount comparable to what I'd been earning in the lunch room at the school."

The shocking news rocked Emily's world, and the two women embraced before Emily finished her meal.

❧

After Laura made her announcement about leaving, Emily spent the next few weeks thinking about her situation with Frank and praying about it. When Laura did leave, it was heartbreaking for Emily. She drove her stepmother to the airport and promised that if she found adequate help on the farm, she'd come and visit Laura and her family within the next year. She still participated in her church book club, and she was still involved in the singles ministry. She kept a busy routine, trying to figure out what to do about Frank. She didn't mention the matter anymore to Laura, Kelly, or Christine, but left it solely in the Lord's hands.

When Frank had been in town for a month and a half, Emily fell to her knees before bedtime, continuing to seek the Lord's guidance. "Lord," she whispered, "let me know what You want me to do. I keep thinking about Frank. When I see him at church, worshipping and praising You on Sunday, I just want to walk up the aisle, sit beside him, and praise You with him. I want to spend time with him and get to know him all over again now that he's a Christian. Does this mean he's the right man for me, Lord?" When she finished her prayer, calming peace flowed through her.

She slid between her crisp, clean cotton sheets, and when she awakened the next morning, she knew what she had to do.

Chapter 14

The next day was Saturday, and after Emily milked her cows and did some errands, she showered and changed into her favorite blue jeans and red shirt.

She had already discovered the location of Frank's new apartment from the gossip she'd heard through the church grapevine. She'd also heard that he volunteered every other Saturday at the rec center in a nearby town. She drove to his apartment building in Monkton, saying a silent prayer during the entire journey. She took a deep breath and knocked on his door, wondering if she should have called before traipsing to his apartment unannounced.

The rusty hinges creaked when the door swung open. "Emily!"

Emily clenched her hands together, staring at Frank. "Frank, I wanted to talk with you. I hope it's all right."

He smiled, stroking his beard. "Emily, you're always welcome in my home. Come in." She stepped into the living room, trying to ignore the clothes and newspapers scattered on the hardwood floor. A heavenly scent of tomatoes and spices spilled from the small kitchen. "What are you cooking?"

"Spaghetti and meatballs. I made some garlic bread, too."

Surprised, she glanced into the kitchen before looking at Frank again. A disturbing thought fluttered through her mind. "You made all this for lunch?"

"Yes."

"Are you expecting somebody?" Had she waited too long to give him an answer, and he'd already started dating? She noticed how the single women at church swarmed after Frank like bees to honey.

"No."

"Then why did you make all this for lunch?"

He motioned toward the kitchen, not answering her question. "I'm getting ready to eat right now if you're interested." He caressed her with his dark brown eyes, and her heart thudded. When her tummy rumbled, he chuckled. "You still haven't changed. I see you still have a noisy stomach."

She chuckled, and he led her into the kitchen and pulled out a chair for her. She sat, and he served up plates of spaghetti and meatballs, salad, and garlic bread. "I've missed having home-cooked food since Laura's been gone."

Frank nodded. "I can understand that. Have you heard from her?"

"We call each other regularly. She sounds happy, and I think she's glad that she's growing closer to her daughter and her grandchildren." Frank took her hand and bowed his head. In his deep, strong voice, he thanked the Lord for their food. Emily said amen and squeezed his hand. She took a bite of the food and moaned. "Oh my!"

"What's the matter?"

She licked her lips, taking another bite of spaghetti before sampling the crunchy garlic bread. "This is the best spaghetti I've ever had." She sampled more food. "Mmm. This garlic bread is excellent!"

He laughed, watching her eat. "I'm glad you like it so much."

"I can't believe you made all this yourself."

"I don't use spaghetti sauce out of a jar. I make my own, and I made the garlic bread myself, too."

"You cook?" She looked at him, and she felt as if she was seeing a new Frank, a different Frank from the way he was eight months ago.

"Yes, I cook."

"But when I went to your old apartment, you had pizza boxes and empty take-out containers all over the room. I thought you didn't know how to cook."

They ate in silence, enjoying their meal. When they were finished, they took their lemonade into the living room, and Frank invited her to sit. "I'm glad you came by. I wanted to talk to you about something."

She sat on the expensive leather couch. "Good, I wanted to talk to you, too."

"You were asking about my cooking earlier?"

"Yes."

"Well, cooking is something I used to do all the time before Julie died. When she died, I started drinking, and I just stopped doing the things I loved, like cooking and working out." He sipped his lemonade. "I was so bitter and angry that the only thing that brought me pleasure was alcohol. You know when I left you for six months and my dad died?"

She nodded, encouraging him to continue.

"Well, I was a real mess back then."

"I know, you told me that."

"No, I didn't tell you how bad of a mess I was. When my dad died, I was so afraid that I was going to start drinking again that I took a month-long leave of absence from work. Even though I was saved, the urge to drink consumed me so much that I went to a medical doctor, and he had to give me medicine to help with my cravings."

She touched his arm. "Are you still on the medicine?"

"No, I stopped taking it a few months before I decided to come back here. But I was off work for a whole month, helping my mother out and just straightening out my life. There's an alcoholic support group that meets each day in Chicago. It's not always the same people, but I made sure I was there every day. Being with the other members helped me stay sober. I read my Bible like crazy. I was drinking in the Word, and I had so many questions about the scriptures. My church in Chicago was awesome, and they answered all my questions about God and the Bible. I found that I had a lot of learning to do." He pointed toward his Bible. "I don't think I could've made it through this whole ordeal if it weren't for God."

He paused for a moment, then said softly, "You know, Emily, I love reading the scriptures. There's so much wisdom between those pages." He looked toward the window for a minute, as if thinking of what he should say. "Anyway, during my absence, I learned that I not only had to continue placing my faith in God, but I also had to get into the things that brought me pleasure."

"Like cooking?"

He squeezed her hand. "Yes, like cooking. It's something to do to keep my mind off drinking."

"Do you still have the urge to drink?"

He looked at her. "Honey, the urge to drink never goes away; you just have to learn to be strong and not act on it. It's scary thinking about not ever having another drink, but you have to take it one day at a time."

She blew air through her lips. "I didn't realize that."

"I had to let you know all this. I'd still like us to get to know each other again. I'm different now."

"That's what I wanted to talk to you about."

"Oh?"

"Yes. I think I'd like to give us a chance. I wondered if we could get to know each other as friends again."

His lips touched her nose. "I'm too attracted to you to be just your friend, but I'd like to spend time with you again."

She smiled at him. "I'm attracted to you, too. And I have an admission of my own to make."

He chuckled. "What's that?"

"I'm a lousy cook."

He laughed. "I know. You told me that when I first met you. Maybe my cooking skills will balance everything out between us."

She smiled. "Yes, maybe your cooking skills will balance everything out."

❧

During the next few months, Frank continued to struggle with his decision to ask Emily to marry him. Even though they were getting to know each other better, he still faltered as far as his alcoholism was concerned. It was a daily struggle, and he prayed each day for the strength to let go and trust himself and believe in the Lord enough to trust his decision to marry Emily.

As he got to know Emily again, he found his love for her grew as the days passed. Since Laura was gone, Emily was out at the farm alone, and he often worried about her living by herself in the country, running the farm solo. He visited often after work, and he realized she wasn't kidding when she said she couldn't cook. His frequent late-evening visits often included takeout. Sometimes in the evenings, while she was in the barn milking the cows, he'd stop at the grocery store to buy food to make dinner for her.

He knew he had really fallen hard for her when he arrived unexpectedly at five in the morning on a Saturday. He'd worn his oldest clothing and a pair of battered sneakers. After parking in the driveway, he traipsed to the familiar barn. The cows were chained in their stalls, eating their piles of food. He recalled Emily telling him about the corn, soybeans, and alfalfa they grew to make feed for the cows. A clear liquid squished through the pipes, and Frank found Emily in the room where the milk tank and sink were located. "Frank!" Her eyes shone with delight as they embraced. "What are you doing here?"

"I know you like having somebody to help you milk the cows, so I came to give you a hand." Since Emily had been milking the cows most of her life, he figured he'd be more of a hindrance than a help. But he was determined to learn how to milk so he could help her eventually. He gestured toward the sink. "What are you doing?"

She explained that she was cleaning the pipes and the equipment with an acid and water solution before she started milking. He washed his hands before he followed her as she went into the barn carrying the mobile milking units. She gave him a pair of gloves, patiently explaining how she cleaned the udders of each cow using an iodine dipper. She left and returned with a steaming bucket of liquid. "I could have carried that in here for you," he said.

She smiled, patiently explaining he could carry it next time if he came back to milk again. Since he felt so uneasy cleaning the teats and udders of each cow and attaching the units, Emily ended up doing most of the milking herself. Nevertheless, it felt good to be out in the barn with her, watching her do the chores. He found that he was a better help once the cows were milked. She pushed a cart full of feed and handed him a shovel. "After milking we feed the cows grain, soybeans, and corn feed." She told him what to do. "Just shovel some in front of each stall. After they're done, we need to let them out to graze a bit. I'm going to clean the milking equipment." As he shoveled feed, he glanced at the pipes, noting that clear liquid again swished through them as Emily did her cleanup. Once they'd cleaned the floor and let the cows out, he followed her to the porch. She removed her barn boots, and he took off his shoes, wiggling his toes.

"Thanks for helping me this morning, Frank."

He shrugged. "I'm not sure if I was much help."

She touched his arm. "You were a big help." When they'd washed up, Frank made bacon, eggs, and toast for breakfast. Once he said grace over their meal and they were eating, Emily told him something. "My sister, Sarah, called me last night."

"Did she want money?"

"Yes."

"How much did she want?"

"She said she needed two hundred dollars to pay her phone bill. If she doesn't pay it soon, they're going to turn her phone off."

"Are you going to give it to her?"

Emily shrugged. "I don't know. I told her I'd have to think and pray about it. I said I'd call her back in a couple of days to let her know what I'd decided to do." She sipped her juice. "Have you spoken to your mother lately?"

He sighed, spreading butter and jelly on his toast. "Yes."

"How is she doing?"

"She's doing okay." He didn't bother to mention that his mother had not been vocal about his dating life in a long time. He still wasn't sure if she was learning to accept his choices or if she had more pressing things on her mind. "Trish spends time with her every week, so I'm glad about that."

"How are the kids doing?"

"They're doing fine. Next month is Regina's birthday. I'm flying up to Chicago for that." He stopped eating and took her hand. "I'd like for you to come with me if you can get somebody to do the milking for you."

"I'd love to come with you, Frank, but I can't make any promises. I'll see if I can find somebody to do the chores for me the weekend of the party."

They continued to eat in silence for a few minutes before he mentioned he was going to the rec center later on. "You know, I didn't realize how much I missed spending time with young people until I started doing it again."

"Yeah, I can tell you enjoy it. It's nice of you to spend time mentoring the kids at the center." After a few moments, she touched his arm. "I enjoyed having you with me this morning to milk the cows. It was nice."

He took her hand, squeezing her fingers. "I enjoyed doing it with you. Is it okay if I come and help you milk on the weekends?"

Emily returned his squeeze. "Yes, I'd like that very much."

Later that day, Frank found a store in Monkton that sold barn boots. When he returned to Emily's for the next milking, he brought his new footwear with him. He left his new barn boots at Emily's, placing them right beside hers.

❧

When Frank had been helping Emily milk cows for a couple of months, he finally felt it was time to ask her to marry him. On the day he purchased the ring from the jeweler, he called his mother. "Hello, Franklin." His mother was one of the few relatives who still called him by his full name.

He hesitated. "Mom, hi."

"You've got a worried tone in your voice, son."

"How are you?"

His mother spoke for five minutes about her health and how her regular visits with Trish and her grandchildren were going. Frank blurted his news before he lost his courage. "I'm going to ask Emily to marry me."

"Emily? That farmer you told me about when you came home?"

"Yes, Mom. You can't treat her the way you treated Julie. I don't like that kind of behavior." He failed to mention that his parents' actions had intensified his grief after Julie's violent death. "I love her too much to hurt her like that. She's a strong, proud woman, and she's running that farm by herself right now." When she remained silent, he mentally said a quick prayer before he reminded her how he'd met Emily through his job and how they'd grown closer in recent months. "If she says yes, then she'll be a part of the family."

"This is so sudden," she began.

Frank still wondered what was going through his mother's brain. "It's not so sudden. I just explained how long I've known her. I love her, Mom, and it'll hurt me if you reject her for superficial reasons." When his mother remained silent, he finally ended the call. Once he'd hung up the phone, he fell to his knees. "Lord, please, if this is your will and Emily says yes, please make everything work out with my mom. Amen."

❧

When Emily arrived at Frank's apartment for their Saturday night dinner date, the sight of the lit tapered candles on the table made her stop and stare. "Why are we eating by candlelight?" She had been a bit suspicious when he'd called earlier, saying he would not be by that evening to help her with the milking.

He pulled her into his arms, kissing her nose. "I just wanted to share a romantic dinner with you. What's wrong with that?"

She shook her head. "Nothing."

"I think you sometimes forget how much I enjoy your company." He led her to the table. "Let's eat."

When he placed the shrimp cocktail on the table, she looked at him. "Shrimp cocktail?"

He took her hand, asking the Lord to bless their food. Once they said their amens, he commented, "I made crab cakes and rice pilaf for dinner."

"All my favorites." When he continued to hold her hand, she wondered when they were going to dig into their meal. He kissed her fingers, and she closed her eyes, enjoying the feel of his lips against her skin.

"I have a question for you." His voice was low and husky, and his dark eyes shone in the candlelight.

He released her hand and pulled a small velvet box out of his pocket. He presented it to her. When she popped the box open, the diamond solitaire ring glittered. "Frank!"

"Will you marry me, Emily? You know how much I love you."

"Yes, I'll marry you. I love you, Frank!"

He pulled her into his arms, and they shared a blissful kiss.

Epilogue

F rank stood at the altar of Monkton Christian Church, his smile so wide he thought his face would split apart. Christine, Kelly, Trish, and Emily's sister, Sarah, served in the wedding as bridesmaids. Their canary yellow dresses looked becoming as the bright sunlight streamed through the church's stained glass windows. Mark, decked out in his tuxedo, was a junior groomsman, and Regina served as a junior bridesmaid.

His mother sat in the front of the church, looking uncomfortable as she scanned the crowd. Both he and Trish were trying to convince their mother that her strict way of judging others was wrong, and so far she'd been cordial to Emily, not shunning her the way she'd shunned Julie.

Laura Cooper sat in the front row, crying openly. Since Frank was going to live with Emily on her dairy farm, Laura had confided to him that she felt better about her decision to leave and move in with her daughter.

Frank's heart palpitated when Emily walked down the aisle. Her white silky dress complemented her smooth brown skin. As Devon Crandall and his other friends from church served as ushers, Frank and Emily vowed to love each other forever.

BITTERSWEET MEMORIES

Dedication

To my sister, Joanna.
Thanks for helping me iron out the wrinkles in this manuscript.

Prologue

K aren burst through the church doors, tears streaming down her face. "Pastor Smith, I can't believe Lionel is still missing!"

The reverend and his wife, Candace, pulled the hysterical woman into a hug, patting her back. After they released her, Candace stroked Karen's hair. "Honey, thanks for coming as soon as we called. The police detective is in the boardroom, waiting to talk to you. Are you sure you're up for this?"

Karen wiped her eyes, struggling to gather her thoughts as the events from the past couple of weeks played through her mind like a nonstop movie. Her fiancé, Lionel Adams, had been fired as church treasurer after being accused of stealing thousands of dollars from their megachurch. And it was rumored that the assistant treasurer, Michelle James, who had recently resigned, had aided him with the theft.

Like the rest of the congregation, Karen had been shocked when the allegations against Lionel were announced at church two weeks ago. And since Lionel had left town the day before, she hadn't been able to contact him to find out what was going on.

Karen turned toward Candace, her trembling lips attempting a smile. "I'll—I'll do the best I can to—to answer his questions."

The threesome began walking slowly down the hallway, toward the boardroom. A moment later, the pastor stopped outside a closed door, placing his hand on Karen's shoulder. "Karen, Michelle is missing also."

Karen gasped, stepping away from the pastor. "That. . .that can't be true."

He nodded. "Unfortunately, it is." Speaking softly, he said, "The church leadership team is concerned for both her and Lionel's welfare. We want to find them, but we can't ignore what's happened."

Candace took her hand. "Honey, we have to do all we can to locate them. What if there was foul play involved? Don't you want to make sure Lionel is safe?"

Tears rushed from Karen's eyes, and she wiped the moisture away. Her head pounded as she leaned against the cool wall, the contact bringing relief to her heated skin.

"Are you okay?" asked Pastor Smith.

Pulling herself away from the wall, she silently prayed, *God, give me strength*. "I–I'm okay now."

The pastor's kind dark eyes offered comfort. "The detective is in here. We called you to be questioned first since you know Lionel so well."

Karen glanced at Candace. "Nobody told the congregation exactly how much money Lionel may have stolen. We just know it was thousands of dollars. How much cash was missing?"

The woman released Karen's hand and looked at her husband, frowning.

In a calm voice, the pastor paused before speaking. "Fifty thousand dollars."

Karen's head started spinning. With a muffled sob, Karen turned away, wiping her eyes. "Lord, please help me deal with this pain."

"We'll take this one day at a time," Candace said. "The Lord will see us through."

Karen looked back at the closed door, hesitating. "Is it okay if I go to the restroom be–before talking to the detective?"

"Of course," Candace said with an understanding smile.

Leaving the couple, Karen walked to the bathroom, pushed the door open, and entered the room, desperately seeking a private moment with the Lord. Her heart skipped a beat when Tara Baker, the church secretary, dressed in an immaculate cream-colored suit and sporting stylish hair and polished fingernails, stepped out of the stall. Spotting Karen, her dark eyes widened.

While the secretary wordlessly washed her hands, Karen regarded her own worn jeans and faded T-shirt before touching her hair, which she'd pulled into a ponytail in her haste to get to the church. She suddenly felt rumpled and dowdy.

"I always thought Lionel and Michelle were up to no good," Tara finally mumbled, drying her hands with a paper towel while glaring at Karen.

Karen gritted her teeth, shocked at the rudeness of a woman who'd once flirted with Lionel.

"I find it hard to believe that you had no clue what your fiancé was doing behind your back," Tara said then turned on her heels and strode out of the restroom.

Waves of pain floated through Karen's head as she struggled to blot out the secretary's words. Turning her focus to the Lord, she prayed, "God, please help me. Help us to find Lionel and Michelle. And keep them safe. Amen." Somewhat soothed, she rejoined the pastor and his wife.

Pastor Smith gestured toward the now-open door. "Karen, I'm so sorry about this."

Karen gave him a halfhearted smile then entered the room, praying for strength. The detective sat in a chair near the front of the room.

The minister spoke, his voice full of kindness, "Detective Ramsey, this is Karen Brown."

"Good morning, Karen," greeted the detective.

"Good morning," Karen mumbled, taking a seat near the detective. She turned to her minister. "Can you stay here with me, Pastor Smith?"

The clergyman touched her arm, gazing at the detective. "Is that okay with you, detective?"

Ramsey shrugged, opening his notebook. "If she wants you to stay, that's fine."

Pastor Smith settled into the empty chair beside her.

The investigator asked his first question. "Do you know where Lionel is?"

"I. . ." She paused, chewing on her lower lip. "The day before the church announced he was fired, he told me he was going to go out of town to visit his cousin. I haven't talked to him since, and th–that was two weeks ago." She paused, gripping the arms of the chair. "I—I haven't been able to contact him since he left." She took a deep breath. "He won't answer his cell phone. I figured he wanted some time alone and I would see him when he returned for his hearing."

The detective looked up from the notes he was writing. "Where does his cousin live?"

As Ramsey's questions went on and on, Karen felt overwhelmed with worry, fatigue, and nausea. Hot tears flowing down her cheeks, she prayed, *Lord, will I ever feel normal again?*

Her head pounded with pain, and she began rubbing her temples.

Pastor Smith touched her elbow. "Are you all right?"

"My head. . .hurts."

"Detective, is it okay if we stop the questioning for a few minutes while I get Karen some aspirin?"

"I don't mind at all," said Ramsey.

Karen heard Pastor Smith's retreating footsteps as she closed her eyes and rubbed her aching head. Her pain worsened as she leaned back into the chair. And then the world faded out.

Chapter 1

One month later

Karen pulled into her mother's driveway, gravel crunching beneath her car's tires. Yellow, pink, and white tulips dominated the front yard, their enticing sweet scent beckoning, welcoming her home. Staring at the blossoms, she tried to relax after the two-and-a-half-hour drive from Ocean City.

She took a deep breath, stepped out of the car, and walked to the front steps of her childhood home. It had been over a year since she'd been here, and with her present state of mind, the sudden comforting and nostalgic feelings gave her unexpected strength, making her glad she'd decided to return to Annapolis.

Continuing to enjoy the heady scent of the flowers, she unlocked the door and entered the living room. A thud sounded from the kitchen, and she rushed into the adjoining room. "Mom!" Her heart stopped when a large, brown-skinned man pulled his head out from beneath the kitchen sink and turned toward her, his eyes twinkling behind his round-framed glasses.

"Who are you?" she demanded.

He dropped his tool and rose from the floor. "I'm Keith Baxter, your mother's next-door neighbor. You must be Karen."

Surprised, she tried not to stare at the tall, attractive stranger. "My mother never mentioned you to me before." Caution filled her voice.

"Well, she's mentioned you to me, dozens of times."

She placed her hands on her hips. "Where is my mother?"

"She's at Bible study over at the church. She asked me to stay and fix her sink while she was out. Said she'd be gone about an hour."

Karen huffed, dropping her purse on the table. *Great, just great. When I need Mom the most, I'm left here alone with a complete stranger.* She sank into a kitchen chair, arms folded, foot tapping. "How much longer are you going to be?"

The plumber narrowed his gorgeous eyes, scanning her from head to toe. "Did you wake up on the wrong side of the bed this morning? You're sure in a sour mood."

She closed her eyes, mentally counting to ten, then silently prayed, *Lord, forgive me for my sharp words.* Since Lionel's disappearance, Karen's moods had

248

altered drastically. She'd hoped and prayed she'd be over Lionel's deception by now, but so far, animosity toward her fiancé consumed her, affecting her interactions with others. She opened her tear-filled eyes and blinked, again realizing that Lionel was gone. Did that mean they were no longer engaged? How did you break a commitment when your future mate disappeared?

The repairman pressed a tissue into her hand.

Resigned, Karen blew her nose, wondering if she would ever stop crying over Lionel. She turned away, ashamed of her abrupt and rude behavior. After wiping her tears, she glanced at the stranger. "Look, what's your name again?"

He plopped into the empty chair beside her. The delicious scent of his cologne teased her nose, and she tried to ignore the smell while getting her emotions under control.

"I'm Keith Baxter," he said, his deep voice now soft and somehow comforting.

"Well, Keith, I'm sorry I snapped at you. It wasn't intentional, but I just really wanted to spend some quiet time with my mom." Sniffling, she glanced around the spotless kitchen. "I'm just surprised she's not here."

"Did she know you were coming?"

Karen shook her head. "Not really. I'd told her I was coming the day after tomorrow, but I decided to make the trip a little earlier." She paused for a few seconds. "If she'd invest in voice mail, I could've left her a message when I called last night."

"She was at the church until late. The women's choir is rehearsing for the Easter Sunday service in a few weeks."

She fingered her engagement ring, wondering if she should remove it. "I didn't realize my mother had joined the choir."

Curiosity shone from his caramel-colored eyes. "So how long are you going to visit?"

She continued toying with her ring. "I'm not here to visit. I'm here to stay."

"You're going to live here? For how long?"

She shrugged. "I don't know. It's hard to say."

"Your mom told me you've been going through a lot with your ex and all."

She gasped. "Why would she tell you about that?" Then she said half to herself, "I wonder if she told anybody else."

"I'm not sure why your mom confided to me, but I don't think she told anybody else."

Well, that's a small measure of comfort. Wonder why Mom would tell this guy anything about my life. Just how close is Mom to Keith Baxter, anyway? Before she could voice her thoughts, the front door opened.

"Karen!" Her mother rushed into the kitchen.

"Mom!" She hugged her mother tightly, glad to finally be home and in her arms. For a long moment, they continued to hold each other. A loud clunk resounded from under the sink as Keith resumed his repair.

Her mother finally released Karen and walked toward Keith, touching him on the shoulder. "Hi, Keith. Thanks for staying to fix my sink."

He poked his head out from underneath the sink, giving her mother a warm smile. "You're welcome. I shouldn't be too much longer."

As he continued his work, her mother led Karen into the living room.

Karen fingered her mother's short, stylish gray tresses. "Mom, you cut your hair."

"Do you like it? I got so tired of wearing my hair back in that bun. I'm much too old to have that much hair anyway."

"It looks nice. It's just such a big surprise." Karen smiled, recalling how her father loved her mother's long hair. "Keith told me you've joined the choir, too."

"Well, it was time for me to get out of my rut."

The women were silent for a few seconds before her mother spoke again. "When I saw your car in the driveway, I was surprised. Why didn't you tell me you were coming today?"

Before she could answer, her mother looked at her closely as they took a seat on the couch. "You look thinner! Karen, if you don't start eating something, you'll fade away to nothing!"

"Mom, so much has been happening." Karen glanced toward the kitchen, lowering her voice. "And I don't feel comfortable talking to you with that guy in the kitchen. He might hear us. Can we go into my old bedroom where there's more privacy?"

"Of course, dear, if you'd like."

Seconds later, they entered her childhood bedroom. The familiar twin bed and cream-colored walls soothed her frazzled nerves. Lying back onto the mattress, Karen rested her head on the fluffy pillow. "I feel so tired."

"You look tired." The older woman peered at Karen. "Now tell me what's on your mind, child. You've barely spoken to me since Lionel disappeared. And the few times I've managed to get you on the phone, you just tell me that you're fine." She sighed. "But I know better."

"I'm handling things, Mom."

"Humph. No, you're not. You didn't even want to tell me what had happened with Lionel. If it hadn't been for your friends Monica and Anna, I wouldn't have known a thing."

Karen frowned, her eyes resting on the emerald green curtains. "They should have minded their own business. I would have told you when I was ready."

"Pumpkin, they were worried about you. I'm glad they told me."

"Listen, Mom, before we start talking about Lionel, I want to know why *you* have some strange man in your house when you're out at Bible study."

Her mother wrinkled her nose. "Strange man? Keith is my friend. And my next-door neighbor." Touching her daughter's hand, she continued to speak. "Remember I told you I joined a new church?"

"I remember."

"Well, Keith is a member there."

"Mom, the man had the nerve to mention Lionel." Her voice wavered. "H–he's a stranger to me, and you–you've aired my dirty laundry to him?"

"Karen, I happened to mention it to Keith the day after Monica and Anna called. I didn't tell anybody that you know."

Karen blew air through her lips, still upset. "Well, how do you know he didn't tell anybody? In this neighborhood everybody seems to know everyone else's business."

Her mom touched her shoulder. "Honey, please don't get so worked up over such a small thing. Keith is very blunt, and he doesn't always think before he speaks. But he's a good Christian man, and his heart is in the right place." She rubbed her daughter's shoulder. "He's been a blessing since he moved in six months ago. He's a plumber, and he's good at fixing other things, too. This house is over fifty years old, and things are falling apart. He's been helping me out a lot." She pulled Karen into a hug. "That's enough talk about Keith. I'm sorry I told him your business. Now why don't you tell me about Lionel? I've been praying for you, hoping you would find the courage to tell me how you've been doing. It hurts that you shut me out of your life after Lionel disappeared."

Taking her mother's hand, Karen's voice softened. "Mom, I'm sorry. I—I haven't really spoken to anybody about what happened, except for Monica and Anna—and the police. They know all about it, but I—I haven't told them how I feel." She lowered her voice. "I've stopped going to church. Mom, it just hurts too much. A lot of the people look at me like they feel sorry for me, and some people act like I'm responsible for Lionel's actions! The church secretary wonders why I didn't realize that Lionel was so dishonest. I overheard one woman talking to somebody when I was in the bathroom stall. She wondered if I'd helped Lionel steal from the church and if I knew of his whereabouts." She shivered. "I don't need their false accusations, and I certainly don't want their pity. I can't go back there, Mom."

A brisk knock at the door interrupted Karen's tirade.

Keith's voice resounded from behind the closed door. "Ms. Doris, your sink works. You can give it a try if you like."

"Thanks, Keith. Is it okay if I come to your house later to pay the bill?"

"No problem." Seconds later, the heavy clomp of boots against hardwood floors echoed in the house.

After hearing the door shut, Karen said, "Oh, Mom, he gets on my nerves! Couldn't he have waited until we were done talking before he interrupted us?"

Doris's brow furrowed. "Lionel's disappearance has gotten you into a tizzy. You're usually not so sour."

Karen stood and walked to the window. She lifted the curtain and spotted Keith going to his driveway. In front of his house, an ivory van, emblazoned with BAXTER'S PLUMBING in black script lettering, rested next to a sporty black car. After placing a toolbox into the back of his van, he turned toward her window and looked right at her. He waved before getting into his work van and driving away. Somewhat embarrassed, she dropped the curtain.

Pushing the plumber out of her mind, she refocused on her dilemma. "Mom, I'm having the hardest time forgetting about Lionel. I don't think I ever want to go back to his church."

"You don't have to go back if you don't want to. The Lord won't mind if you choose to worship elsewhere. What about your old church home? The one you used to attend with Anna and Monica."

"I went back a few times, but everybody there had heard about Lionel's she-nanigans. I just felt so embarrassed, wondering what they were thinking about him, me. . .everything."

"Honey, you shouldn't feel that way. As Christians, we're supposed to be there to support each other during bad times."

Karen shrugged her mother's comment away. She sat on the bed, bittersweet memories of Lionel littering her brain. The scenes from their time together played in her mind constantly, trapped inside her head. "I loved Lionel so much. It–it's hard for me to let him go."

"Pumpkin, I'm not surprised. You're in love with him, and you were plan-ning on getting married, raising a family."

"I feel terrible. Sometimes I wonder. . ." She gripped the pillow. "I wonder if he was taken against his will. Maybe he was forced to take that money, and he's being held captive."

"Oh, Karen."

Karen squeezed her hands together. "Mom, I can't help it! What if Lionel didn't take that money and he's innocent?" Even as she said the words, she sensed they were untrue. Before he was fired, the evidence was gathered, and it appeared he'd taken the money. He certainly didn't deny it after he was accused. She frowned, recalling other things members of the congregation speculated about. Some of the accusations they'd been flinging against Lionel made Karen again wonder if she should remove her engagement ring.

"What's wrong?" asked her mother.

Karen stroked the floral bedspread, finding the courage to reveal the recent news. "Remember when Lionel disappeared, the assistant treasurer, Michelle James, disappeared also?"

"Yes?"

"Well, the police and Pastor Smith finally found Michelle's mother. Mrs. James has been out of the country for the last month. She didn't even realize her daughter was missing until she returned to the States."

"How awful! What happened?"

"Michelle's mother told the police her daughter was having an affair with Lionel."

Doris gasped. "Honey, that can't be true. Lionel loved you—"

"I'd like to believe that, but I'm starting to feel like he didn't. Maybe he was going to break our engagement and marry Michelle."

"Did Michelle's mother have any proof of these allegations?"

Karen nodded. "She had personal e-mails that Lionel had sent to her daughter. Michelle had forwarded them to her."

"Have you seen these e-mails?"

"No, but I've heard about what's in them. It's quite obvious they were sharing more than just a business relationship." Karen couldn't help the bitter tone in her voice. Silently she prayed, *Oh God, why have You allowed this?*

Her mom pulled her into another hug. "Just leave it in the Lord's hands, and He'll help you through this," she advised before releasing her.

Karen grunted. "That's easy for you to say."

"You know, I suffered a lot when your father passed away a couple of years ago. Remember, I couldn't work for a few weeks, I was so devastated."

"Mom, I'm sorry. It's wrong of me to be so self-centered right now. I've been so irritable and rude since Lionel disappeared, and I shouldn't be acting like I'm the only person on this earth who's suffered pain."

"That's okay. In time, the pain will lessen, and you'll be able to move on with your life." She paused. "Besides, you should thank the Lord that you found this out *before* you got married. Can you imagine if you discovered these facts about him after you wed and had children?"

Karen cringed.

"Well," her mom said, patting her daughter's hand then rising from the bed, "why don't we shelve this discussion for now and have dinner?"

"I'm not hungry."

"Well, you've got to eat. Come on, you can watch me fix dinner, like you used to do when you were a little girl."

Moments later, an exhausted Karen sat slumped in a kitchen chair, watching her mother prepare dinner. Soon, childhood memories swept through her as the scent of meat, onions, tomatoes, and garlic filled the room. As steam rose from the mound of spaghetti her mother placed on the table, Karen's mouth watered. Garlic bread and salad completed the meal.

After they'd said grace, Karen broached the subject weighing on her mind. "Mom, do—do you like living alone?"

Her mom poured two glasses of iced tea. "Well, actually. . .no. Since your father passed, this house has seemed so big. . .and empty. Too empty. But now that Keith has moved in next door and joined my church, I've discovered I like having someone else around."

"Does he visit you every day?"

"He'll stop through often enough. Plus, since I don't drive, I get a ride with him to service every Sunday. He's nice, compassionate, and caring."

Karen sampled her food, savoring the tangy taste of the spices. Smiling, she ate for a few minutes, thinking about her mother's words and the handsome plumber who'd handed her a tissue when she'd cried.

Her mom took a sip of iced tea then said, "He also takes me grocery shopping every week. We usually do our shopping together."

Karen immediately bristled with jealousy and then found herself saying, "Well, he won't have to take you grocery shopping anymore. I'm here to do that now."

"Pumpkin, he likes doing these things for me. And you know, *he's* the one who encouraged me to join the choir."

"What?" She couldn't believe this. "*Keith* got you to join the choir? How many times have I tried to convince you, since Dad died, that you needed to get out more? *And* join the choir. You have such an awesome voice. But you kept telling me you were too shy to get up in front of the entire church. But now this stranger moves in next door, and like that"—she snapped her fingers—"you're joining the choir?" Karen stabbed a meatball with her fork and lifted it to her mouth, wondering if Keith would be coming by all the time, intruding upon her time with her mother.

Doris raised her brows then ate a few bites of spaghetti and garlic bread, giving Karen a few minutes to calm down. "Well, the main thing is I joined the choir. You should be glad. I know I am. I truly love singing."

Karen mumbled, "You're right, Mom. Sorry for getting so worked up. I'm glad you're getting out there."

"That's quite all right, honey. I understand." She paused. "You know, after your friends called me about Lionel, I was tempted to take the train down to Ocean City and drag you home for a visit. A mother's impulse, I guess. Even though I was covering you in prayer, I wanted to do more. I wanted to take care of you."

Karen shrugged. "Well, I'm here now. I—I need this time. . . . Time to try to heal from all that's happened."

"I love that you decided to come home, but I did wonder how long you'll be staying. And what about your job at the hair salon in Ocean City? You told me you have a huge clientele."

"I do, but I can always find new clients here. I already contacted the manager at Hair Care Salon in downtown Annapolis, and they said I can start once I'm settled. Besides, the place where I used to work went out of business."

"Really?"

"Yes, the owner sold the property, so I was going to lose clients anyway if I'd stayed." She sipped her tea. "Mom, I've been so depressed lately that I don't even feel like working anymore. That's when I thought of coming home. I thought a change in scenery would help me to heal."

"Have you been praying about it?"

Karen winced, recalling how the situation with Lionel had caused a rift in her relationship with God. "I do pray, occasionally. But for the last month, I haven't even felt like reading my Bible. I just can't seem to concentrate." Her shoulders slumped.

Doris squeezed her daughter's shoulder. "It hurts me knowing you're hurting so much. I could just strangle that man for all he's done." Her voice hardened with anger.

Karen sat silently, biting her lip, then said, "Mom. . .where did I go wrong?"

"What do you mean?"

"How did I ever make the mistake of getting involved with Lionel? He seemed so genuine, honest, and trustworthy." She put her fork down, thinking about her failed relationship.

"I notice you're still wearing your engagement ring."

Karen toyed with the large diamond, recalling Lionel's bright smile when he'd proposed. Whenever they were out at a social event, he'd always wanted her to show off her diamond. She used to think it was because he was proud of being engaged to her; now she wondered if he just wanted to flaunt the oversized stone. "Yes, I'm still wearing his ring. I've gotten so used to having it on my finger that my hand would feel empty without it." Twirling the ring clockwise, she positioned the diamond so that it faced her palm. "I guess I should remove it. It's just hard to do, especially since I haven't heard Lionel's side of the story."

"They still don't know where he is?"

"No." She fingered the rim of her plate. "The judge issued a warrant for his arrest since he failed to show for his court hearing."

"I'm sorry, Karen." She squeezed her daughter's hand and remained silent for a few seconds.

Karen changed the subject, asking her mother about her job for the county government, a topic her mother was glad to take up. When that subject was exhausted, Doris mentioned her church.

"Karen, Pastor Bolton has been asking about you. I told him you'd been going through some difficult times—"

"Mom, I thought you said you didn't tell anybody, except Keith Baxter, about what had happened with Lionel."

She patted her hand. "I didn't. I'm just saying that I was talking to Pastor Bolton and I told him you were having some problems. I asked him to pray for you. I also placed your name on the church's prayer list a few weeks ago, and"— she dropped her fork onto her plate—"here you are on my doorstep! I know the Lord must have wanted you to come home and spend some time with your mama!"

"Oh brother, Mom, I'm not so sure that's true."

She shrugged. "Sure it is."

"I'm still wondering why God let me fall in love with a good-looking, smooth-talking man like Lionel, not allowing me to see his true colors until it was too late."

Doris stared at her plate for a few seconds. "Honey, you can't necessarily blame God for everything. There was no indication at all that Lionel was dishonest?"

Karen thought about it then shrugged. "If there were any clues about the flaws in Lionel's character, love made me blind to them."

They finished their dinner in silence.

Chapter 2

Keith tossed and turned, finally getting out of bed at 2:00 a.m., his head pounding with pain from lack of sleep. He reached for a plastic bottle on his nightstand and poured two aspirin tablets into his palm.

As he rolled out of bed, disturbing thoughts continued to haunt his mind like a bad dream. He traipsed to the kitchen for a drink of water. *Lord, please mend the rift between my brother and me.* Pulling the gallon water jug from the refrigerator, he poured some into a glass, popped the tablets into his mouth, and guzzled the cool liquid. After a second glass, he lifted the window curtain to see Ms. Doris's house. The light was on in Karen's bedroom. *Wonder if her problems are keeping her awake, too.*

He put his glass in the sink and found his way into the living room, turning on the light as he went. He lifted the picture of him and his twin brother, Kyle, studying it closely. The photo had been taken right after they'd graduated from high school. He thought about that joyous day and their college years as well—doing some heavy drinking, eating tons of food, and getting together with his brother regularly to discuss problems, women, and class assignments. Their close relationship shifted when Keith had found Christ shortly before they finished grad school. Kyle didn't understand Keith's deep devotion to the Lord and couldn't comprehend why he no longer wanted to go out regularly to get sloshed.

He sighed and plopped into a chair, thinking about Aaron—a friend, lawyer, and member of Keith's church who ran into Kyle occasionally since they were in the same profession. Aaron mentioned having seen Kyle the previous day at a restaurant in downtown Annapolis. His brother was with a bunch of people and obviously drunk. Keith hoped Kyle hadn't driven home that way, and Aaron assured him that he hadn't. "I saw him leave with a woman, and she appeared sober. I followed them outside and saw her get behind the wheel," he explained.

A relieved Keith then told Aaron, "I'd appreciate it if you'd let me know whenever you run into Kyle. He and I have been. . .somewhat estranged since we graduated from college. And since our father died, it's gotten even worse. He doesn't answer my phone calls or e-mails. So I finally gave up contacting him." He'd frowned. "We haven't talked in six months."

Keith placed the photo back on the table and reclined in the chair, staring at the ceiling, his thoughts revolving around Kyle. His brother had always had a drinking problem, even when they were teenagers. Now he tended to drink heavily in the evenings, after he got off from work. Keith wished there was a way to get him to control himself.

He closed his eyes, silently praying, *God, please help Kyle. May he come to know You and get help for his drinking problem. And, Lord, my own incessant worrying about Kyle isn't helping anything. Help me to curb that tendency, to leave everything in Your hands.* He soon relaxed, breathing steadily.

Drifting to sleep, he thought about his meeting with Ms. Doris's daughter. Goodness, she was pretty! Her smooth dark skin and large eyes were refreshing like a glass of lemonade on a hot day. Funny how she'd stayed on his mind since he'd met her. He wanted to take the sadness away from her dark eyes and make her smile. He hoped he hadn't offended her when he'd commented about her problems. He really needed to think before he spoke.

His thoughts full of Karen, Keith fell asleep, still sitting in his living room chair.

✃

Karen forced her eyes open and glanced at her alarm clock: 6:00 a.m. She blinked, the effects of another sleepless night rippling through her exhausted body. After dragging herself out from between the ivory sheets, twisted and wrinkled from her endless tossing and turning, she dressed then ran her fingers through her hair. Minutes later she entered the kitchen and lifted the window curtain. Her mother's array of spring flowers adorned the backyard, creating a carpet of color amid the grass.

Smiling, she reminisced about one of her childhood chores: Always an early riser, she'd watered her mother's flower garden each morning before going to school. She dropped the curtain and turned, her eyes drawn to the canister of coffee that beckoned. Sighing, she decided to water her mother's plants before having her morning cup of java.

Grabbing a light jacket, she stepped onto the small porch at the back of the house and met the cool early April breeze. She stopped, closed her eyes, and inhaled the delicate scent of tulips, daffodils, and lilies. She walked to the side of the house and unwrapped the hose. Pulling the lever on the nozzle, she sprayed a fan of water over her mother's beloved flowers. As the plants bobbed in the early morning breeze, Karen realized how much she appreciated taking care of her mother's garden, spending time alone, basking in the scent of flowers.

When the blossoms were well watered, she turned the spigot off and wrapped the hose around the plastic stand. As she turned to go back into the house, a movement caught her attention. Frozen, she stared into Keith Baxter's backyard.

Barefoot, wearing blue jeans with a white T-shirt, he'd stepped onto the porch, seemingly unaware of Karen's presence in the adjoining yard. A book clutched in one hand, he took a seat, closed his eyes, and tilted his head toward the sky.

Karen was finding it hard not to gawk. Was he relaxing or praying? She stepped back, wondering if she should return to the house. *No matter what he's doing, I shouldn't be staring at him like a lovesick teenager.* Quickly turning around, she slipped on a wet patch of grass. "Oh!" She fell, her chest hitting the ground. After lying there for several seconds, eyes open, gasping for breath, she spied an ant crawling across the blades of grass in front of her. She jumped up and felt herself falling backward into a solidly built body. Her heart thudded as masculine arms wrapped around her.

"You okay?" Keith's charmingly deep voice resonated in the small yard.

"Yes!" Stepping out of his arms, she was unhappily aware of the pleasure of their brief physical contact.

His gorgeous eyes crinkled with amusement behind his glasses.

Feeling the need to explain why she was standing in a wet lawn at six in the morning, she blurted, "I was watering my mother's flower garden."

He glanced at the moist buds then turned back to Karen. "Yes, I can see that."

Silence surrounded them, and Karen wondered if she should make an effort to continue the conversation. Keith beat her to it.

"Have you had breakfast yet?"

"Breakfast this early in the morning?"

He nodded then folded his muscular arms in front of him. "I normally get up at a quarter to five to exercise before going to work, so I'm usually hungry around now."

"Oh." Karen didn't know what else to say.

"So have you had breakfast yet?"

She shook her head, mesmerized by his presence. He beckoned her toward his house. "Come on, I'll fix us something to eat. I know Doris usually doesn't get up until seven." He glanced at his watch. "And I don't have to be at my first job until seven thirty, so we've got a little time."

Slightly dazed, she followed him to his house, shocked when he stopped beside a clump of tulips near his home. Snatching up the pair of clippers resting on the porch, he snipped one of the flowers, pressing the bloom into her hand. "This is for you. I—I want to apologize for yesterday. Some of the things I said. . . may have been. . .out of line. And since we're neighbors, well, sort of neighbors, for now anyway, I'd like us to be friends."

The warmth from the contact was comforting, and for some insane reason, she wanted Keith to hold her hand and tell her everything would be okay.

As he continued standing in front of her, Karen realized he was probably awaiting her response. She clutched the flower. "Thanks. It's okay. I shouldn't have gotten so upset."

He tilted his head toward his house, again inviting her to follow. They stepped onto the large walnut-colored porch, and Karen observed the classy wooden lawn furniture and old-fashioned porch swing swaying in the light breeze. A loud bark resonated from the kitchen, and she stepped back, startled.

Keith looked toward her, reaching for the handle of the screen door. "Are you scared of dogs?"

"No." She regarded the large brown-and-white Saint Bernard, its nose pressed up against the screen. "I don't mind dogs if they don't bite." Her voice faltered as she focused on the large pink canine tongue hanging out of the dog's mouth. "D–does he bite?"

He laughed, a smooth loud bellow that carried over the early morning wind. "It's a she, not a he. And no, Suzie wouldn't hurt anybody!" He opened the door, and the canine bounded out of the house.

Karen gasped when the dog pounced upon her, knocked her to the ground, and then began licking her face.

"Suzie!" Keith yelled, his tone filled with exasperation, as he pulled the dog off her.

Standing, Karen caught her breath while Suzie jumped up and down, barking.

Keith focused on Karen, his eyes full of concern. "I'm so sorry. Suzie hardly ever acts up like that when she first meets somebody." His full lips broke into a charming smile. "She must like you. Must mean you're okay, 'cause Suzie's a great judge of character."

The screen door creaked when he opened it. Karen followed the twosome into the house. "Do you mean to tell me you trust a dog to judge the character of people?"

Suzie sat on the floor, her dark eyes scrutinizing her master.

He poured dry dog food into a bright yellow dish and loaded a red bowl with water. Suzie dove into the food. "Not just any dog. I trust Suzie. She knows a good person when she sees one."

Keith washed his hands at the sink then dried them on a paper towel. As Karen watched him remove a carton of eggs from the refrigerator, the wetness of Suzie's unexpected greeting made her cheek tingle. "Do you mind if I use your restroom to clean up?"

"It's right down the hall on your left."

"Thanks." Karen exited the kitchen, stopping in the living room, observing the black leather furniture and TV coated with dust. On the mahogany end table rested two photos in silver frames. Lifting one picture, she observed two identical handsome faces grinning at the camera. The boys appeared to be around five years old, and one of them was missing a front tooth. She inspected the photo but could not determine which twin was Keith.

She returned the picture to the table and lifted the other. The warmth of the duplicate faces made her stare. This photo appeared to be taken at Keith's high school graduation. The twins' blue graduation robes cascaded around them, and each had an arm draped around the shoulder of the other. She again could not tell which boy was Keith. She finally returned the picture to its spot.

Not wanting to be caught snooping, she made a beeline to the bathroom. While washing and drying her face, she wondered about her mother's next-door neighbor. Did he have a girlfriend? If so, she didn't want the woman to stop by and find her significant other fixing breakfast for Karen. She dismissed the surprising thought, realizing Keith's personal affairs were none of her business.

Seconds later, she returned to the kitchen. Spices lined the counter and the smell of bacon filled the room. He grinned when she entered, his milky white teeth a nice contrast to his nut-brown skin. The effect made her heart race.

He turned a few slices of the meat. "There you are. I was starting to wonder what was taking you so long. I was about to come back there to check up on you." He gestured toward the table. "Have a seat. We'll eat in about ten minutes."

Karen was pleased to have somebody cook breakfast for her. Lionel never cooked. He always expected her to make meals according to his specifications. At the time, it never bothered her, because she loved him and wanted to please him. Absentmindedly, she began fingering her engagement ring.

"Are you okay?" Keith's strong voice interrupted her musings.

Karen mentally shook herself. Since Lionel's disappearance, her friends Anna and Monica said they could always tell when she was thinking about her fiancé. "Your eyes get sad, and you look like you're about to cry," Monica had told her.

She tried to smile, forcing thoughts of Lionel out of her mind. "I—I'm fine." She sniffed the alluring scent of bacon and omelets, mingled with brewing coffee. "I guess I'm a little hungry."

"Good, because breakfast is just about ready." He gestured toward the loaf of bread on the counter. "Do you want toast?" He glanced at her, his eyes twinkling with warmth. "You look like you could use some meat on your bones."

Normally Karen would have been offended by the comment, but the way Keith said it amused her. She smiled. "Toast is fine."

He prepared two pieces of toast for each of them then opened the refrigerator and removed butter and jelly. He placed both containers on the table, and seconds later he presented her a meal, served on a paper plate. As he poured coffee into Styrofoam cups, Karen realized she'd seen no dishes in the kitchen. She couldn't resist asking the question that was burning in the back of her mind. "Don't you have any real plates and silverware?"

He gestured toward a closed door at the edge of the kitchen. "My dishes and silverware are down in the basement."

She gazed at the door, still confused. "How come?"

"I hate washing dishes."

She shrugged. "Just use your dishwasher."

"I do sometimes, but it seems like a waste to run the dishwasher for just one person."

He sat beside her, adding a generous amount of cream and sugar to his coffee. When he touched her hand, warmth traveled up her arm. Sitting in Keith Baxter's home, sharing breakfast, had a charming and intimate quality about it.

"Do you mind if I say the blessing?" he asked.

Karen's throat had gone dry, so she swallowed. "I don't mind at all."

His large fingers wrapped around her hand as he bowed his head and closed his eyes. "Lord, thank You for this beautiful day and for this food. Also, thanks for letting me share my meal with Karen today. Amen." He squeezed her hand, and she returned the gesture.

"Amen," she whispered. Lifting her plastic fork, she sampled the omelet. "Oh man!"

Keith's eyes widened. "What's the matter? Don't you like it?"

"I love it!" She took another bite and chewed slowly, trying to decipher the ingredients. "What's in here?"

He shook his head, smiling. "It's a secret."

"A secret? You've never told anybody?"

He bit into a piece of bacon. "Nope. Although I can't take credit for the recipe."

"Really?" Grinning, she sipped her coffee. "I'll bet your mother taught you how to make this."

His smile faded. "No, not my mother. Ms. Sonya."

"Who's Ms. Sonya?"

"She practically raised my brother and me. If she hadn't had a husband and family of her own, my dad probably would have had her move in with us."

"So Sonya was like a nanny?" His family must've been pretty well-off financially if they could afford a nanny.

"She was nanny, housekeeper, cook, and whatever else you want to call her."

"I'm sure having Sonya around made things a lot easier for your mother," she said, wondering what Keith's mother was like.

"My mom died when I was three. I don't remember her. I think that's when my father hired Ms. Sonya."

"My goodness." Karen couldn't imagine not knowing one's mother. Her parents had always been such a big part of her life that she'd pretty much taken their presence for granted until her father died. "Did your dad talk about your mother a lot? Do you have pictures, stuff like that?"

Nodding, he took another bite of his food then swallowed before saying, "I have lots of pictures, but I don't think my dad liked to talk about Mom very much."

Karen wanted to ask why but didn't want to appear too nosy.

Keith spoke again. "Your mother reminds me of her."

"But I thought you didn't remember your mother."

"What I meant was that Doris reminds me of Ms. Sonya. They don't look at all alike, but your mom's mannerisms, her habits—stuff like that reminds me of Ms. Sonya."

She couldn't stop herself from voicing her next question. "Is that why you're so close to my mom?"

He shrugged. "I guess. I never really thought about it before. The relationship I have with your mother, I mean. It just kind of happened after I moved in. I think our worshipping at the same church, and her needing rides to service, might have had something to do with our spending time together and talking. I know she's proud of you and worries about you a lot."

Karen almost choked on her coffee. "What? She worries about me?"

"Has been, for the past year or so." He hesitated then said, "You haven't been down to visit her."

"Well, she took the train and came to visit me a couple of times. So it's not like I haven't seen her at all for the last year." She decided it was time to bring the subject of her mother to rest. "I saw your pictures in the living room. You have a twin brother?"

"Yes."

When no details were forthcoming, she asked another question. "What's his name?"

"Kyle."

"The two of you look like you're pretty close in the picture."

He continued to eat, not commenting.

"Has my mom ever met your brother?"

"No, she hasn't. He's been pretty busy lately and hasn't visited in a long time."

"That happens sometimes. People get tied up with careers and other things."

Silently they continued to eat. He finished his coffee and poured another cup. When Suzie marched to the table, barking, Keith dropped a piece of bacon on the floor. The dog gobbled it up, begging for more. "That's enough, Suzie." He rose from the table and opened the screen door. "Go on out there and get some air. I'll bring you in before I leave." Suzie ran into the yard, eyed a fluttering butterfly, and began chasing it, barking. The screen door squeaked then banged shut. Keith rejoined Karen at the table.

She wanted to know more about Keith Baxter. Just as she began settling in and sipping her second cup of coffee, he checked his watch.

"Well, I hate to hurry you out, but I have to leave in about twenty minutes to fix a client's sink."

Karen fought to keep her disappointment from showing. Since Lionel's disappearance, this was the first time she'd felt like herself. She wasn't sure if it was being with Keith or being in a different environment, away from the constant reminders of her botched relationship, that made her feel a little bit better.

He gestured toward her cup. "You can take the coffee back to Ms. Doris's with you." They stood. She held the Styrofoam container and plucked her flower off the table.

He touched her shoulder. "Before you leave, I wanted to ask you something."

"Yes?"

"Since you're just back in town, I wasn't sure if your mom has had a chance to ask you to come to church. How about if I give you two a ride over there this Sunday? I think you'll like the service."

Karen frowned.

"Maybe I shouldn't have asked you."

She shook her head, not wanting to give Keith the wrong impression. "No, it's okay. I'm just not sure my going would be a good idea."

Keith furrowed his brow. "Why?"

She sighed. "It's a long story. And I know you have to get to work."

He glanced at Suzie frolicking in the yard. "Why don't you at least think about it?"

"Listen, I–I'm just not ready. . .to go to church."

His frown deepened. "Ready? What's that supposed to mean?"

Suzie barked, and Keith checked his watch again. "Look, I've really got to get going. Is it okay if I stop by sometime over the next few days and talk to you?" He gestured toward her mom's garden. "Maybe I can catch you when you're out watering your mother's flowers?"

She shrugged, cradling her coffee cup, not wanting to hold him up any longer. "That's fine." She went out the door and, once in the yard, managed to skirt a galloping Suzie. She turned back and waved to Keith before heading home.

In her mom's kitchen, dirty dishes and a stained coffee cup littered the sink, verifying her mother had already awakened. Peeking through the kitchen window, Karen spotted Keith yelling for Suzie to return indoors. Minutes later, he drove away in his cream-colored van.

264

Chapter 3

The next day, Karen pulled into the small parking lot of the unisex salon on Maryland Avenue in Annapolis, itching to unload the boxes of hair-care supplies loaded in the trunk of her car.

She entered her new place of employment, which was bustling with activity. Smooth jazz wafted from the oversized speakers, and a ball game played silently on the TV. A group of people waited in the small reception area while ten barbers served customers sitting in black leather chairs. One child fidgeted in his chair as he watched the barber plug in his electric clippers. When the shears made contact with the boy's scalp, the child let out a shriek. As tears began streaming down his face, Karen felt an overwhelming urge to pull the boy into a hug. Instead, she turned her attention to the young dark-skinned woman with plaited hair sitting behind the receptionist's desk.

Karen approached. "Hi, I'm Karen Brown. The manager, I mean, Carol, told me I could start today. Sorry if I'm a little late. I assumed the salon opened at nine. But I noticed the sign outside says eight."

The woman stood. "No problem." She reached out to shake Karen's hand. "I'm Gail. Carol isn't in today, but she told me to expect you. You got your stuff with you? I'll show you where to set up."

"It's out in the car. I'll go and get it."

"I'll help," Gail said then turned and yelled, "Hey, Darren, watch the desk for me! I'm helping the new woman get set up!"

A barber nodded without looking up, continuing to clip his client's hair. Gail followed Karen to the back of the shop then out to her car, where Karen popped open her trunk. Each woman hefted a box and then trekked back into the shop, setting the cartons down at Karen's empty station.

Gail folded her arms in front of her. "We have ten barbers up front. They bring in most of our business. We keep the beauty shop here in the back."

Karen appreciated the space in the large beauty shop area, which boasted eight black-and-steel-colored hair dryers. A separate section held a washer and an already-spinning clothes dryer. The two stylists glanced her way, mumbling a greeting before returning to their clients' hair.

As they returned to the car to get the rest of her stuff, Gail placed her hand on Karen's arm, halting her. "Before you start, I wanted to warn you about one

265

of the other hairstylists."

"Who?"

"Sheronda. She's the heavy one you saw using a flatiron."

Karen held her box, anxious to get back inside. "What about her?"

Gail leaned toward her. "Well, I know Carol told you that you have to provide all of your own supplies except for shampoo and conditioner."

"Yes, she told me that when I talked to her on the phone."

The young woman continued. "Well, Sheronda will sometimes use some of your supplies."

Karen shrugged, used to beauticians borrowing each other's stuff. "So—that's typical."

The girl waved her hand. "No, you don't understand! Sheronda will borrow perm cream, coloring, whatever, and never give it back! You'll have to keep reminding her and practically force her to return your supplies."

"I'll try to remember that," said Karen, smiling.

Gail continued. "Also, she gossips a lot. So if you don't want your business making its way up to the barbers, then you shouldn't say anything around her."

"Okay." Karen clutched her box.

The girl continued to talk, helping Karen carry the rest of her stuff into the shop. "Since we get a lot of customers who are tourists, we get a lot of walk-ins. Carol says business is never too slow, so that should be a good thing for you. By the way, do you do haircuts, too?"

"You mean like men's haircuts, right?"

Gail nodded.

"Sure. No problem."

"Great, because sometimes when the barbers are backed up, we'll send their walk-in clients back here to you guys. Sheronda does an awesome job with men's haircuts, but Deidre, the other stylist, doesn't like barbering, so I don't send any of the male customers her way."

Karen arranged her supplies and Gail returned to the desk, giving Karen the first walk-in beauty appointment. She soon got into the flow of the shop, and she was glad that she had two walk-ins in a row since Deidre and Sheronda were taking care of regular customers.

When a few whoops and hollers erupted from the barbers' area, Karen realized that working in a unisex shop would be a different experience than where she'd worked before, a salon that featured a mostly female clientele.

At midday, some of the barbers ate their lunch, laughing and talking as they watched the game on TV in the front of the shop. A few others continued to service clients.

Sheronda and Deidre had just enough time to grab a bite before their scheduled appointments arrived. They sat with Karen in the large employee break room, eating a Papa John's pizza they'd all chipped in on.

As Karen sipped her soda, Sheronda looked at her engagement ring. "You engaged?"

Karen winced. Why couldn't she find the courage to remove Lionel's ring and fall *out* of love with him?

Deidre came to her rescue. "Stop asking questions, Sheronda. You can see that she doesn't want to talk about it." Deidre plopped two slices of pizza onto her plate.

Karen gave both women a warm smile, not wanting to start her first day on the job on the wrong foot. "It's kind of complicated."

Sheronda folded her arms in front of her chest. "How so?"

"It's a long story."

"Humph. That can only mean one of three things." She held her index finger in the air. "Number one, it's a long-distance relationship." She held up a second finger. "Or number two, you're no longer engaged and just don't want anybody to know." She held up a third finger. "Or number three, the man is in prison and you're too ashamed to admit it."

Karen took a shaky breath. *Sheronda's last assumption isn't far from the truth. If Lionel is ever found, he could end up in prison.*

Gail entered the break room, giving Karen a much-needed reprieve. "Sheronda, your twelve thirty appointment is here."

Sheronda threw her plate away and headed to her station.

Deidre touched Karen's shoulder. "Don't worry about Sheronda. She's just always trying to start trouble."

"Thanks, Deidre. I'm okay."

❧

That evening, after the shop had closed, Karen didn't feel like going home. She drove to the Eastport section of downtown and parked. Wandering the redbrick streets, she stopped at a shop window, admiring the lemon-colored summer dress draped around a mannequin. She toyed with the idea of entering the chic clothing store and trying the item on.

"Do you like it?"

She turned, shocked to see Keith Baxter standing beside her, sporting a pair of jeans and a collared shirt. "What are you doing here?" she blurted.

His caramel-colored eyes twinkled when he looked at her. "I had to get a few things for the church from the Christian bookstore down the street."

"What kinds of things?"

"Stuff for Communion this Sunday, like bottles of grape juice and wafers."

"Is it usually your job to pick up those sorts of things for the church?" she asked, wondering how involved he was within the congregation.

"No. But they're a little short on volunteers this week. So I offered."

"Oh, I see." She glanced toward the dress again.

"Do you like the dress?" he repeated.

"Yes, I like it a lot."

"Why don't you try it on?"

"No, the temptation would be too great."

"Temptation?"

"To buy the dress. I don't think I should spend the money."

"I can understand that." They stood on the redbrick sidewalk, admiring the garment. Keith cleared his throat. "Um, would you like to join me for dinner?"

"Dinner?"

"Yes, dinner." His smile looked warm like sunshine. "You haven't eaten yet, have you?"

She shook her head.

He gestured toward the Spa Creek Bridge. "I was going to walk across the bridge and go to Carrol's Creek for dinner. I love their lobster." He touched her shoulder. "I'll treat."

"A lobster dinner at Carrol's Creek?" A slight breeze blew off the Chesapeake Bay, billowing her light jacket. "That's an awful lot of money to spend on a virtual stranger."

He grinned. "Karen," he said as he steered her toward Spa Creek Bridge, "you're not a stranger to me."

When he said her name, her spine shivered and her mouth went dry. She swallowed, trying to find her voice. "I–I'm not?"

His laughter rumbled. "Of course not. You're Ms. Doris's daughter. She's talked about you so much that I feel like I know you already."

Several minutes later, they entered the crowded restaurant. Scents of shrimp, fish, and lobster filled the air, as well as the din of diners' voices raised in conversation.

The host approached, bearing two menus. "Hi, Keith!" The men shook hands.

"Hey, Jerome."

Jerome smiled, focusing on Karen. "Two for dinner?"

"Yes, this is Karen. Karen, this is Jerome."

Jerome and Karen shook hands.

Keith scanned the room. "Do you have a table available with a view of the water?"

"I can help you out with that." They followed him to a table with an exquisite view of the Chesapeake Bay. "I'll tell your waiter to bring your bread right away."

"Thanks, Jerome."

Keith pulled out her chair, waiting until she sat before he settled into his seat. They studied the menus and Karen glanced outside periodically, watching the ships resting on the tranquil water of the marina. "You seem to know the host pretty well."

"Yes, I come here every week, and when I do, Jerome is usually working." He scanned the room. "I love eating here."

Rays from the bright sun spilled through the window, warming their table with light. Karen glanced at the docked ships before speaking. "I remember when I came here for dinner in high school. My date brought me here before we went to the prom." Fond memories unfurled through her mind like the sail of a ship. "It was a nice night."

The server placed glasses of water, rolls, and butter on their table before taking his exit.

"So you've always lived here in Annapolis?"

"I lived here my whole life until I moved to Ocean City." She sipped from her water glass. "Have you always lived in Annapolis?"

"Pretty much, except for college."

"You've only been living next door to my mother for six months. Where were you living before that?"

"With my father."

"Had you always lived with your dad?"

He shook his head. "No. About a year and a half ago, my dad began suffering from cancer. When he got worse, I moved in with him to help with his care. He died six months ago."

"I'm so sorry." Her voice softened. "I didn't know. . . . Did my mother tell you that my father died two years ago?"

"Yes, and how hard it was for her to adjust afterward."

"Yes, it was. . .difficult." Karen swallowed the lump in her throat. "H–have you been okay since your dad died?"

He sighed, gazing outside for a few seconds. "Honestly? No. I still think about him a lot. I just find it so hard to believe he's gone."

Karen touched his hand. "I know what you mean. I felt the same way when my father died."

They sat in silence for a few minutes; then Keith spoke again. "Before I moved in with my dad, I lived in a condo. Then when I started taking care of him, I rented out my place. After Dad passed, I just felt it was time for me to buy a house."

She paused, considering her next words. "My mother tells me that you can be somewhat blunt."

"Yeah, why?"

"Well, I'm about to be blunt with you."

He frowned. "What do you mean?"

"Well, you seem to be pretty well-off to be a plumber. You have a condo that you're currently renting, and you own the home that's next door to my mother."

He nodded. "I make a pretty good living as a plumber. People don't realize how much we charge by the hour." He sipped his water. "I also inherited money from my dad."

"Oh." Not wanting to appear nosy, Karen decided to change the subject. "Since you've always lived in Annapolis, I'm surprised that I've never run into you before, like in school. How old are you?"

"I'm thirty, the same age as you. We've probably never met before because I always went to private schools."

"How did you know how old I am?" asked Karen.

"Your mom told me."

She again wondered how much her mother had revealed about her, but their waiter returned before she could broach the subject.

"Are you ready to order?"

"Do you mind if I order for us?" Keith asked her.

"Go right ahead."

She was pleased when Keith took the lead. He ordered lemonade, corn on the cob, baked potatoes, and steamed lobsters.

After the waiter departed, taking their menus with him, Keith asked, "Mind if I say grace?"

"No, of course not."

Keith took her hand and blessed the food.

After echoing his "Amen," Karen pulled her hand away, trying to ignore the tingle he'd left behind.

Keith began buttering a roll. "So tell me a little bit more about why you're here staying at your mom's house."

Karen sighed. "Well, for one thing, the hair shop where I used to work closed down."

He shrugged. "So rather than find another job in Ocean City, you decided to come back home to Annapolis?"

"I needed a change." She reached for a roll.

He shrugged again. "But why?"

She bit her lip, wondering if having dinner with Keith was a mistake. "Can we change the subject?"

He held his hands up in the air. "Sure, fine with me." He looked at the marina for a long time. "Doris said that you're a Christian. Tell me a little bit about your church."

"I don't go to church anymore," she said in a small voice.

He frowned. "You mentioned when we had breakfast that you weren't ready to go back to church."

"That's right."

"Why? I know you're hurting because Lionel left, but you can't abandon God because of. . .your situation."

She clutched her roll, wondering if Keith knew all of the sordid details. "You just don't know when to stop, do you?" She threw her bread back onto the plate.

"Take it easy. . . . I was only asking you about your church."

She shook her head. "My church is part of the reason why I left."

Confusion crossed his face. "I—I don't understand."

She tried to calm down. "You can be honest with me. Exactly what did my mother tell you about my fiancé?"

"She said you two were planning on getting married but he left and nobody knows where he is."

"That's all she said?"

He stopped eating his roll, focusing on the ships bobbing on the water before responding. "She said that you implied he'd gotten cold feet."

"There's so much my mother didn't tell you."

His voice softened. "What happened?"

She told him of Lionel's and Michelle's disappearance and the missing money from the church bank account, wrapping up the story by saying, "So it looks like they stole from the church." Tears rolled down her cheeks.

He gave her a napkin and took her hand, his eyes full of kindness. "Karen, I'm sorry about what happened. But you can't abandon your church because of it."

She sniffled then blew her nose, finding a strange comfort in his touch. "You don't understand. I didn't abandon my church. My *church* abandoned *me*."

"Why do you say that?" He squeezed her hand, encouraging her to continue.

"After Lionel disappeared, I couldn't eat and I couldn't sleep. When I'd come to church, people would stare at me and whisper behind my back. Everybody acted so different. I was so. . .embarrassed." She paused. "S–some of the women think I might have helped or encouraged Lionel to commit this crime. But I didn't! I don't even know where Lionel is!"

She wondered if she'd revealed too much. But it seemed she couldn't help it. His warmth and encouragement had caused her to completely spill her soul.

Suddenly realizing she was appreciating Keith's hand-holding too much, she abruptly pulled her hand away.

He glanced down at the table where her hand had been then looked into her eyes. "You know, when you said you'd stopped going to church, I thought about a scripture in Matthew. The one where Jesus talks about building a house on a solid foundation? If the foundation isn't solid, the house is blown away when a storm comes."

She nodded.

"Well, I think people's faith needs to be strong, just like the house built on a rock that Jesus was talking about. If your faith is solid, then you'd keep going to church. Don't let the church members' attitudes prevent you from worshipping the Lord."

Her mouth dropped open. "You're telling me that I should go back to that church, with all those hypocritical people, people who are accusing me of being a thief?" Her warm feelings toward him vanished.

"I'm just saying that you shouldn't let other people's attitudes make you stop worshipping God. You need to go back to Ocean City, not run away from your problems. You need to strengthen your faith in God and keep right on worshipping Him in your church."

Glaring at him, she gritted her teeth. "Have you ever been accused of being a thief and a liar by your church?"

Keith's caramel-colored eyes widened, the question apparently catching him off guard. "Well, no, I—"

She abruptly stood. "Well then, don't tell me what to do and how to act when you've never been through what I've been through!"

Their server approached, bearing two plates with freshly steamed lobster. She shook her head, no longer wanting to be in Keith's presence. "I'm sorry. I've lost my appetite."

She left the restaurant, her stomach roiling in anger. When she got to her car, she realized she'd left Keith sitting at the table alone. She hesitated before she drove away from downtown Annapolis, still trying to calm herself down.

When she arrived home, fatigue swept through her like a tidal wave. She went into the kitchen, knowing she needed to eat something before falling asleep. She made a grilled cheese sandwich and ate half of it, feeling guilty about having abandoned Keith in the restaurant.

She pushed her half-eaten sandwich aside. "Lord, why can't I let this go? Why can't I just get over Lionel and his deceit? I feel so bad about getting mad at Keith when he was only trying to help me." She tossed the remains of her sandwich into the trash before heading for bed.

Chapter 4

After another restless night, Keith awakened at 5:00 a.m. and got out of bed. Plodding to the bathroom, he recalled the events of the previous evening. After his aborted dinner with Karen, he'd eaten his meal alone. Later, driving down Main Street, he'd seen his brother strolling down the sidewalk, his arm draped around a woman. Keith had pulled over, his heart pounding as he watched the couple enter an upscale bar. He'd sat in his vehicle for a few minutes, wondering if the Lord had presented this opportunity so that he could approach Kyle. He'd silently prayed then decided the time wasn't right.

Not wanting to dwell on his problematic relationship with his brother, he turned his thoughts to Karen and her anger against God, hoping he could smooth things over with her. All he'd been trying to do was tell her to remain faithful to Jesus amid her troubles. But she'd obviously misunderstood.

He dressed, put his glasses on, and brushed his teeth. He opened the blinds and glanced over at Ms. Doris's house. The kitchen curtains were open, and he saw movement in the room. Seconds later, Karen appeared in Doris's backyard. After he'd watched her water the flowers, he removed a square Styrofoam container from his refrigerator and hurried over to her house.

Karen abandoned the hose when he approached. Dark circles shadowed her eyes.

He swallowed before speaking. "I'm sorry."

"I'm sorry."

They spoke at the same time, and Keith laughed nervously.

"Want to come in for some coffee?" she asked with a yawn.

"Sounds great."

Karen gestured toward the container as they walked toward the house. "What's that?"

"It's your dinner. I didn't have enough room in my stomach to eat both meals, so I got yours to go." They entered her home, and he plopped the box on the kitchen table. "I've had leftover lobster before. It should be pretty tasty."

"Thanks. I'll take it with me to work and eat it for lunch."

She placed the container in the refrigerator then poured two cups of coffee while he sat at the table.

She fixed him a cup, spicing it up with just the right amount of cream and sugar, then joined him at the table.

Impressed that she'd remembered how he took his coffee, he took a sip, pleased with the way the brew danced on his tongue, waking him up. "Look, I know you got mad at me yesterday for what I said."

She raised her eyebrows. "At first I was mad, but after I thought about it, I realized you were just trying to give me suggestions on how to get through this. . .difficult time." Her long eyelashes fluttered when she glanced down at the table, and he wondered what she was thinking. "Whenever I talk about what happened, why I happen to be living here with my mother, I get upset." She paused before continuing. "I'm just sensitive about what happened with Lionel, and sometimes people dole out advice when they've never been in the same situation. I'm the victim here, and some people, especially those in my church, don't seem to think that."

He frowned. "The whole church is giving you a hard time, or just a few members?"

"Just a few people. The pastor and his wife have been more than loving toward me, encouraging me to come back to church." She shrugged and started looking sad again. "It's just too hard for me to go back there." She looked around the kitchen. "Before I went to sleep last night, Monica called me."

"Who's that?"

"One of my best friends. She told me she'd had her baby."

"Well, that's good news."

"Yeah, I was happy to hear about it. But that wasn't the only reason she called."

"What else did she say?"

"It seems the local paper in Ocean City ran an update on the original story about Lionel's embezzlement."

He placed his cup on the table. "Did you find out anything you didn't already know?"

She nodded. "They've hired an outside firm to audit the church's finances. It appears that Lionel and maybe Michelle have been stealing money from the church for over a year. They've found evidence that both were writing checks drawn on the church bank, then cashing them and using the funds for their own personal use." She touched the large diamond ring gracing her finger. "I'm starting to wonder if Lionel was spending some of that money on me. Did he buy this engagement ring with church money?" She glanced at the window for a few seconds. "Lionel always liked spending money, and I'd assumed the money he was spending was his own. It almost sickens me to wear my engagement ring anymore since it may have been purchased with tainted money."

"You don't know that." He gave the situation some thought then asked, "Is the audit done?"

She shrugged. "I guess so. Who knows? I didn't think to ask Monica what else the article said. I could go online and read it for myself, but I—I just can't do it right now."

"You don't have to if you don't want to."

They sat in silence for a few minutes. Then Karen, her lower lip trembling, said, "I—I just feel so. . .responsible for—for everything that happened. What if Lionel stole that money. . .to buy me things? Like this engagement ring. What if he thought he needed more money. . .to m–make me happy? To buy us a home?"

"But you weren't—you *aren't*—responsible."

"H–how could I have been engaged to a man I didn't even know? How could I have been so blind?"

He paused then said, "Maybe you should start worshipping at our church."

"Our church?"

"Yes. The one your mom and I attend."

His suggestion was met with silence. So he tried another tactic. "Do you feel better since you're living here?"

"Yes, I do."

"Well, our church is small, and we're always looking for some of our members to volunteer in its ministries. If you start coming to our church and find that you like worshipping there, then you might want to consider helping me out with the youth."

She furrowed her brow, frowning. She then stood, topped off their coffee cups, and returned to the table. "Helping you out with the youth?"

"Yes, at Devo every Friday night."

"What's 'Devo'?"

"It's short for *devotional*. Every week we have a youth gathering—it's mostly praise and worship—and the youth can talk about things that are bothering them. My friend Melanie usually helps, but she's been canceling a lot lately. I'm not sure what's been going on with her, but it would be nice to have another pair of hands. We usually have dinner afterward."

"I don't know anything about teenagers."

"Sure you do. You were a teenager yourself once, weren't you?"

She smiled. "Yes."

"So? Just remember what it was like back then. Sometimes young people get confused, and it's easier for them to talk to an adult other than their parents."

"I don't know," she mumbled. "I'm pretty confused myself right now."

He patted her shoulder. "Just give it some thought. I think it would be good for you."

"Why do you say that?"

"My first minister in college used to say that when you're hurting, you should try not to focus on your own pain. One way to do that is to help others. I can tell you're hurting, and I just want to make you feel better." He paused. "It was wrong of me to advise you to go back to your church where you felt uncomfortable. I've never been in your situation, so I probably should have told you that it would be best if you worshipped at another church where you felt more welcome." He looked down at his coffee. "Or I could have just kept my big mouth shut."

"Why do you care about me—my situation?"

He toyed with the salt and pepper shakers on the table then shrugged. "It's the way I am. I feel called to help people."

She frowned. "Do you mean like a pastor?"

"Yes." Looking into her dark eyes, he decided to tell her about his dream. "I don't know how much your mom has told you about me."

Karen took a sip of coffee. "Well, she told me about how much you love the Lord and how devoted you are to the church."

"Well, I'd like to lead a church one day, if God allows. You'd think at thirty years old I'd have this all figured out, but I'm taking it one day at a time."

Raising her eyebrows, she set her mug back onto the table. "You want to be a pastor?"

"Yes, I do. But I still have a lot of things I need to do first."

"Such as?"

He paused, still struggling with what to tell her about his future plans.

"You don't have to tell me if you don't want to."

"Well, for starters, I need to learn how to advise people in such a way that they don't end up leaving restaurants in a huff."

She winced. "I probably overreacted."

"No, I can be quite blunt. I need to work on that. Another thing I'd like to do is go to divinity school to get my degree."

She leaned toward him. "Really?"

"Yes, I'm looking into some schools now."

She sat back. "Have you ever preached?"

"Yes, a few times."

She smiled. "How did it go?"

"Honestly? It wasn't bad, but I felt it could be better." They were silent for a few seconds before Keith reminded her about his earlier question. "Just give my request some thought."

"Your request?"

"To help out at the church. I think it'll be good for you."

"I don't know."

"Our congregation doesn't know what happened to you, so they can't hold it against you. Plus, once you start ministering and fellowshipping with other Christians, it'll take your mind off. . .other things."

"I'll think about it," was all she managed to say.

"Okay, let me know what you decide." He squeezed her hand before he left her home.

Chapter 5

Over the following week Karen worked steadily at her new job. Turning a deaf ear to Sheronda's prying questions and constant gossip, Karen focused on building up her clientele. At home, she spent lots of time with her mother, much of it in the kitchen, where they prepared meals and conversed about life.

One evening they dined at the Aqua Terra on Main Street before buying dessert at the Annapolis Ice Cream Factory, which proudly boasted about baking cobblers and pies on its premises and smashing them into its homemade ice cream. While digging into a dish of the store's unique and luscious-tasting blackberry cobbler ice cream, Karen murmured, "Mmm. This is so good."

"Yes, it is," her mother agreed. "So, Karen, are you going to services this weekend? You know it's Easter. What a great time to begin worshipping again."

Karen ate a few more spoonfuls of her treat before responding to her mother's question. "Yes, Mom, I think I will."

Doris squeezed her daughter's hand. "I'm glad to hear that." She suddenly frowned.

"Mom, what's wrong?"

"I just wondered about Lionel. You haven't mentioned him since Monica called about the church's audit."

Karen abandoned her spoon. "I'm still angry, but I don't hurt as much as I used to."

Doris hugged her daughter. "Give your anger over to God," she whispered.

‿❧

Karen awoke at dawn to a sunny and unseasonably warm Easter Sunday. She stretched and smiled, having slept well.

Hearing a knock on her bedroom door, she yelled out, "Mom. . . ? Come on in!"

Her mother poked her head in. "You awake?"

"Yes, just. You're up early."

"Yes. For an hour or so already. I just wanted to let you know that Keith is picking me up soon to take me to church."

"You're leaving already?" Karen asked with a yawn.

278

Her mother nodded. "We need to be there early to prepare for the holiday services."

"Are you excited about singing in the choir today?"

"Well, I don't know about excited," her mother said with a somewhat nervous smile. "There's bound to be a big crowd."

"Believe me, Mom. You'll do just great."

"I hope so. . . . Well, I've got to get going. I'll see you later?"

"Wouldn't miss it for the world," Karen said.

An hour later, Karen pulled into the parking lot of the small house of worship in nearby Gambrills, Maryland. Bible in hand, she approached the steps to the recently renovated building. Tulips nodded in the spring breeze, creating a rainbow of color beside the whitewashed structure. The steeple gleamed in the early morning sun as if Jesus was smiling down on the church.

Taking a deep breath, she entered the vestibule, admiring the cranberry carpet and paneled walls. Karen's heart stopped when she spotted Keith standing at the sanctuary door, holding a stack of programs. The dark suit, crisp white shirt, and midnight blue tie accented his broad chest and shoulders. His eyes sparkled when he saw her.

"Karen." He wrapped his arms around her.

Somewhat stunned, Karen returned his embrace then stepped out of his arms. "Hi, Keith."

"I didn't know you were coming."

"My mom didn't tell you?"

"No." He grinned. "She spent the entire ride going over her choir music." He pressed a program into her hand. "You look beautiful."

She touched her hair. "Thanks, you look nice, too."

He glanced toward the other usher. "Aaron, this is Karen Brown. She's Ms. Doris's daughter. Karen, this is Aaron."

She smiled, shaking Aaron's hand before Keith spoke again. "Can you handle things alone for a minute, Aaron?"

The tall, dark-skinned man grinned. "I've got things covered. Take your time."

Keith pulled Karen aside. "You're wearing the dress."

Puzzled, she tried to make sense of his words. "The dress?" The delicious musky scent of his cologne surrounded her, and when she peered into his eyes, she realized his face looked different.

"Yes, the dress you were looking at the night we had dinner together?" He paused. "I mean the night we *almost* had dinner together."

Karen recalled their aborted meal with some embarrassment. "Yes, well. . . I guess I couldn't resist. . . . I'm surprised you remembered," she said, suddenly glad she'd given in to her impulse.

"There's not much about you that I forget." He gave her a warm smile.

For the first time Karen realized Keith had a dimple in his left cheek. But something else about him was different today. *Hmm. He is so nice, and handsome, and. . .* Karen nervously cleared her throat. As she stuffed her program into her Bible, she tried to focus on his altered appearance instead of the effect he seemed to be having on her. "There's something different about you today. What is it?"

"Huh?"

She frowned in concentration while he continued to grin. And then it hit her. "You're not wearing your glasses!"

"Nope. I'm wearing my contact lenses."

His light brown eyes were warm and rich like hot caramel sauce. She looked away, needing to get into the sanctuary to find her seat. She glanced at Aaron, who was looking a bit overwhelmed at the huge crowd of parishioners coming through the doors.

As if reading her thoughts, Keith said, "Look, I've got to help Aaron. But I'll talk to you at your house later."

"At my house?"

He led her back to the sanctuary door. "Yes, didn't your mom tell you?"

"Tell me what?"

"She invited me over for lunch after service."

With a parting smile, he resumed his station at the door while Karen entered the sanctuary, both floored and excited about their unexpected lunch guest.

❧

Trying hard not to stare at Karen's retreating form, Keith forced himself to focus on the churchgoers entering the sanctuary. He could just kick himself for admitting he remembered almost everything about her! He was sure she didn't want to hear that.

Finally, as the prelude began and the ushers were about to close the double doors, Aaron drew closer to Keith, saying softly, "Karen's a cute little thing. Are you two involved?"

Rolling his eyes, Keith entered the room behind his friend. "No," he whispered, not wanting Aaron to get the wrong idea. "You know how I feel about dating right now."

Aaron and Keith sat in the back, ready to assist latecomers who would be looking for seats. The choir voices lifted in song and Keith closed his eyes, taking delight in the joyful melody resounding throughout the church, wrapping the audience with God's Holy Spirit. He finally opened his eyes and focused on Ms. Doris. Her robe drifted as she swayed with the rest of the choral members. Her dark eyes appeared nervous, but when her gaze met his, she smiled, giving him a quick wink, continuing to sing.

The tune carried on and he clapped his hands, swaying to the rhythm. Parishioners stood in their seats, heartily singing along, clapping, and praising the Lord. Keith smiled, joy filling his soul on this Easter morning.

Sunlight streamed through the stained-glass windows, warming the church with light. When the chorus finally ended, Pastor Bolton stepped up to the podium, his deep booming voice filling the sanctuary. "Happy Easter, everybody!"

Several members responded, "Praise the Lord! Happy Easter!"

"It's a pleasure to have all of you here today." He stared at the audience before speaking. "I'd like to invite Keith Baxter to step forward and lead the opening prayer."

Wiping his sweaty palms on his pants, Keith went to the pulpit, trying to calm his frazzled nerves. He walked onto the platform. "Good morning, everybody."

"Good morning, Keith! Praise the Lord!"

"We are here to praise Jesus today." He bowed his head. "Lord, thank You for this beautiful Easter morning, for this day of life, and for the sacrifice You made by sending Your Son. Please be with us as we continue through the day, worshipping You and praising You. And if there are any souls suffering here today, may Your Holy Spirit comfort them." He gripped the podium, his eyes still closed. "In Jesus' name, amen."

"Amen," several parishioners responded.

Pastor Bolton stepped to the pulpit and shook Keith's hand. "Wonderful job, Keith."

"Thanks for letting me lead the prayer, Pastor," Keith said softly to the minister; then he rejoined Aaron in the back of the church.

As Pastor Bolton read the account of Jesus' resurrection in the Gospels, many members expressed their joy over the event that granted eternal life to those who accepted Jesus as their Savior.

"Amen!" cried members from the pews.

When the sermon was over, the pastor gripped the pulpit. "If there is any-body present who has not accepted Jesus, or if you're a believer with something on your heart that you want to let go and bring to Jesus, please come forward."

Keith and Aaron, part of the four-member prayer and encouragement team, stood and walked forward. This was one of Keith's favorite moments during a service. His heart lifted with gladness when a person came forward, wanting to accept Jesus as his Savior.

Several "Praise Gods" and "Halleujahs" sounded from the audience. They continued to chant the song "Oh, What a Mighty God We Serve" along with the choir as people came forward. Keith's heart stopped when Karen walked down the aisle, tears streaming from her pretty brown eyes. She looked like a wounded dove, and all he wanted to do was lift her up and help take away her pain.

A total of eighteen people stepped forward. Pastor Bolton's wife divided the lot into four groups, one group for each member of the prayer and encouragement team. When Keith led his group away to the prayer room, he said a silent prayer for Karen, who'd been assigned to Aaron's group. *Lord, may her time in prayer with You heal her spirit.*

୬ଈ

Before going to Ms. Doris's house, Keith changed into his best jeans and collared shirt, still thinking about the events that occurred after the service. He'd prayed with his assigned group before searching for Karen. Aaron found him and gave him the message that Ms. Doris had ridden home with her daughter and was looking forward to seeing him later for lunch.

Still wondering if Karen was okay, Keith strolled toward her house. A light breeze blew, rustling the new green leaves budding on the trees. He rapped on Ms. Doris's back door. Karen opened it, her petite frame sporting a pair of jeans and a pink T-shirt. Resisting the urge to kiss her cheek, he stepped into the kitchen. The scents of cheese, ham, and tomatoes filled the space, making his mouth water. "Smells good in here."

"Thanks. The food is almost ready." She tapped his arm, and his skin sizzled from the brief touch. "Come into the dining room."

A small platter of cheese and crackers rested in the center of the dining room table, along with smaller empty plates. "Where's your mom?"

"She's on the phone. She'll be out shortly." She gestured toward the platter. "Help yourself. Would you like something to drink?"

"A Coke, if you have it."

She exited the dining room and returned with his soda. He thanked her before he sat, wanting to relish their time alone before her mother returned. "I was glad you stepped forward at church today. Did the prayer session afterward help?" When she didn't respond, he rushed on, wanting to put her at ease. "You don't have to answer if you don't want to. I know it's none of my business."

"That's okay. It's sweet of you to ask." Sighing, she sat in the empty chair beside him.

He admired her crimson-colored nails when she placed cheese and crackers onto a plate for herself, his heart skipping upon realizing that Lionel's engagement ring was now absent from her finger.

"You know, my mom told me to give my anger over to God."

"And that's why you came forward?"

She nodded.

"Do you still feel angry?"

"Yes. But Aaron told me it would probably take some time for my anger to go away completely. I do feel better about returning to church, and I'm going to start reading my Bible again."

"You haven't read your Bible since Lionel disappeared?" He found this hard to believe.

"Keith, I've all but forsaken God after what happened. I feel bad about it, and I know my anger and resentment toward God, Lionel, and Michelle was making me bitter."

He touched her shoulder, fighting the urge to pull her into his arms. "Don't feel bad about it, Karen. The Lord's already forgiven you." He dropped some cheese and crackers onto his own plate, suddenly feeling awkward. "I know it's hard to lean on God during difficult times. There are things that have happened to me over the last six months that have tested my own faith."

"Like what?" She looked at him, her dark eyes full of curiosity.

"Mostly issues with my family."

"Are you talking about the death of your father and the situation with your brother?"

He frowned. "How do you know about the situation with Kyle?"

She shrugged, immediately putting him at ease. "I don't. I just sensed things were not well between you two. When I commented on the photo of you and Kyle, you didn't say anything. I almost felt like you were hiding something."

"I wasn't hiding anything. I just don't like talking about it. I've been praying about it though."

"But it does bother you."

"How did you know?"

"Because I know you. You're so intent about getting me to renew my faith in God and not let my anger toward Lionel control my life. You've also told me you're concerned about other people in your congregation. If you're so concerned about me, my mother, and the rest of your congregation, then I sense that you care a great deal about your brother simply because he is your brother."

He was silent as he thought about her words.

A few seconds later, she asked, "Do you ever talk to him?"

He didn't like the way this conversation was playing out. "No."

"Why not? Maybe the Lord wants you to call your brother and try to rectify the situation."

"I don't think that's a good idea."

"Why not?" she asked again.

He didn't feel like mentioning that his brother never wanted to speak to him again. Karen wouldn't understand, and he didn't feel like ruining their Easter lunch by rehashing the family drama that had spanned the last several months.

"I don't think Kyle wants to hear from me right now. I know my brother, and when he's ready to talk, he'll let me know."

"I hope things work out with you two. I'll be praying for you."

Doris entered. "Keith, I'm glad you could join us."

"Thanks for inviting me, Ms. Doris." He stood. "Do you two need help carrying the food from the kitchen?"

Doris shook her head. "Karen and I can handle it."

The mahogany table was soon filled with the delicious-looking food.

"Keith, before we eat, would you say grace?" asked Doris.

As they bowed their heads and joined hands, he asked the Lord to bless their food.

Chapter 6

A couple of weeks later, on a Friday night, Keith rapped on the back door of Karen's house. This would be her first night helping him with Devo. When Karen opened the door, she smiled warmly.

He touched her arm, entering the house. "Hi."

"Hi, Keith." She brushed his hand with her fingertips. "I'll be right back."

He watched her go, his hand still burning from her touch. There was something about this girl that sent his heart and mind whirling. *Karen, do you have any clue what you do to me?*

Minutes later she returned, holding her purse and Bible. "I'm ready." Her velvety smooth voice broke into his thoughts.

"Okay then," he said, smiling. "Let's go." They headed out the back door and into his car. Pulling the car onto the street, he said, "You know, I'm glad you agreed to help me with this."

"My pleasure."

"How's the job going?"

She rolled her eyes. "One of my coworkers gets on my nerves, but otherwise, it's fine."

"Maybe you might want to look for a job at another salon if this one doesn't seem right."

She groaned.

"What's wrong?"

"Nothing. I know I should feel blessed to have a job, but I'm tired of working in salons."

He stopped at a light. "You don't want to be a hairdresser?"

"I love doing hair, but I'm tired of dealing with crazy coworkers."

He pulled away from the light. "Well, if you had your choice, what would you do?"

She stared out the window, hesitating. Then she turned to him and said softly, "I—I'd like to own my own salon."

He couldn't help smiling.

She slapped his shoulder. "What are you smiling about? You don't think I can do it?"

"I *know* you can. Tell me all about it."

"What?"

"Tell me how you envision your salon."

"Well. . .it would be large and roomy. Glossy pine floors, great lighting, with plenty of mirrors. We'd have somebody specializing in natural hair. Then the others would focus on doing perms and touch-ups, maybe a weave or two. We'd have high-quality hair dryers and blow dryers. There'd be a washer and dryer in the back to wash the tons of towels we'd use." She settled back into the seat, and when he pulled into the church parking lot, it appeared that Karen barely noticed their surroundings as she continued. "My stylists and beauticians would be so good that we'd be booked solid weeks in advance, and word in town would be that my place would be the best place to go to get your next touch-up or perm."

Pride filled her voice and her full, pretty lips curved into a delicate smile. Keith longed to kiss her. His eyes on her lips, he asked, softly, "What would you name your shop?"

Her grin widened, her dark eyes shining with warmth. "I'd call it Karen's Classy Salon." She grabbed his forearm.

"Karen's Classy Salon." He returned her smile, loving her enthusiasm. "I like that."

She still held his arm in a tight grip, and he didn't want her to let go.

Her smile faded as she glanced down at her hand clamping his arm in excitement. She released him, looking away. "I'm sorry. I get so excited when I talk about my dreams that I don't always pay attention to what I'm doing." She turned back to him with an uncertain smile.

He stared at her lovely face, wondering about the cause of her mood swing. "There's nothing to apologize for, Karen. I like seeing you so enthusiastic."

"You do?"

"Yes, I do," he said quietly.

"Lionel never liked it when I got excited." She frowned. "He hated when I spoke about my dream of owning my own salon."

He sounds like the biggest fool who ever walked the face of the earth, Keith thought to himself.

"Mr. Keith, are you coming inside or are you going to sit in that car all evening?" Amanda, one of the teens, shouted at him from the steps of the church. Keith inwardly groaned, saddened that the romantic mood had been shattered.

Keith opened his door while Karen exited the car.

"Hi, Amanda." He squeezed the young girl's shoulder.

"Hi, Mr. Keith," Amanda greeted.

He gestured toward Karen. "This is Karen Brown. You know Ms. Doris? This is her daughter. She's going to be one of the youth group volunteers."

"Hi, Amanda." Karen smiled, trying to put the girl at ease.

Amanda muttered a hello and fidgeted, so Keith took her a few feet away from Karen. "Amanda, what's the matter?"

Tears came to the girl's eyes, and she grabbed Keith's elbow. "My foster parents are getting a divorce. I'm so tired of them arguing all the time. I don't know what to do about it."

"I'm sorry." He didn't point out that he wasn't surprised.

"I feel so worthless at home. I've been listening to them argue for the last few years. They get on my nerves." She pulled a tissue from her pocket and blew her nose. "My eighteenth birthday is coming up, and you know what that means."

"I know, Amanda. I've already spoken to the pastor, and we're checking around to see what we can come up with within the church."

"I'm so scared. Everybody else looks forward to their eighteenth birthday, but I dread it. The only person who makes me feel good about myself is Ron. He loves me, and he just wants me to be happy."

Gently he advised her, "Amanda, be careful about Ron. Don't hang all of your hopes of happiness on him. Remember to focus on Jesus. All of us here at church who care about you—"

She shook her head, cutting him off. "It's not the same. I'm special to Ron. He focuses on *me*. He makes me feel good about myself."

Keith sensed impending doom. He'd met Ron and was not pleased with Amanda's choice of a boyfriend. "Amanda, why don't you come out to the church one day after school so that we can talk? I can arrange for Melanie, Karen, or the pastor's wife to be there." He couldn't meet with her alone since their church forbade one-on-one counseling with opposite sexes.

She pushed one of her plaits behind her ear. "I'll think about it."

"Do more than just think about it—I want you to pray about it. How about I ask the youth to say a prayer for you tonight?"

The girl looked mortified. "No, don't let them know about my problems!"

"Okay. But I'll be praying for you."

"Okay," she mumbled before she entered the church.

Karen approached. "What's wrong?"

They headed for the stairs. "That's Amanda. She's upset because her foster parents are getting a divorce and her eighteenth birthday is coming up."

"What happens when she turns eighteen?"

"When you're a foster kid, who knows?"

Karen held her hand over her quivering mouth. "Oh my goodness. Her foster parents won't be getting paid from the state anymore."

Keith nodded. "That's right. I've been trying to find out what I can do for her through the church, but so far I've come up empty. You know, I would let her live with me, but that wouldn't be appropriate."

"I'm assuming she's graduating from high school this year?"

"That's right. But she's not sure what'll happen after that."

"Is she looking for a job?"

Keith sighed, the problem weighing heavily on his mind. "I think the whole situation is so overwhelming that it's hard for her to focus on what to do."

"Has she been a foster child her whole life?"

"Yes, she's been through a lot of homes."

"The poor girl."

"Don't let her hear you say that."

Karen furrowed her brow. "Say what?"

"What you just said about her being poor. She hates pity. And being a foster kid already makes her feel like a misfit." He shook his head, the thought of Amanda's boyfriend making him angry.

Karen touched his arm, her cool fingers calming his frazzled nerves. "Keith, what's wrong?"

Her voice sounded soothing, and for a brief moment, he daydreamed about Karen being by his side when they mentored the youth of the congregation. "I'll tell you later," he mumbled, entering the church. The youth stood in the foyer, several greeting him by name. He shook hands with several of the teens, beckoning them into the sanctuary so they could begin their devotional time.

Chapter 7

Once they entered the church, the band warmed up, holy notes filling the sanctuary. "I'm surprised you have a band here tonight," Karen commented.

"A few of the teens play instruments, so they accompany us during praise and worship." As Karen and Keith headed to the front of the sanctuary, they were stopped by a striking woman with brown skin and midnight black hair that cascaded down her back. The woman smiled at Keith, draping her hand on his arm.

Karen stared, jealousy slicing through her as Keith and the stranger spoke in low voices. Feeling like an intruder, Karen began to step away.

"Karen, don't go!" Keith took her hand, glancing at the beautiful woman beside him. "This is Melanie Richards. She's one of the most awesome women you'll meet at this church." His voice filled with pride. "Melanie, this is Karen Brown, Ms. Doris's daughter."

Melanie shook Karen's hand. "It's so nice to meet you, Karen. How long will you be in town?"

"I–I'm not sure. I just needed to get away from Ocean City and spend some time with my mother."

Melanie's eyes widened. "Oh, well, I hope you have a nice visit." Somebody beckoned Melanie, so she left Karen and Keith to walk to the front of the sanctuary.

Keith led Karen to a seat, continuing to praise Melanie. "She's really a great woman. I don't know what the youth ministry would do without her." Karen wondered if Keith was interested in Melanie romantically.

More teens arrived, filling the sanctuary with noise. When the band strummed the notes to a popular gospel song, the young people swayed, singing to the music. After the praise and worship, a few of the young people stepped forward, telling of recent battles they had been facing. Keith then stepped to the front of the stage, Melanie beside him, gazing at him like a woman smitten.

Keith spoke. "I just want all of you to remember never to give up. Most of you know what I went through as a teenager, and I want to remind you to stay focused on God. Let Him lead you in your life."

As Melanie said a few words to the large group, Karen barely listened. Her mind was full of curiosity about Keith. . .his younger years. . .his family. . .his relationship with Melanie. She realized she knew so little about her mother's next-door neighbor, and she longed to find out more.

After Devo, a middle-aged woman approached Melanie and Keith, telling them that the pizzas had been delivered and were awaiting them downstairs. Karen assumed the woman was a church employee or a volunteer. After Keith made the appropriate announcement, the group trekked down to the basement. Melanie and Keith set the pizza boxes in a row on the long table, then set out plates, paper cups, napkins, a bucket of ice, and sodas. Watching them work together, Karen felt like a third wheel.

After Keith said grace, everybody got plates of food and broke up into groups to share the meal. Since Karen didn't know anybody, she sat at a table near the end and was surprised when Amanda sat beside her with her plate of pepperoni pizza and cup of orange soda.

"Hi," said Amanda.

"Hi, Amanda."

"I usually sit with my best friend Cassandra, but she's not here today."

"Oh. Well, thanks for joining me." Hoping they could get better acquainted, Karen asked, "So where do you live?"

As they feasted on pizza and sodas, Amanda told Karen about the neighborhood she lived in, how she'd been best friends with Cassandra since she'd entered high school, and about her impending eighteenth birthday. "I just wish God would open up the sky and money would pour into my lap."

"If that were to happen, what would you do?"

"I would buy myself a place to live. Then I wouldn't have to deal with crazy foster parents. I would take care of myself."

"Then what?"

"What do you mean?" The girl furrowed her brow.

"If you were living alone, what would you do with yourself during the day? Would you want to go to college or get a job?"

The girl, attractive but wearing too much makeup, shook her head, looking at Karen as if she were crazy. "Oh no! You've got it all wrong. I wouldn't be living alone."

"Oh? You'd have a roommate?"

Amanda again gave Karen a befuddled look. "No, I'd have Ron with me."

Karen didn't like the way this conversation was playing out. "Who's Ron?"

"He's my boyfriend. We'd get married and then we'd live in the house together."

Karen inwardly groaned, finishing her pizza. "Well, Amanda, even if you were to marry Ron, it would still be a good idea for you to think about what you'd like to do for a living."

"Yeah, I guess you're right. Maybe I could get a job as a waitress." After a few bites of pizza, Amanda asked, "What do you do?"

Surprised, Karen began telling Amanda about being a hairdresser, winding up her shoptalk with, "One day maybe you could come down to the salon. I know they've been advertising for a shampoo girl."

"Okay, I might do that," Amanda agreed.

Sometime later, the teenagers assisted Melanie, Keith, and Karen with cleanup. Once the youth left, Karen heard Keith telling Melanie to go home and rest, his deep voice full of concern, and Karen again wondered if Keith was interested in Melanie.

Soon, when Keith and Karen were alone in the empty basement room, he checked to make sure everything was put away then locked the doors on their way out. Touching her shoulder, he said, "Thanks so much for coming tonight."

"You're welcome. But I felt a little like a third wheel. I mean. . . Well, why did you need me when Melanie was here to help you?"

He raised his eyebrows, leading her to his vehicle. He opened her door before sliding into the driver's seat. "I wasn't sure if Melanie could come. I told you that she doesn't make it very often anymore." He started the engine. "This church is so blessed to have Melanie helping to lead the youth."

"You're a great youth leader, too. The kids really seem to look up to you. And it's obvious how much they like you."

"Yes, but it's nice to have an extra pair of hands." He played praise and worship music as he drove the short distance home. Gravel crunched when he pulled the car into his driveway. Cutting the ignition, he asked, "Do you mind if we sit on my porch for a while?"

She nodded, looking forward to spending some time alone with Keith. Soon, they sat on his porch, relaxing in lawn chairs. A gentle breeze blew and Karen tilted her head, relishing the wind kissing her skin.

He continued talking about Melanie. "You know, Melanie was apprehensive about helping at first. But since she came on board, we've managed to increase the youth membership. In fact, it was her idea to have dinner after the service."

"Can the church afford to feed the teens each week?"

"The way they eat? No."

She laughed. "So who pays for the pizza every Friday?"

"I do."

"Wow," Karen said, again briefly wondering about Keith's financial situation. But there was a more pressing subject she wanted to broach. So she asked the question that had been burning in her mind since she'd met Melanie. "Keith. . . are—are the two of you dating?"

He jerked back. "Who, me and Melanie?"

Karen nodded.

"Of course not. Why do you ask?"

"Well, you keep singing her praises, s–so I just wondered. . ."

He grinned. "If I didn't know any better, I'd think you were jealous."

Karen's mouth dropped open. "Jealous! Huh! No, this has *nothing* to do with jealousy. You just keep talking about how great Melanie is, so I—I assumed. . . Well, never mind what I assumed." Feeling heat flare in her cheeks, Karen looked away for a few minutes, but her curiosity about Melanie soon got the better of her. She turned back to face Keith. "So. . .Melanie joined the church after you did?"

"Yeah, I ran into her downtown one day. I hadn't talked to her since my father's funeral, and I told her about the new church I'd joined."

"She came to your father's funeral?"

"Yeah, Melanie and I go way back. I've known her since I was a kid. We went to the same private school."

"I think she has feelings for you. You should have seen the way she was looking at you during Devo."

Keith scoffed. "Melanie's not interested in me. She's over that now."

Karen's heart skipped a beat. "What do you mean?"

"I took her to the prom in high school, and we used to hang out as friends. When I was about to go to college, she told me she'd always wished we could be more than friends. To tell you the truth, I was surprised she wanted to have anything to do with me romantically, considering my reputation."

"What reputation?"

He hesitated then said, "Well, I didn't have the best of reputations in high school. Anyway, I told her I'd always thought of her as a sister. My dad and her parents were so close, the idea of her being a girlfriend never entered my mind."

"What did she say when you told her how you felt?"

"She started crying. It was rough. I felt bad, but I thought she needed to know the truth."

"So after that, you two kept in touch?"

"Yeah, when we went to college, we talked on the phone once in a while. But the boyfriend-girlfriend thing was never brought up again, so I figured it wasn't an issue anymore."

"Was she a Christian back in high school?"

"No, she told me she got saved in college."

"I think she likes you."

Keith huffed. "You're a woman, so I'm surprised you didn't notice."

"Notice what?" Karen threw her hands up in the air, exasperated.

"Melanie's engagement ring."

Karen touched her finger, which no longer sported Lionel's ring. Bittersweet memories of her fiancé fluttered through her mind, but she pushed the recollections aside, focusing on their conversation. "Melanie's engaged?"

"She's been engaged for a few months. She's marrying a businessman named Duane. He owns a chain of restaurants in Maryland."

"Really? Which one?"

"The Blue Crab Grille."

"Wow. That's one of the most famous chains in Maryland. And Melanie is engaged to the owner?"

Keith nodded.

"Have you met him?"

"Yes. He seems to be a decent Christian man, and Melanie seems happy with him, most of the time, at least."

She mentally sighed with relief, knowing Keith was not involved with Melanie.

"I think it's kind of funny that you thought I was dating Melanie."

"Why?"

"Because I don't date." His deep voice rang with a note of finality.

Karen's heart sank. "You don't date? How come?"

A loud bark interrupted them. "Oh, I forgot to let Suzie out." He opened the screen door and the dog raced out, holding a leash in her mouth, her brown eyes pleading with Keith.

"I haven't taken Suzie out for a walk in days. I think she wants some exercise." He removed the leash from her mouth. "Want to come along?"

She chuckled, amused. "I could use the exercise, too."

"Great." He attached the leash to the dog's collar, and seconds later, they headed out of his gate. Streetlights shone on the sidewalk as they strolled through the neighborhood.

Karen was still curious about Keith's previous comment. "So why don't you date?" she asked, somewhat breathless as she tried to keep up with Keith and Suzie's rapid pace. "Do—do you think you guys could slow down? Wha–what are we racing to? A fire?"

Keith smiled as Suzie dragged him toward a hydrant. "Well, maybe not a fire exactly." He pulled back on the leash. "Okay, Suzie, come on. Let's slow down." Once they'd reached an easier gait, he said, "The reason I don't date is because I'm not very good at relationships."

"You mean you've dated a lot in the past?"

They rounded a corner and passed another couple out walking their dog. Suzie greeted her fellow canine with a bark. "Suzie, be quiet." Keith continued,

"I don't know if you'd call it dating. You see, I didn't accept Christ until I was almost out of grad school. My brother and I went to the same school as undergrads and, well, we had some pretty wild times."

"Are you talking about drinking, parties, stuff like that?"

"Yes, pretty much. I'm ashamed to say this, but when I was in high school and college, I slept with so many women that I can't even remember them all. Looking back at how irresponsible I was, I'm just glad I had enough sense to wear protection."

"You did all of this before you were saved?"

Suzie stopped at a large tree, sniffing the trunk. "Yes. You know, Karen, even though I was doing all of those things, I wasn't happy. My roommate, Steve, was a Christian, and he—"

"You and Kyle didn't share a dorm room?"

He shook his head. "No. We weren't roommates." He glanced at Suzie. "Anyway, Steve invited me to Bible study. I'd never really read the Bible much before, and I didn't think I would understand it." Suzie abandoned the tree, and they continued their stroll. "But once I'd started studying the Word, I found what was missing in my life." He paused a few seconds before continuing. "Remember the woman I told you about, the one who raised me and my brother?"

"Ms. Sonya?"

"Yes. She tried to share her faith with me and Kyle several times throughout the years, but we never listened. She asked my dad if we could go to church with her, and Kyle never wanted to go, but I went with her at least once a month."

"But. . .it didn't stick?"

"No, it didn't. I'm sorry to say I never even listened to the sermons. I mostly used church as another social outlet. I was so busy paying attention to the pretty women all dressed up that I didn't hear a word the pastor said. Once I got my driver's license, I had more freedom to go to the places I wanted, so I stopped going to church with her." He shook his head. "Ms. Sonya would fuss at us about our behavior. But after a while her lectures became like so much background noise."

"Your dad didn't know about your being gone all the time?"

"At the time, I didn't think he cared or even noticed."

Karen thought about his words for a while. "Since you never listened to Ms. Sonya about God, what prompted you to listen to your roommate?"

Keith sighed. "While I was in college, Ms. Sonya was in a car accident. At first, the doctors didn't think she was going to make it. She was in the hospital for weeks. During that time, I realized life could be cut short so suddenly, and I really wanted her to get better. I'd never been so depressed. When my roommate asked what was wrong, I told him about Ms. Sonya's accident and that I felt bad about never listening to what she said about God." Keith squeezed the leash as they continued to walk. "Steve said it was never too late to start studying God's Word, and that's when I started going to the Bible study on campus."

"Wow, it looks like you really went through a lot."

"Yeah. I'm just glad I finally made the right decision."

"So is that why you're not close to your brother anymore? He doesn't understand your Christianity?"

He tensed. "I don't want to talk about my brother right now."

"O–okay, sorry." She paused then said, "But I still don't understand what all of this has to do with your decision not to date."

"Well, I told you that I was very promiscuous."

"Yes?" She wasn't sure what to say about that.

"The attention I was able to get so easily from women. . ." He shook his head. "You know I got into some big trouble back then. . . . . I broke up a lot of relationships. Once I even slept with a married woman. And I'm ashamed of that."

She attempted to reason with him. "But you're a Christian now. Jesus has forgiven you."

"I know. But we should resist temptation. And I guess that's what I'm doing."

"I don't understand."

"When my college pastor studied the Word with me, he said new Christians needed to resist temptation, which for me meant avoiding women and romantic entanglements."

"When did you become a Christian?"

"I was twenty-four at the time. I started going to church and reading the Bible when I was an undergrad, but I didn't accept Christ until shortly before I received my MBA."

"You have an MBA?"

"Don't sound so surprised."

"But you're a plumber."

"Tell me about it. My dad gave me grief about that for years. He said he didn't pay for my college education to throw it away on a blue-collar job."

"Why did you want to be a plumber?"

"I didn't want to sit in an office all day. I love going to different houses, driving around, fixing things."

She changed the subject. "So you've been saved for six years? I'd hardly consider you a new Christian, and I don't think God would mind if you found a nice Christian woman to settle down with." They turned a corner, and he clutched the leash when Suzie saw another dog and tried to approach the animal.

"Suzie, calm down." The dog slowed and he continued speaking. "I don't trust myself. What if I get involved with somebody and revert back to my old womanizing ways? What if I get married and I find I wouldn't be a good husband? I don't want anybody to get their feelings hurt, and I'm not sure if I'm strong enough to be committed."

She imagined Keith would make a kind, loving husband.

"Since I've been involved with the church, I've found joy in ministering to the youth. I think the reason I have such affection for teens is because I remember what it's like to be young and confused." He looked at her. "Since I accepted Christ and cut out all romantic relationships, my life has been on track, and I don't want to mess up." He paused. "The Lord will probably change my mind, but right now I feel He's calling me to stay single and to work toward getting my degree at divinity school."

They finished the rest of their walk in silence, both lost in their own thoughts.

Chapter 8

Over the next month, Karen continued assisting Keith with the youth on Fridays. The girls liked her, and one night she gave a successful session on beauty tips. As Amanda and Karen grew closer together, Karen promised she'd help her find a job since the girl's high school graduation and eighteenth birthday were just around the corner.

Keith found himself enjoying spending time with Karen and seeing her interact with the youth. As he continued praying about his relationship with Kyle, he imagined seeing his twin again, boasting about the beautiful woman who was slowly capturing his heart.

One day, Keith drove through Gambrills, Maryland, to see Ms. Sonya. He approached her home, pulling into the driveway. Before he could exit the car, Ms. Sonya opened the door of her house, rushing toward his vehicle.

"Keith, it's been a long time since you've visited." Hearing her Jamaican accent filled him with pleasure. The petite woman's hair was now partially gray, but her dark face was wrinkle-free. She pulled him into a hug.

"It's good to see you again," he said once they ended their embrace.

Seconds later, her husband, Terrance, joined them, his bald head shining in the late afternoon sun. "Keith, you haven't been to see us in months. We wondered when you were going to drop by again." The men shook hands.

Sonya's perceptive dark eyes pierced into Keith's. "I can tell something heavy is on your mind. Come in. We were about to eat."

He stepped into their home and the scents of curried goat, fried plantains, and an assortment of other food met his nostrils. After they fixed their plates, Terrance blessed their meal. As they ate, Keith asked them about their two college-aged children, and Ms. Sonya and Terrance were more than happy to fill him in on all the details.

After dinner, during which Keith downed two helpings of Ms. Sonya's delicious fare, Terrance announced he was going into the den to watch the ball game. "You're welcome to watch with me, Keith."

"How about I join you later? I wanted to talk to Ms. Sonya about something."

"Okay, but you'd better watch out. My team is going to beat yours!" He clapped Keith on the shoulder, and Keith reminisced about their good-natured rivalry since they were fans of opposing teams.

Once Terrance took his exit, Sonya refilled their coffee cups before rejoining Keith at the table. "What's bothering you?"

Keith sipped his coffee, wondering how to start. "I'm worried about something." He ran his fingers through his hair. "And I've been losing sleep over it."

"You know what the Lord says about worrying."

"I know, but I can't seem to help it."

"Has Kyle contacted you?"

Keith shook his head. "No, I haven't heard from him."

"If nothing's changed with your brother, what more is weighing you down?"

"Remember I told you about Ms. Doris, my next-door neighbor?"

"Yes, I remember. What about her?"

"Well, she has a daughter." Keith told her about Karen and how much he loved having her help with the teenagers. "I'd like to spend some time with her outside of the youth ministry."

"You want to date her?"

"Yes, but I'm not sure if that's a good idea."

"Why not? She's not married, is she?"

Keith scoffed. "No, but she came pretty close." He told of Lionel's deception and Karen's renewed faith, then said, "Ms. Sonya, I told you about how wild I was in college. I've never had a steady girlfriend. Me being with one woman, I don't know if that'll work."

"Keith, stop worrying about it so much. You've really grown as a Christian. I think if things work out with Karen, you would be okay."

"I don't know. . . . Sometimes I wonder if she still has feelings for Lionel. With all of my doubts, maybe the Lord is trying to tell me not to pursue this relationship."

She touched his arm. "Or maybe He's telling you to pursue her, but to take it slow."

Keith squeezed Ms. Sonya's hand. "Maybe."

The two sat in silence for a while. Then Ms. Sonya asked about his divinity school search. He told her about the colleges he was considering. "There's a place over in Lanham that looks interesting. I'd like to go there for their open house this summer."

"When are you thinking of enrolling?"

"I'll probably start applying soon. Hopefully I can begin classes somewhere next fall."

"Well, you should pray about that. And while you're at it, you should be praying about your situation with Karen. You know, honey, if you never let her know how you feel, you might regret it. Let me ask you something."

"What?"

"How would you feel if Karen started dating somebody else in your congregation?"

He'd noticed some of the men admiring her during Sunday services. Aaron always mentioned how classy Karen looked when she stepped into church every week. "It would bother me a lot if I saw Karen with another man."

"Well, I think you know what you need to do." Sonya cleared the table, telling him he should watch the game with Terrance and that they'd have dessert in the den.

Feasting on banana pudding, Keith spent the remainder of the evening watching the ball game with Terrance, contemplating Sonya's advice.

Chapter 9

Clutching a box of party decorations, Karen stepped into the private dining room of the Rockfish Restaurant. "Giving Amanda a surprise party was a great idea," said Karen, pulling a tablecloth out of the box.

Keith stood on a chair, hanging blue and white streamers on the wall. Sunlight splashed through the wide windows, lending the place a festive feel. He stepped down from the chair. "I wish there was more I could do for her."

"I'm worried about her, too. Hopefully everything will work out."

"Yes, after asking around, I did find a couple who were willing to let Amanda stay with them at the end of the summer."

Karen placed the cloth over the table then turned to glance at Keith. "I'm glad everybody's been praying for her."

Her eyes were drawn to his muscular calves, revealed by his knee-length shorts. She looked away, not wanting to be caught staring. Since they'd been working together in the youth ministry over the last couple of months, her thoughts about Lionel were fading.

She pulled a gift from the shopping bag, placing it on the table. Turning, she caught Keith staring at her. He smiled.

"What's so funny?" she asked.

He laughed. "Nothing. I was thinking how much you've changed since you moved back to Annapolis. Remember you didn't want to go back to church because of. . ." His smile faltered. "Well, you know what I'm talking about."

She knew, but she didn't want to ruin a nice day by talking about Lionel. The door opened and some of the teenagers arrived.

"Hey, Karen," said Sharon, one of the youth, "I picked up the cake you ordered from Cakes and Confections!" She glanced around the space, her curls gleaming in the sunlight. "Where should I put it?"

Karen nodded toward a table. "Right there is fine." Sharon opened the bakery box. The delicate roses and vines outlining the chocolate icing were beautiful. The words HAPPY BIRTHDAY, AMANDA were scrolled across the triple-chocolate mousse cake. "Well, I hope Cassandra was right about chocolate being Amanda's favorite flavor."

They had barely finished setting up when Amanda arrived with one of the youth members. When she entered, everybody bellowed, "Surprise!"

"Oh my goodness." Amanda smiled, tears streaming from her eyes. Karen looked closely at the girl, noting her thick makeup. A few minutes later, she pulled her aside, shocked when she saw the shadow under her eye.

"What happened to your eye?" Karen touched the dark bruise.

Looking away, Amanda didn't respond.

Karen's anger bubbled. "Did Ron hit you?"

Amanda frowned. "He didn't mean to."

Keith approached. "Is everything okay here?" He looked closely at Amanda's face then scowled. "What happened to your eye?"

Tears slid down Amanda's cheeks. "This is my birthday, and both of you are ruining it with your questions." She abandoned Keith and Karen, rejoining her party.

Karen touched his arm. "Keith, I don't know what to do. She says Ron didn't mean to hit her—"

He took her hand. "Honey, we'll talk to her another time."

"But Ron—"

He hugged her. "I know. We'll talk to her later."

Karen blinked away tears, saying a silent prayer for Amanda's well-being.

Soon the party was in full swing. As the teens filled up on an exorbitant amount of crab cakes and pasta, Karen's head rolled thinking about the bill Keith would be paying at the end of the evening.

Once the food and most of the cake had been eaten, the teens left the party. Amanda followed, grinning as she carried off her bundle of gifts. Karen still wished they could have talked about Ron, but she figured she would broach the subject again during their next Devo night. Right now she was too exhausted to do anything.

"Tired?" asked Keith.

"Very." Rubbing her eyes, she continued thinking about Amanda. "I hope Amanda's not seeing Ron today."

"I know. We can advise her, but we can't force her to break up with him."

"I know."

He stood and stretched. "It shouldn't take us long to clean up."

As they worked in companionable silence, Karen realized she could really get used to spending time with Keith. Being around him gave her a warm fuzzy feeling.

After they boxed up their stuff, they exited the private room, carrying their containers, and headed to the front of the restaurant. Karen nearly tripped when Keith's twin stumbled through the door. He looked at them, sneering.

"Well, if it isn't my little brother." He stood on unstable feet, slouching toward them. Kyle had already slipped into the old habit of calling him "little brother." He'd been doing that sporadically since their father told them that Kyle was ten minutes older than Keith. "If I'd known you were going to be here, I wouldn't have come."

Speechless, Karen leaned toward Keith as they set their boxes on a nearby table.

Placing his arm around Karen, Keith said, "We were just leaving." He glanced around then turned back to his brother. "Are you here alone?"

Kyle's mouth hardened. "That's none of your business." His breath reeked of alcohol. Kyle looked at Karen. "Who's this?" He leered, and Karen jumped when Kyle clapped his hand on her shoulder.

Keith shoved his hand away. "Don't touch her."

" 'Don't touch her,' " Kyle mimicked his brother. "She's a pretty little thing." Kyle grinned. "Don't worry, little brother. I wouldn't try to steal your woman." He glared at Keith. "I don't steal things, unlike you."

Abandoning Karen, Keith forced Kyle outside. The day had turned overcast, and it looked like it was going to rain. While Keith stood outside with his brother, Karen watched them, wondering if Keith could have a civilized conversation with Kyle since he was so sloshed.

An attractive woman exited the restroom, glancing around the restaurant. She noticed the twins outside. "What in the world?" she mumbled.

"Are you here with Kyle?" Karen asked.

"What's it to you?" The woman gave her a cold look.

"I'm friends with his brother. Keith is concerned that Kyle might try to drive home drunk."

"I didn't even know he had a brother." She went outside and Karen followed. Keith spoke with Kyle's date for a few minutes. After Kyle and his date reentered the restaurant, Keith joined Karen. As thunder cracked from the cloudy sky, Keith frowned, his shoulders slumped. "Come on, let's go," he mumbled. They walked back into the restaurant to retrieve their boxes then headed out to Keith's vehicle.

They dumped the boxes into the car. Once they were both inside, Keith drove off as rain splattered against the windshield.

They were silent during their ride, and when he pulled into his driveway, he gripped the steering wheel.

Karen glanced over at him. "Do you want to talk about it?"

He sighed, his shoulders slumped. "I've been praying for my brother for the last nine months."

She remained silent, unsure of what to say. The rain continued to pound against the window. "I'll start praying for your brother, too. Maybe with both of us praying, it'll make a difference."

"Sometimes I think it'll take a miracle to help him."

"Sometimes God does miracles. I'm sure you know that. . . . D–do you want me to go home?"

He held her hand. "Could we sit in the house for a while?"

She turned to look over at her mother's house, its windows dark. "Well, doesn't look like Mom's home. . .so sure. Why not?" She glanced around his car.

"What are you looking for?"

"Do you have an umbrella? I don't want to get my hair wet."

"No, but there's an old newspaper in the back. You can cover your head with that." Karen shielded her hair with the paper as they bounded onto his porch. He unlocked the door and, after they'd stepped inside, turned on the lights.

Thunder cracked, prompting Suzie to bark. The lights flickered before they extinguished. Keith led her to the couch. "Sit down. I'm getting some candles."

Soon after he lit the scented candles, the smells of vanilla and strawberry permeated the room. Suzie plodded into the living room and rested on the floor.

"I hope things work out with your brother."

He leaned back against the couch. "Thanks. That makes two of us."

"Do you see him often?"

"That was the first time I've spoken to him since the trial."

"What trial?"

"I already told you that my dad passed away."

"Yes. . ."

"Well, tonight you heard my brother say that I stole from him."

Karen nodded. "I assumed Kyle was talking crazy since he was drunk."

"Nope. He believes every word he said."

"Well, I know you didn't steal from your brother."

He folded his arms in front of his chest. "I didn't, but he doesn't see it that way."

"Okay, now I'm really confused. Do you want to clue me in?"

"It's a long story."

Rain continued to batter against the window. "I'm listening."

Keith began to explain, his voice sounding distant in the shadowy room. "After Kyle and I were in college, he decided he wanted to join my father in his law practice. Our dad wanted both of us to work with him, but I didn't want to be a lawyer." He shrugged. "After I'd gotten my bachelor's, I told my dad how I felt, and he wasn't pleased. Kyle was in law school, so my dad convinced me to get my MBA. While earning that, I got to know a lot of people in a local church. The pastor was a plumber. As a new Christian, I spent a lot of time with him and his family. . . . I liked the idea of having my own business, and he showed me what to do to get started. My father was horrified when he found out."

She nodded.

"My dad said I brought shame to the family because I wanted to be a plumber. But he admired Kyle for joining the family law practice." His mouth set in a firm line. "I always felt my dad favored my brother over me because of his career choice." He frowned. "Anyway, sometime later, when I accepted Christ, I had to stop doing certain things. Kyle didn't get that. That's when things started getting tense between him and me."

He sighed, looking at her, the candlelight wavering in the darkness. "Then when my dad got sick with cancer, he couldn't work anymore. So I moved in with him to help with his care." He took her hand. "I lived with my father for a year, sharing the gospel with him." He squeezed her hand. "I bonded with my dad. His cancer changed him."

"Did Kyle visit when your father was ill?"

He nodded. "Yes, but he didn't spend much time with him. I think seeing our father sick like that affected him. It—it was hard for him to be around Dad, knowing he was going to die. Kyle always did have a hard time dealing with death." He sighed. "Plus, he'd fallen in love and almost got engaged when my dad was sick."

"Really?"

"Yes. When Kyle started dating Andrea, I saw some changes in him. He was nicer, and their personalities seemed to click. Then he told me he was going to ask Andrea to marry him."

"What happened?"

"She left him for another man."

"He must've been devastated."

He nodded. "A few months later, our father died. Kyle has been bitter ever since. That's when he started drinking more heavily." He paused for a few seconds. "When my dad's will was read, the *real* trouble started. Dad had gathered a lot of money over the years from his successful law practice and from some smart investments. He left me most of his wealth."

"You mentioned that to me when we had dinner."

"He only willed 15 percent of his estate to Kyle."

"Why such a small amount?"

"I don't know. I've asked myself that question a million times. It appears that he changed his will while I was living with him. Kyle thinks it was my doing, that I'd influenced Dad with my Christian talk. But I was as shocked as my brother when I heard Dad's will."

Karen shrugged. "If that's what's causing so much animosity between you two, then why don't you just give Kyle an amount equal to half the estate?"

"I wanted to, but not if my dad did this for a reason."

"Why didn't he tell you about this before he died?"

"I think he tried. The day before he passed, he said he had something important to discuss about his finances. But then the nurse gave him his medicine, and he—he just wanted to go to sleep."

"And never woke up?"

"Right." He stared at the candles. "After today's performance, it's obvious Kyle's drinking has gotten worse. He usually doesn't get so sloshed that early in the day. If he keeps this up, it'll affect his job."

"Earlier you mentioned a trial."

"Kyle took me to court, trying to prove I'd influenced Dad to change his will. But he lost the case. I don't blame him for being angry, but I'm still wondering why my father did this."

Walking home later that night, Karen thought about Keith's rocky relationship with his brother, hoping he'd find the answers to his questions soon so that he could heal the rift.

Chapter 10

The following morning, Keith awakened and walked into his kitchen. Glancing out the window, he noticed Karen watering her mother's flowers. The buds danced in the breeze as the moisture rushed from the hose. He found himself staring at Karen, unable to tear his eyes away. When she returned to her house, he roused himself from his reverie. *Time to wash up and get dressed.*

Minutes later, he pulled into the parking lot of his brother's trendy town house in an upscale Annapolis neighborhood. He knocked on the door, but when nobody answered, he used the spare key Kyle had given him years ago.

"Kyle!"

His brother stumbled down the steps minutes later, his face still lazy with sleep. "What are you doing here?"

"I came to talk to you."

Kyle shook his head. "Not now."

Keith sighed. "Man, I've been worried about you."

"My head hurts."

"Take some aspirin. I'll make some coffee."

Several minutes later, the twins sat at the kitchen table. Kyle, having already downed two aspirins with a cold glass of water, sat sipping his hot black coffee.

Keith looked at his brother. "Your eyes are red."

"So?"

"Do you remember running into me at the Rockfish Restaurant yesterday?"

Kyle winced. "Barely."

"What's up with you? You never get that drunk in the middle of the day."

Kyle remained silent, sipping his coffee.

"Kyle, you need help. And you know you don't have to walk this road alone."

Kyle shook his head. "Don't start talking to me about Jesus."

"Listen, part of your trouble is you're trying to handle all of your problems under your own power. You're still mad because Andrea left, you're still not over Dad's death—"

"Are you over his death?"

Keith shook his head. "No. . .but I take everything to the Lord, knowing He'll work everything out. That's what you need to do—lean on the Lord to help you with your problems."

"Some of my problems would be solved if you'd give me my half of the money."

"Kyle, I don't like it any better than you do. But Dad changed his will for a reason. And until I figure out why he arranged things the way he did, we're both stuck."

The brothers were silent as Kyle sipped his coffee. Then a bleary-eyed Kyle asked, "Who was that woman with you at the Rockfish?"

"What?" Keith was surprised Kyle even remembered seeing Karen.

"Are you deaf? I asked who you were with at the Rockfish yesterday."

"Karen. And I don't like the way you talked to her. You can act pretty ugly when you're drunk."

Kyle hung his head. "I'm sorry about that," he mumbled. Lifting his head, he asked, "So what's up with you and this Karen?"

Keith frowned. "What do you mean?"

"I haven't seen you out with a woman since you turned religious. Are you two dating, engaged, or what?"

"She's my friend. Karen helps me with the youth ministry."

"That's it?" Kyle looked at Keith. "You like her. I can tell."

"So what if I do?"

"I'm shocked! My brother has been living like a monk for six years, and now he's finally spending time with a woman."

Keith shrugged. "We're just friends for now. I'm not sure how she would feel about dating me."

Kyle stood, walked to the sink, and rinsed his mug. "My only advice to you is be careful. You know how I fell for Andrea. Days before I plan on asking her to marry me, she dumps me for another man. You'd better make sure Karen doesn't do that to you."

Keith knew Karen wouldn't be so callous, but he didn't think Kyle would understand, so he decided to change the subject. "I just stopped by to check up on you. You haven't talked to me since Dad died, and. . .well, I'm concerned about you. I want you to promise me you'll at least try to get some help. You could go to AA or something like that."

Kyle was silent as he placed his cup in the dishwasher.

Keith spoke again. "Is it okay if I call you once in a while to. . .touch base?"

Kyle leaned against the counter, looking at his twin. "I guess, if that's what you want to do."

Keith inwardly cringed, still wishing there were more he could do to help his brother. At least Kyle had agreed to speak with him again, so it looked like the Lord had answered one of his prayers after all.

Chapter 11

The alarm sounded, waking Keith from a deep sleep. Forcing his eyes open, he gazed at his clock, remembering he had set the alarm for 4:45 a.m. He lay back on his pillow, taking pleasure in knowing he was off from work today.

Eventually he got out of bed and, after a rough workout, showered then brushed his teeth. When he entered his kitchen, Suzie plodded over, begging for breakfast. "I'll feed you in a minute, girl." After starting a pot of coffee, he poured water and food into Suzie's dishes.

Hearing the water spurting from the hose at Ms. Doris's house, he opened the blinds in his kitchen and saw Karen outside, watering her mother's plants. Her slender arms held the hose over the flowers. She turned the faucet off and wrapped the hose around the stand. An idea formed in his head, and seconds later, he was approaching Karen in her mother's backyard.

"Hi there."

She jumped. "Oh, Keith. You scared me." She smiled. "What's up?"

He shrugged, still looking at her. Her hair was swept into a bun, a few curls dangling at the side. "You're off today, aren't you?"

"Yes, I am. Why?"

He relaxed against the oak tree. "If you don't have any plans, I was wondering if you wanted to take a ride with me today."

"A ride?"

"Yeah, remember I told you that I'm researching different divinity schools?"

She nodded.

"Well, I'm visiting Washington Bible College in Lanham. They're having an open house today. Do you want to come?"

"You really want me to?"

"Yes, if you're not busy. I know it's last minute and all, but it didn't occur to me to ask you to come until this morning."

"What time are you leaving?"

"In an hour or so. I know that's early, but I wanted to get a jump on rush-hour traffic. I was going to stop and have breakfast on the way. My treat. So—you interested?"

She grinned. "Yes, I'd like that. I promise I'll be ready in about an hour."

He watched her as she headed back inside; then he returned to his own house, guzzled his coffee, and changed into slacks and a collared shirt. An hour later, Karen met him in his driveway. The heavenly scent of her perfume enticed him as he opened the car door for her. After she stepped into the vehicle, he walked around to his side, got behind the wheel, and turned the radio to his favorite gospel station.

They were silent for part of the way before Karen spoke. "I saw Melanie yesterday."

"Really? I heard she's been worshipping at her fiancé's church lately. How is she?"

"She came into the shop, asking me to give her a haircut."

Keith frowned. "Do you mean a short haircut?"

"Yes, and you know how long her hair is. It's so pretty, but I cut it like she wanted me to."

Keith shrugged. "Maybe she just needed a change."

"Well, after I cut her hair, she started crying, like she really hadn't wanted me to do it."

"That's strange."

"Yes. She said she messed up. Then she paid her bill and left the shop."

"That doesn't sound like Melanie. She's a tough woman who knows her own mind. I can't imagine her getting her hair cut like that unless she really wanted to. I think I'll call her soon to make sure she's okay."

"I still think she has feelings for you, Keith."

He huffed, wondering why Karen continued to think that Melanie had a crush on him. "You know that she's engaged. What more do you want me to say?"

Karen shrugged. "I saw the way she looked at you the few times she's shown up for Devo. Even though she's engaged, I don't think her feelings for you ever disappeared. . . . And I've also noticed that you're very protective of her."

"Karen, I already explained that Melanie is almost like a sister to me. There's nothing romantic between us."

Karen changed the subject. "Have you heard from your brother?"

He stopped at a light. "I went to see him the day after Amanda's birthday party."

She grabbed his arm. "Why didn't you mention it to me? How is he doing?"

"Horrible. We talked a little bit, but I don't think he was very glad to see me."

"So does this mean you're going to start talking to him again?"

"He told me that I could call him, but things are still strained between us. And I think they'll stay that way until I figure out why my father put me in charge of the inheritance."

The traffic slowed, and Keith glanced at the clock on his dashboard.

"Do you have to be there at a certain time?" asked Karen.

He nodded. "I'm supposed to meet the dean for an hour." He looked at the cars packed on the highway. He turned the radio to a traffic station and discovered there had been an accident farther ahead. "I think I'll be able to make it in time, but we won't be able to stop for breakfast."

The traffic continued to creep along, and almost an hour later, they were going at a steady pace. Once they reached Lanham, Keith checked the time. "I have to meet the dean in a half hour." He drove past the entrance to Washington Bible College. The sign whizzed by, and seconds later he pulled into a 7-Eleven. "I'm going to run in here and get us something to eat."

He entered the store and soon returned with two sweet rolls and two containers of juice. Before they ate, he pulled out of the parking lot of the 7-Eleven and drove across the street to the college. He pulled out a map and found his way to the parking lot outside the dean's office, where they feasted on the rolls and juice.

After finishing her breakfast and placing her trash into a bag, Karen said, "If you're interviewing with the dean, I'm not sure you'll want me tagging along."

"I know what you mean. I guess 'interview' is kind of a strong word. It's really just a meeting to find out more about the school." He pulled a piece of paper out of his glove compartment. "I even have a list of questions that I need to ask him. . . . I don't think it would be a problem if you come with me."

She shook her head. "That's okay." She glanced around the campus. "This is a small school."

Keith chuckled. "Yeah, I know. I'm not even sure if I'm going to enroll here. It's just one of many schools I'm checking out. Then I'll pray about it and see what God wants me to do."

A middle-aged man glanced at their car before strolling into the building.

"That's the dean," commented Keith.

"How do you know?"

"I saw his picture on the Web site." He glanced at his watch. "I'm supposed to meet with him in five minutes, so I'm going to head inside." He looked at her, feeling funny about leaving her sitting in the car. "I don't mind if you come inside with me."

She shook her head. "That's okay. Do you know how long you'll be?"

"They said the whole process should only take about an hour. He said it depended on how many questions I have."

She shrugged. "Take your time. I think I'll just walk around the campus and browse around the bookstore. I'll be back here in an hour. If you're not back, I'll wait."

"Okay." He handed her the car keys.

After his meeting with the dean was over and he'd had a tour around the campus, he returned to the car an hour and a half later and found Karen waiting. She was reading a novel, and she looked so pretty he could have just stared at her for hours.

She looked up and he smiled, trying to get his suddenly pounding heart to slow down. He approached the car and entered the vehicle. "What are you reading?"

She lifted the book for him to see. "It's a Christian romance novel."

"Is it a good story?"

She shrugged. "Pretty good."

He drove around the campus, showing her the different buildings and telling her about the tour he'd taken. When he was finished, he exited the campus.

"Where are we going now?" asked Karen.

"I just want to drive around the area and get a feel for it." Cruising through New Carrollton, he showed Karen where the metro station was. He then explored nearby College Park and Greenbelt and drove through the University of Maryland. Several minutes later, he stopped at a quaint sandwich shop in the heart of town.

"Are we eating lunch here? I'm starved." Karen's stomach rumbled.

Keith chuckled. "I've already ordered our lunch."

Her pretty brown eyes widened. "You have?"

He smiled, touching her shoulder. "Yeah, I ordered it to go right after my meeting with the dean. There's a park nearby and we can eat there. Stay right here. I'll be back in a second." He entered the establishment and soon afterward returned to the car with two bags of food.

Several minutes later, they entered Greenbelt Park. He parked in the lot, grabbed the two bags of food, and strolled to Karen's side of the car. He opened her door for her, taking her hand as she exited the vehicle. He nodded toward one of the picnic tables beneath the huge trees. "Let's sit over there."

He held her hand as they sat at the table. The green leaves on the trees created an umbrella of shade, and the warm breeze blew, kissing their skin.

"It sure feels nice out here," commented Karen. A few signs were posted, advertising the upcoming Fourth of July fireworks in Greenbelt.

It was a perfect day. It wasn't too hot or too cold, and he was having a great time just being alone with Karen. He released her hand and opened the bags of food, pleased to see the restaurant had followed his instructions. The cold cut sandwiches were made on fresh sourdough bread and had been packaged with potato chips, sodas, and two thick slabs of chocolate cake.

Keith again took Karen's small hand and bowed his head. "Lord, thank You for this beautiful day and for providing us with this wonderful meal." He paused, squeezing her fingers. "And, Lord, thank You for allowing me to spend the day with my friend Karen. Amen."

Karen squeezed his hand. "Amen."

After they'd eaten their tasty meal, Karen glanced around the park. "I'm going over there to the restroom. I'll be back in a few minutes."

"Take your time," he said, gathering their trash and placing it into the bin.

Once Karen was out of sight, Keith plopped back down at the picnic table. He sighed before closing his eyes, whispering another prayer. "Lord, I'm falling for Karen and I don't know what to do about it. I'm not sure if I should tell her how I feel." He paused for a few seconds. "Please guide me in saying the right words to her, Lord. Amen."

He opened his eyes, delighting in the warm weather. Minutes later, Karen approached, giving him a small smile.

"Are you okay?" she asked.

His heart nearly flopped when he heard the note of concern in her pretty voice. "Why do you ask?"

She shrugged. "You look a little worried."

When she sat beside him, he smiled, taking her small hand into his. He struggled with trying to find the right words to tell her his feelings, but decided he would wait until they returned to his house. "I'm fine. Just relaxing."

"Are you ready to go home?" she asked.

If it were up to him, he'd sit out here with Karen all day. He checked his watch. "Not really. Actually, I've got another surprise. Remember I told you about my old college roommate, Steve?"

"Yes?"

"Well, he lives around here. I told him I'd stop by and visit today. We don't have to stay for long."

❧

When Keith pulled into Steve's driveway, a man rushed out to the car. "Keith! What's up, man?"

Keith laughed, exiting the car. The men shared a brief hug and a hearty handshake. "Nothing much. Just came from checking out a Bible college."

Steve glanced inside the car, seeing Karen for the first time. "You brought somebody with you?"

Karen stepped out of the vehicle, amused by Steve's jovial nature. "I'm Karen."

"Pleased to meet you, Karen." Steve squeezed her hand before pulling her into a brief hug. He gazed at her with his warm brown eyes. "Keith! She's beautiful." Steve gave Karen a playful wink. "Where in the world have you been hiding her?"

A short woman, her belly swollen with child, stepped through the front door. "Steve, aren't you going to invite your friends inside?" Exasperation tinged her voice, but her smile was bright like the sun.

The group strolled into the house. Keith pulled the pregnant woman into a hug. "You look like you're about to deliver, Dianne!" The young woman laughed, swatting Keith on the arm.

After the women were introduced, Keith sat in the living room with Steve, telling him about his divinity school visit.

While the men were engrossed in conversation, Dianne whisked Karen into the kitchen. "Please, Karen, have a seat. Would you like anything to eat or drink?"

"We just ate lunch, so I'm stuffed, but thanks for asking." Karen glanced at Dianne's stomach. "When are you due?"

Dianne chuckled. "Tomorrow."

Karen gasped. "No way! Really?"

"Yeah, really!"

Mesmerized, Karen watched Dianne's stomach move. "Can I touch?"

"Sure!" Dianne took Karen's hand, placing it over her belly.

Karen laughed, feeling a solid kick to her palm. "That was hard."

"Yeah, he's a strong little guy." She poured a glass of milk then joined Karen at the table. "So do you have any children, Karen?"

"No, but I'd like to someday, if I ever find the right person to settle down with." She toyed with the strap of her purse. "Monica, one of my best friends, just had a baby. I haven't had a chance to visit her in Ocean City since the baby was born, but I can't wait to see her *and* her new little girl."

The two women sat in silence for a few minutes before Dianne spoke. "So you're Keith's next-door neighbor?"

Karen nodded. "That's right. A few months ago, I moved from Ocean City back home to my mother's house in Annapolis, right next door to Keith. He and my mother are friends and worship at the same church."

"It appears you and Keith became friends, too."

"Yes, we work together in the youth ministry at the church."

Dianne sipped her milk. "Well, you can be honest with me. I know that the two of you are more than just friends."

Karen frowned. "Not really."

"You don't like him?"

Karen suddenly felt like she was fourteen again, gossiping at a slumber party with a girlfriend. She glanced toward the living room, not wanting the men to overhear.

Dianne waved toward the other room. "They're not paying us any attention.

313

When Steve and Keith get together, they talk forever."

"What do they talk about?"

"Everything! The Bible, churches, sports, problems, you name it. I'll bet Keith said you guys weren't going to stay long, didn't he?"

Surprised, Karen responded, "Yes, he did."

"Well, if I know those two, you'll be fortunate if you get home before ten o'clock."

"You're kidding."

"Nope." She took another sip of milk. "So do you like Keith?"

Chuckling, Karen evaded answering by asking a question of her own. "How old are you, Dianne?"

"I'm twenty-three. Steve's thirty, but our age difference doesn't bother me."

"Is this your first child?"

"Yes, and I'm so excited!" She finished her drink, placing the glass into the sink. "Would you like to see our nursery?"

"Sure."

Dianne chatted all the way up the stairs. She then opened the door, and a profusion of blue, green, and yellow surrounded the space, enveloping the room with warmth. "Look at this!" Dianne said, grinning as she stepped over to the cherrywood crib, then turned the knob on a mobile. Soon a lullaby filled the room, and animals twirled in a circle, in tune with the music.

"It's lovely, Dianne."

"Thanks! We're having a boy, but I didn't want the room to be all blue. That's why I made it blue, green, and yellow."

Karen continued to relish the nursery, admiring the animals and cartoon characters stenciled on the wall.

Dianne interrupted her thoughts. "So what's up with you and Keith Baxter?"

Karen laughed, immediately liking Dianne's easygoing personality, in spite of her persistent curiosity. "I told you, we're friends."

"Just friends?"

"Yes, we're just friends."

"Don't you like him?"

"He's nice," Karen admitted.

"Don't you think he's cute?"

"Dianne!"

"Well, he is! Don't get me wrong, Steve is my number one man, but at my wedding. . ."

When Dianne didn't continue, Karen's own curiosity was aroused. "What about your wedding?"

"Keith was Steve's best man at our wedding two and a half years ago. Every unmarried woman in my bridal party wanted his phone number. Keith got hit on so many times that I felt sorry for him." The mobile stopped, so Dianne turned the knob again, continuing to speak. "The whole time I've known Keith, he's never brought anybody over to meet us. He always comes alone and never mentions that he's dating anybody. Do you know if he's still having issues with his brother?"

Karen nodded. "They still have some things unresolved. Keith did go to visit Kyle recently, so at least they're speaking a little bit."

Dianne looked away. "That's so sad. I wish they would just make up. Steve told me that Keith's rift with his brother really breaks his heart."

"Yes, it does."

She beckoned Karen out of the room. "Come on. I want to show you our wedding album. You can see what Keith looks like in a tux!"

Karen smiled as she followed the waddling woman to a room down the hall. After they'd gone through the wedding album, Dianne shared photos of her family, telling funny stories about things that had happened when she was a little girl. One childhood anecdote caused Karen to laugh so hard that tears rolled down her cheeks.

"Dianne, what in the world are you women doing up here? You sound like you're having too good of a time," commented Steve.

Keith entered behind his friend. "I don't think I've ever seen you laugh so hard, Karen."

"What are you two talking about?" asked Steve.

Dianne raised her eyebrows. "Just a little girl talk. I'll bet the only reason you guys came up here is because you're hungry."

Karen glanced at her watch, shocked that so much time had passed. Her stomach rumbled with hunger, reminding her that it had been hours since they'd eaten lunch.

Steve playfully hugged his wife. "I'm ready for some grub!"

The foursome climbed down the stairs and entered the kitchen. Dianne opened the freezer and pulled out a package of frozen hamburger patties. "We were going to have hamburgers and chips for dinner. These patties will cook up in a few minutes on our electric grill."

Karen helped Dianne fix dinner. Soon they'd grilled the meat and served up burgers and chips for everyone. Steve took Dianne's hand. "I'll bless the table before we eat," he announced. Everyone bowed their heads and joined hands. Steve's strong voice soon filled the kitchen. "Lord, thank You for this wonderful day and for the blessing of having friends like Keith and Karen. And, Lord, please be with Dianne. Let your Holy Spirit protect her as we get closer to the time of our baby's birth. Amen."

"Amen," everybody mumbled.

Steve clapped his hands. "Now I'm ready to eat!"

Karen delighted in the fabulous fare and the friendly conversation at the table. Before she knew it, it was almost nine o'clock, and Keith suggested they head home. Both Dianne and Steve pulled Karen into a hug.

Dianne gave Karen a wide smile. "I want you to come back and visit us again. I had a good time today."

"Thanks, Dianne. I had a good time, too. Maybe I can ride over when Keith comes back to visit."

Shaking Keith's hand, Steve said, "Listen, buddy, don't keep Karen all to yourself anymore. Be sure to bring her by sometime after the baby is born."

Keith chuckled as he wrapped Steve up in a bear hug, saying, "We'll come back to visit soon."

While Keith drove away from the house, Karen waved to his friends standing in the driveway.

❧

As he pulled into his driveway late that night, Keith glanced at Karen, savoring the wonderful day they'd had together. A sense of contentment had filled his soul when he'd introduced her to Steve and Dianne. Keith loved spending time with Karen, and since they'd met his feelings had deepened. *Perhaps now is the time. . . .*

They exited the car and he looked up, amazed at the brilliant stars in the heavens. The stars twinkled a bit brighter this evening. They stood in front of his car, observing the sky.

"It's so pretty tonight," Karen said.

"Yes, it is."

"I had a great time. I especially loved meeting Steve and Dianne."

Saying a silent prayer, he pulled Karen into his arms. "Maybe we can drive down another time and visit again. I'm sure Dianne would like you to see her baby."

He released her, taking her hands.

"Keith—"

"Karen—"

She chuckled, and their eyes met. Keith spoke first. "I guess both of us have something to say."

"Why don't you go first?"

Grinning, he squeezed her fingers, wanting to share his feelings. "Well, I—"

"Karen!"

Doris Brown's voice carried across the yard, and Keith winced. *Talk about bad timing.*

"Mom, what is it?"

As Doris hurried over to Keith's driveway, he dropped Karen's hands then stepped away, his euphoric mood shattered.

Doris approached Karen. "Honey, there's an important phone message for you."

Karen grabbed her mother's arm. "Did something happen to Monica or Anna?"

Doris shook her head. "No, nothing like that. But Monica phoned about ten minutes ago. Karen. . . She says Lionel turned himself in to the police last week. He's already had a hearing and. . .he's in jail."

"Are you sure?" asked Karen.

Ms. Doris nodded. "Monica claims they won't issue bail for him since he disappeared before his first hearing." She touched her daughter's face. "You might want to call Monica back."

Karen broke away from her mother and hurried over to her house.

Keith couldn't help himself. He had to find out if Karen still had feelings for Lionel. He followed the two women into Ms. Doris's home.

Chapter 12

Karen rushed to the telephone and punched in Monica's phone number. Monica answered on the first ring.

"Monica, it's Karen. What's happened? Lionel turned himself in?"

"Yes. Both he and Michelle. Last week—"

"Last week? Why didn't you call me then?"

"I wasn't sure if I should. I know he hurt you a lot, and Anna and I struggled with telling you. . . ."

Karen rolled her eyes. "Monica, I'm a big girl now. You and Anna don't have to protect me. So. . .where has Lionel been all this time?"

"I'm not sure. But he's back and in jail. He hasn't had his trial yet, only the hearing."

"I have to see him. Is he allowed to have visitors?"

"As far as I know, yes." A baby's cry carried over the wire. Monica sighed wearily then said, "Karen, I have to go. Mica is hungry. You might want to think and pray about seeing Lionel again. Make sure this is what you want to do. . . . Your mother told me you're involved with somebody else now—"

"No. I—I am not."

"But she said—"

"I don't care what she said. It's not true. Keith and I are. . .just friends, that's all." Karen clutched the receiver, her thoughts reeling. The baby cried again.

"Listen, I've really gotta go. Call me later if you want to talk." With that, Monica hung up the phone.

Karen continued holding the receiver then turned toward her mother. "I'm going to Ocean City tomorrow."

"I can't believe it! You're going down there to see him?" Keith's deep voice thundered through the kitchen.

Karen dropped the phone, turning toward him in surprise. "What are *you* doing here?"

"I followed you. I—I had to know. . ."

Her mother touched her arm. "Honey, are you sure this is what you want to do?"

Karen huffed, staring at her mother's face etched with concern. And at Keith, whose lips were set in a hard line and eyes sparkled with anger. Didn't they understand why she needed to do this?

"I'm going to Ocean City tomorrow, and that's final. I'll just call the salon and ask Deidre and Sheronda to cover for me."

Keith folded his arms in front of his chest. "I don't think you should go."

Karen glared at him. "And I don't think *you* should be telling me what to do."

His mouth dropped open. An instant later he turned on his heels and strode from the kitchen, the screen door banging shut behind him.

Karen watched him storm back to his house. "What's his problem?"

Her mother sat at the table. "Honey, don't you realize that Keith is falling for you?"

She grunted. "Mom, you're letting your imagination run wild."

"Why do you say that?"

She shrugged. "Well, Keith and I have a good time together, but that's all it is. Besides, right now he's focusing on finding the right divinity school and fixing his relationship with his brother. On top of that, he's already told me he doesn't date." She kept the fact of Keith's promiscuous past to herself, not sure it was hers to share.

"Karen, you just *went* on a date with Keith—today."

"Today's outing was not a date! He just wanted somebody to ride with him to Lanham to see the college. And frankly, Mom, I don't want to talk about this right now. My mind is on. . .other things."

"There's nothing more you can do tonight about tomorrow's visit to Lionel. But you *can* come here, sit down, and tell me what you two did today." She patted the empty chair beside her.

Resigned, Karen sighed and plopped down. "Mom, really, I don't want—"

"Just talk to me. It'll keep your mind off other things, help calm your nerves."

"Yeah, okay, whatever." Karen took another deep, calming breath. "When I was watering your flowers this morning, Keith came over and asked me to go to the Bible college with him." She shrugged. "I didn't have any plans, so I went. You got the note I left you, right?"

"Yes. So what did the two of you do?"

Karen struggled to sort her scrambling thoughts. *Lord, give me peace and patience.* "It was no big deal. We went to the campus and Keith interviewed with the dean. Afterward, he picked up this special lunch he'd ordered, and we ate it in the park." Fiddling with the salt and pepper shakers on the table, she continued to tell about her day. "I met Keith's college roommate Steve and his wife, Dianne. They're so much fun, and they're friendly, too. I'd like to visit them again sometime after Dianne has her baby. . . ." She gazed at her mother. "We ate dinner with Steve and Dianne; then we drove home. And that's all there was to it."

Her mother smiled. "Karen, Keith has feelings for you, but you're just having a hard time seeing that. I mean, you go on this road trip together for the day, and then he introduces you to his friends. It's obvious he likes being with you and was anxious for you to meet Steve and Dianne."

Karen shook her head. "Mom, he just wanted to have some company today, that's all." She thought back to her and Keith's previous conversations. "He just wants to be there for me like a friend, to help me get over Lionel."

"Well, I don't know what else I can say to convince you. But that man is falling for you. And whether you realize it or not, I think you're falling for him."

Karen sighed, ignoring her mother's observations, yet suddenly feeling ashamed for lashing out at Keith. "Maybe I overreacted earlier. Maybe I shouldn't have yelled at him. It's just that after that phone conversation with Monica. . .I can't seem to think straight." She glanced through the kitchen window, noting that the lights in Keith's house were on. "Do you think I should go over and apologize?"

Her mom shook her head. "No. Give him some time to cool off. Maybe you can talk to him in the morning. Both of you seem to be early risers."

Her mother stood and stretched. "Well, I'm going to get ready for bed. You should go to bed, too. You've got a big day tomorrow." When her comment was met with silence, she squeezed her daughter's shoulder. "Good night, pumpkin. Don't stay up too late."

After her mom left the kitchen, Karen sighed, staring at the ceiling. The brief conversation she'd had with her mother about Keith made her temporarily forget about her planned mission: to go to Ocean City and visit Lionel Adams, desperate to find the answers to the questions that plagued her. She prayed, "Lord, please be with me. Give me wisdom and courage for tomorrow. And if there's any sleep to be had tonight, please help me find it. Amen."

❧

The entire night, Karen tossed and turned as she mentally relived the horrid day when she'd found out about Lionel's crime against their church. Between short, pleading prayers for direction and healing, snatches of bittersweet memories wove through her mind. . .the days Lionel courted her and the day he asked her to marry him. How loving and caring he'd been when she'd grieved over her father's death. His sweetness, tenderness. . .all the traits that had caused her to fall in love with him.

When the rays of the early morning sun began to lighten her room, she sat up in bed, rubbing her eyes with a tired sigh. Fatigue washed through her body, but there wasn't anything she could do about it now. She was too wired up to sleep, and she wondered if she was strong enough to drive the two and a half hours to Ocean City.

She finally pulled herself out of bed then washed and got dressed. When she opened the door to the backyard, ready to water her mother's flowers, she saw Keith standing on his porch, looking at her. He remained silent as he climbed down his steps and walked over to her house. His brown eyes had softened from the previous night, and his mouth drooped as he placed his hand on her shoulder. "Are you okay? You have circles under your eyes."

"I—I didn't sleep very well," Karen said, finding comfort in his touch.

"I'm sorry for losing my temper last night," he said.

"I'm sorry for yelling at you, too."

"I was just trying to protect you from. . ." He squeezed her shoulder. "Karen, I—I don't think you should visit Lionel."

She sighed. "Keith, this is something that I have to do."

"Why?" His voice softened and his eyes pleaded with her.

"I have to try to put this whole thing behind me, and seeing Lionel will help me to do that."

"Is he allowed to have visitors?"

"Monica says she thinks so."

He removed his hand from her shoulder, looking away. "When are you leaving?"

"This morning."

"I don't want you driving down there by yourself." His authoritative tone surprised her. "You still look half asleep. Are you sure you're up to the trip?"

"I can make it down there just fine. If I get too tired, I'll stop and rest."

"You sure are stubborn." He hesitated then said, "Listen, can you wait a few hours before you leave? I'd like to come with you." He glanced at his watch. "I have to fix somebody's toilet early this morning; then I'll have to call George, a colleague of mine. He can handle the rest of today's jobs for me."

Her mouth dropped open. "I don't want you rearranging your whole schedule because of me. You have a business to run."

He nodded. "That's true, but I have to make sure you're okay, too."

"I'm not your responsibility."

"I know you're not, but. . ." He sighed, his eyes scanning the houses lining their street. "Karen, there's something you should know."

She frowned. "What?"

"Last night, before your mother interrupted us, I was going to tell you that I had a great time with you yesterday."

"I had a good time, too."

He sighed. "Well, I wanted to know if you'd be open to the idea of spending more time with me, out–outside of doing the youth ministry." He paused. "I like you, Karen, and I. . .I care about you." His voice turned gruff. "I can't bear to see

321

you get hurt. Please. Don't go to see Lionel."

Karen's heart skipped a beat. She didn't know what to say.

When she remained silent, he rushed on. "You don't have to tell me what you think about my idea right now. I know you've got a lot on your mind. But once you have everything sorted out, I'd like you to think about what I'm asking you."

She nodded. "I will. I promise. But right now I have to go to Ocean City." She paced the small yard in silence, gathering her thoughts as pansies, marigolds, and roses swayed in the warm breeze. Finally, she spoke. "I was engaged to Lionel. I was in love with him."

Keith winced.

She hurried on. "I—I need to talk to him, find out why he proposed to me and then apparently had an affair with somebody else."

"He's a loser, Karen. That's why. Men do that all the time." He stepped toward her, taking her hand.

Warmth traveled up her arm from his touch.

"Nobody knows better than I do how irresponsible some men can be. But, Karen, you and me. That's something special. If you'll just give me a chance, I guarantee I'll do my best to treat you the way you deserve."

Mere inches separated them. Keith's head leaned in closer to hers but then stopped. Staring into her eyes, he brushed his finger against her cheek, a gesture as sweet and endearing as a kiss.

Karen took a few steps away, removing her hand from his. "I—I have to go."

"Let me ask you something. If Lionel had disappeared forever, not to be found, do you think you'd ever be able to put this whole thing behind you and move on?"

She gritted her teeth. "That's not a fair question."

"Why not?"

"Because Lionel *hasn't* disappeared. So that point is moot. But there's one thing you haven't even considered. Have you even thought about the fact that maybe God wants me to do this?"

"What?"

"Maybe God moved Lionel to turn himself in and allowed me to find out about it so that I can go confront him and get some answers."

"Maybe," Keith mumbled, but the future pastor sounded doubtful.

"Well, let me ask you something else."

"Go ahead. Ask me anything you want."

"If you had a member of your church with my problem, how would you advise her?"

He frowned, his brown eyes crinkled with confusion. "What do you mean?"

She threw her hands up in the air. "I mean what I just said. Pretend you're pastoring a church, and one of the members comes to you with this problem. Her fiancé has disappeared with the church's funds. It's rumored he's had an affair with the assistant treasurer who's also disappeared. He's turned himself in and is now in custody. She wants to go and visit him. Would you advise this person *not* to see her ex-fiancé?"

He turned away, running his fingers over his short hair. Finally turning back toward her, he said grimly, "I would tell her to pray about it and do as she felt led."

She touched his arm, wishing she could wipe the sullen expression from his beautiful face. "Keith, I've done that. I spent part of the night reminiscing about the time I've spent with Lionel, and another part seeking God's will. I feel led to do this, Keith, but when you get angry and upset with me, I feel like you're interfering with God's plan for my life."

"I don't mean to make you feel that way. If I do, then I'm sorry."

She nodded, accepting his apology.

"Will you at least let me take you to Ocean City? I don't think you should be going down there by yourself." He glanced at his watch. "Just give me a couple of hours to get everything together with my clients, and then I'll pick you up."

She was touched that Keith insisted on coming with her, even though he didn't approve of her decision. "Okay, that's fine. To tell you the truth, it'll be nice having someone else do the driving," she said, trying to stifle a yawn.

He checked his watch again, and they agreed to meet in a few hours.

Chapter 13

When Keith returned to his house, he called George, his friend in the business who handled his workload when he needed to take time off. Then he left to do the repair at his client's house.

Returning home, he was happy to see Karen sitting on his porch, waiting for him.

"Are you ready?" she asked.

I'll never be ready to take you to see another man. Brushing that thought aside, he said, "Let me just get out of these work clothes and wash up a bit. Then we can get going. I'll only be a minute."

When they were finally settled into his car and had buckled their seat belts, he pulled out of his driveway. Once on the highway, he worked up the nerve to ask, "When we get to Ocean City, where do you want to head first—to see your friends. . .or Lionel?"

When his question was met with silence, he glanced at Karen and noticed she was fast asleep. The urge to kiss her cheek and cover her with a light blanket flowed through him, reminding him how his feelings for Karen had grown in such a short time.

Hours later, when they entered Ocean City, Karen sat up blinking, looking around. "I can't believe I slept the whole way here."

"You were tired. You needed it." He pulled onto the main road. "Fortunately, you woke up just in time. From this point on, you'll need to give me some directions. Where are we headed first?" He couldn't bring himself to ask where the jail was located.

"I called Monica and Anna this morning. They said they would meet me over at Monica's house."

He swallowed, still wondering how this whole thing was going to play out. "Are you three going to visit for a while before you go. . ." He struggled to say the next words. "Before you go to see Lionel?"

"Oh no. After meeting at Monica's, we're going over to see Lionel right away. . . . Make a right here."

He sighed, wincing as he turned.

She touched his shoulder. "I'm sorry, Keith. But this is something that I have to do."

"I know." He swallowed hard. "And if this is what you need to do, then so be it."

Minutes later, they pulled into the driveway of a charming house up the street from the waterfront. A multitude of flowers bloomed in front of the massive porch, and sounds of a baby crying wafted through the open windows. Female voices followed by a deep male chuckle drifted into the yard, where white lawn furniture was arranged around the porch.

Karen rapped against the screen door a few times then opened the door. "Hey, guys, I'm here."

A tall pretty woman stood, patting the back of the infant in her arms. The baby whimpered before she stopped crying completely. "Karen! I was so worried about you!"

Karen and the woman shared a one-armed hug. "You shouldn't have been."

A large woman with long, cornrowed plaits stood. "Well, somebody needs to! I think your going to see Lionel is a cuckoo idea!"

Keith decided he liked this woman. *Maybe I can convince* her *to talk some sense into Karen.*

The other male in the room stood, speaking to the three women. "Y'all need to leave Karen alone. She's only doing what she feels she needs to do."

"Thanks, John," Karen commented.

The tall man approached Keith, offering his hand. "I'm John French."

Keith shook his hand. "I'm Keith Baxter."

Karen gasped, looking at Keith with her pretty eyes. "I'm sorry. I've got so much on my mind that I forgot to introduce you. Keith, this is Monica and her husband, John, and this is Anna. And this little one is John and Monica's baby girl, Mica."

Keith shook hands with each adult, trying to ignore Anna's and Monica's curious stares. Feeling the need to explain his presence, he said, "Karen was tired this morning, so I told her I would drive her over here."

"Hmm," murmured Anna. "She was probably tired because she was tossing and turning all night, thinking about this trip." The large woman shook her head, her plaits swinging with the movement. "I'm telling you, Karen, this whole visit is a big mistake. You need to put that no-good man out of your mind."

Keith couldn't help the next words that slipped from his mouth. "Amen to that." He turned toward Karen. "Why don't you listen to Anna?"

Karen gritted her teeth then said, "Keith, I already explained everything to you this morning." She turned to Anna, looking her up and down as the large woman placed her hands on her ample hips. When Karen shrieked then hugged Anna, Keith wondered if she'd lost her mind.

"Anna, what a pretty engagement ring!"

Anna proudly modeled her left hand, showing the huge square-cut diamond ring on her finger. "Yes, Dean Love and I are getting married."

"When did you get engaged?" Karen sat on the couch.

"A few weeks ago."

Karen frowned. "Why didn't you tell me?"

"I wasn't sure if this was news you wanted to hear since. . .well, since Lionel was missing and all. Didn't want to make you feel bad since your engagement. . . ended on a bad note."

"But this is *good* news. This is something I wanted to know." After admiring the ring for a while, Karen took the baby from Monica. "Hi, Mica," Karen said with a smile. "Oh, Monica, she's so precious."

Monica grinned. "Can you believe she's already three and a half months old?"

Karen cooed and played with the infant until the child gurgled with laughter.

Keith relished watching Karen with the baby. "Do you like babies?" he asked.

Karen smiled and nodded before giving the baby back to Monica. Then, focusing on her best friends, she gestured toward the door. "Come on, let's go."

"Okay. I'll drive." Monica handed Mica off to her husband. "John, there's three bottles of breast milk in the refrigerator. If that's not enough, then there's a can of formula on the counter. Do you want me to make a few bottles of formula in case you run out?"

John smiled at his wife. "No, I think I can handle mixing formula if I need to."

"When you warm up her bottle, don't forget to test it on your wrist before you feed her." She looked at Karen. "I'm not sure how long we'll be gone."

"We shouldn't even be going," muttered Anna, lifting her large purse from the floor.

Karen glared at Anna. "I need some answers. And you're my moral support. Can't you understand that?"

The three women continued talking as they exited the house. Seconds later, Monica popped back into the living room. "John, the box of diapers in the nursery is almost empty. I already bought some more, and they're still in the bag over there in the corner." She gestured toward the back of the living room.

"Monica, go. Mica and I will be fine."

She gave him a warm smile and kissed his cheek, then ran outside to join the other women.

Moments later, Keith sighed, watching the car disappear around the corner. "I almost feel like I made this trip for nothing."

"You really didn't want her to go, did you?"

"Of course not! That heel doesn't deserve any visits from Karen after all he's put her through." He shook his head, watching as John placed Mica in an infant seat on the floor. She gurgled, clutching a yellow rattle. "I should've stayed home. When Karen saw her friends, it's like I no longer existed."

John shrugged. "I know how you feel. When the three of them get together, it's almost like they're in a world of their own. That's just the way they are. They've been friends for such a long time, they're more like sisters than friends."

Keith huffed, still feeling dejected. "That doesn't make me feel any better."

John changed the subject. "Hungry?"

Keith shook his head. "As a matter of fact, I am. I had something at McDonald's early this morning before I did a repair, but I haven't had anything to eat since. I would've stopped on the drive down here, but Karen slept in the car the whole way." He frowned. "Said she didn't sleep much last night."

John shrugged. "I'm not surprised. Did you want to go and get something?"

"Yeah." He looked at Mica. "Won't Monica object to your taking Mica out of the house? She seemed to be a little worried about leaving her alone with you."

John's laughter filled the room as he took a large bag from the corner. He opened the sack of diapers and placed several into the black tote. "No, she won't care. I've taken Mica out lots of times. Monica's just a worried new mother." He took two bottles from the refrigerator and placed them in the bag. "I don't think she'll be hungry for a few hours. Monica just fed her, but I have to take a couple of bottles just in case."

Minutes later, John had Mica strapped into the car seat and Keith was sitting in the front seat with John. They pulled out of the driveway and John started talking about his family. "My life has really changed since I got married, but in a good way." Keith remained silent as John continued to speak. "Mica still gets up in the middle of the night to be fed at least two times. But according to the pediatrician, we can start giving her rice cereal within the next couple of weeks."

Keith grunted. "I'd start giving her the cereal now. Maybe it'll fill her up so she's not waking you guys up hungry in the middle of the night."

John chuckled. "That's what I told Monica, and she had a fit! She said that as new parents, we need to do follow doctor's orders."

Keith shrugged. "I guess you need to do what you feel is best."

John turned a corner. "You like seafood?"

"I love eating—and making—just about any kind of food. I do a lot of cooking in my spare time."

They pulled into the parking lot of Phillips Seafood Restaurant. John took a little time to unhook Mica's car seat, which doubled as a baby carrier. He then hoisted the diaper bag onto his shoulder, picked up the carrier, and locked the van before they walked into the restaurant. After they were seated, he placed Mica's carrier between them. The brown-skinned baby looked at Keith, her mocha-colored eyes full of curiosity. Her full lips reminded him of a rosebud, and when she opened her mouth and smiled, drool spilled down her chin, prompting John to wipe it with a cloth.

The baby continued to smile at Keith, gripping a rattle. Keith, returning her grin, stroked her cheek. Her skin was soft like feathers. "She's a cute little thing," he commented.

"Thanks," said John, opening his menu. "I think she resembles Monica, but Monica said she looks like me." He shrugged. "I guess we'll find out who she takes after when she grows up."

"You don't have any other kids?" asked Keith.

John shook his head. "No, this is our first."

Their waitress arrived, and Keith opened his menu. "I haven't even read the menu yet."

John closed his. "I can tell you what's good. Order the clam chowder and soft-shell crabs with potatoes and vegetables."

Keith gave his menu back to the waitress. "I'll have everything he just suggested."

"Make that two," John said to their server. Nodding, their waitress left, returning moments later with their drinks and a basket of bread and butter.

Keith's stomach rumbled with hunger. "Do you mind if I pray before we eat?"

"Not at all. Go ahead."

Keith bowed his head. "Lord, thank You for this day of life and for the food we're about to eat. Also, Lord, I'd like to ask you to please watch over Mica, John, and Monica. Be with these new parents as they raise their first child." He paused, gathering his thoughts. After a deep breath, he prayed, "And, Lord, please let your Holy Spirit be with my friend Karen. I'm sure you know this is a difficult day for her. May she truly feel Your strength and guidance today. Amen."

"Amen," John responded. He looked at Keith as if trying to figure him out. "Thanks for praying for Monica and me. Parenthood is really taking a toll on us. It's not a bad toll, just different."

"I can imagine. I hear that all the time."

John buttered a piece of bread. "So a lot of your friends have kids?"

Keith shook his head, squeezing lemon juice into his water. He took a sip before responding. "I have one close friend who's expecting his first. But I hear a lot of new parents from my church talk about how their lives have changed."

"Do you and Karen worship at the same church? Is that how you two know each other?"

Keith's heart skipped a beat, realizing that Karen had probably not even mentioned him to her friends. *Maybe she has no feelings for me at all. Maybe she's still in love with Lionel.* Shaking off his thoughts, Keith finally responded to John's question. "I'm Karen's mother's next-door neighbor. When I moved in, Karen's mom, Doris, and I became friends and started attending the same church. She doesn't drive, so sometimes I'd take her grocery shopping and back and forth to services. Then Karen moved in with her mom, and she and I became. . .acquainted. For a while now, she's been helping me out with the youth ministry. I love working with teenagers, and I'd like to lead a church one day, Lord willing."

Soon their food arrived. As they ate, Keith told John about the day he'd spent with Karen at the divinity school. "We had a great time together, but. . . well, I'm afraid she's still in love with Lionel. Maybe after this visit, she'll be able to get him out of her system."

As they were finishing up, John finally spoke. "Wow, it sounds like you have a lot on your plate. Do you know where you want to go to school?"

"I'm still not sure. I'm researching colleges, trying to decide which is best for me. If I have to relocate, then I'll do it. I'm hoping by the time I decide, I'll know if there's any chance between Karen and me. I wouldn't be able to ask her to come with me if she still has feelings for Lionel."

John sighed. "I was once in a similar situation, in more ways than one."

"Really? How so?"

They were interrupted by the waitress bringing the bill. John pulled out his wallet.

Keith shook his head. "I've got it."

"No, that's okay. I've got it."

After they agreed to split the bill, paid it, and were back in the car, John said, "I used to be an agnostic."

Keith frowned. "Really?"

"Yes."

"How did you hook up with Monica?"

"Monica has a blind nephew. She had to take care of him for a while. When he started having trouble in school, Monica brought him to me. I tutor blind children in my spare time. As soon as we met, Monica and I were attracted to each other, but we couldn't date because of my agnostic beliefs."

"Sounds rough."

"It was. Keith, the most important day of my life was when I finally accepted Jesus as my Lord and Savior." John turned off the street and pulled the car into his driveway.

"That's an awesome testimony, John."

John removed a sleeping Mica from her car seat and took her into the house. After the child was situated in her nursery, he returned to Keith. "After I got saved, I wanted to join a traveling ministry to speak to other agnostics around the world." He shrugged. "I wanted to make up for lost time, but I finally saw that was a skewed way of thinking and that God was calling me to stay right here and minister to the kids on the college campus. . .and marry Monica." He paused, joining Keith on the couch. "So I can understand your feeling called to serve God in ministry. And I also know what you're going through as far as Lionel is concerned."

Keith frowned. "What do you mean?"

"Well, two years before I met Monica, she was involved with a guy named Kevin. I think she was still in love with him when they called it quits. Kevin got engaged months after their breakup, and when I met Monica, he still worshipped at her church. He'd bring his wife and infant to the services."

Keith shook his head. John's situation certainly did mirror his own, and he had to wonder if the Lord had led him to John today. "So what did you do?"

"I confronted her about it. I think part of the problem was she never really had a conversation with Kevin about what had happened between them. He just broke up with her, and there wasn't really any closure." He glanced at the family photo gracing the wall. "As I think about it, Karen's in the same situation. She was in love with Lionel, she switched churches—"

"She switched churches?" Karen had not told him that. He'd just assumed she'd met Lionel through her church home.

John nodded. "Yeah, Karen used to worship at Monica and Anna's church. The three of them had gone there for years. That's how they met, doing the soup kitchen together. But when Lionel came along, he insisted Karen worship with him at his large megachurch, especially since they'd gotten engaged and all, and Karen agreed." John paused for a few seconds. "Anyway, since he disappeared, there was no way for Karen to have closure with Lionel. At least in Monica's situation, Kevin was still here, although she was never engaged to him—unlike Karen, who thought she was going to be spending the rest of her life with Lionel. Then Karen found out Lionel was being accused of embezzlement and, on top of that, a womanizer. Man, desertion, embezzlement, and two-timing. Talk about a triple blow!" John shook his head. "That's a lot for somebody to go through, to find out those things about your future mate, somebody you proclaim to love—and who proclaimed to love you. No wonder she wants to see Lionel. How else is she going to put it all behind her?"

Keith thought about John's words. "I guess I can kind of understand why she'd do it, but it's kind of scary in a way, too."

"Scary how?" asked John.

"Well, I almost feel like she'll see that dude and then she'll find that she still has feelings for him. That in spite of the fact that he stole money and cheated on her, she'll still want to get back with him and work things out, especially since they're engaged and all. Then he'll just end up hurting her again. That's something I couldn't bear to witness."

"Man, you don't know that'll happen. We'll just have to wait and see what God has in store. If you want my opinion, I honestly don't think Karen will take Lionel back. She's intelligent and has high self-esteem. I think she'll see Lionel's true colors and put the whole situation into perspective. That'll help her bring closure to their relationship. Then, once Lionel is out of her system, she'll be ready to move on."

Keith closed his eyes for a few seconds, silently praying that there was truth to John's words.

Chapter 14

As Monica pulled into the parking lot of the police station, Karen began wringing her hands, her heart beating a mile a minute. "I feel so angry and nervous right now."

Anna folded her arms in front of her. "Humph. Maybe the Lord is telling you that you don't need to be seeing that no-good man."

Monica glared at Anna. "Anna, Karen has already made up her mind. What she needs now is our support." The three women unbuckled their seat belts, but before they got out of the car, Monica made a suggestion. "Don't you think we need to ask God for some help this afternoon?"

Karen sighed, giving Monica a small smile. "Thanks, Monica. I'm so nervous that I didn't even think about praying."

The three women joined hands and bowed their heads. Monica then prayed, "Lord, please be with Karen as she visits Lionel this afternoon. Please let Your Holy Spirit guide her and protect her during this difficult time. Amen."

"Amen," both Karen and Anna responded.

The three women exited the vehicle and entered the police station. When they approached, the female worker sitting behind the desk pushed her glasses up on her nose, giving them a bored look. "Can I help you?"

Karen nodded. "We're here to see Lionel Adams."

The woman glanced at the threesome. "The inmate can only have one visitor at a time."

Monica pulled Karen into a hug. "We'll be waiting out here for you, praying while you're back there, okay?"

Karen nodded, gazing at her two best friends. "Thanks." After checking Karen's ID and searching her purse, the attendant led Karen into a room with three tables. Each table had two chairs. Karen clutched her hands together, silently praying, her heart beating faster. The female attendant left, and seconds later, the door squeaked open. Karen turned to see a police officer leading Lionel into the room.

She gasped at Lionel, hardly recognizing him with his hair, now longer and being worn in dreadlocks, full mustache, and beard. His scruffy, haggard appearance was a stark contrast to the neat, immaculate, clean-shaven man she used to date.

Surprise tingeing his dark brown eyes, he said, "Karen! I didn't think you'd come to visit me."

She remained speechless as Lionel sat in the chair.

The officer said, "You've got twenty minutes."

Karen nodded toward the retreating officer then turned toward Lionel. "I can't believe it," she said softly.

"Can't believe what?"

She sighed. "You look terrible." She shook her head, not wanting to waste any of her precious twenty minutes asking questions about his drastically altered appearance. "Lionel, I've come for some answers. First off, why did you steal the money? And why did you date me while you had feelings for Michelle?"

Lionel frowned, rubbing his eyes. "The church owes me."

"What?"

"I said the church owes me. God owes me."

"What are you talking about?"

He folded his arms in front of him, his expression angry. "You know I mentioned to you that while I was growing up, my mom got involved with a weird church?"

Karen nodded. "What's that got to do with your embezzling church funds?"

He sighed. "What I didn't tell you was that my mother gave those church people everything! Everything! They said all members needed to support each other." He stared at the wall, his voice becoming rough. "Soon there was nothing left to give. My mom got sick, and they didn't do anything to help her. Instead of finding a doctor, they said we could just pray over her and make her better. They said the money belonged to the church, and we didn't need to be wasting it on a doctor."

Karen swallowed, shocked. "Then what happened?" she asked softly.

Tears slid from Lionel's dark brown eyes as he continued to speak. "She got worse and then she died. God died that day for me, too."

Karen sniffled, her eyes welling with tears. She took Lionel's hand. "Lionel, that doesn't sound like a church. That sounds like a cult."

He waved her comment away. "Church, cult, religion. It's all the same."

Karen shook her head, sending up a silent prayer for Lionel's soul. "No, it's not all the same. You can't blame God because your mom got mixed up with the wrong religion." She squeezed his hand. "Why didn't you tell me all this before?"

"Nobody knows now except you and Michelle."

She dropped his hand, feeling as if she were going to faint. Trying to quell the anger and sorrow welling up within her, she closed her eyes and said a silent prayer, asking for God's guidance. When she felt a bit calmer, she opened her eyes. "Lionel, when did you start dating Michelle? Were you—*are* you—having an affair with her?"

He wiped his wet eyes, and seconds later, he'd regained his composure. "Yes, I am. Remember when I went to a finance seminar downtown about a year ago?"

Karen frowned, recalling the event. "Yes, what about it?"

"That's where I first met Michelle. I was attracted to her and we started talking. That's when we exchanged phone numbers and I started seeing her. Remember when I told you I was working late on the weekends and in the evenings?"

"Yes." Karen's heart skipped a beat.

"Well, I wasn't always working. I'd be with Michelle sometimes." He continued to glance at Karen, propping his chin in his hand. "As I got to know her better, I finally told her about my religious background and how I was angry about my mother's death. After we'd had sex one night, she told me that her family had been mixed up with a strange religion, too."

Karen's mind was spinning. She checked her watch, aware of the seconds ticking away. "Why did you start going to church in the first place if—if you're not a Christian?"

"I joined because I planned on stealing from the church eventually." He lowered his voice. "I've stolen from a church before, but it wasn't for this amount of money. They never prosecuted me because they never found out about what I'd done."

"How could they not know?"

He sighed. "There are ways to hide those kinds of crimes. When I told Michelle about what I needed to do, and that the assistant treasurer position was open, I had her apply. And they hired her. She wanted to help me steal the funds, but when she saw the amount of money they had in the church, she didn't want to pilfer the small amounts that I was taking." He folded his arms in front of his chest. "She convinced me to steal a much larger amount. I told her it was harder to cover your tracks when you steal thousands of dollars like that, but she told me we could pull it off."

Karen's mouth dropped open. "And you believed her?"

"Yes. We figured we'd steal the funds and then resign from our jobs a few months later."

"Then what? Find another church to steal from?"

He shrugged. "Probably."

"Are you even sorry for what you've done?"

He sighed. "Like I said, the church owes me. Do you realize how much money my mother gave to the one we used to belong to? They said prayers and

God could cure my mama, but she's dead now. These churches owe me for my pain and suffering!"

"Oh, Lionel. Don't be angry at God. You need to give Him a chance—"

"Don't talk to me about God! I don't want to hear it," he said slowly.

"What about Michelle? Did she turn herself in, too? Where have the two of you been all this time?" She rushed to ask her questions because time was running short.

"I'm almost ashamed to tell you, but since I've put you through so much, I believe you have a right to know."

"Know what?"

"When I discovered the church had found out about our crime, Michelle contacted her brother in Washington State. He's an ex-con. He told us we could stay with him until we figured out what we were going to do. Since I've been over in Washington for the last few months, I've had time to think. I found out about the warrant for my arrest, and. . ." His face hardened as he turned to gaze at the wall; then he looked back at her. "Karen, even though Michelle and I had lots of money in Washington, we were arguing all the time. And then when I started thinking things would be worse for me if I got caught, I got scared. So I turned myself in. So did Michelle." He shook his head. "I'm still scared about going to prison, but I did what I had to do."

The guard spoke from behind the closed door. "You got two more minutes."

The next words rushed from Karen's mouth. "Did you care about me?"

His brown eyes glistened. "Karen, I did have feelings for you."

"Then why, Lionel? Why did you turn to someone else?"

He looked down at the table. "I had an affair with Michelle because I knew you wouldn't have a sexual relationship with me because of your religious beliefs. But while I was hiding out with Michelle, I still thought about you."

The news rocked Karen's world, and she struggled to keep her feelings in check. "Do you love her?"

"Who, Michelle?"

She nodded.

He sighed. "Not really. The only reason I ran away with her was because, well, when the church found out about what we'd done, I was scared."

"Lionel, be honest with me when you answer this next question. Did you ever love me?"

"Yes," he whispered.

"Are you serious?"

"Yes, I loved you and I thought we'd have a decent life together."

She narrowed her eyes. "But you're not a believer. Plus, what about stealing from the church? How would we have had a marriage if you were a thief?"

"Karen, I didn't think I'd get caught. I didn't think you'd ever find out about my deceit."

She removed the engagement ring from her purse. "I think it's only fair that I sell your engagement ring and give the money back to the church." She squeezed her palm hard, enclosing the ring within her hand. Tears rushed to her eyes, and she blinked the moisture away.

The officer stepped into the room. "Time's up!"

Karen stood and walked out of the room.

꒰ꔛ꒱

Karen rushed into the lobby, wiping her eyes. Monica and Anna rose as one, pulling her into their arms. Anna gave Karen a few tissues as they made their way to Monica's vehicle.

"Are you okay?" asked Monica.

Karen shook her head. "No, I'm not okay. Monica, I know you want to get back to Mica, but could we stop for coffee for a few minutes? I really need to talk to you guys alone right now."

"No problem," Monica responded.

Soon they were sitting in Starbucks, drinking steaming cups of coffee. Karen cradled her mug, trying to stop her hands from shaking.

Anna finally broke the silence. "What did Lionel say?"

Karen took a deep breath then told them what Lionel had said about his mother's religion and her death.

Monica gasped. "That sounds like a cult to me."

Karen nodded. "That's what I told him. He just sounded so angry and bitter. Because of all that's happened, this is going to be hard for me to do, but I'm going to continue to pray that Lionel finds Jesus."

"Amen to that," mumbled Monica. "What else did he say?"

Karen then told them about his meeting Michelle and getting her on board as the assistant treasurer.

Anna sipped her coffee before speaking. "So Michelle joined the church, too, just to steal money?"

Karen shrugged. "Apparently. I only had twenty minutes to talk to Lionel, so the information he gave me was kind of sketchy."

After Karen finished relating the rest of her conversation with Lionel, Anna asked, "Do you think he was really telling you the truth about loving you?"

"I don't know. I guess. Everything he said is like this huge knot in my head. I need to think about it, sort everything out. I guess I should praise God for allowing me to find these things out about Lionel before we were ever married. It's a blessing that the church discovered his crime."

Monica touched her hand. "Now that you've visited him, do you think you can put this whole thing behind you?"

"I already put it behind me for the most part." She spoke of how she'd come forward at her mother's church, asking God to help her with the pain and bitterness she harbored against Lionel. "Since Lionel turned himself in, I felt the Lord leading me to come and see him and get some answers."

Anna placed her cup on the table. "And now you have all your answers. Do you think you'll be going back to visit Lionel?"

Karen shook her head. "No. I just wanted to speak with him one last time." She glanced at her watch. "I know Keith wanted to get back to Annapolis today. He rearranged all of his clients so that he could bring me down here today."

Anna gasped. "Oh my goodness. We've been so busy discussing your meeting with Lionel that you haven't even told us about that cute man who drove you down here! What's his name again? Keith?"

Karen nodded. "Yes, Keith Baxter. He's a good friend of mine."

Monica asked, "Is he the man your mom was telling me you were involved with?"

"We're *not* involved."

As Anna threw her head back, laughing, her body bumped the table, causing Karen's coffee cup to topple. The hot coffee splashed onto the table and Karen's clothes.

Karen jumped up. "Ouch!"

Anna hurried for napkins to mop up the spill. "I'm sorry, Karen."

Karen waved her comment away. "That's okay."

"Let me buy you another cup," Anna offered.

She shook her head. "I didn't even really want that one." After they had resettled into their seats, Karen told them about Keith. "He's just a good friend who's been there for me. We work together in the youth ministry at his church."

Anna said, "Well, you're more than just friends if he's rearranged his work schedule and driven you down here."

She shook her head. "No, we're just. . .friends." Her brow furrowed.

"What are you thinking about?" asked Monica.

"This morning, Keith tried to talk me out of visiting Lionel. Then he wanted to know if we could be more than just friends."

Anna folded her arms in front of her chest. "If you ask me, I think he's already a better man for you than Lionel. I can tell that he likes you. Is he honest and trustworthy, and, even more importantly, is he a Christian?"

Karen shifted in her chair, uncomfortable in her damp, coffee-stained pants. "Yes. He wants to be a preacher and is searching for a divinity school. He and his twin brother have had a falling out, but he's working to heal the rift. You know, it's funny. Initially, I didn't think he was interested in me. But now, after our conversation this morning, I know that he'd like for us to date."

"Are you going to?" asked Monica.

Karen shrugged. "I'll have to think and pray about it. I do like him." Karen was silent as she played with her empty coffee cup, still trying to digest all that she'd discovered about Lionel that day.

❧

When they returned to Monica's house, the new mother immediately scooped up her baby while Anna pulled Karen into a hug. "I have to go. You know you can call me if you need anything."

Karen returned her friend's hug. "Thanks for coming with me today, Anna. It really meant a lot to me."

Monica was occupied with Mica as Keith rushed toward Karen, his eyes full of questions, questions she didn't feel like answering. She touched his arm. "I'll be right back."

She went upstairs and used the restroom. Afterward, she entered John and Monica's guest bedroom, wanting to spend some time alone. Fatigue swept through her as she sat in the wooden chair by the desk. She wanted to change into a fresh pair of pants since the huge coffee stain was still a little damp. Perhaps she could borrow Keith's car and drive to Wal-Mart to purchase a new pair of pants before they drove home. She again thought about the conversation she'd had with Lionel, and a tear escaped from her eyes. While she was wiping the moisture away, a strong knock sounded on the door. Figuring it was Monica, she said, "Come in."

Her heart skipped a beat when Keith strolled through the door. The scent of his aftershave filled the small room with musky sweetness, and his warm caramel-colored eyes were full of concern. "Are you okay?"

Remaining silent, she stood and walked to the window, where she lifted the bright yellow curtain and stared down at the street. Keith walked to the window and stood beside her. She blinked several times, refusing to look at him, hoping to hold any further tears at bay.

"You're crying. What did that. . . What did Lionel say to you?" he softly demanded.

Karen dropped the curtain and plopped down onto the queen-sized bed. "He said lots of things."

He sat on the bed beside her, taking her hand. "Like what?"

Taking a deep breath, she told him about her conversation with Lionel, eliminating his proclamation of love.

"Karen, that's terrible."

She nodded. "I know. I feel so bad for Lionel. I never realized he'd been

338

through so much. I knew his mom had died when he was a child, but he never told me what really happened until today. At least now I know the reason why he stole from the church. He blames God and all religions for what happened to his mother. It's wrong for him to think that way, but I'm glad he finally told me."

"Do you still have feelings for Lionel?"

She squeezed his hand. "I feel bad for him, and I'll pray for him to accept Jesus, but I—I don't love him romantically." She took a few moments to gather her thoughts. "I started to let my bitterness go the day I came forward at church. I did the best that I could without having Lionel around to talk to and find out what happened. I feel even better now that I've spoken to him."

Keith paused for a few minutes. "Do you think he still has feelings for you, even though he ran away with another woman?"

She sighed. "He said that he loved me but felt forced to flee with Michelle because of the church finding out about his theft."

"Do you believe him?"

She shrugged. "I suppose. It's hard to say."

"Well, thanks for telling me about your meeting with Lionel. That means a lot to me." He looked away, his shoulders drooping.

"What's the matter?" Karen asked.

Continuing to hold her hand, he turned back toward her. "I know you have a lot on your mind with all that Lionel has told you, but I wondered if you would consider what I asked you this morning."

"You mean about us seeing each other more, outside of the youth ministry?"

He nodded. "I really like you, Karen. Since I've accepted Christ and made a lot of changes in my lifestyle, you're the first woman I've liked enough to pursue a relationship with."

When she remained silent, he continued. "We can take it slow. We can see each other as friends. Is that okay with you? Karen, don't you like spending time with me?"

"Yes, Keith, I do, and I'd like to get to know you better, but. . .are you sure you don't have any feelings for Melanie?"

"I already told you she's like a sister to me and that's it. I wouldn't lie to you about something like that, Karen. Nor about anything else for that matter."

She touched his shoulder, feeling bad about offending him. "I'm sorry, Keith. I'm afraid my experience with Lionel has made me skeptical as far as men are concerned."

"Well, I'm not Lionel. I already told you that I'd never disrespect you like that."

Suddenly Karen realized how good a friend Keith had been to her since she'd relocated to Annapolis, and how well he'd treated her. "Keith, I'm sorry."

Her voice wavered as she struggled to keep her emotions in control.

"Sorry? Why?"

"Because you've done so much for me. You've shuffled your clients just to drive me to Ocean City." She didn't mention the fact that he'd done that just so she could see another man. "I've been ignoring you since you've been here, and I never even said thank you for doing this for me." She again touched his shoulder. "So thank you. I appreciate all you've done."

"You're welcome. But don't you understand, Karen? I'd do anything for you."

She nodded as a tear ran down her cheek.

Keith brushed the water away with his finger. "Are you sure you're okay?"

She sighed and nodded again. Keith got up and pulled a few tissues from the box on the desk. He gave her the tissues and she wiped her eyes. Then he pulled her into his arms. He glanced down at her pants. "What happened to your clothes?"

"After my visit with Lionel, Monica, Anna, and I went out for coffee, and Anna bumped the table." Karen pulled at her damp pants. "My coffee spilled on my clothes. I wondered if I could borrow your car and go to Wal-Mart to get some new pants before we head home."

"Want me to go to Wal-Mart for you?"

"No, I'd rather get them."

"I'll drive you over there if you want." He continued to caress her with his amazing eyes. "Have you eaten today?"

She thought about the toast she'd had for breakfast. "Not since early this morning."

"Aren't you hungry?"

She shook her head. "No, not really."

"Well, you need to eat something." He pulled his keys from his pocket. "We'll say good-bye to your friends, and then I'll take you over to Wal-Mart. Afterward we'll stop and get you something to eat."

She grabbed her purse and followed him out the door.

❧

At Wal-Mart, Keith watched Karen rifle through racks of clothing. He could tell she wasn't really paying attention to the items. Her body was in Wal-Mart, but her mind was obviously elsewhere.

"Couldn't you have borrowed some pants from Monica? And returned them when you saw her again?"

She gestured toward her petite, cute frame. "Well, Keith, we're not exactly the same size. Plus, I'm not sure when I'm coming back to Ocean City."

He supposed that was a stupid question on his part. Monica's clothes would probably fall right off Karen.

"Would you like me to help you look?"

She quickly shook her head. "No, that's okay. I'll be done in a minute." She finally settled on a pair of blue jeans. "After I buy these, I'll change, and then we can get something to eat."

"Okay."

She glanced around the store.

He touched her shoulder. "Are you sure you're okay? Did you need anything else?"

"No, that's it."

After she had paid for the jeans and changed in the restroom at Wal-Mart, they got back in his car. "Where did you want to go and eat?"

"There's a fast food place not too far from here. Why don't we eat there?"

He started the ignition. "I have no idea where I'm going, so you'll need to tell me how to get to the restaurant."

"Sure."

As Karen gave him directions, Keith noticed the town was full of tourists trekking along the busy sidewalks. Curious about Karen's past, he asked, "So how did you happen to be living here in Ocean City if you were raised in Annapolis?"

"I went to the University of Maryland at Eastern Shore for college."

"You have a bachelor's?" he asked in astonishment.

Her pretty eyes widened at his reaction. "Yes, I'm sure you're surprised about my degree since I'm a hairdresser, just like I was surprised to find out you have an MBA and you're a plumber."

He chuckled. "That's true. So how did you happen to become a hairdresser?"

He continued to drive, savoring the sweet sound of her voice as she recalled her college years. "Girls that lived in my dorm used to come to my room and get their hair done. I was doing it so regularly that I had to start charging people for it."

Keith interrupted her. "So you were doing hair without a license?"

"Yes. But since I wasn't working in a salon, it wasn't an issue at the time. I taught myself how to do hair, and I guess it was a natural talent I had." She continued, "When I graduated, I realized I liked doing hair more than studying to receive my degree in business administration. I wanted to work in a salon as a beautician, but I couldn't do that without a license."

He shrugged. "So what did you do?"

"I went to cosmetology school. While I was there, I apprenticed in a salon under another hairdresser in Ocean City."

"So you moved to Ocean City after you graduated from college?"

"Yes. Since the University of Maryland isn't too far from here, I decided

341

to move to this area after graduation. Then I started worshipping in the same church as Anna and Monica. We worked in the church's soup kitchen regularly, and that's how we became friends."

He pulled into the parking lot of the fast-food place and cut the ignition, still lulled by the sound of her voice. "When did you accept Christ?"

"When I was in college. My mom and dad were always regular churchgoers, but I never truly placed Him first in my life until I was living in the dorm."

"Did something happen to make you accept Him, or did you just finally bite the bullet and decide you wanted to follow Jesus?"

"Well, the whole story is kind of long."

"I'd like to hear it if you don't mind."

"Okay, well, when I was away from home, in college, I realized I'd only gone to school because it was expected of me, and although I then found I had a great outlet by doing hair and finally getting paid for it, I still felt like my life was missing something." Passion began to fill her voice. "Then my roommate started socializing and studying with a campus Christian group. They had a Bible study in my dorm room sometimes. My roommate invited me to come, and I found that through the Bible study, my questions about God and salvation were answered. I started poring over the scriptures because, even though I'd been to church all my life, I'd only read a few verses here and there. I'd never read the entire Bible, nor actually spoken with others who knew so much about the scriptures. So one night during Bible study, I told the group that I'd accepted Christ." Her voice wavered, and tears now filled her eyes. "I'd found the piece that was missing from my life. A passionate relationship with Him." She wiped her eyes. "You know, I'm glad you asked me that question, Keith."

He smiled, taking her hand. "Why?"

"Because you've just reminded me about the most important day of my life."

He smiled then gestured at the restaurant. "Come on, let's go get something to eat."

Hand in hand, they walked toward the restaurant.

Chapter 15

After seeing Lionel, Karen continued to pray for his salvation and that he would find help for the bitterness he still harbored against those who were responsible for his mother's death. As the trial came near, both Monica and Anna kept her abreast of what was transpiring in Ocean City. She eventually learned that Lionel had been sentenced to two years in prison. She felt a little sad but held out the hope that Lionel would seek religious counsel while in prison and one day accept Christ.

During the late summer, Karen and Keith helped with the annual youth picnic held on the church grounds. Karen watched Keith as he poured charcoal onto the grill. As the teens munched on pretzels and chips while waiting for the meat to get done, Karen thought about Keith's divinity school search. She knew he was narrowing down his choices and would, within a few months, make his final decision.

"Hey, Karen." Amanda approached, sipping a soda.

Karen smiled at the young girl. "Hi, Amanda."

Amanda grinned. "I saw you staring at Mr. Keith."

Karen looked away, wishing the teen hadn't caught her gawking at Keith. Wanting to steer the conversation in another direction, Karen asked, "How have you been lately, Amanda?"

Amanda shook her head, still smiling. "No, you can't go changing the subject by asking about me. What's up with you and Mr. Keith?" She gestured toward the teens eating their snacks. "We've all been wondering if you two are dating or what?"

Karen thought about the frank and honest discussion she'd had with Keith after their impromptu day trip to Ocean City. "Yes, we're dating, but we're taking it slow."

The girl furrowed her brow. "Taking it slow?"

Karen had noticed that since Amanda had broken up with Ron, she'd stopped wearing so much makeup and so little clothing. "Yes, we're getting to know each other as friends."

The girl pursed her lips. "I wish me and Ron had done that. Maybe if we'd taken things slow, we'd still be together. He called me last night, wanting to reconcile, but I told him no, even though it was hard."

Karen sighed. "I know we've talked about this before—"

"I know, I know, I need to stay celibate until I get married. I've learned my lesson. Believe me."

Karen mentally sighed, saying a quick prayer for Amanda's well-being.

Keith approached, pulling Karen into his arms, kissing her cheek. "I got one of the guys to man the grill for a few minutes. What are you two ladies talking about?"

Amanda giggled then said, "Girl talk," before rejoining the other teens.

Keith chuckled. "I hope I didn't interrupt anything."

Karen sighed, basking in the scent of Keith's aftershave as she settled into his strong arms. "We were just talking about. . .stuff."

"What kind of stuff?"

Karen swatted his shoulder. "Girl talk, like she said."

One of the teens turned on the radio, and praise and worship music soon floated on the warm summer breeze.

Later, Karen watched Keith as he served up burgers and hot dogs. Afterward, they played a competitive game of softball. Once the picnic was over and all of the food had been put away, Keith and Karen drove home in his car.

After he pulled into his driveway, he turned to Karen. "I was going to watch the game tonight. Want to join me?"

"Sure."

Suzie greeted them as they entered his house. After letting the large dog out into the backyard, he threw a bag of popcorn into the microwave and grabbed two sodas from the refrigerator. He plunked ice cubes into the Styrofoam cups before pouring their beverages. Moments later the scent of buttered popcorn filled the room.

After they were settled into the living room and he'd turned on the game, Karen ate a few kernels of corn before taking a sip of soda. Headlights shone into the living room, announcing an unexpected visitor.

"Who in the world can that be?" Keith mumbled, standing. Before he opened the curtain, a faint smile graced his lips. "Maybe it's my brother."

Karen's heart skipped a beat, hoping that it was, indeed, Keith's brother coming to make amends with his twin.

"Oh man!" Disappointment filled his voice as he dropped the white curtain.

"What's wrong?"

"It's Melanie."

"Oh." Karen wondered about Melanie often. After Karen had told Keith about Melanie's behavior following her haircut, he'd called her to check up on her. It turned out Melanie's fiancé was too controlling and was constantly telling her what she needed to do to change herself. After her fiancé had forced her to lose her locks and then quit the youth ministry, Karen wondered what else he would make her give up.

She rapped on the front door and Keith opened it. "Hi, Melanie, I'm kind of—"

She stormed into the house, not giving him a chance to finish. After wiping her tear-streaked eyes, she noticed the popcorn, sodas—and Karen. "Oh!" Her brown eyes widened. "I didn't realize you had company."

Keith's expression softened as he looked at Melanie. Jealousy, as thick as pea soup, flowed through Karen.

Melanie turned to Keith. "I—I could come back later if you want."

Karen sighed, gathering her purse. "That's okay. I need to get going anyway."

Keith shook his head. "No, Karen, don't leave." He looked at Melanie. "You can tell me anything you want in front of Karen. There are no secrets between us."

Melanie sat down, wiping away her tears. Karen brought her a box of tissues.

"I'm sorry to interrupt," Melanie said through her tears.

Sitting beside her, Karen said, "It's okay. Melanie, Amanda was just asking me about you today. She said a lot of the teens have missed you since you quit the youth ministry."

Keith sat across from the women in a chair, staring at Melanie. "What's the matter? Why are you crying?" His deep voice was full of concern.

Melanie glanced at both of them before responding. "I just gave Duane his engagement ring back."

Karen gasped. "You broke your engagement?"

The woman nodded. "Yes."

"Why?" asked Karen.

Melanie sighed. "It just got to the point where he'd criticize everything I said or did. I—I couldn't do a thing without wondering if Duane would get upset or angry. After you live like that for a while, it makes you tired."

Keith shifted in his chair. "What did Duane say?"

Melanie frowned. "You don't want to know. Let's just say he wasn't pleased."

"So you're not going to see him anymore, at all?" asked Karen.

Melanie shook her head. "Karen, I can't. He made me cut all my hair off. He hated my talking to my friends. He just wanted me to focus on him and do whatever he told me to do."

Keith stood and squeezed Melanie's shoulder. "I'm glad you broke things off with him. We're here for you if you need anybody to talk to."

For the rest of the evening, Melanie unburdened her heart to Keith and Karen.

The following Tuesday, Karen entered the salon and was greeted by her coworkers. After placing her equipment out on her station, she removed her bucket of curlers and made sure she had enough supplies for touch-ups and hair colorings for the day.

When it was almost time to break for lunch, Deidre spoke in an amused tone. "Karen, you have a visitor."

Karen turned, pleasantly surprised to find Keith standing at the receptionist's desk. He walked back to her station, holding a dozen brilliant scarlet roses surrounded by baby's breath. "Keith! I didn't realize you were coming."

He shrugged. "I came to see you."

"But you never come to visit me at work."

He glanced around the shop for a few seconds, as if he was nervous. He gave her the bouquet. "Here, these are for you."

"Thanks." She sniffed the flowers before laying them on her counter.

"Mmm, mmm, mmm," mumbled Sheronda. "Your man must've done something wrong if he brought you those flowers for no reason."

Karen gritted her teeth, having grown tired of Sheronda's unfounded innuendos. Ignoring the remark, she focused on Keith.

"Actually, I, uh, came by to get a haircut."

Karen chuckled. "You want me to cut your hair?"

"Yeah, if you don't mind. My barber's out of town and I need a cut." He touched his head, and Karen gestured him over to the chair.

"Sit down."

Keith sat and Karen placed a cape around him. She looked until she found her clippers in the bin. She then plugged them in and turned them on. As the light buzz filled the space, she found herself admiring Keith's profile as he waited for her to cut his hair. Warmth enveloped her when he glanced toward her, catching her staring at him. She swallowed, saying the first thing that came to her mind. "Sit still."

He chuckled, giving her a warm smile. "You don't have to tell me to sit still. When I was five, I moved around in the chair so much that the barber accidentally nicked my ear with his clippers."

While smooth jazz floated from the speakers, she smiled at him, touching his hair before running the clippers over his perfectly shaped head. They continued to buzz as she cut his hair low. She glanced at his face periodically, and when she gazed at his full lips, she wondered how it would feel to kiss Keith Baxter.

She pushed the thought from her mind, finishing her task. "All done."

Keith glanced in the mirror. "It looks perfect." His caramel-brown eyes shone with warmth as he turned his gaze to her. "It's the best haircut I've ever had."

After they had settled the bill and he'd paid the receptionist, he came back to Karen's station. "Do you want to go out to lunch?"

Karen checked her watch. "I only have a half hour."

Keith shrugged. "That's enough time. We can get hot dogs from the vendor outside and sit on the bench to eat."

After they'd gotten their food, Keith blessed their simple meal and told her what was on his mind. "I'm sorry about the other night."

"Do you mean when Melanie came over?"

He nodded. "I know we were going to watch the game together, but I didn't want to make her leave when she was so upset."

"That's okay. I understand."

"I'm glad that you stayed."

"I just hope things work out for her now that Duane is out of the picture."

"Yeah, she called me last night and told me that she's moving."

"Moving?"

"Yes. She quit her job and she's moving to Idaho to open a health food store with her cousin. She'd talked about doing this before she met Duane, but after they got engaged, it was just one more dream he'd squelched."

"A health food store. . . That's a big switch."

"I think it'll be good for her. This is something she's passionate about, and I think it'll help her to heal. She wants to keep in touch with both of us." They ate in silence for a few minutes before Keith spoke again. "You know, I wanted to ask you something."

"What's that?"

"Both of us get up pretty early in the morning. . . ."

Karen shrugged. "Yeah, so?"

He finished his hot dog before taking her hand, squeezing her fingers. "You know how much I love cooking, especially after my early morning workouts."

Karen furrowed her brow, wondering where this whole conversation was leading. "I know." She fondly recalled the first time she was in Keith's kitchen and the way he'd fixed breakfast for her.

"Well, I hate cooking just for one. So. . .I was wondering if you wanted to come by for breakfast."

She smiled. "Sure, when? Tomorrow?"

He squeezed her hand. "Not just tomorrow, but. . .every day."

Karen widened her eyes, wondering if she'd misheard him. "You want me to come to your house every day for breakfast?"

"Why not?"

"It would just seem weird, my coming to your house every day to eat breakfast."

"Really?" He was silent for a few minutes as he continued to hold her hand. "I think it'd be kind of nice. But if you don't want to see me so often, that's okay."

He frowned, and Karen wondered if she'd hurt his feelings, so she rushed to explain herself. "I didn't mean it would be weird in a bad sort of way, just weird as in different."

He tilted his head. "What do you mean?"

She balled up the paper from her hot dog, tossing it into the bin beside their bench. "Keith, in my thirty years of life, I've never seen anybody I was dating every day."

"What about Lionel? Didn't you see him every day?"

Karen shook her head. "No, not even Lionel. I guess the thought of my seeing somebody every day is just so new, I–I'm not used to it." She squeezed his hand, giving him a huge smile. "But I think I like the idea."

His frown eased into a smile. "Really?"

"Yes. Although we're already seeing each other once or twice a week, I have wanted to spend more time with you, but I just wasn't sure how often you wanted to see me."

"So is that a yes? You'll start coming by for breakfast every morning?"

Her smile widened. "That's a yes." Her heart pounded as Keith leaned closer, and then he kissed her.

Chapter 16

O ver the following couple of weeks, Keith eagerly awaited Karen's coming to his home and sharing breakfast with him. He soon found that the more time he spent with Karen and the better he got to know her, the deeper he was falling in love with her.

As September rolled around, he took Ms. Doris out to the nursery to get her fall chrysanthemums on sale. It had been the first time he'd needed to take Ms. Doris anyplace in months. Since it was Saturday, Karen was busy at the hair salon, and Ms. Doris had been anxious to get her flowers planted.

"Keith, don't these look lovely?" she said, fingering the nursery's white and orange blossoms. "I'm going to set these out in my backyard as soon as we get home. My plants have really been thriving since Karen's been watering them every day."

Keith just smiled, his mind elsewhere.

As they drove back to his house, Ms. Doris said, "Too bad Karen had to work today. It would've been nice having her along."

"Mmm," Keith said absentmindedly.

Doris continued, "I've noticed that Karen has been eating breakfast at your house lately."

Keith smiled, nodding while he drove. "Yes." He was falling in love with Karen, but he wasn't sure if he should tell Ms. Doris his true feelings.

"Karen seems much happier now. She's changed since she's renewed her faith and started spending more time with you."

"Yeah. . . . And you know, although I didn't like the idea at first, I think it helped her to visit Lionel. She obviously needed closure. And now that he's out of her life for good, I think she's on the road to healing." *And hopefully falling in love with me.*

Doris chuckled.

Taking his eyes off the road for a second, Keith caught her smile, which made him smile in return. "What are we grinning about?"

Doris hesitated a moment then said, "Keith. . .we're not just neighbors, but friends, right?"

"Right." *Where is this leading?*

"And friends can discuss anything with each other, right?"

Suddenly feeling uncomfortable, Keith replied with a hesitant "Right. . ."

"So I'm going to come right out and ask you. Are—are you in love with my daughter?"

While Keith's mind began to scramble for an answer, he felt the heat rise in his cheeks.

Doris smiled knowingly. "You *are*, aren't you?"

Keith grimaced. "Is it that obvious?"

"To me it is. I take it you haven't told Karen yet."

Keith took a deep breath. "Here's the thing. . . . I don't know if I should. . . yet."

"Why not?"

"Well, for one thing, I've only known her for six months."

"Well, that's true, but—"

"And for another, she's on the rebound. I mean, she just came out of a really bad relationship with a man who deceived her in so many ways. He cheated on her, committed a crime, and then disappeared."

"Yes, Keith, but—"

"Well, I really find it hard to believe that she would be ready to hear words of love spoken by another man."

Doris was silent, her smile now faded, her brow furrowed. Finally, she said, "Well, all you say is certainly true. So there's really only one piece of advice I can give you."

"What's that?"

"Pray about it."

"I have. But I haven't gotten a clear answer to that, nor to. . ."

"Nor to what?"

"Kyle. My brother."

"Oh, right. Kyle. Have you seen him since that day you stopped in at his town house?"

"No. I call him occasionally, and he sometimes answers the phone, which I guess is a good sign. But our conversations are so stilted. It's like we're strangers instead of brothers."

"Hmm. Any new ideas of why your father arranged the inheritance the way he did?"

"Well, I did stop in to see Dad's lawyer, hoping he'd remember something—anything—any reason as to why Dad changed his will. But I came up empty-handed." He sighed heavily. "I tell you, Doris, my plate is full. Between my feelings for Karen, the issues with Kyle, the search for a school, and taking care of my own business, I feel like I've got so much more than I can handle," he said, pulling into his driveway.

"What you need, Keith, is to spend an entire day alone with the Lord."

"You think? An entire day?"

"Sometimes that's what it takes. Trust me. I know what I'm talking about."

❧

The following Wednesday, Keith took Doris's advice. He got into his car and drove to Sandy Point State Park. Bible in hand, he grabbed a beach chair from the back of his car and set it up beneath the trees, staring at the Chesapeake Bay in the distance. Since it was near the end of the season, the place was almost deserted. Sitting in the cool breeze, listening to the leaves rustle in the early autumn wind, he read his well-worn Bible, gaining comfort from the scriptures.

Finally, he bowed his head and folded his hands. *Lord, I've got quite a load on my shoulders. I want to discuss it with You, one item at a time.* He sighed then continued praying silently. *Okay, Lord. . . . First, You know I want to tell Karen that. . . that I love her. But I don't know if she's ready to hear it right now. Give me wisdom in this situation, Lord. Let me know when the timing is right.* He paused, pressing his hands tighter together. *And, Lord, I miss my brother, Kyle. I don't know how to heal the rift between us. On top of that, he hasn't accepted You, Lord. Touch his heart. Give me the right words to say. Help me to convince him of the gift of eternal life. I ask all these things in Jesus' name. Amen.*

Feeling as if a huge weight had been lifted, Keith raised his head, his eyes taking in the billowy clouds above him. As he reveled in the cool breeze, the sounds of the water slapping the shore, and the wonder of God's creation, his cell phone rang, pulling him out of his reverie. Removing the phone from his pocket, he glanced at the display, noting the unfamiliar number. "Hello?"

A professional female voice sounded. "I'm looking for Keith Baxter?"

"Speaking. How can I help you?"

"You're listed as a contact for Lawrence Baxter."

Keith's heart skipped a beat when he heard his father's name. "Contact for what?"

The female sighed. "For his safe-deposit box here at the bank. He needs to make a payment if he wants to keep it open. We've called his phone number, but it's been disconnected. And the payment notice we sent to his house came back as undeliverable."

"Which bank is this?"

"Annapolis Bank and Trust."

"Ma'am, my father died almost a year ago. Is it possible for me to have access to his safe-deposit box?"

"Sir, that's fine since you're listed as a point of contact. It'll also help us if you'd bring a copy of your father's death certificate as well as your driver's license." She then told him the address of the bank.

Keith packed up his chair and Bible, jumped in his car, and drove away, trying not to break the speed limit, anxious to find out what was in his father's safe-deposit box. After stopping at his house to get his father's death certificate, he drove to the bank. When he arrived, he was ushered into the back of the building, where an employee opened the box for him then pointed to an empty room.

"You're welcome to go in there and look at the contents of the box."

Keith stepped into the room and opened the small box. Inside were a few pieces of jewelry as well as a cream-colored envelope. He opened the envelope and found a notarized letter addressed to him, dated a few weeks before his father's death. Keith read:

> *Dear Keith,*
>
> *I know that my remaining days upon this earth are few. With that in mind, I feel called to write this letter, to tell you some things I seem unable to say.*
>
> *First, thank you for showing me the way to the Lord. That is something for which I will be eternally grateful. How I wish I could change the past, but I feel content in knowing my future lies in heaven with God.*
>
> *Second, I know that Kyle has been troubled since his breakup with Andrea. And my being diagnosed with cancer seems to have sunk him into an even deeper depression. I also know he hasn't been handling his finances very well lately. Keith, I'm worried about your brother's physical and spiritual well-being. Please be there for him. Help him sort things out. And try to show him he needs to lean on Jesus.*
>
> *And lastly, because of your brother's erratic behavior, I don't feel comfortable leaving him a lot of money right now. So I'm leaving the bulk of my estate to you, hoping and trusting that you will allocate your brother's half whenever you feel he is responsible enough to handle it.*
>
> *Keith, you are an extremely levelheaded young man, and I'm proud of you. I trust that you will seek the Lord's guidance in this matter.*
>
> *I love both you and Kyle with all my heart. May God bless you both, in this world and the next.*
>
> > *In Christ,*
> > *Your father,*
> > *Lawrence Baxter*

Keith held the letter, wondering why their father chose to leave it in the safe-deposit box and not tell him about it. *Perhaps this is what Dad was going to tell me about just before he died.* Keith stood in the room, lost in thought.

A knock sounded on the door. "Sir, we're about to close the bank."

Keith stepped out of the room, holding the contents of the box. "May I take these things with me?"

The woman nodded. "Yes, when your father filled out the paperwork for the box, he listed you as the party who should have possession of the contents in case of his death. Can you step to my desk for a few minutes? I'll need you to sign some forms."

After Keith had signed the appropriate papers, the banker placed the safe-deposit contents into a large padded envelope. Keith carried the envelope to his car and drove home.

When he arrived at his house, he brought his vehicle to a screeching halt. "Lord, You've certainly been busy today answering my prayers," he muttered, recognizing the classy black Lexus sitting in the driveway.

Taking a deep breath, he exited his car and walked toward the front door of the house. Kyle sat on the porch, beer bottle in hand. Placing the bottle on the wooden planks, he then stood, staring at Keith.

Keith swallowed, unsure of how to greet his twin. He eyed the beer bottle again, recalling that the last time he'd seen Kyle, he'd been hung over from a drinking binge. He lifted the bottle, noting it was empty. He set it back down then examined his brother's eyes. "You're sober."

Kyle lifted his dark eyebrows. "I only had one beer. Give me a break." The brothers stood on the porch observing one another until Kyle spoke again. "Come on, I wanted to talk to you about something." He gestured toward the house.

Keith thought it weird, Kyle inviting him into his own home. But his brother had always been like that, taking the lead, trying to tell Keith what to do.

"Go on in," said Keith.

Kyle grunted. "You're not thinking, little brother—the door is locked. I tried it when I got here."

Rattled, Keith pulled the keys out of the pocket of his faded blue jeans. Keith walked the few steps to the door, opened it, and strolled inside, his brother following close behind. Suzie ran up, tail wagging as she barked a greeting to the brothers.

Bending down to pet the dog, Kyle's gaze swept the room as if appraising the value of its contents. "Have you been spending the money that Dad should've left for me in his will?"

Keith gritted his teeth, trying not to lose his temper. This was not the best way to start this visit. Placing the padded envelope on the coffee table, he decided to change the subject. "I haven't eaten all day. Did you want to order a pizza or something?"

"You don't cook anymore?"

Keith shrugged. "I still cook, but I don't feel like making anything right now. Do you want to get a pizza or not?" he asked with a note of impatience.

Kyle looked away for a few seconds before responding. "Yeah, that's okay with me."

Keith ordered the pizza then grabbed a couple of Styrofoam cups. After putting ice and soda into the containers, he brought them into the living room.

Kyle looked at the soda then stood. "I've got to get something out of my car," he said. He soon returned with the rest of his six-pack of beer.

"Man, take that beer out of this house!"

"I'm not going to get drunk and act stupid. I promise."

"I don't want alcohol in this house. Take it out, now." Standing face-to-face, the brothers glared at one another until Kyle eventually left the house and returned empty-handed.

For a few moments, they sat in tense silence, Kyle continuing his survey of the living room. Spotting the brochures for divinity schools on the coffee table, Kyle picked one up and began flipping through it. "You plan on going back to school or something?"

Kyle had always been good about doing that. After they'd had an argument or disagreement, he smoothly changed the subject, almost as if he was trying to make Keith forget about what had just transpired.

Between sips of soda, Keith told Kyle about his search for the right divinity school, ending with, "It's something I feel called to do."

Kyle scoffed, tossing the brochure back onto the coffee table. "What's that mean anyway?"

Before Keith could respond, a knock sounded on the door. "That must be the pizza," he said. He strolled to the door and moments later returned to the living room, pie in hand. "Let's go into the kitchen to eat," he said. After Kyle was seated, Keith removed two paper plates and napkins from the cupboard. He sat down, silently blessing their meal, then opened the box.

For a few moments, the brothers ate. Then Kyle broke their silence by repeating the question he'd asked earlier. "What do you mean by you feel *called* to go to divinity school?"

Keith chewed and swallowed, carefully choosing his words. "I feel this is what God wants me to do."

Kyle removed another slice of pizza from the greasy box. With a smirk, he asked, "How do you know God wants you to do it? Did He knock on your door, come in, and say, 'Keith, I want you to go to divinity school'?"

Striving to overcome a growing feeling of exasperation, Keith spoke calmly. "I just feel in my heart that this is the direction the Lord wants me to go, the path He wants me to take."

Kyle grunted, finishing another slice of pizza.

Questions continued to riddle Keith's brain like popping kernels of corn, and he again wondered why his brother had chosen to show up on this day. Before asking what Kyle wanted, he decided to tell him about what happened earlier. "I got a phone call from the bank."

Kyle frowned. "What bank? What are you talking about?"

He stood, gesturing toward the living room. "Come on, I'll show you."

He opened the envelope and dumped the contents on the coffee table. "Dad left me this letter. It was in a safe-deposit box. I didn't even know the box existed until today. The letter. . . I—I want you to read it."

Kyle read in silence, his mouth set in a tense line. When he finished, he lowered the letter, his hands dropping to his sides.

For a few minutes, no words were spoken. Then Kyle said, "I didn't realize Dad knew about my finances."

Knowing their father wouldn't lie, but wanting Kyle to admit he had a problem, Keith said, "So it's true?"

Kyle nodded. "The part about my finances is, but not the part about my being. . ." He picked up the letter again and read, " 'Troubled.' "

"Kyle, we both know your drinking has gotten worse." When Kyle remained silent, Keith asked the question that had been burning in his mind ever since he'd seen Kyle's car in his driveway. "Why are you here?"

Kyle hesitated, suddenly looking unsure. "I—I came to ask you a favor."

"Well. . .what is it?"

"I'm in a. . .a little bit of a bind."

Keith narrowed his eyes. "What do you mean by *little*?"

"Well, maybe it's not so little."

"Well, what's the matter?" asked Keith.

"My home is in danger of being foreclosed."

Keith widened his eyes. Shaking his head, he sank into the nearest chair, feeling like a fool. *And I actually thought you'd come over to patch things up between us.* He sighed then looked up at his brother. "So I guess you want money."

"Well, yeah. I'm glad to find out you weren't dishonest about getting Dad to change his will." He pointed to the letter. "He said you could disperse the funds as you see fit. I think you should give me my half of the money now. No matter what Dad thought, I'm not a child."

"Listen, Kyle. For a minute, let's forget about the money. Let's talk about us, about your not trusting me, about your having barely spoken to me since Dad died. You never even gave me a chance to tell you my side of the story."

Kyle rolled his eyes. "Okay, little brother, what's your side?"

"Remember the day that Dad died?"

Kyle frowned. "Is this your way of giving me a guilt trip?"

"A guilt trip?" Keith echoed.

"Yeah. Are you deliberately trying to make me feel guilty because I was in the Virgin Islands while you stayed here, taking care of Dad?"

Keith sighed. "No. I'm just trying to get you to understand where I'm coming from."

"Whatever," Kyle said as he took a seat across from Keith. "So go ahead. I'm listening."

Keith struggled to gather his thoughts, recalling their father's last month of life, then said, "The day Dad died, he wasn't feeling well. Remember how he didn't want to go into a nursing home?"

"I remember," Kyle whispered, his face softening. "He said he wanted to die at home."

"Right. Well, he'd been feeling worse than usual that day. The hospice nurse came, checked him out, gave him some medicine. He told me he wanted to talk to me about something important, but he'd been in so much pain the day before that he was very tired. He managed to tell me he felt bad about the way he'd raised us, and he wished that we could have been tighter. . .as a family."

"Dad never cared about being closer to us."

"Yes, he did. He just never showed us. . . . You know, I learned a lot about Dad that last year. Anyway, he always figured that having a lot of money would prove how much he cared for us." Keith paused, his eyes misting with tears.

"What else did he say?"

"H–he told me he'd made some changes to improve things in the household."

"Huh?"

"I know. He started talking to me like I was a little boy instead of a grown man. Said things were going to change around here. At first I thought the medicine was affecting his mind, so I told him to take a nap and we'd talk about it later."

"And when you went back to check on him, he was gone," Kyle said softly.

"Yeah. I never got a chance to ask him what he'd meant. When the will was read, I was just as floored as you were. But I honestly think that he was going to tell me about this letter, or maybe give me the key to the safe-deposit box."

"So you didn't have the key?"

Keith shook his head. "No. I didn't even know the box existed until today. But now we know why he did what he did." He gazed at his twin. "It looks like it was a smart move, too, especially with your present situation." He paused. "Listen, Kyle, I hate that this money issue has come between us. I miss talking to you. I—I miss your being in my life."

Suzie, having awakened from a nap, sauntered into the living room and placed her large head on Kyle's lap.

"See, even Suzie notices you're not around anymore." Keith tried to make light of a serious situation. But his brother didn't even crack a smile. Keith hesitated then said, "Kyle, now that we both know what happened, can't we just move past this and start. . .well, start being brothers again?"

Kyle remained silent, petting Suzie's fur, then said, "We'll always be brothers. I just don't know about us being. . .friends."

For a moment, Keith was stunned, his heart cut to the quick. Then he said softly, "Kyle, the very fact that you thought I lied in order to cheat you out of your inheritance. . ." He shook his head then said, "Have I *ever* given you a reason to mistrust me before? I mean, have I ever lied to you?"

The room filled with silence, each brother lost in thought. Abandoning Kyle, Suzie approached her master, begging for food. Keith went into the kitchen and poured food and water into the dog's dishes before returning to the living room.

Kyle sighed. "Look, I know you've never lied to me, but you still need to give me my part of the inheritance." He glanced around the house again. "Have you been spending my share of the money?"

"Kyle, I told you all this in the letters and e-mails I sent you the first few months after Dad died. I haven't touched a dime of your money."

"Well, I need it. If I lose my house, I might end up having to move in here with you. Do you really think that's a good idea?"

Exhaustion, mingled with exasperation, racked Keith's body. *Lord, give me strength.* He ran his fingers through his hair. "What happened to your money anyway? Dad left you some in his will, plus you're running a law firm, and I know what salary you're bringing home. Why—and on what—are you spending so much money?"

Kyle shrugged. "It's something to do, I guess."

Keith frowned.

"I like spending money. . .traveling, buying things, taking women out. You know me, Keith."

"The Kyle I knew spent lavishly but always paid his bills. What happened to you?"

Kyle shrugged. "I—I guess it all started when Andrea left. I was so hurt. . . . I couldn't stop thinking about her. So I started drinking. Just a little at first. Then when I realized that wasn't enough, I started doing anything to take my mind off of her—trips, extravagant gifts for women, you name it. The bills started coming in fast and furious. I just let them pile up, I guess. Next thing I know, Dad gets sick and dies. Then guilt piled on top of the pain, and I just got further and further behind on the bills. . .and I started drinking more heavily." Kyle sat slumped in his chair.

"Well, big brother, let's take it one step at a time. First, how long do you have before you lose the house, and how much do you need to keep it?"

"Six weeks before they foreclose." He then told him the amount of money he needed.

The exorbitant sum made Keith's head spin. He whistled. "Well, I don't want you to lose your house, but I need to think and pray about it."

"You're asking God about giving me money that's rightfully mine?"

"Yes, like I've told you, I go to God for all of my major decisions."

The twins sat silently for a few minutes before Kyle spoke. "Well, I guess I have no choice but to wait for your answer." After an uncomfortable silence, Kyle cleared his throat then asked, "So are you still seeing the woman I saw you with at the Rockfish?"

"Yes," Keith said, his eyes lighting up. "I'm in love with her."

"That's great! Does she feel the same way?"

Keith frowned. "I don't know. Haven't told her how I feel. . .yet."

"Why not?" asked Kyle.

"I think the Lord wants me to wait a bit."

"Well, be careful, little brother. Remember what happened between me and Andrea."

"I'll be careful. Karen's been through a lot over the last year, and I just want to be sure she's ready to hear what I have to say." He paused for a few seconds. "She's been coming over every morning for breakfast."

Kyle raised his thick eyebrows. "Really? She drives over here every day just to eat with you?" He playfully swatted Keith's shoulder.

Keith grinned, shaking his head. "She doesn't drive over; she walks."

"Huh?"

Keith pointed toward the kitchen window. "She lives right next door. I was friends with her mother before I ever met Karen. She moved in this past spring. She'd just gotten out of a really bad relationship. Turns out her *ex*-fiancé was not only an embezzler but a two-timer."

"Man, and I thought I had a bad breakup."

"Yeah, well, she's doing a lot better now than when she first came to Annapolis. She's been helping me with the youth at church. And then somewhere along the line, we started dating." He smiled again. "And every day we have early morning breakfasts, then evening walks with Suzie. If everything works out the way I'd like it to—I mean, if it turns out she feels the same way about me—then I'm hoping she'll be my wife and come with me when I start divinity school. But we'll just have to wait and see."

Kyle stood. "Well, I've got to get going. I hope things work out with you and Karen."

Keith nodded, pulling his brother into an impulsive hug. "Thanks. I love you, bro. I'll be in touch. And you. . . Don't be a stranger."

Chapter 17

On her way over to Keith's house, Karen decided that tonight was the night. She was determined to find out what had been bothering Keith over the last few weeks. Just as she was about to knock on his front door, it opened.

"Hey there, gorgeous," Keith said, his initially brooding frown turning up into a smile. "Suzie's ready for our evening stroll. Are you?"

"Yep!" she said, returning his smile.

Starting down the sidewalk together, a comfortable silence soon descended as each strolled along, lost in thought. As they turned a corner, Karen glanced at Keith's face in the streetlight. Suddenly it hit her. *Keith Baxter, I am falling for you. . .hard.*

As if reading her thoughts, he lurched to a halt, pulled her into his arms, and began kissing her. At first, Karen was stunned, as was Suzie, who began barking and nudging her nose in between them. Then all sense of time and place was lost as Karen melted in Keith's embrace. What seemed like hours later, he released her.

"Well," she said, trying to catch her breath.

Keith, grinning from ear to ear, grabbed her hand and held on tight.

As they continued their stroll, Karen's wits began to return. But Keith was soon back to brooding, prompting Karen to ask, "Keith. . .are you okay? Is anything wrong?"

No response.

"Keith?"

He suddenly looked up from his study of the sidewalk. "Huh?"

"I asked you a question."

"Oh," he said with a halfhearted smile. "Sorry. What was it?"

"I asked if anything was wrong?"

"Wrong? No, everything's fine." He lifted her hand to his lips, giving her a gentle kiss.

Hmm. Okay. . . . Let's try some small talk. "I've got some news."

"Yes?"

"I got Amanda a job as a shampoo girl at the salon."

"That's nice," he said absentmindedly.

"Yes. She seems to like it."

"That's good."

"Yeah, she's a great girl. I'm so glad you got me involved in the youth program at church. I like spending time with them once a week."

"Mmm. . . Yes. Me, too."

Finally, Karen gave up trying to have a conversation with Keith. *But when we get back to the house, I'm going to sit you down and find out what's going on.*

When they had circled back to Keith's house and approached the end of his driveway, he would have walked right past had Karen not stopped dead in her tracks.

"Did you want to make another loop around the neighborhood?"

Keith, suddenly pulled from his reverie, lurched to a halt, then said, "Uh, no. Sorry." He cleared his throat. "Want to sit on the back porch for a while?"

"Sure."

Suzie played in the backyard while Keith and Karen sat in silence, the brightly colored leaves tumbling from the trees in the autumn breeze.

Finally, Karen said, "Keith, if we're going to be having a relationship, you need to be open with me. What's been bothering you lately?"

Their hands again interlocked, he began playing with her fingers. "Sorry, I know I've been a little moody lately. I've. . .had a lot on my mind."

Karen shifted in her seat, suddenly uncomfortable. "L–like what?"

"Oh. . .things. . .problems."

Karen cleared her throat. "Um, we're okay, aren't we? I mean, you don't have a problem with us, do you?" *Oh, please say you don't.*

Keith smiled and squeezed her hand. "No, honey. We're fine. It's just that I've been trying to figure out what to do about my brother's money. I know I need to let him have it, but I'm not sure how to go about giving it to him. . . . Do I wait a month? A year?"

"Is that all?" she asked, relieved.

"Well, to me it's a pretty big deal. I mean, if I give him too much all at once, there's no telling what he'll do with it. What if he takes off to Cancun or goes on a drinking binge? And do I give him just enough to save the house now, see how he handles it, and then wait until next year to give him more?"

"Sorry. I know it's important, and I wish I could help you. But the only thing I think we can do is take it to the Lord and see where He leads."

Keith's eyes lit up. "You know, you're right! Do you remember the verse from Matthew, the one where Jesus says, 'If two of you on earth agree about anything you ask for, it will be done for you by my Father in heaven. For where two or three come together in my name, there am I with them'?"

"Yes. That's the one we've been focusing on at Devo."

"Right. Well, let's pray together right now and lift this problem up to God."

"Sounds great." *Lord, this man is a keeper.*

Keith took Karen's other hand, and beneath the light of a harvest moon, they lifted his concerns to God.

✌

A week later, Karen headed over to Keith's house early in the morning, eager to see him. She walked right past her mother's autumn chrysanthemums, which needed no watering today since God had taken care of it the night before with a blessing of heavy rains.

Last night, Keith had told her he was making blueberry muffins, bacon, and eggs this morning, and she was looking forward to the meal—and seeing him. After she rapped on his door, Keith opened it, beckoning her inside. Suzie barked excitedly as Keith let the dog out to play in the yard.

"Hi, Karen." His full lips touched her cheek.

With a contented sigh, Karen stepped into the kitchen, the scent of blueberry muffins filling the air. Removing her light jacket, she said, "It's starting to get colder in the morning."

"I know. We're going to have to start wearing our heavy coats soon."

"Smells wonderful in here."

He chuckled. "Yes, this is Ms. Sonya's recipe. You know, I'd like to take you over to meet her and Mr. Terrance soon." He pulled the muffins out of the oven. "This is a lot of food. Maybe you can take some muffins over to your mom."

"Yes, I'm sure she'd like some."

He removed eggs from the refrigerator.

"You seem to be in a good mood," Karen commented.

He placed the eggs on the counter and returned to the table, temporarily abandoning his task. "Let's have a seat while the muffins are cooling off. I—I want to talk to you about something."

Curious, Karen sat at the table.

Keith took her hand, squeezing her fingers. "I think I've found a solution to my problem."

"Do you mean the problem with your brother's money?"

He nodded.

"What are you going to do?" she asked.

"Well, I called him last night. I'm going to give him his half of the money."

"Do you think he can handle that much cash all at once?"

"No, but I've worked that out, too. I'm going to give it to him over the next ten years in equal annual installments. But even before he sees one red cent, he's got to give me proof that he's getting financial counseling."

"Do you think that's the right thing to do?"

"Karen, I've done the best that I could. The rest is up to God. But you know, I feel like a huge burden has been lifted. This money issue has weighed heavily on my mind since my dad died. But since I've made my decision, I feel happier. And Kyle was definitely agreeable to the terms."

"I'm glad." She squeezed his hand. "Do you think he'd consider coming to church with you sometime?"

"I can't see that happening anytime soon. But we'll just have to wait and see. Meanwhile, we'll pray on it. At least my relationship with Kyle is a little bit better now."

Karen smiled, loving Keith's jovial mood.

He returned her smile. "I had something else I wanted to talk to you about, too."

"Really?"

"Yes." He pulled her onto his lap, kissing her cheek. "I love holding you, Karen."

She giggled, her heart beating wildly. "I like having you hold me, Keith."

He hugged her for a few seconds before releasing her. "Karen, I just want you to know that you're one special lady and that I'm in love with you."

Her heart skipped a beat. "What?"

He kissed her nose. "I love you, Karen Brown."

She smiled, euphoria filling her soul. "And I love you, too, Keith Baxter."

As the months passed and Christmas rolled around, Keith invited Karen over for a festive holiday dinner. After they'd feasted on roasted chicken and potatoes, they sat in his living room, gazing at his Christmas tree. "It's so pretty," Karen gushed. "Do you get a tree every year?"

"No, this is the first time I've purchased one since I've been living alone." He pulled her into his arms. "I wanted to ask you something."

She smiled. "What's that?"

He reached into his pocket and pulled out a velvet box. When she opened the lid, her excited grin made his head spin. "Will you marry me?"

"Yes, I'll marry you!" She pulled him into her arms and kissed his lips. "I love you, Keith," she whispered.

"I love you, too, Karen."

She admired the ring now gracing her finger. "We need to go let my mother know!" Karen pulled her cell phone from her pocket. "She went out to dinner with some of the women from church, but I've got to call her and tell her the news." She put the phone on speaker after she dialed the number.

"Hi, Karen." Her mom's voice sounded in the living room.

"Mom, I'm engaged!"

"Oh, Karen." Her mother's voice wavered. "I'm so happy for you."

"Hi, Ms. Doris."

Her mother chuckled. "Keith, I already know you'll be a nice, respectable husband for my daughter. Congratulations, both of you."

After they rang off with her mother, Keith said, "Our news wasn't a surprise for her."

"Of course it was!"

His eyes twinkled as he looked at her. "No, it wasn't. I asked your mother last week if it was okay if I asked you to marry me."

She playfully swatted his arm. "Oh, Keith, I'm not some young teenager. You didn't have to ask my mother's permission."

"I know, but I just wanted to be sure she approved."

"Well, you knew she would. My mother thinks highly of you, and I know she's grown fond of you since you moved in next door."

"Yes, that's true."

"Oh, Keith. I'm so excited! Do you think your brother will come to our wedding?"

"I hope so. You know, I asked Kyle to come by for dinner today, but he told me he couldn't make it. He said he had a date."

"Maybe he should have brought his date with him." She took Keith's hand. "I hope, eventually, that I'll be able to spend some time with your brother and get to know him. Is he still getting help for his drinking?"

Keith nodded. "He's been going to AA meetings and says he hasn't had a drink in weeks. And. . .well. . ."

"Well, what?" she said, continuing to admire her ring.

Keith hesitated then said, "Kyle told me he'd come to church with us this Sunday."

Karen's mouth dropped open as she stared at Keith. "You're kidding," she said softly.

Keith shrugged. "But don't get your hopes up. Kyle is known for breaking promises and changing his mind."

"That may be true, but to have him to agree to come to church with us at all is a big deal if you ask me."

"Yes, you're right." Keith dropped her hand and stood. "I'll be right back." He returned minutes later with a colorful brochure. "If you're agreeable, I'd like to enroll in Calvary Christian College for their fall term."

Karen smiled, glancing at the catalog, admiring the picturesque campus. "Where is Calvary Christian College?"

"It's in Waldorf, about an hour from here. We could move there if you'd like, but if you'd prefer staying here next door to your mom, I'll understand.

I also wasn't sure how you'd feel about trying to find another job as a hairdresser in Waldorf. If you want, we can stay here and I can always commute."

Karen hugged him. "Keith, if you feel the Lord is calling you to move to Waldorf, I'm okay with that. From my experience, it's usually pretty easy to find another job at a salon in a new area, but I'll admit that I have gotten used to seeing my mother every day."

"How about we compromise? We can move to Waldorf, but we'll drive down every Sunday to take your mom to church and spend the afternoon with her."

"That sounds good to me. Thanks, Keith." Happy tears slid down her cheeks as she hugged him.

Epilogue

Eight months later

A re you ready, little brother?"

Keith paced the dressing room at the church, feeling stiff and unnatural in his tux. He stopped walking and looked at Kyle, who was also in a tuxedo, ready for the wedding that was going to start in an hour. After a few moments, he answered his brother's question. "I'm about as ready as I'll ever be. I'm just grateful and blessed that the Lord brought Karen into my life. I am nervous, though."

Kyle pulled on his collar. "Yeah, I saw Karen and the rest of her bridal party arriving awhile ago. Karen's a nice woman. I like her."

Keith nodded. "I'm glad you and Karen hit it off so well." He paused before continuing. "I know the wedding's going to start soon, but I just wanted to tell you that I'm glad we're getting along now and that you agreed to be the best man at my wedding."

Kyle looked away for a few seconds, continuing to tug nervously on his collar. "Yeah, since I've stopped drinking and started getting my life back on track, I guess it made it easier for us to settle our differences."

"Are you happy, Kyle?"

His brother sighed. "I feel better than I did eight months ago."

"But are you happy?"

"I know you're going to tell me that I'll only find true happiness by accepting Jesus."

Keith mentally sighed with relief. Although Kyle had not accepted Jesus, he had attended services with him and Karen a few times. And his voice was no longer full of disdain when they conversed about the gospel. Not wanting to push the issue, Keith simply clapped his brother on the shoulder. "Just keep my advice in mind."

"I will," Kyle answered.

One hour later, the quartet played the "Wedding March" as Keith watched Kyle, Steve, and his church friend, Aaron, walk down the aisle. Anna, Monica, and Amanda then slowly followed, their matching royal blue gowns flowing behind them. Keith smiled with pride when Karen came forward. Her long lacy white dress contrasted nicely against her dark skin. Her large eyes were full of tears as she approached, holding a red floral bouquet in her small hands. She was so beautiful that Keith knew he could sit and look at Karen Brown forever. After Pastor Bolton performed the ceremony and they'd said their wedding vows, they shared a long, blissful kiss.

A Letter to Our Readers

Dear Readers:

In order that we might better contribute to your reading enjoyment, we would appreciate you taking a few minutes to respond to the following questions. When completed, please return to the following: Fiction Editor, Barbour Publishing, Inc., P.O. Box 719, Uhrichsville, OH 44683.

1. Did you enjoy reading *Chesapeake Weddings* by Cecelia Dowdy?
   ❑ Very much. I would like to see more books like this.
   ❑ Moderately—I would have enjoyed it more if _____
   _____
   _____

2. What influenced your decision to purchase this book?
   (Check those that apply.)
   ❑ Cover   ❑ Back cover copy   ❑ Title   ❑ Price
   ❑ Friends   ❑ Publicity   ❑ Other

3. Which story was your favorite?
   ❑ *John's Quest*   ❑ *Bittersweet Memories*
   ❑ *Milk Money*

4. Please check your age range:
   ❑ Under 18   ❑ 18–24   ❑ 25–34
   ❑ 35–45   ❑ 46–55   ❑ Over 55

5. How many hours per week do you read? _____

Name _____

Occupation _____

Address _____

City_____ State_____ Zip_____

E-mail _____